Dragon Crown Books presents

NEVADA NIGHTMARES

VOL. 2

More Weird Tales of the Silver
State from the Masters of Horror

DRAGON CROWN BOOKS

Contents

Images

Unattributed images are in the public domain

Introduction

What lies before you is an excursion into some of Nevada's weirdest, scariest, and most offbeat stories, assembled by the editors of Dragon Crown Books. This two-volume set features new stories from some of the Silver State's most acclaimed contemporary authors, set alongside vintage tales from Nevada's literary legends.

We've delved into the archives to find celebrated and lesser-known tales from the likes of Mark Twain, Dan De Quille, Sarah Winnemucca, and Sam Davis. We've also included tales award-winning authors and seasoned paranormal investigators. Sprinkled among these stories are a number of newspaper articles from the halcyon days of Nevada's youth: some deliberate hoaxes, others legends, still others reports that may or may not have held some degree of truth. As the original writers did, we leave these matters for the reader to judge.

In these pages, you'll find tales that span a century and a half of history—and legends that date back far earlier. Tales of ghosts, sea serpents, demons, vampires, and phenomena peculiar to this neck of the woods (or sagebrush). You'll read about water babies, oo'doo stones, quickie divorces, nuclear tests, outlaws, serial killers, and more.

Many of the contemporary entries in this anthology were inspired by and incorporate elements of Nevada's rich history, its vivid settings, and its folklore. In some cases, writings from the likes of Twain and De Quille, both masters of news hoaxes they called "quaints," have been incorporated into modern, fictional tales.

Details such as free-range cows, lonely highways, old saloons, pronghorns, coyotes, and casinos will be familiar to many Nevadans, gleaned from travels to all corners of the state. For readers unfamiliar with Nevada, it is our hope that these stories spark an interest in a place shared by ghost towns and neon lights, by abandoned mines and cities that never sleep. Whether you're interested in the reliving the history of the Old West, exploring for ghosts, heading off-road, or challenging a one-armed bandit to a duel, there's something here for everyone.

We trust you'll find the same is true of this two-volume set. Dragon Crown Books is proud to present *Nevada Nightmares*, a collection of tales best read by candlelight in a haunted hotel room. We assure you it's all fiction... or is it?

The best way to keep nightmares at bay is to sleep with one eye open.

We humbly suggest you do so.

—Stephen H. Provost
June 19, 2025

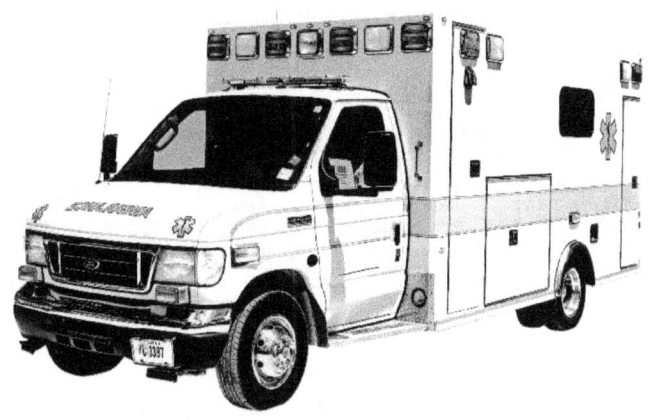

Sharon Marie Provost

The Road to Oblivion

Ramona had been walking for days, or at least it felt that way. No matter what road she took, she never saw any landmark that looked familiar. At one point, she even turned around and went back the way she had come, but it looked entirely different, in a strange nondescript way, than it had when she'd passed it before, even if it had only been two minutes ago.

She'd begun to wonder if dehydration was causing her to hallucinate, except for some reason she wasn't thirsty. Nor was she hungry. She wasn't wearing sunscreen, but her skin hadn't blistered or turned lobster-red. She didn't feel weary and her feet weren't sore, even though she'd been walking nonstop. She really had no complaints, other than her inability to find Pascal or a way home.

But then, her head began to ache, dully at first. The ache became an all-consuming throb, like her head was being crushed within a vice. She clutched her head and stumbled down the rutted track. Her foot caught a rock, and she tumbled to the ground, blacking out.

"Fuck, man. Did you see that?"

"Why'd she do that, dude?"

"Hello," Ramona called out.

"I didn't mean for that to happen. I didn't see the car on the road till the last minute as I jumped the berm, and I thought she'd just stop."

"Dude, your parents are going to be so pissed."

"Help me. I can't find my way back to the highway. My husband is missing," Ramona begged.

"I'm out of here, man. I ain't going down for this. She's the one who almost hit two kids. Fuck that!"

"Wait for me, Tim!"

"No, don't go," Ramona said through sniffles.

In the darkness, Ramona heard the two voices and kept trying to interject, but they ignored her, no matter how much she pleaded. She couldn't tell where they were coming from—it was too dark with no moonlight shining down on the barren landscape. She tried to sit up, but she didn't seem to have the energy.

The sounds of the two boys' voices faded into the distance along with the rumble of their ATVs. Ramona slumped back into the dirt and drifted off into unconsciousness.

Ramona heard other voices around her, but she couldn't make out what they were saying.

"Miss..."

"Help you..." or something to that effect.

Then she heard a loud whine and the sound of rending metal. Her head pounded harder—it seemed like that noise was cutting into her brain. The car shook each time it was hit.

But with what?

What kept hitting it over and over? Why didn't they stop? Couldn't they tell she was hurt?

That was when it dawned on her that her *entire body* hurt. The pain in her head had taken over her whole world, so it hadn't been apparent before. She couldn't seem to open her eyes and see the people who were talking or what was happening around her.

"Pascal?"

Nothing.

"Hey, you guys, what happened?"

There was no response. Maybe she wasn't yelling loud enough over the noise of that heavy equipment.

"HELLO! CAN YOU HEAR ME?"

Still there was no response.

She tried to slam her fist against something... anything, but she couldn't move.

Oh, God! Am I paralyzed?

The sounds grew fainter, and her head begin to spin. Were they moving away from her?

And then there was nothing.

The siren slowed and then stopped as the ambulance pulled up to the scene of the crash at the junction of NF-401 and U.S. 50. Two Nevada Highway Patrol cars and a fire truck were pulled off to the side, with flares and cones set up. One of the officers was directing traffic through the single open lane.

The ambulance driver jumped out and ran around to the back to help his coworker pull out the stretcher and the medical bags. They jogged over to the officer in charge.

"Hey, Sergeant Ames. What's the story? Are we clear to go in?"

"One female victim in the driver's seat. The firefighters had to use the jaws of life to breach the car, and they cleared the scene. It is safe for you to approach."

The two attendants began rendering aid as the sergeant walked over to the officer in the highway.

"It's the damnedest thing. There were no witnesses. No skid marks showing she tried to avoid another car or wildlife. I have no idea why she turned the wheel so hard that she flipped her RAV4. All I can figure is maybe she fell asleep and drifted, then overcorrected when she hit the rumble lines on the shoulder."

"How's she doing? That was a bad crash."

"The EMT with fire said she doesn't look good. She has pretty severe head trauma from hitting the windshield. I guess we'll see once she gets to the hospital."

"Got an ID?"

"Ramona Carlton. Her purse was in the front—the contents scattered about, but I found her wallet. I'll be calling the family when we get back to the office. Then I'll check in with the hospital and have them contact me when she is up for questioning."

Ramona felt like she was swimming upward from the depths of a dark ocean. As she neared the surface, the light became brighter and brighter until she crested the water and saw a blurry form standing in front of her. It held her forearm, shaking it lightly.

"Ms. Carlton, please stay calm. You're okay. You're at Renown Regional Medical Center in Reno."

"What? Where?"

"You're okay, Ms. Carlton. Just lie back and rest for a bit. I'll be back later, and I will explain everything to you."

"Carlton? Who's that?"

"You are, Ms. Carlton."

"It's Ramona Fischer. Fis-cher! *Fischer* for fuck's sake!"

"We'll sort this out later. Just lie back, Ms. Carlton."

Ramona began to hyperventilate as tears etched paths down her cheek. "No. Tell me what happened?"

"I'm going to give you a sedative. You've been through a serious trauma, and you need to remain calm."

A nurse, who'd been standing behind the doctor, came forward, syringe in hand. She injected a clear solution into a port on an IV line that fed into the back of Ramona's right hand. A few seconds later, Ramona's eyes felt like they were made of lead.

They closed against her will.

Ramona awoke sometime later, and the light in the room had changed. It was nearly sunset outside. She reached down and found the call light. The nurse entered the room quickly.

"I'll go let the doctor know you've awakened. How're you feeling? Can I get you something?"

Ramona's throat felt dry and scratchy. "Water," she croaked.

"I'll be right back. Ms...." The nurse saw Ramona's eyes glow ominously. "Ramona." She exited the room quickly.

"Hello, Ms. Carlton. Are you feeling a little calmer now? It can be quite disconcerting to wake up after a coma."

"Coma? What happened to us? And why do you keep calling me Ms. Carlton? Where is my husband? Where did you say I was again?"

"Please calm down, or I will have to sedate you again. Would you prefer I call you Ramona?"

"Yes. Or how about Mrs. Fischer? That *is* my name? Like I said, where's my husband?"

"Let's start slow. You were transported here on Care Flight a week ago. 'Here' being Renown Medical Center in Reno. You had a traumatic brain injury from a car accident. There was swelling on the brain so you've been in a medically induced coma for a little over a week."

"Car accident?"

"Yes, Ms.... uh... Ramona. Do you have any memory of the accident?"

"No, that can't be. My husband and I got lost trying to make it back to the highway after visiting Hamilton. We ran out of gas."

"I don't know all the specifics. That's a matter for the police. I just know what they told me."

"Whatever. I'll deal with that later. But where is my husband?"

The doctor frowned, looking confused. He looked at the computer screen by the bed and tapped a few keys. "Hmm. I'm just going to say this plainly: Our records show you aren't married."

"How would you have any records on me? I've never been here before now. This is fucking ridiculous! You must be looking at the wrong patient."

"I just mean the police were here and gave us the information from your identification and insurance cards, so we could get you checked in and reach next of kin to make important medical decisions. Everything has you listed as single with a name of Ramona Carlton."

"What the fuck? Is this a joke?"

"We called your family as well. Your mother has been involved in making decisions about your care. She never mentioned a spouse. She's awaiting a call from me to let her know how you are doing."

"My mother has no right to be making any decisions about my life. We've been estranged for years. She's quite aware that I'm married, but she doesn't approve of him. This is bullshit! I want to talk to the police now.

"Oh fuck! You said it's been over a week? My husband's been

out there all this time, alone, with no food or water. He could be hurt. Somebody needs to get out there now and find him. Call them NOW!" Ramona rocked forward in the bed and turned to get up. Her eyes blazed with anger from a blood-red face.

The doctor backed up, unnerved by her aggression.

"You must calm down. I'll have the nurse call them right now."

Ramona slumped back against the bed. Her anger dissipated, superseded by a lightning bolt of pain shooting through her head and then through her eyeballs. She felt weak, and the room was spinning. She took a couple of calming breaths and strained to think back to the last memory she had before she woke up at the hospital.

The voices of the boys talking about a crash... one that seemed to be their fault.

Then the loud metallic noise. The car shaking. Men talking about a woman.

Her? Had she been in an accident? But how? The car had been out of gas. And where was Pascal?

She anxiously awaited the two hours it took for the Highway Patrol sergeant to arrive and talk to her.

"Hello, Ramona. I'm Sergeant Ames from the Nevada Highway Patrol. I spoke to Dr. Carruthers, He said there seems to be some confusion, and you wanted all the details of what happened. How does that sound?"

"But...?"

"We'll get to everything as quickly as possible, but it's always best to start at the beginning."

Ramona nodded, her frustration mounting.

"We received a call from a motorist on Sunday, July 20th, at 11 a.m., reporting an overturned RAV4 off the side of Highway 50 at the NF-401 junction. When we arrived on the scene, we found you in the driver's seat..."

"But what about...?"

Sergeant Ames talked right over Ramona. "There was no one in the car with you... no sign that there had been. There was a bag in the backseat, presumably yours, containing women's clothing. We found your purse containing a driver's license, credit cards, a medical insurance card, et cetera, all identifying you as Ramona Carlton."

"But I'm Ramona Fischer. I've been married to Pascal Fischer for the past ten years. We left our hotel on Thursday, July 17th, and drove out to the ruins of Hamilton to take pictures, but we got lost. I lost track of my husband on Friday when we finally found the town again just after we ran out of gas. He walked up to see if anyone was there to help us. He never came back. I walked for days—I guess two, from what you're saying—trying to find him until I collapsed and was found. But I wasn't driving... the car was out of gas. This doesn't make any sense!"

"I have to agree with you there, Ramona. Brain injuries can be tricky things, from what the doctor told me. Like I said, all your identification shows you unmarried. Your mother says you've never been married.

"I'm not trying to call you a liar, but you couldn't have been out to Hamilton. Your car would have been covered in road dust, and it looked like it had been freshly washed. Not only that, but we found a receipt in your purse from the Hotel Nevada showing you had checked out that morning: Sunday, about an hour and a half before we received that call. That would be consistent with the location where you were found."

"You're wrong. All of you are wrong. I haven't talked to my mother in ten years because she didn't agree with my marriage to Pascal. Where's the camera? I'll show you the pictures of Hamilton."

"I believe they put your belongings in the wardrobe over

there. Let me see." Sgt. Ames walked over and retrieved the camera, handing it to her.

Ramona turned it on and madly pressed the button to flip through the pictures. "No, no, no. Fuck! Who deleted them? They were there. The last pictures we took. I don't remember these pictures of me at the train museum in Ely. We didn't go there. Where are the ones of Pascal at Lehman Caves? And at the Ward Charcoal Ovens? The two of us together drinking cheap frozen margaritas at the Hotel Nevada? Is someone messing with me, and why?"

"Maybe I should call the doctor, Ms...."

"So help me God, if one more person calls me Ms. Carlton, I'm going to scream. Aaaaaargh!" Ramona yelled as she threw the camera down on the bed.

"I'm truly sorry. I don't know what to say."

"Wait! What's the date?"

"It's Thursday, July 31st. Why?"

"Oh my God! Pascal has been out there alone without water for two weeks. You have to go out there and search for him. Please! I'm sure you'll find him. I love him more than my own life. Please save him."

"Ma'am, I've been trying to be understanding here, but there are limits. You were alone. All the evidence shows you were alone."

"Call his phone. Call his family. They'll tell you that we're married. Call his work. I'll give you all the numbers. Please believe me."

"Okay, ma'am. Write the numbers down for me. I'll put my office on tracking him down. And I'll see if I can get some locals together to form a search party. I know some guys who know the area like the back of their hand."

"Thank you so much! I'll pay whatever costs you incur. Money is no object."

Ramona waited on pins and needles for a phone call or a return visit from the sergeant. But she didn't hear anything for the rest of the day. Whenever she asked for any info, the nurse reported that there had been no news.

That must mean they've taken me seriously. They must be deep in the search. Surely they'll find Pascal any moment.

Exhaustion overtook her sometime in the wee hours of the morning. She awoke to find the doctor and nurse standing over her, with the sergeant standing on the other side of the bed.

"Hello, Ramona," Sgt. Ames said when she met his eyes.

"Did you find him yet? Please tell me he's okay."

Sgt. Ames sat down in the chair next to the bed, looking somber.

"Oh God, no. Don't tell me he's dead." Tears streamed from Ramona's eyes.

"No, sweetheart. I don't know how to break this to you, but I'm not going to beat around the bush here. There is no Pascal Fischer. I can't find any record of one having ever been born in San Luis Obispo, or any other city, for that matter, in California.

"The people who answered the phone at the number you gave me for his parents are childless and named Osbourne. The number you gave me for him hasn't been assigned to anyone for over two years. The number for his employer, Google, is valid, but they've never had an employee with his name."

"That's impossible. You're lying to me. But why? What did we ever do to you?"

"That's just not true, darling."

"What about the search party?"

"They searched through the night. They're very good, dedicated men. They found no sign of him. Several of them had been in that very area during the days you say the two of you were stranded, and they never saw either one of you."

"Liar! You fucking asshole! You're just letting him die out there. You can't do that. I'll do whatever you want. Pay you whatever you want."

"I just can't waste any more resources on this, ma'am. This is a medical matter now," Sgt. Ames said, rising from the chair, his hat in hand.

Sgt. Ames walked out of the room without looking back.

"Ms. Carlton, I assure you everything will be okay. You've had a severe traumatic brain injury. Confusion is quite common after an event such as this. With proper treatment and time, you will come to realize this is all just a side effect of the injury."

"Where's my phone? I need to make a call."

"I'll give you your phone if you promise to calm down."

"Yes. Whatever. Just give it to me." She saw the hard looks pass between the doctor and the nurse. "Please," she said, softening her tone.

Ramona pressed the button on the side to activate the screen. A picture of Pascal popped up. "See, look. Here he is. That's my husband..."

Her voice trailed off as the picture melted away and turned into a picture of her in what appeared to be Hawaii.

"No!" Her eyes flicked back and forth between the doctor and her phone.

Then she paused when she caught sight of her wedding ring.

"My wedding ring!" She held up her hand in triumph, only to see it was suddenly devoid of jewelry.

"Fuck! No!"

"Ms. Carlton, I'm going to sedate you now. You're getting much too worked up, which is going to set back your recovery."

"Please don't!"

The nurse appeared at her side and plunged the needle into her IV line.

Sgt. Ames heard a desperate scream as he entered the elevator.

"Pascal! He's in Hamilllllltoooooon! PASCAL!"

"Poor sick woman," he muttered as the doors whooshed closed.

"The Road to Oblivion" by Sharon Marie Provost is a sequel to "The Road to Nowhere," which appeared in Nevada Nightmares, Vol. 1. *It appears here for the first time.*

Stephen H. Provost

The Nevada Nightmare

The Laniers had driven all night and arrived in Ely just before dawn. They didn't have a place to stay there; it was a day stop before heading on to Carson City, but they wanted enough time to see some of the sights: the old cemetery, the historic depot with its feline caretaker "Dirt," and the courthouse.

They hit the cemetery first, at the crack of dawn. That made it seem spookier, then grabbed a bite at Denny's in the Hotel Nevada before stopping at the courthouse.

"Darn, it's still closed," Kitty Lanier said. "I told you we left too early."

Daniel Lanier looked down at the pamphlet he'd picked up at the convenience store. The letters were blurry, so he squinted, but he still couldn't make them out. He kept hoping his eyesight would miraculously revert to form the next time he tried to read something, because he refused to acknowledge his nearsightedness. He wasn't *that* old yet.

Daniel reached back onto the dashboard and pulled his glasses out, pushing them up onto his nose with a defiant grunt. He pulled his hand back across his balding head, a nervous habit he'd developed when he first discovered his long-outdated Elvis pompadour had begun to thin. There it was in blue and white: The museum opened at 8 a.m. every weekday, and here it was just a few ticks past 7:15.

"What's wrong, Daddy?" Little Lisa looked up at him with those 5-year-old baby brown eyes of hers. He never could hide his stormy moods from her; he loved that she was so sensitive, and he hated that he was so inept at shielding her from his dark side.

"Oh, for Pete's sake, Daniel," Kitty huffed. "Can we just skip this one? We've been to every single place on that ridiculous list of yours. It won't kill us to miss this one. I'm tired, and I'm not about to stand around for an hour to see another old courthouse."

"It's *less* than an hour. And how can you be tired this early in the morning?"

"We've been driving all night, that's how."

"You mean *I've* been driving all night. You were *sleeping* most of that time."

"I was not."

Lisa started to cry. "Don't fight, Mommy," she whimpered. "I wanna *see* it. There's ghosties."

"Yes, there are." The voice came from an old man with a drooping gray mustache who stood behind them. Daniel and Kitty had been too busy arguing to notice him approach. He was dressed in a dusty long brown jacket and a matching wide-brimmed hat, with a narrow black tie hanging down from his neck over a white shirt that appeared to have been worn so often that it was now closer to cream-colored.

Daniel looked behind him and saw the door to the courthouse was open.

The man bowed slightly and touched the brim of his hat. "I'm the morning docent. I reckon you're here 'cause you're wantin' to take the tour."

"Yes!" Lisa cried. "And to see the ghosties. Is Casper here?"

The docent smiled broadly but shook his head as he bent down to speak to her. "I'm afraid not, sweetie," he said. "But there *are* ghosts. I can guarantee you that."

Lisa clapped excitedly, but the docent put a finger to his lips. "But you have to be very quiet," he whispered, "or you'll perturb them. And some of them have a right nasty temper when they're provoked."

"Like Daddy?" Lisa whispered.

Daniel scowled, while Kitty made no effort to contain a satisfied smile.

"Oh, much worse than that," the docent said. "In fact, if you'll come inside with me, I'll tell you the story of one particular ghost who haunts this place. When he was alive, he'd shoot you sooner'n look at you if you crossed him. And he ain't any more agreeable now that he's dead. I'll tell you about him, but don't get his dander up or you'll probably regret it."

Lisa shivered.

Kitty rolled her eyes.

Daniel just nodded and pursed his lips.

"All right, then, let's get going," the docent said. "And once we're inside, I'll tell you all about him."

The courthouse was still dark inside. "I like to keep the lights off 'cause it ain't polite to wake a ghost out of a sound sleep with a flick of one of these modern switches," the docent explained.

Daniel turned as he heard the front door close behind them. The docent hadn't moved, and his wife and daughter were both standing right beside him. They huddled in a little closer as the room became nearly pitch black.

Then the docent lit a match and touched it to the wick of an old-fashioned lantern he held, creating a dim, golden glow. "Now," he said, "that's more like it. Miners hereabouts used this very lantern to light their way when they was lookin' for silver way down deep. I prefer it to these newfangled 'lectric contraptions they have here." He chuckled.

"This is ridiculous," Kitty whispered to Daniel.

"It's a Chautauqua," her husband snapped in a whisper. "Actors put on period garb and talk about the history of a place like they would have a hundred years ago. It makes the stories come alive."

"That's right," the docent said. "And do I have a story for you!"

He put the lantern down on the table, and it flared brightly for a minute, then flickered. There was no wind, and the room was still.

"He's here," the docent whispered.

Kitty looked around her. "I don't see anyone," she said.

"But you *feel* him. I know you do."

"I do," Lisa said timidly before her mother could respond. "He's not very nice, is he?"

"Shhh," the docent said. "He doesn't like bein' insulted..." The old man cupped his ear for a moment. "He says he'll pretend you didn't say that," he translated. "But be careful. You never know what might set him off."

"Who is he?" Daniel asked, and Kitty rolled her eyes.

"I'm gettin' to that," the docent whispered conspiratorially.

"Now, whenever ya talk about serial killers, certain names come up right away. John Wayne Gacy. Ted Bundy. Jeffrey Dahmer. Jack the Ripper. The Skid Row Slasher."

"But nobody talks about the Nevada Nightmare... Well, no one else calls him that. I made that up. Pretty catchy, eh?"

Kitty shrugged, and the docent continued.

"I'm his official biographer, and I'm here to inform my dear readers that old Hank here killed as many as 19 people in his day." He lowered his voice. "He wouldn't want me tellin' it like that. He hired me to write the story from *his* point of view, but then he got himself hanged before he could pay up, so I figured I could tell the story my own way... *Ouch!*"

The docent jumped and reached up to rub his shoulder.

"Yeah, that was him. He just hit me in the arm: His way of tellin' me I needed to tell it *his way* and he'd pay me later. But in his current state, he ain't exactly solvent, if you know what I mean." He winked, then cupped his hand to his ear and said, seemingly to no one, "What's that?"

He turned back to the Laniers. "Oh, now he's threatening to blow my head off if I don't tell it his way. Typical. I might have been scared back in the day, but he happens to be unarmed at present. No gun. No knife. No nothing. But I'll make him sound good anyway... in a bad way. First, though, his side of the story. And I quote:

'I have been charged with a great many crimes,' he says. 'I killed three men, and I was right in doing it. The last man I killed, he assisted in stringing me up three times. They say I have a wife and family that I have not treated right, but my wife has been dead thirteen years. I have two children in Oregon, well fixed.

'I'm an ignorant man, have always been persecuted, and am innocent of crime. All this will appear in Mr.

Murphy's book of my life, and I want you to believe it.'

"Mr. Murphy, that's me," the docent explained. "But these days, I go by Murph."

"Why are you playing the part of this Mr. Murphy and not this Hank person?" Kitty sighed, sounding bored. "He seems a lot more interesting."

Murph laughed a short laugh. "I'm sure he'd agree with that," he said. "But ya see, he don't like people impersonatin' him. He's ornery enough about folks tellin' the story of his life, but he tolerates it for the fun of messin' with 'em."

Kitty seemed unimpressed. "Hmph."

Somehow, in the still and stale air of the courthouse, a cloud of dust billowed up right under her nose and sent her into a coughing fit.

Murph offered her a tissue, which she took without bothering to thank him. He just nodded once and resumed his story. "I never got a chance to finish that book he was talking about, which is probably why 'the Nevada Nightmare' ain't right up there with the Boston Strangler in terms of bein' famous. I don't regret it, though. Not really. Should someone be famous for all the wrong reasons? I ain't too sure about that. So why am I tellin' you Hank's story now? Well, it's just you and me here, and I *do* want the truth to be known, even it stays on the Q.T." He put his finger to his lips, and Lisa mimicked him, giggling. She was staring at him, enthralled.

"Therefore," he said, "without further ado…

⌘ ⌘ ⌘

Hank's story begins in Nova Scotia in 1840, but I won't bore you with the details of his not-particularly-tragic upbringing.

What happened over the first few decades of his life doesn't matter much.

What matters is what happened when he became the Nevada Nightmare.

Don't take that name I pinned on him wrong. Word has it he killed folks all over the West: Idaho, Montana, Wyoming, Arizona... But he did his worst in Nevada, which is why I settled on that name.

It's not as though Hank didn't try to make an honest living. In 1879, he was down in El Dorado Canyon on the Colorado River. He set to work mining there with a partner named Paddock and defined a ledge of ore aggregating four feet that assayed $276 per ton. He and Paddock got into a scuffle: Words were exchanged, weapons were drawn, and—long story short—Paddock was shot and wounded.

Paddock skedaddled across the river into Arizona Territory and commenced to emptying his revolver shootin' at jackrabbits, thinkin' the desert was gonna kill him. But it wasn't the desert what got him, it was Hank. You see, he wasn't going to let the matter go. He and another man saddled up their horses and, sure as shootin', they caught up to poor ol' Paddock just eighteen miles into the desert.

Out of bullets, Paddock threw up his hands, but Hank wasn't havin' none of it. He emptied his revolver into the man, sending him to the hereafter. They put out a warrant for his arrest in Arizona, but he was never apprehended—even though he went right back to El Dorado Canyon and picked up right where he'd left off.

Hank was lucky like that. He was a slippery varmint, and he always managed to stay one step ahead of the law. Of course, it wasn't a minute before he got himself into trouble again, this time in an El Dorado saloon. It happened like this: James B. "J.B." Greenwood, who'd traveled down from Tybo by way of Bristol, was engaged in a game of poker with Hank and a man named

Clark into the wee hours of the morning.

Sometime between 3 and 4 o'clock, Hank got dealt a honey of a hand: a full house of aces over kings. But Greenwood went him one better: Holding four jacks, he called Hank and beat him.

Hank didn't take too kindly to this. He accused the others of cheating and walked out of the saloon then and there, swearing he'd "come back a-shootin'"—which is exactly what he did. He returned a few minutes later with two pistols drawn and commenced to firin'. The first shot hit Clark, and J.B. tried to grab his arm. Hank, bein' further agitated, turned on him and shot him through the arm and into his chest. Then, for good measure, he delivered a second bullet to his abdomen.

J.B. was taken home, where a fella named Andy Fife saw to his wounds. You'd think Hank would have let well enough alone, but he didn't. Instead of skipping town and lyin' low until things blew over, he marched himself right on over to J.B.'s house and demanded that the wounded man fork over $100. Should he fail to do so, Hank told him, he'd never make it alive to the boat for Fort Mohave—where medical treatment awaited him.

Fife handed him the money, and Hank left. The crazy thing was, there were six men in the house at the time, who might easily have overpowered him, but not one of them lifted a finger to stop him.

Like I said, Hank was lucky. Unnaturally so.

J.B. made it to the boat, but he didn't share Hank's luck— not by a long shot. The minute he got into the boat, it was plagued by headwinds, and they didn't arrive at Fort Mohave until midnight. The next day, a pony rider brought word to El Dorado that Greenwood had expired and that Clark wasn't expected to live.

Hank? He was back at work in his mine as though nothing had happened.

Funny thing was, you'd think holding four jacks in your

hand would be lucky. But not long before, some hombre in Bodie was killed for the same affrontery. So not long after, a man who was dealt four jacks in Pioche decided not to press his luck. Instead of bettin' big on his hand, he folded like a tent in a boomtown that's gone bust. The tragic fate of his fellow jack-holders was enough to dissuade him from betting on *that* kind of hand.

⌘ ⌘ ⌘

Lisa giggled, and Murph smiled down at her. "I like Jack," she said. "He's cute."

"He means in a deck of cards, Lisa," Kitty said in a sour tone. "Can we please just get on with it?"

A noise that sounded like a growl came from somewhere back in the darkness. Murph's lips hadn't moved.

"Is there an animal in here?" Kitty said. "Please don't tell me there's an animal in here?"

"It's just Hank gettin' testy," Murph said. "Try not to make him angry. You wouldn't like him when he's angry."

Kitty whispered up at Daniel: "It's probably some foul possum or squirrel," she hissed. "Like that dirty old cat at the depot. If we don't get out of here soon, we won't be able to see him." Her tone wasn't one of regret, but almost glee. She was taunting him now: She didn't want to stay here any longer than necessary, but if it spared her a stop at the depot, it would almost be worth it.

"Then why don't we let him get on with his story, *dear*?"

"*Fine*."

Murph continued without skipping a beat:

⌘ ⌘ ⌘

That business at El Dorado wasn't the only trouble he got himself in down in Arizona, neither. Another unfortunate

27

soul nearly fell victim to his deadly temper at Mineral Park, north of Kingman. It ain't there no more, but at the time, it was the biggest mining camp in Mohave County. That meant it had plenty of saloons and plenty of men getting' drunk. Hank had a beef with one of these men, who he found lyin' at the edge of the sidewalk, passed out from partakin' too liberally of the bottle. Hank picks up a thirty-pound rock, strides up to him, brash as a king rooster, an' holds it up over the man's head like a guillotine. But just then, a miner named Smith pulls his pistol and threatens to shoot him if he lets the rock fall.

Hank cleared out then. That time, he didn't get away with anything, but he still got away, which was what always seemed to happen with Hank.

He didn't care who you were: If you crossed him—wittingly or not—you put your life at immediate risk. Take the case of Hank's run-in with a man who walked with the use of crutches. The man, a certain Enos Blancett, came up to Hank in McDonald's saloon at Eureka and accused him of a particularly heinous crime. I should point out that this was the Eureka in the Tintic district of Utah, not the one in Nevada, nor the one in California. There are far too many towns of this name for my liking, as they're easily confused with one another unless one makes plain exactly where they are.

Be that as it may, Blancett had come to this particular Eureka two months previous from Colorado, where he said Hank had robbed a bank and shot a man named Major Graham for good measure as he lay dead, having already been killed by others. Not caring a whit for Mr. Blancett's crutches, Hank hauls off an hits the man, knocking him to the ground. Hank had been out hunting the day before, so he grabs his shotgun and aims it at Blancett. It so happened, however, that a certain John Watts was passing by and prevented him from using it.

Rather than have it out then and there, the two men agreed

to meet and decide matters with shotguns behind Pat O'Shea's corral the following day. But that wasn't good enough for Hank, whose itchy trigger finger never left a single thing to chance. Blancett went home to fetch his shotgun—and a revolver for good measure—and was on his way to the appointed meeting place when a gunshot sounded. A bullet slammed into one of his crutches, knocking it free and sending Blancett to the ground. It had come from behind a nearby house, where Hank had been lying in wait for him.

"You have not got me yet!" Blancett shouted.

This, of course, encouraged Hank to empty the second barrel of his shotgun into Blancett, who was struck by five buckshot. One entered his chest near the heart, which proved to be his undoing.

Hank, of course, claimed that Blancett had shot at him first, notwithstanding the fact that both barrels of his shotgun were still loaded, as were all six chambers of his revolver. Eyewitnesses, likewise, contravened his account. Blancett, they said, had never even raised his gun to shoot. Blancett's death left his wife a widow.

Hank was arrested and held on $2,000 bond, but once again, nothing came of it, and before long, he was a free man.

⌘　⌘　⌘

"The cops weren't very good at their job back then, were they?" Daniel quipped.

"Oh, it wasn't that so much as the state of things in those days," Murph said. "Take Silver Reef, for instance. Hank wound up there after he quit El Dorado, but it weren't as though he was the only rabble-rouser in town. There was a thousand crusty, mangy sons of the devil all packed into one place, fightin' and carousin' at nine saloons, a billiard room, and out in the streets. One fella named Bateson tried to kill a Catholic priest at the Reef, and his only regret was he'd failed in the attempt. 'I intended to kill him at the altar,' he boasted."

Lisa gasped.

"Another time, at the faro table, a dealer named Saxey and a player named Clark got into a row, each accusin' the other of cheating. Now, you may never've heard of faro, but let me tell you, it's *very* easy to cheat at that particular game, so anything was possible. No one ever found out who was tellin' the truth, though, because the men both drew their guns at the very same time and shot each other straight through the heart."

Lisa hugged herself and pushed in closer to Daniel, who put his arm around her. "It's okay, Leelee," he soothed. "This all happened a very long time ago."

"I'm amazed that Mr. Murphy here can talk about it all in such *excruciating* detail."

"He's a docent," Daniel said flatly. "They're paid to know their stuff."

Murph nodded, a tiny smile forming at the corners of his lips before returning to his story. "Hank's dust-ups didn't always happen in the heat of the moment, like in El Dorado," he said. "Other times, he plotted them out beforehand (though he would certainly deny this)."

There was a muffled noise from somewhere beyond the lantern's glow.

Murph ignored it and went on with his tale:

⌘   ⌘   ⌘

Whether he held up that bank in Colorado or not, old Hank *was* implicated in various stagecoach holdups.

One such incident occurred back in '85. Hank was workin' for the Christy Mining Company over in Utah at Silver Reef—the place I was just tellin' you about—which was comin' near the end of its boom. Christy was still spittin' out 50 tons of ore every day that year, but things started goin' downhill after that. Maybe Hank saw the writing on the wall, but more'n likely he just wanted to supplement his income with a little extracurricular fun.

He'd kept buildin' on his reputation as a bully and a ruffian, especially when he was drunk, an' that was a lot of the time. So people steered clear of him.

Hank's shenanigans, however, took place a ways outside the city limits and involved a stage that arrived in the Stockton Hill camp north of Kingman carrying a package loaded with $340 in gold and silver coins, which had been set for delivery to a merchant there. But when they went to unload it, the package was missing. The driver, Ed Gilbert, accused a stranger named Wickert of absconding with the money. Hank just happened to be standing there, and it was hardly surprising that he became involved in the quarrel that followed—a quarrel that left Wickert badly beaten around the head and face.

Gilbert was placed under arrest.

Then, the next morning, the package miraculously turned up. A search party led by Gilbert found it back aways near the roadside, where it was supposed to have fallen from the stage. It was curious that Gilbert knew exactly where to look, and even more curious that no one had made off with the package if it had simply been lying there in plain sight. Had Hank, at Gilbert's direction, surreptitiously returned to that spot and put it back where it was supposed to have been?

He's givin' me the side-eye right as I tell you this, refusin' to talk. But if the safe's propitious "discovery" was an attempt to undo the damage already done, it didn't work out that way. Wickert swore out a warrant against both Hank and Gilbert, and they were bound over on $1,000 bond, having been charged with intent to commit murder. Still, Hank, bein' the slippery snake he was, wriggled out of it somehow and was soon a free man again.

But that wasn't even Hank's most famous highway robbery.

Kitty groaned. "Don't tell me there's more."

Murph pursed his lips and forced a congenial smile. "Well," he said, "You've heard of Las Vegas, right?"

"Who hasn't?" Daniel chuckled.

Kitty's eyes brightened a little. She'd much rather have been out on the floor of the Bellagio, dancing with a one-armed bandit, or sitting in the front row for a Cirque du Soleil show than *here* in the dusty middle-of-nowhere. Daniel had promised he'd take her to Sin City, but he'd saved that stop for the end of the trip, when she'd be too tired to even enjoy it. "Typical," she'd told him when he'd announced their itinerary—without her input, of course. "You get to do what you want first, and then, if there's time, we'll get around to what I wanna do!"

"What about Vegas?" she asked Murph. "Was Hank there?"

"Indeed he was, but a long time before it looked anything like it does now." He returned to his narrative before Kitty could ask any more questions.

⌘ ⌘ ⌘

You might not know that, back in the day, it was called *Los Vegas*, because they already had a post office in Las Vegas, New Mexico, and they didn't want the two of them conflictin'. In Hank's time, it wasn't a city at all, but a Mormon fort set up at the midway point between Los Angeles and the Great Salt Lake. As time passed, a ranch was built on the site. There was a vineyard (the first in the state), a peach orchard, a few apple, apricot, and plum trees... and not much else.

By 1879, a fella named Octavius Gass had built up a 640-acre ranch there called the Los Vegas Rancho. It was a big spread, but unfortunately for Mr. Gass, he had an even bigger debt: $5,000, which he owed to a friend of his who'd fronted him the money to pay off a tax bill. The friend's name was Archibald Stewart, who lived in Pioche at the time with his wife, Helen. Gass was counting on a bumper crop to pay off his debt to Archie, but when the harvest he'd been countin' on was spoiled by bad weather, he found himself on the wrong end of foreclosure. Not only did he lose the ranch, but 320 more acres to boot, along with his livestock.

Archie and Helen then packed up and moved down there. The two of them began growing crops again, addin' alfalfa to the mix, which they sold to miners from the El Dorado district, some fifty miles away. Archie would haul food and supplies from his ranch down to the miners there on a regular basis, taking back with him hefty payments in the form of El Dorado gold.

While he was away on one of these trips, trouble began when a ranch hand named Schyler Henry quit and demanded to be paid for his work immediately. Helen told the man Archie would deal with the matter when he got back, but this wasn't good enough for Henry, who went over to a nearby ranch owned by Conrad Kiel—which also happened to be a haven for outlaws.

Now, you might be askin', what does any of this have to do with our friend Hank? Well, I'm gettin' to that. As I previously mentioned, Hank owned a mine in El Dorado, which is where Archie was doin' business. He saw the supplies come in and the gold go out, and he and some like-minded confederates soon hatched a plan to enrich themselves at Archie's expense. One of their number stole some horses headed down to the Kiel Ranch, the same place where Mr. Henry happened to be stayin'.

Suddenly, Henry's abrupt resignation and demand for payment made a lot more sense: He'd been in league with Hank all along.

When Archie returned, he grabbed his rifle and went lookin' for Henry at the Kiel Ranch... only to be ambushed by Hank and his men. It had all been a set-up. Hank's gang robbed Archie of the gold he'd collected at El Dorado, then they killed him and sent a note back to Helen that read: "Mrs. Sturd send a team and take Mr. Sturd away he is dead."

Making their getaway on the horses they'd stolen was a simple matter: Bein' close to the place where Nevada touches California and Arizona, some of them fled to each place, while one of them wound up in Utah.

"This guy must have been born under a lucky star, eh Kit?" Daniel was needling her. She knew he didn't believe her astrology readings any more than she believed in ghosts.

"But eventually," Murph said, "everyone's luck runs out. And so did Hank's."

There was another growl back in the darkness.

Murph continued:

⌘　⌘　⌘

He finally got his comeuppance in 1890, back at Royal City, sixteen miles north of Pioche, where another game of poker ended in bloodshed. You might've heard the place called Jackrabbit, if you've heard of it at all. Ain't nothin' there these days but some broken-down cabins and headframes.

Anyway, Hank—who had moved up to Pioche after Silver Reef folded up—wasn't involved in this particular card game. He was just standin' there in Jimmy Curtis' saloon, lookin' over the shoulder of a miner named Pete Thompson. Folks who was there say Hank was standin' a little too close and pushin' a little too hard on Thompson's back, so he turned and asked Hank to kindly step back. Hank muttered some fake apology, then came right back up and started hoverin' over the table again, disruptin' the game. This happened yet a third time, and things might've settled down after that if one of the players hadn't gotten so drunk he passed out at the table, and that everyone started havin' a laugh at his expense. Hank, thinking the whole durned world revolved around his fat behind, was certain Pete was laughin' at *him*, so he started cursin' him out right there. Bein' naturally offended, Pete told Hank he didn't care two bits for him and went back to lookin' at his cards.

But Hank upped the ante, so to speak, by slammin' his right hand down on the table, then bringin' it back up again to connect with Pete's mouth. When Pete stood up to defend himself, he saw Hank's eyes "glarin' at him like a mad bull." That's how he himself put it. In a flash, Hank socked Pete in the jaw with his right hand and pulled out his pocket knife with his left, stabbin' him just above the belly button and braggin' about how he'd done the same thing to another man in Montana.

"There's another sonofabitch that I stabbed in the heart," he said, "and he'll go off in the sagebrush and die like the rest of 'em."

The wound weren't more than half an inch long, but it was enough to spell curtains for Thompson, who passed a couple of days later.

Hank, meanwhile, got paranoid about the people who'd seen him do the deed. While still there in the saloon, he waved a knife in one man's face and slugged another—one of the men who'd been playin' poker at the table—accusing them both of bein' one of "those lynchin' SOBs." He told them both he'd been put on trial four times for his life, and on each occasion had got himself acquitted. This was to make sure they knew he expected the same this time, and that he'd be comin' after any man who spoke against him at his trial.

After this, Hank made a run for it, but Lady Luck didn't follow him this time. He scaled the side of Bristol Mountain and found a tunnel to hide in. But Sheriff Turner formed a posse and went after him. They found him in his hideout, but even though he wasn't armed, none of the posse wanted anything to do with apprehending him: They were *that* scared of him. So the sheriff went in and did the deed himself, then he brought Hank back to stand trial in Lincoln County.

The whole place was abuzz with people speakin' their mind about how Hank deserved to get himself hanged, so he demanded that the trial be moved here to Ely at the courthouse—not this particular one, but a one made outta wood that stood here afore this one was built. The two men he'd accused of bein' lynchin' SOBs both testified against him, and the jury came back after 75 minutes, sayin' he deserved to be hanged.

And so he was, right in front of the jail here. Hank climbed up onto the scaffold at 2 minutes before high noon and was cut down at 10 minutes after, his pulse racin' at 142 beats a minute just before he died.

An' that's my story folks. Whaddya think?

⌘ ⌘ ⌘

"Is that it?" Kitty asked. "We've been standing here all this time, and you haven't even shown us the courthouse yet." She turned to Daniel. "What time is it, anyway?"

Daniel pulled out his phone and activated the screen. The flame in Murph's lantern flashed and danced in a wild frenzy.

"Whoa!" Daniel exclaimed and took a step backward.

"Whoa is right," Kitty scoffed. "It's almost 8:30, and this place was supposed to open at 8. Where is everyone?"

"I think we need to get going," Daniel said, sliding the phone back into his pocket.

"But the ghosts!" Lisa blurted out.

"What about them, Leelee?" Kitty said impatiently, not even bothering to look at her daughter.

"Mommy, they want us t'pologize."

"For what?" Daniel asked.

"For bein' rude."

Kitty and Daniel looked up together, toward the place where Lisa was already looking: directly at Murph.

"Now, I'm a reasonable sort," he said, spreading his arms wide. "All we're askin' for is a little common courtesy. You can understand that, right? We invited you into our house, and the least you could do is show a little appreciation."

"We?" Daniel said.

Kitty ignored the question and leaned into him, whispering, "I think he wants a tip."

As Daniel began digging in his pocket, the lantern flared and went out.

"Daddy, no!" Lisa pleaded.

"I don't want your durned money," Murph spat in the darkness. "Hank does, but he can't use it... and remindin' him of that fact weren't such a good idea."

"I'm sorry," Daniel stammered. "We didn't mean to offend..."

There was a loud clattering that sounded like a tin can or teapot crashing to the floor.

"Dagburnit!" Murph shouted. "Watch where you're going!"

"It's pitch dark in here!" Kitty objected. "We can't see a thing!"

"But Mommy," Lisa said. "I can see. The ghosties are right over there. That nice Mr. Murphy and his friend Hank."

"Honey, Mr. Murphy is not a ghost," Kitty said patiently, reaching out for her daughter's hand and grasping it in the dark. "He's... what did you call him before? A chatty man?"

"*Chau-tau-quan*," Daniel said, spelling out the syllables like he was speaking to a child. "Like an actor."

Murph burst out laughing. "Now ain't that a hoot?" he said. "He thinks I'm one of them fools from the melodeon!"

"It ain't funny," another voice said. "It's downright insultin'!"

"Who said that?" Daniel said, looking around frantically into the unyielding darkness.

"You're so gullible, *Daniel*," Kitty said dismissively, emphasizing the first syllable of his name the way she did when she was annoyed with him.

"Babe, I was just…"

"I know, I know. Asking a question. Blah blah blah. That's all you ever do. God forbid you ever actually *made a decision!*" She added, under her breath, "unless it suits *you* and you put it on a goddamn itinerary."

"Stop fighting!" Lisa wailed, sounding frightened. "It's Hank. You're making him mad."

"Too late for that, little girl. I'm already good an' fired up."

"Oh, piss off!" Kitty snarled at Murph. "I don't know if you're trying to be scary or funny, but whatever. You're not fooling anybody by throwing your voice like that. Turn the lights out and pretend there's some disembodied spirit back in the shadows. Or is some fucking coward hiding back there in the darkness, helping you?" She peered around it.

"Babe, language," Daniel chided. "Lisa…"

"…Has heard you use that word a hundred times. But when *I* use it, I'm the Billie Eilish bad guy! Well fuckety fuck fuck, and fuck you too!"

She'd barely finished when a single shot rang out, and something fell to the floor with a thud.

Or someone.

Lisa screamed and began sobbing.

"Oh, now you done it," Murph groused. "And I told 'em you didn't have no weapon. I guess that's an even twenty notches for you now."

"I only killed *three* people," Hank muttered. "And all of them had it coming. So did he."

"How do you figure? *She* was the one bein' disrespectful."

"I ain't never killed no woman afore, an' I weren't about to start now. When I shut *him* up, I shut *her* up in the bargain. I just done it in a roundabout way."

"What about the little girl, though? Look at her! You just killed her father!"

A light switch was flipped, and the room was flooded with artificial light.

Murph and Hank were gone.

"Oh, God," said the watchman, who looked not a day over 21, as he stared in horror at Daniel's motionless body on the floor. "I gotta call 911. I swear to God it was an accident. I pulled my gun when I heard voices and it... just went off. It's my first night on the job... Oh God, oh God, oh God... It's Saturday. Oh God! There wasn't supposed to be anyone here! We're closed!"

Lisa shivered as she walked through the Ely Cemetery, searching for Hank Parish's final resting place.

She couldn't find it.

Not that it mattered. She hadn't really wanted to find it anyway.

They'd put that poor security guard, Nate Whisler, behind bars for killing her father, but no one could ever convince her it wasn't Hank who'd pulled the trigger.

A lot had happened since then. She was on her way to Reno on a tour to promote her breakout paranormal romance bestseller, *Ghost of a Chance*.

It had been years since she'd seen her mother. Kitty Lanier had moved on quickly after Lisa's dad died, becoming Kitty Lynn when she remarried a much older man who owned a few casinos. Well, more than a few.

Lisa had petitioned for emancipation when she was sixteen and had made her own way as a writer.

She walked farther into the cemetery and found her father's grave, kneeling down and placing a bouquet of roses beside his headstone.

"How ya doin', little miss?"

Lisa felt a light breeze on her shoulder, or was it the gentle touch of a hand?

"Hi, Murph," she said, smiling wistfully.

He smiled back. "I was hoping I might see you again. I got a question to ask you. I think I finally wanna write that book about Hank, and I hear you've become an author. I was hopin' you might help me tell everyone what a sonofabitch he was."

He winked at Lisa.

"Aren't you friends?" she asked.

He shook his head. "Never were, really. Just shared a place at the courthouse 'cause neither of us had anywhere better to be. But I moved out after he killed your pops. He can have the place. I like it better here."

"I'm sorry, Murph," Lisa said, shaking her head. "I don't want him taking up any more space in my head, right, Daddy?"

"That's right, Leelee," her father said. "But Murph's a good guy. I've come to know him since we've both been living here in the graveyard."

Lisa's face brightened. "I have an idea," she said. "Murph, what if I write a book about *your* life?"

"Me?"

"Sure. I bet it would be a lot more interesting."

Lisa's father hugged her. "That's a wonderful idea. I smell another bestseller."

"Me too," said Lisa. "C'mon, Murph, let's get to work."

The stories Murph told in this account are based on actual historical records and press clippings of Hank Parish's misdeeds. Parish's claim that a certain Mr. Murphy was to write an account of his life is also historical, as stated at his execution in his final words, presented above. Mr. Murphy himself, however, is an enigmatic figure, only referred to in Parish's final statements and nowhere else in the historical record that I could find. Likewise, I could find no record of him ever completing the book Parish had commissioned him to write. That, and sightings of Parish's ghost at the White Pine County Courthouse, formed the inspiration for this story, which appears here for the first time.

Michael K. Falciani

Hell Hath No Fury

It was a hot summer night in Nevada when I found out demons were real.

I should have known—that whole week was riddled with problems, First-world problems, Dec would say. Dec, short for Decland—that's my boyfriend, or ex-boyfriend. I'm not rightly sure since I break up with him every other week. Not his fault, mind you. He loves me proper, like a man should. I'm the crazy one. Still, can't find any peace around him—but that's a story for another time.

Like I said, the day started with problems. I flew home to Nevada to see my daddy in Las Vegas. I needed a place to think. Can't gather my thoughts to save my life in San Francisco. Everybody's in a rush all the time, and everything's a competition.

It's all, "My daughter is the first chair for the piccolo in the middle school orchestra." Or, "My son just made the varsity football team and he's only 14 years old."

I mean, whoopty-do, right? So, your daughter beat out the one other piccolo player in school? Did you know your husband's sleeping with that piccolo tutor you pay for? She told her hairdresser, so now it's all over the neighborhood.

You say your son made the varsity football team? 'Course he did. We all know his real daddy is a former NFL tight end. Well, all of us 'cept your husband, the banker.

Lord howdy, those people drive me insane. I had to get outta there.

I'm Maria, by the way. Maria Addison Donnelli. Used to be Maria Shank, until I had enough of being ignored by my now ex-husband. He was a looker, I'll give him that, but Lord Jesus, a more arrogant man I've never met. Good riddance to him.

Anyway, back to the demons.

Now, I'm a god-fearing woman, always have been. I sleep with the good book right next to me every night. I read from it too. I'm not just one of those pretenders who goes around spouting the word of God like they are one of his disciples back in the days of fire and brimstone. I try to walk the walk, if you take my meaning.

Still, nothing in that book prepared me for what I saw last night.

I apologize. Here I am starting at the end of the story when I know I should bring you up to speed. I warn you though, best fasten your seatbelt, because it's a hell of a ride.

I drove up to the town of Pahrump from Las Vegas after spending a few days with my daddy. He's a good man, raised me right. I'm lucky in that regard.

On my third day home, I got word one of my old high school friends, Jeanna, had lost her parents. She was living in Pahrump, some sixty miles west of Vegas.

"Go visit your friend," my daddy said to me, waving me off with a smile. After fifty years of living in Sin City, he still speaks with an Italian accent. He emigrated here from Rome back in the sixties. He's lived here ever since. Used to own a chain of restaurants up and down the strip. I spent my entire life growing up in them. Good food and good company, he used to say.

He took every Sunday off though. Called it, "family time."

That's my daddy for you.

On my drive to Pahrump, I heard my phone vibrate.

Decland.

I hate to admit this, but my heart does a little flip in my chest every time he calls. He's the best man, outside my father that I've ever known. You know those great guys you see on Netflix or Amazon Prime, the ones you know are going to end up with the girl in the end because of how great they are? He's like that, only better, because he's real.

"Hello," I answered, knowing exactly what he was gonna say.

"How's the most beautiful girl on Earth?" he asked.

You see what I mean?

"Thank you for saying that, but you know it's not true," I sniped back, trying not to gush.

I heard him laugh on the other end. "A blind man could sense your beauty, my love."

"What do you want?" I asked, before he had the chance to turn my good sense into mush.

"Why did you leave?" he asked. "I mean, I had to contact your work to find out what happened to you."

"I needed to get out of town," I answered, a bit too defensively. "I just need a few days away from... everything."

"You mean away from me," he guessed, reading my thoughts.

"I don't know what you see in me," I told him for the millionth time. "I keep telling you, I'm no good for you."

He laughed again. It's irritating how nothing gets him down.

"Think what you want, Nevada girl, but I'm going to marry you as soon as you figure your life out."

"No, you're not," I practically shouted. "I'm never getting married again."

"Okay," he replied affably. "We'll just live together for the rest of our lives. That's perfectly fine with me."

He's so infuriating.

"What are you doing anyway? Your dad said you left town?"

"You called my father?" I asked, more than a little annoyed.

"Well, you don't pick up your phone half the time, and when you do, you're Miss Grumpy Pants, so yes, I called your dad. We had a good talk."

"Maybe you can call him back and ask him where I went!" I yelled, growing angry. "Stop calling me. We are done!"

"Will you calm..."

I pushed the end call button before he could say more.

Yes, I'm temperamental, but I'm never going to be stuck in a relationship with another person again. I'd be lying if I said there weren't times when I wanted to be with Decland forever. Other times... I just don't understand what he sees in me. I'm a simple girl, an assistant manager of the local grocery outlet, nobody of importance. Decland, he's this big shot college professor who teaches ancient history over at the university where the college girls all *swoon* over him.

One day I'm at work and he just walks up to me out of the blue and says, "You have the face of Aphrodite," and gives me this beautiful smile, full of kindness.

Of course, I thought he said, "Hermaphrodite," so I cold-cocked him in the jaw.

As he was lying there on the ground, laughing himself silly with a big hunk of top sirloin on his face while I stammered out an apology, I knew he was a good fit for me.

I put him out of my mind once I got close to my destination.

I got off Highway 95 and turned onto 160 South. Half a mile later, I took a right on State 372 until I saw West Street. One more turn, and I pulled into the driveway of the second house on the left. I got out of my car and heard the front door of the house swing open.

A woman of color, medium sized in height and build, came outside and gave me a bear hug. Jeanna had been my best friend since high school. I hadn't seen her in over ten years. She had a few more wrinkles than I remembered and had become a bit heavier, but her dark eyes were the same.

"God, it's been too long, girl," she said to me, stepping back and taking a look. She shook her head and smiled. "How do you do it, Maria? You haven't aged at all. Still the same dark-haired beauty you were in school. You don't look a day over thirty."

"I'm forty-four, love, same as you," I responded. "But thank you for saying that."

Clasping her hand tightly in mine I dropped my voice. "I am sorry to hear about your folks. They were good people, always kind to me."

Jeanna glanced around and took me by the hand. "I don't think you got my true message. My folks aren't dead, just... missing. Best you come inside. We've got a few things to discuss. I'll send one of the boys out to fetch your things."

Pahrump was a decent-sized town—but small enough where you had to drive nearly an hour to get to the nearest In-N-Out. There were four churches within walking distance. That might seem excessive, but many folks here had the reputation of being professional sinners and found comfort in the house of

God.

I was led into the living room. I sat on a second-hand couch of brown suede. It was comfortable enough, though it smelled of cigarettes. I met Jeanna's two sons, Glen and Jason, neither of whom took after their mother. Both were lighter skinned on account of their daddy and both looked to be in their early twenties. The older of the two, Glen, carried in my duffle bag, while Jason handed me a glass of ice-cold sweet tea.

"Thank you," I said, watching him sit on his chair, polishing a shotgun. He glanced from time to time at a green camouflage walkie-talkie sitting upright on the table.

Glen dropped the bag on the floor, took out a six-inch hunting knife and began to sharpen it.

"Ya'll expectin' a war?" I joked, grinning at them both.

Neither smiled back. They just looked up at their momma.

"I'm sorry, Maria. Don't mind them," Jeanna said, lighting a Camel. "They're worried about their sister."

"Sierra?" I guessed, trying to remember her name. "She's got to be, what? Ten by now?"

"Eleven last Sunday," Jeanna corrected, exhaling smoke out the side of her mouth.

"Why the concern?" I asked, curious.

All three looked at me without speaking. After a moment, the boys went back to their weapons while Jeanna leaned forward.

"Well, you've come to the heart of the matter. The boys and I didn't want to involve anyone else, but you came all the way up here from Vegas, and I could use the help."

"You know I'll do whatever I can."

I saw Jeanna tense up as she took another drag of her cigarette.

"You should go," said a deep voice. I was shocked to hear it come from Glen, as he was the slighter of build, lean and wiry.

"We need her," Jason argued, frowning at his brother.

"We talked about this," Jeanna snapped, looking at both of them. "It's her choice, she can leave or stay, but I will not lose help when we can use it."

"Is Sierra okay?" I asked, starting to worry.

"She's fine," Jeanna answered, looking weary. "Tell her," she said, nodding to Glen. "Tell her everything."

The older child nodded, while continuing to sharpen his knife.

"It started a week ago," he began. "A new preacher came to town—a man named Matthias."

"There's a fifth church now?" I asked, surprised.

"I wouldn't say that," Jason snorted.

Jeanna swatted him on the leg. "Hush now. Let your brother talk."

"Matthias brought two followers with him," Glen continued. "A man and a woman. He went to the town hall last Thursday and was awarded rights to start his services the very next day."

Glen paused, licking his lips. "Jason and me were walking home from the food mart and saw his female companion from a ways off. Something about her, it was, I don't know—magnetic, like I was drawn to her."

I took a drink of sweet tea from my glass. It felt like heaven on the way down my throat.

"Nothing wrong with being drawn to an attractive woman," I said. "Your mother turned more than a few heads in her day."

Glen looked down and blushed. "I don't much care for women," he muttered.

Feeling like an idiot, I reached out and touched his hand. "You'll excuse me, Glen, I forgot."

"S'okay," he shrugged. "It's not important. We have other concerns, just now."

"Keep going," Jeanna encouraged.

Glen took a deep breath and continued. "Ain't natural what I felt toward her, but it was nothin' compared to Jason's reaction. He damn near ran across the road trying to jump on her."

Jason, the younger, stockier brother, was nodding in affirmation. "I never felt anything like it before," he said. "If Glen hadn't clamped on to me, lord knows what would have happened."

I took another drink and set the tea on the coffee table. "I still don't see the problem, boys."

"You will," Jason said quietly.

Setting aside his knife, Glen continued. "At first, we didn't think much of it. Hormones runnin' wild and such. On Sunday, after folks attended service at the new church, people started to go missing."

"What do you mean, they went missing?" I asked.

"He means they're dead," Jason cut in harshly.

"Dammit Jay, we don't know that," Jeanna snapped, looking at her younger son angrily.

"Sierra said..."

"I don't give a rat's ass what she said," Jeanna continued. "They may still be alive!"

"Calm down, the both of you," Glen ordered, looking at them in frustration. "We don't know anything for certain."

He turned and stared at me. "That's why we need you."

I frowned at Jeanna. I didn't understand a lick of what was going on. "What do you need me for?"

Glen sighed. "She's never going to believe us," he muttered again.

"Just tell her," Jeanna insisted. "She's smarter than all of us put together."

Glen scratched his chin and shook his head. "We think

Matthias' followers are some kind of supernatural beings. Creatures that prey upon those of the opposite sex."

The house went quiet for ten of the longest seconds of my life.

"Ya'll are messing with me," I laughed, looking straight at Jeanna.

"I know it sounds crazy," she answered, the smoke from her cigarette dancing in the air in front of her. "But hear the boys out."

"You know how I went crazy with lust when I saw that woman?" Jason asked, putting aside his gun. "Sierra says that Widow Pickens had that same look on her face when she was talking to the man Matthias brought with him."

"That doesn't mean..."

"Widow Pickens is ninety-eight years old," Jeanna cut in. "She hasn't lusted after a man in nearly half a century. When she saw the fellow, she damn near jumped his bones at the service."

"Widow Pickens is one of the folks that's come up missing," Jason chimed in. "No one's seen her since Sunday. The same day our grandparents went missing."

I looked carefully at each of them. All three were deadly serious. I took another drink of sweet tea, swirling the information in my mind.

"What do you think is going on?" I asked.

Jason let out another sigh. "We think Matthias and his followers are abducting these people, though no one knows why, but our guess is that they are drawn to his followers... sexually."

"What about Sierra?" I asked, after a moment's hesitation. "Aren't you worried about her?"

It was Glen who answered. "Sierra's only eleven years old. She—well, she hasn't gone through puberty yet. I figured she'd have the best chance at resisting Matthias' followers."

"So far it has worked," Glen continued. "She's outside the church now, hiding in a tree with her walkie-talkie, giving us updates."

I exhaled deeply. "Let's say I believe you for a second," I offered. "What is it you want me to do?"

"Well," Jeanna said, taking a last drag of her cigarette, "I thought, you being so smart and all, you might know something about this stuff. Men and women being... seduced against their will? Did you ever hear about anything like that in Sunday School or one of your fancy colleges?"

The crazy thing was, I *had* heard about this kind of thing, though it hadn't been at Sunday School or the university.

"Well shoot," I swore under my breath.

"What's the matter?" Jeanna asked.

I shook my head, annoyed as all get-out. "I don't know much myself, but..."

They all looked at me, waiting to hear what I was going to say.

"I know someone who does."

Jeanna leaned her head forward. "Who is it?"

Lord Jesus, I did not want to call Decland back, not for this. "It's a good thing I love you, Jeanna," I snapped, knowing I needed his knowledge. "I wouldn't call for anyone else."

I whipped out my cell and pressed Decland's number. It rang twice before he picked up.

"I was just thinking about you," I heard his voice say sarcastically. "Still mad at me for loving you?"

"Decland, shut up," I hissed, casting at furtive look at Jeanna. "I have you on speaker, and I need your help."

There was a moment of silence on the other end.

"Why am I on speaker? Who's in the room with you?"

Sweat began to drip down my face. "I'm with my friend Jeanna, and her two sons Glen and Jason."

"Ahh, the infamous Jeanna," he replied, his voice friendly. "It's a pleasure to make your acquaintance."

"Are... are you Maria's boyfriend?" Jeanna asked, giving me a small smile.

"Well, we've been seeing one another for almost a year..."

"Shut up, Dec, no one is interested in my love life."

"I am," Jeanna said, her smile widening.

I covered the speaker with my hand. "Do you want my help or not?"

"He said he was in love with you," she replied, raising her eyebrows.

"He is not in love with me. He just likes to..." I stopped, nearly saying too much.

Jason leaned forward. "Likes to what?" he asked.

"I enjoy everything about her," Decland's voice said loudly over the phone. "She loves me too—though she won't admit it. She's the most incredible..."

"Decland, shut up!" I screamed, cutting him off.

"What? It's true. No matter what you..."

"Dec, I swear to god, if you say one more word, I'm going to stab you in the neck," I threatened, sweat beading down my face.

There was silence on the other end. "Dammit, Dec, did you hear me?" I demanded.

"You just told me not to speak or you'd stab me in the neck," he answered, sarcasm dripping from his voice. "How am I supposed to answer with that kind of threat hanging over my head?"

Jeanna began to laugh. "I like him."

"Ask him," encouraged Glen, who still looked focused.

"Look, Dec, we can talk later. Right now, I need your help."

"I'm listening."

I took a deep breath. "This is gonna sound crazy, but I want you to answer my questions, okay?"

"Fire away."

"You used to play that Dungeons and Dragons game, right?"

"Sure did. That's how I got interested in ancient cultures."

"Did you ever hear about any supernatural creatures that could seduce men and women?"

There was a pause.

"There's all kinds," he answered. "The ancient Greeks believed in sea creatures called Sirens. They would lull sailors in with their songs. There are nymphs, and fairies too, all rumored..."

"What about a type of being that uses lust to lure in their prey?" Glen interrupted.

Another pause.

"There is one," Dec confirmed. "It's called a succubus. They often work with powerful demons to lure men to their deaths with a single kiss. They were said to take the form of voluptuous, beautiful women."

"Could they make a man go crazy? Like a dog in heat?" Jason asked.

"Yes—but, what's this about?"

"Are there... boy succ-u-buses?" Glen asked, stumbling over the word.

"Succubi—and yes, a male is called an incubus. Are you playing a game or something?"

All of us sat there quietly.

"Hello? Are you still there?" Decland asked.

"I have to go, baby, I..." I hesitated, glancing at Jeanna. "I love you, Decland. I'll call you later."

"Wait, what? You love me? What the hell is wron..."

I pressed the "end call" button.

Each of us sat, blinking at one another.

"Do ya'll have WiFi here?" I asked.

"Yes," Jeanna answered. "You believe me, don't you?"

"I don't know," I replied honestly. "But it won't hurt to do some research, see what we might be up against."

"Why didn't you ask your boyfriend?" Jason asked. "He seemed to know all about them."

I couldn't tell them why. The answer was terrifying. As sure as I know Decland, I knew if he suspected I was in trouble, no force on Earth could keep him from me. I couldn't take the risk of losing him.

"You love him," Jeanna said.

It was not a question.

"Let's get to work," I replied, ignoring my old friend.

We decided the best thing for it was to go to the new church and see for ourselves. After some fierce negotiations, I talked Jeanna and her sons into letting me go with Sierra. All of us were vulnerable in some way, but not her.

Jason contacted Sierra on the walkie-talkie and let her know I was coming.

"What's she look like?" I heard Sierra ask her brother.

"A short woman, with light skin and jet-black hair. She has a kind face and," I saw him glance over at me, but I pretended not to notice. "She's a stunner Double C. Like something out of a movie. Even Glen thinks so."

There was a pause on the other end. "Well, maybe she's a succubus too," Sierra said harshly. "Fooled you all with her womanly wiles. Not me, I'm hard core, tougher than you milksops."

The walkie-talkie went dead on the other end, evidence that Sierra was done talking.

"Sorry about that," Glen said, shuffling over. "Sierra can be... difficult sometimes."

"She can be a pain in the ass, is what she can be," Jason said, shaking his head. "But she's smart and strong-willed. Last year she chased after me with a shovel when I touched her science project. Damn near knocked me unconscious."

"Don't worry about her," Jeanna said, crushing her latest cigarette in an ashtray. "You'll get on just fine." She looked up at the computer screen in front of her. "What is it exactly I'm supposed to be looking for online?"

"See if these creatures have a weakness," I answered. "In case they are what you think, we'd best know how to fight them."

"Take this," Jason said, handing me a four-inch knife.

I smiled at him and his naivete. "What kind of girl do you think I am?" I asked. Raising up my white pastel dress, I showed him the small but powerful handgun I kept strapped against my thigh.

"Decland know about that?" Jeanna asked quietly.

I gave her the naughtiest smile I could. "He's familiar."

The plan was to drop me a block away from the church and have Sierra meet me outside. I'd go in and pay my respects, pretending like I was new in town. Sierra would use that time to see if she could sneak in the back and find out what was happening at the new church.

Jason let me out of the car a quarter of a mile away from our meetup. I started to walk east along Wilson Road till I saw the church. It was a small building with a faded red exterior. Outside on the street was a white sign with bold lettering that read, "Church of Orphanim, and the Lord's Philosophy."

Giving a sideways glance, I saw a tall gangly girl with skin the color of coconut rum walk up next to me.

"I don't think you're that pretty," she said, looking me up and down, a sour expression on her face.

I almost laughed. I could smell the jealousy oozing off of her. "I think you're beautiful," I replied kindly. It was the last thing she expected to hear.

I was being honest. Yes, she was a tomboy, with scuffed knees and elbows. Her hair was a virtual rat's nest, and she was a bit awkward with those gangly legs. Underneath all that, I could see flawless skin, the kind folks pay a heap of money to maintain back in San Francisco. Her face was that of her mother, before the weariness of the world wore it down. Any fool could see she would grow to be a lovely young woman.

"Hmmph," she snorted, unsure of how to respond.

Sierra unclipped a walkie-talkie from the side of her belt. "Big Jay, this is double C. You read me? Over."

There was a moment of quiet before her brother responded. "This is Big Jay, I copy, over."

"I've made contact with the movie star, over."

"Very funny C, just be safe. Over."

"Ya ya, I'll be fine. Over and out."

I looked over at Sierra with one of my eyebrows cocked. "Double C?"

"He couldn't say my name proper when I was born," she explained, "called me CC."

She frowned at me.

"How do you do that?" she asked, nodding at my eye. "Raise just one brow?"

"We pull this off and I'll teach you," I answered with a wink. "Now, how about you tell me your plan?"

She gave me a long look. "You want to know *my* plan?"

I shrugged. "It's your town. You're the one keeping an eye on things. I think it best I listen to you."

I could tell what I'd said meant something to her. She tried not to let on, but I could see she was pleased.

Sierra leaned over and spoke quietly. "I haven't seen the soul suckers for a while now," she said. "They left more than an hour ago. Matthias was out front before you got here, singing a hymn I ain't never heard. After that, he went back inside."

"I'll go in the front door," I said, nodding at her. "Wait a minute or so, and you can sneak in the back."

Sierra nodded and slipped off an old, ratty backpack. Tucking her hand inside, I saw her pull out a canister of honey.

"What's that for?"

"Never you mind," she answered crossly. "I got plans you don't need to know about."

I couldn't help but smile at her bravado.

She slipped into the woods next to the church and waited for me to go in. I took a deep breath, walked past the sign and opened the church door.

You know that old sayin', don't judge a book by its cover? I don't know who came up with that, but they were dead wrong. That dilapidated little building on the outside looked brand spanking new compared to the inside. There were three rows of pews, six in each, running from the front of the room to the back. The pews were all worn with time, barely holding together.

At the front of the room was an arched ceiling, a podium of pure white underneath. On the front of the podium was a wooden carving. It depicted a soldier wearing a ducal crown, riding atop a griffon.

I know from experience most holy places can give a body a sense of peace.

This one most certainly did not.

I took a few steps forward, wondering where Matthias had gone.

"Welcome," came a voice from behind me.

I think it's safe to say I nearly jumped out of my skin. I turned around and laid my eyes on a kindly looking older man. He had frosted red hair and the greenest eyes I'd ever seen. His face turned with a smile.

"I must apologize," he began. "I didn't mean to frighten you."

He spoke with the voice of a saint, a learned man, for certain.

"That's alright," I gasped, trying to get my heart under control. "You startled me."

He raised his hands in apology, and his smile widened. "I was tending to our prayer candles," he said, stretching his hand to the back of the room.

There was a small alcove to the right, next to the door. It was lined with two tiers of votive prayer candles. The place smelled of cinnamon, though I could detect a hint of *something* underneath it, a smell I couldn't put my finger on.

"I'm Matthias," he said, inclining his head, placing a hand to his heart. "What brings you in today?" he inquired.

I took a deep breath. I don't care for lying in the house of God as a general principle, but today was an exception.

"I don't rightly know," I began. "I'm new to the area, thinking of moving here. I heard there was a new church in town, and it just sort of called to me."

Mattias smiled again. "I see," he said.

I frowned at him. "You don't believe in divine inspiration?" I asked.

He laughed aloud. "Oh, I've *seen* divine inspiration," he answered. "But not today."

Nothing about this felt right. I needed to get out of there. "If I'm not welcome here...," I began, starting for the door.

His hand shot up, faster than I would have believed possible, and grabbed onto my wrist.

"On the contrary," he said, his red hair beginning to smoke. "I've been expecting you—Maria Donnelli."

My heart lurched in my chest.

"Let me go," I yelled, trying to rip away from him.

"Oh no, my dear," he replied, his voice becoming deeper, more sinister. "Your corrupt heart will burn for the sins committed against the Erinye."

He blinked once, and his eyes changed from deep green to ghostly white.

"Get off me!" I screamed, kicking out, landing a sharp blow against his shin.

Normally a blow like that would drop a person to the ground. Not him. Matthias' smile vanished, and his hair burst into flames.

"Rabid animal," he hissed, releasing his hold. "Run if you will. You cannot hide from me. Even the protection of *Origen* cannot save you."

I didn't know what he was talking about, but I came to recognize what I'd been smelling.

Sulphur and brimstone—oozing from Matthias.

I needed to get out of that church.

I tore past him, opened the door, and walked straight into the hands of the most beautiful man I'd ever seen.

"She's yours, Salem," Matthais said from behind me. "Feed if you like, but make it slow. I want to bathe in her screams."

"My pleasure," the newcomer replied, his eyes an icy blue.

I could feel it then, a warm rush of physical desire building in my chest. I knew this creature, the incubus, was using his power on me. A picture of Decland flashed in my mind, and I managed to turn away.

"She is strong," another voice said, stepping into view.

A woman, with curves a Kardashian would envy, stepped forward and touched my face. "She is in love," the woman smiled, with soft, pouty lips.

"She is protected by the Oathbreaker," Matthias warned. I could hear him draw close behind me, the smell of brimstone overwhelming. "Leave the girl to your brother, Valais—Maria's will cannot hold out against an immortal."

I hate to admit this, but Matthias was right. Every second Salem held me in his grip, I could feel my will to fight against him weaken. If I looked back into those blue eyes, it was all over.

Thankfully, it never came to that.

I heard something buzz past my ear.

A crossbow bolt buried itself in Salem's eye.

"What the...?" I heard Matthias gasp from behind me as the incubus staggered backward.

"Eat this, devil spawn!" Sierra shouted from the front of the room. She ran up the aisle, throwing a balloon filled with liquid at Matthias. He reached his hand out to catch it, and the balloon burst open, drenching him in a sticky, golden substance.

Honey.

"We need to get out of here!" Sierra screamed, grabbing my hand.

"Not so fast," Valais snarled, drawing a wicked-looking knife from under her dress.

"Your wiles won't work on me, succu-bitch," Sierra threatened, drawing a knife of her own.

"I don't need them to," Valais hissed back.

Free of Salem's spell, I pulled out my gun and fired.

Three shots to the chest knocked Valais to the ground, her dress smoking with gunpowder.

I turned back and saw Matthias staring at us, hatred etched on his face. "Your assault will avail you nothing. I command legions of..."

He stopped, his eyes widening, and yelped in pain.

"We need to run," Sierra urged, tugging my arm.

"What did you do?" I asked, glancing down at her as Matthias began slapping himself on the face and neck, yowling in pain.

"I kicked a hornets nest behind the church and doused him in honey-water," Sierra shouted. "Let's go!"

I didn't resist her pull on my hand, and both of us lit out of there. I looked back only once as we were tearing down the street. I caught a glimpse of Matthias unceremoniously whacking away at himself as an entire hive of angry insects exacted vengeance for the attack on their colony.

It might have been funny, except for two things.

Valais was sitting up, looking angry. Next to her, Salem did the same, furiously ripping the bolt from his eye.

Knowing we'd quite literally stirred up a hornet's nest, Sierra and I raced home.

It was twilight when we skidded to a halt in front of Jeanna's double-wide.

Glen and Jason were sitting out on the porch, polishing their shotguns.

"What happened?" Glen asked, his eyes wide at the sight of my pistol.

"They... knew who... I was," I panted, out of breath from the half-mile run.

"I... saved her," Sierra gasped from next to me.

"Girl, where'd you get that crossbow from?" Jason asked, stepping toward his sister. "Did you... you used my credit card last month, didn't you? Goddammit, I knew it!" he stormed.

"Don't," I said raising my hand, still trying to catch my breath. "She... saved my life."

"What did you mean when you said they knew who you were?" Glen asked.

I shook my head, my hands on my hips. Lord almighty, it was a good thing I'd been taking spinning classes this past month, otherwise I would have collapsed on the way back.

"I don't rightly know," I answered honestly. "Something about... *Origen's* protection and I'd committed a sin against something called... the Erinye."

He looked like he wanted me to say more, but Sierra waved him off. "We don't have time for this Q and A. I reckon we've about five minutes till they come here after us. We done gone and pissed them off."

Glen looked at his sister and nodded. "Alright, best we get inside. Jason, keep a lookout."

Jason, never taking his eyes from Sierra, nodded once and sat back down. "Drunk purchase, my ass," he muttered as Sierra walked by. "You owe me fifty-one dollars for that crossbow, little girl."

"I'll pay for it," I offered, thankful to be alive.

Once inside, Jeanna took one look at me and bade us sit down. "What happened?" she asked. "Are you alright?"

"I met Matthias and his underlings," I started, with a shiver.

"And?"

"The incubus took a bolt to the eye and got up like he'd been bit by a mosquito," I answered. "I put three 9 mm rounds in the female's chest from my Smith & Wesson, and she brushed it off like it was nothing."

Jeanna blinked in disbelief.

"I'm glad you're okay," she said at last, reaching out and clasping hold of my hand tightly.

"I'm fine, by the way," Sierra groused, annoyed at being ignored.

Jeanna frowned. "You'd be as fine as a fox in a hen house," her mother said. "No matter what you were up against."

"She saved me," I offered, knowing it was important to Sierra that her momma knew. "Otherwise, I'd be dead."

Jeanna's face softened somewhat. "Alright then, that's fine. Thank you, child."

"Hmmph," Sierra snorted, crossing her arms over her chest defiantly.

"Did you make any headway finding their weaknesses?" I asked, changing the subject.

Glen scratched his head. "Well, yes and no," he replied. "The bad news is, they don't have much in the way of weaknesses. They suck life from humans and feed off sexual energy. There's plenty of that here in Pahrump, as its, well... it's home to professional establishments that cater to..."

"Whorehouses," Sierra muttered, rolling her eyes. "They are called whorehouses."

I glanced outside and then back to Glen.

"You said there was good news?"

He nodded, grimly. "According to supernatural-being.com, they *can* be killed."

"How?"

He paused before answering.

"Decapitation or ripping out the heart."

I looked at him, wondering if he was being serious.

"Well, that sounds pleasant," Sierra muttered under her breath. "Speaking of unpleasant, I saw what was going on behind that church."

"What was it?" I asked, forgetting her objective in all the

excitement.

"It was bad," she explained. "Them town folk that are missing? They ain't dead. He's got them all in the back. I went to rouse Grandma, and she didn't move. She was glossed over like a..."

The door banged open and Jason backed in, eyes wide with shock. "Ya'll better come see this," he said, beckoning to the rest of us. "Glen, get your shotgun."

"The Weatherby?"

Jason shook his head. "The 590."

Glen blinked twice in surprise before he ducked into the back of the house.

The rest of us stepped onto the porch and gaped.

Hovering above the yard against the backdrop of a purple sky was a demon. There's no other way to put it. It was big, nearly seven feet tall, as close as I could figure. It glowed with fire smoldering all along its wings and torso. It wore some kind of bone armor and carried a curved sword, flames along the blade.

It would have been cool as all get-out if it hadn't been there to kill us.

With a roar, it dove toward us, its sword leading the way.

"MOVE!" bellowed Jason, who blasted at it with his shotgun.

I jumped down the steps, rolling to my feet, pistol in hand. I saw Jason's grapeshot tear into the demon, knocking it from the sky, but causing no lasting damage.

Jason, looking grimly determined, pumped his shotgun again as he strode down the stairs. He fired again, but this time the creature rolled to the side, dodging the salvo.

Before he could get a third volley off, the demon leapt to its feet and grabbed the gun out of Jason's hands, tossing it aside. Cool as a winter's wind, Jason slid his knife out of its sheath and stabbed the demon through the heart.

The demon looked down at the knife and snorted in contempt.

"What the fu..." Jason began, until the monster tossed him aside like a rag doll. He rolled to the ground, coming to rest some twenty feet away, crying out in pain.

"Double C!" Jeanna barked. "See to your brother."

My childhood friend whipped out two ivory-handled Colts and opened fire. I squeezed the trigger of my own gun and emptied the magazine.

Whatever this demon was, it wasn't stupid. It folded its wings around its body like a shield, deflecting every bullet we fired.

"Damn," I cursed, knowing my extra magazines were still in my car.

"Double C!" Jeanna screamed, trying desperately to reload her guns. "Get a move on."

I tried to make for the house, but the demon leapt forward, cutting me off. I backed up, until I could feel the solid wall of the double-wide behind me.

Sierra tried. Staggering as she was under the weight of her older brother, she snapped off a shot with her crossbow. The demon didn't even look her way, catching the bolt out of the air.

The demon reached out, merely inches from my face.

A gun blast sounded from the porch, jolting the creature away from me.

I took the opportunity and sprinted over to Sierra, lifting Jason under the armpit.

"Everybody inside," Glen said calmly, the barrel of his shotgun smoking.

The demon stepped forward again, and Glen sent another shot toward it. This time the creature fell to the ground.

"I can't kill it, not at this range," Glen said. "Get in the house. We'll force it to use the door, and I'll hit him when he comes in."

With Jeanna helping us, we managed to get Jason inside on the couch. He was dazed more than anything, though he was bleeding from a wound at his temple.

Sierra ran into the bedroom and grabbed a can that read, "Big Sexy Hair," along with her momma's lighter. Determined, Sierra held the can up, ready to immolate the demon as soon as it came into the room.

I picked up a kitchen knife lying on the dinner table as Glen backed through the front door.

"Stay behind me," Glen said, licking his lips nervously.

The demon leapt up on the porch, roaring at us once again.

It stabbed its blade at Glen, who backed away reflexively, raising his gun to his shoulder.

Then, quite unexpectedly, the demon stopped its advance. It half turned its head in confusion before being thrown out of the doorway to slam onto the front lawn.

We all looked at one another wordlessly before moving to the porch.

It was a sight I'll never forget.

There was a man, clean-cut and handsome, with a sword in his hand, fighting the demon.

"Who is that?" Sierra asked, awed.

Decland.

I don't know why, but somehow, someway, Decland was here. Not just here, but fighting like mad to save our lives.

"Is this the best Matthias could do?" Dec was saying. "A Hell Knight? I've killed scores of your kind."

In answer, the demon swung its fiery blade at Dec's head. Like a cat on a hot tin roof, Decland blocked the strike with his sword and danced to the side. Before that supernatural hellspawn knew what had happened, my boyfriend slashed it across the neck. The demon let out an earth-shattering scream as molten blood poured from the wound.

Unlike when Jason had stabbed the demon, this time the creature fell to the ground and turned to ash.

Decland spun around to look at me and flashed one of his crooked smiles. "Hello, gorgeous. I'd have been here sooner, but, you know, traffic."

"What, in the name of all that is holy in this world, are you doing here?" I asked, both thrilled and annoyed to see Decland.

"I've been in Nevada since this morning," he answered, cool as a cucumber.

"Why?"

"Who cares?" Sierra asked, looking at him dreamily. "If I had a boyfriend that looked like that, I'd marry him twice."

"Hush now," Jeanna said absently, stroking her daughter's hair.

"I'm just sayin', I wouldn't kick him outta bed for getting crumbs in the sheets," Sierra continued.

Apparently, Glen and his mother were of the same mind as Sierra—none of them could take their eyes off Decland.

"Have you all lost your goddamn minds?" Jason asked, holding a bag of ice on the back of his head. "We just got our asses whooped by a demon! Why is it me and the movie star are the only ones who give two shits about that?"

Jason was right, of course, but the others were right too. I forget sometimes I live in San Francisco. Big city like that has gorgeous folk all over the place. In Pahrump, well, men that look like Dec are a mite less common. Plus, I'd been seeing the man for some time now. They were just getting their first dose of him.

"He's right," Dec said, nodding at Jason. "We have much to discuss."

"Hold on just a minute," I said, narrowing my eyes. "How did you know where to find me?"

"I tracked your phone," Decland answered simply. "It's no great mystery. We've been tracking each other since you thought I was cheating on you with that English professor at the university, remember?"

"You cheated on Maria?" Jason asked, glowering at Decland.

Decland shook his head with a chuckle. "Of course not. I love Maria more than I've ever loved anyone. It would take a force beyond this world to tear me away from her."

Decland moved closer to Jason. "I understand you were the first to fight the Hell Knight. You managed to stab it in the heart. That's no easy feat. If your knife had been blessed like my sword, you'd have killed it without me."

Just like that, silver-tongued as he is, Decland won over his last objector.

"How is it that you know so much about this?" I asked, rather pointedly. "Did you teach a class on demons or something?"

Dec became serious. "There's no time to explain it all, but you're in danger. A powerful demon lord has come to Earth."

"You mean Matthias?" Sierra scoffed. "He's just an old man."

Decland shook his head. "Matthias was his name in heaven. In hell he is known as Murmur—once the foremost of the Orphanim, angels that carried the throne of God. Now he's a duke of hell."

Dec paused, looking at each of us. "He knows I am here now, and he will be coming for us all."

"How do you know who it is?" I asked.

"I just do," he answered evasively.

"Can't you walk down to the church and kill him?" Glen asked.

Decland shrugged his shoulders. "Maybe, but this goes beyond him. Murmur can open a portal to hell on his own. The question is, why is he capturing humans?"

"That's what he's doing!" Sierra cut in. "I've seen it with my own eyes. The townsfolk, they ain't dead, but I think—I think he's draining their energy, or life force, or whatever you call it."

Decland looked at her sharply. "Why do you say that?" he asked.

"Because that's what I saw behind that church," she explained. "Thirteen people, all laying there, exhausted as all get out. I tried to rouse Grandma, but she glossed over me like I was a ghost."

Her words jogged my memory.

"Matthias said something strange to me, something I didn't understand," I said, looking at Dec. "That the protection of *Origen* couldn't save me—that I'd committed a sin against the Erinye."

For the first time since I'd known him, Decland looked worried.

"The Erinye?" he asked quietly.

"Yes, what's he talking about?"

"So, *that's* what this is about," Decland sighed. He shook his head and looked out the window. "The Erinyes are spirits of vengeance and retribution," he explained. "Also known as Furies."

"Dec?" I asked, suspecting there was more.

"There are three," he continued. "The first is Alecto, known for her endless anger. The second is Tisiphone, whose name means 'vengeful destruction.'"

"The third?" I asked, sweat dripping down my face.

Decland did not speak for the span of a few heartbeats. "The last is Megaera."

"What was she known for?" Jeanna asked.

"Jealous rage."

I wiped the sweat from my forehead. "What does she want

with me?" I asked.

Decland sat there, flush with guilt. "I am sorry, my love. I have put you all in danger."

"What are you talking about?" I asked, reaching out, taking his hand.

"Maybe I should have told you from the start, but—I didn't think you'd believe me."

"It's okay," I replied, squeezing his hand tightly.

"No, it isn't," he muttered, standing up.

He ran his hand through his hair. "I never thought it would come to this. All of you should run. Get away from here as fast as you can."

"Hey," I said, standing up next to him. "That's enough. You've stood by me through everything, my divorce, my kids—I'm not about to throw away the only man I'd ever consider marrying again."

A small smile crept onto his face. "You'd marry me? After all the times you've refused?"

"Maybe," I countered. "But only if you tell us what's going on."

He pressed his lips together, making his decision. "Megaera is angry with me," he began. "I—well, I spurned her a long time ago."

"I've read about the Furies in my ancient history class," Glen said. "They are archaic beings. They've been around for millennia."

"Yes," Decland agreed. "They date back to the first days of creation. I was called *Origen* then. It means, 'Of the Mountain.'"

"Wait a minute," Sierra said. "Are you saying *you're* thousands of years old?"

"Yes," he answered. "When I broke things off with Megaera, she cursed me to walk the Earth for eternity, never to find love again."

He paused and looked at me. "I never did, until I met you."
He paused, his gaze grim. "It seems she wants to take what I did
not give her away from me, torturing me yet again."

I stared at Decland, seeing the truth of his words. With a
snort, I started walking toward the door.

"Wait, where are you going?" asked Jeanna.

"Some immortal bitch from thousands of years ago has it in
for my man?" I clucked over my shoulder. "I'm fixin' to reload my
gun. I'm not going down without a fight."

There was no leaving the rest behind, as Matthias, or
Murmur, or whatever the hell he's called, wasn't about to let
Jeanna's folks go free. Having Decland was a huge help. I found
out he was stronger than I thought. 'Course I figured as much
when he tossed the Hell Knight off the porch with one
hand. Still, it was nice to go into a fight with a heavy hitter on
your side.

Decland confirmed that Glen was right about the life
stealers, decapitation and heart ripping would do just fine.

The demons from hell were another matter. He said only fire,
distilled from a pure source, could harm them. Jason, god bless
his soul, got out a bottle of the purest moonshine in the county
and filled up a bunch of bottles to make Molotov cocktails. Sierra
was designated as the fire starter of those explosions.

Most important were the blessed weapons. In addition to
his sword, Dec handed over a pair of knives. He gave one each to
the brothers.

Finally, he handed me a sawed-off shotgun.

"Consecrated by the archbishop of San Francisco," he said.

"Cordileone?" I asked, admiring its walnut stock.

"Some years before him," Dec confessed, giving me a brief
smile.

We came up with a makeshift plan, based on Sierra's intel of the church. Jeanna would drive her pickup and rescue her folks and the others behind the church. Sierra, Jason, and me were going to go with Dec and see how much hell we could raise.

Pun intended.

"What about those life suckers?" Jason pointed out.

"I have an idea," Sierra said, a rapacious look in her eyes.

"By all means," Dec smiled. "It's your show."

We all huddled round to listen to her plan.

"Here they come," Valais whispered to her brother.

"I want the child," the incubus hissed, rubbing a knuckle at his ruined eye.

"You'll get your wish," Valais noted, pointing at the two humans approaching from the left. The first was shorter, clearly in her youth. The succubus could see long, dark hair flowing from the other's hood. Her eyes narrowed. "The young one is with the bitch that shot me." She sniffed. "They think they can flank us."

She turned and looked to Salem. "Both female. Kill them for me, brother," Valais answered, steel in her voice.

"The others are moving on the opposite side. Go, both of you," Murmur stated, staring coldly at *Origen*, who was walking directly toward them. "Kill the others, I will leave *Origen* for the Fury. He will kneel before her in chains."

With inhuman speed, Salem and Valais raced to their prospective marks.

Both Sierra and her companion halted as Salem stopped in front of them. "Let me deal with your friend first, child," he hissed, grabbing Maria in his hands. "Then you are mine."

Salem reached out with his power. "Come to me, woman. I will drink your life force until all that is left is a withered husk."

He was met with a wall of fury that could come from only one source.

"You're a dead man," Sierra snarled, a malicious smile on her face.

Shaking off the hood, Salem was stunned to see the face of Jason, a long black wig on his head. Moving quickly, he rammed his blessed knife deep into the chest of the incubus.

"Rot in hell," Sierra quipped, wiggling her fingers at Salem, as Jason carved out the creature's heart.

A moment later, the incubus turned to dust, a look of disbelief on his face.

Valais felt a pang of loss at the death of her brother.

Impossible! No mortal woman could resist him.

Turning around, she saw Jason take off the wig he'd been wearing and throw it to the ground. Shocked, Valais blinked and looked at the pair in front of her. If Maria wasn't over there, then that meant..."

"Hey there, sugar pie," the figure in front of Valais said, removing the hood from her head. The woman, Maria, gave her a look of pure venom. "Looks like brother done gone and got himself killed."

Standing next to Maria was Glen, a blessed knife in his hand.

Valais grabbed onto his arms. She reached out with her powers—and was met with a dark look of anger in the man's eyes.

"You're barking up the wrong tree there, sweetie," Maria said. "Glen here likes men. Don't take it personal."

Valais was in shock. She barely felt the cold steel of the man's knife slice its way along her throat, all the way through her neck.

The succubus fell to the ground, her head rolling clear.

"Thank you for visiting the great state of Nevada," Maria continued, stepping over the succubus. "Don't let the gates of hell hit that fine ass of yours on the way out."

"Come forth, my children," Murmur shouted. "Come and drink your fill!"

From behind the church, a dozen demons shot forward, summoned from the beyond.

Two, one with the face of a toad and the other a goat, made for Decland. He cut them down with consummate ease.

"You fight well, mortal," Murmur growled, "but the lost blade of Durandal will not save you."

"We shall see," Decland replied.

Murmur transformed. One moment he was an old man with graying red hair, the next he was a flame-haired soldier wearing a ducal crown who carried a spear of fire.

The two adversaries moved forward, their weapons ringing like a clarion bell as they clashed time and time again on unholy ground.

"We've got company," Glen stated in his calm voice.

A half score of demons came charging at us. I readied my sanctified shotgun, as Glen drew his 590. Before they got too close, a Molotov cocktail struck.

"Burn, you bastards!" Sierra screamed in delight.

That got their attention, as two of the creatures went up in blue flames. Four of the demons peeled away from us and raced toward Jason and his sister.

That left the last four to us. I leveled my shot gun and went to work.

Glen blasted the first one to dust, and I shot a second that spun out of control and landed off to my left, dead as a doornail. The other two were on us faster than Charlie Daniels could sing, "Chicken in the bread pan picking out dough."

One with a reptilian head jumped, knocking me to the ground. I jammed my shotgun lengthwise in its mouth, fighting like mad to keep it at bay. We rolled around in the dirt for a few seconds, cursing and swearing at one another. I felt its claw dig into my side and pain erupted along my ribs.

An explosion of sound echoed above me. The demon jolted left and ceased its struggling. I shifted its weight off of me and saw a hand covered in blood floating in front of my face. I took it, as Glen helped me to my feet.

"Thanks," I said, meaning it.

"Look there," he nodded in answer.

Decland was bleeding from wounds on his hip and bicep. However, Murmur looked to have taken the worst of it, as he bled deeply from a cut on his chest, near the heart.

"How?" Murmur asked, looking at his bleeding torso in disbelief.

"Because I'm better than you," Decland panted, triumphantly. "Now, summon her so we can end this."

Despite his imminent demise, Murmur smiled. "She doesn't love you anymore, *Origen*. She will bathe in your blood."

The demon lord tilted his head back and screamed out a single name. "Megaera!"

Decland swept his blade across Murmur's neck, sending him back to hell.

An instant later, the Fury appeared.

I wish I could tell you she was as ugly as a three-headed snake, but that would be a lie. Megaera was tall, sporting a full figure, tits and all. She reminded me of an Amazon princess, if the truth be told. With hair as black as mine and a face of unearthly beauty, she cut an inspiring figure.

I was more than a little jealous.

"That's enough," Decland said, looking at her with pity. "Your jealous rage has gone on for too long."

Megaera walked past him until she stood across from me.

"*This* is the creature you've chosen?" she shrieked. "A subspecies, barely able to speak?"

"Immortal or not," I snarled, gathering an anger of my own. "I'm ten times the woman you are, honey. You best get on out of here while you're still in one piece."

Glen strode up next to me, his 590 ready to rock.

The Fury turned to Decland. "I cursed you for the sins you committed against me. We could have lived together, forever. We could have loved for all eternity!"

"Hey, psycho," Sierra called from behind Megaera. "It's been thirty seconds, and I already despise you. How'd you expect *Origen* to deal with your crazy ass for all eternity?"

The Fury, apparently, wasn't used to hearing those kinds of insults. That's when the shit hit the fan.

"Infidel!" Megaera screamed. The Fury raised her hands and two curved swords, pulsing with darkness, appeared in each hand.

"Get back, all of you!" Decland shouted, rushing to attack.

He ran forward, and Megaera swatted him aside. Dec slammed into the church wall, his sword flying wide. "You cannot stand against me," she thundered. "No one can!"

Jason tossed the last Molotov cocktail to his sister and sprinted forward, leaping at the Fury. Megaera laughed aloud, dropped her sword and caught Jason in midair. Casually, she tossed him aside where he slammed into Decland, who was fighting to rise.

"Your screams will echo throughout Hell," the Fury promised, lifting her sword.

"Glen, give me a leg up," I shouted, struck with a desperate thought.

I crouched down and ran toward him.

"Double C," I screamed, arms pumping at my sides. "Light the last salvo!"

I jumped on Glen's back using it as a launching pad, and he thrust me forward toward Megaera. Sierra, understanding my intent, lit the last Molotov cocktail and heaved it at the Fury. I waited till it was directly in front of Megaera's face and fired the last round of my blessed shotgun.

An explosion like I'd never seen erupted, blasting us all backward. I covered my eyes with my arm as best I could just as the explosion went off. Between the fire of the purest moonshine in the Silver State and my blessed shotgun, Megaera and that pretty face of hers exploded in a ball of fire.

I landed some thirty feet away and rolled, my back to the explosion.

When I looked up, I turned in time to see Megaera crash to the knees, her face alight with flame.

A scream, full of anguish and loss, roared from her mouth and shook the very air around us.

"Noooooooo!"

Glen rose to his feet and threw his blessed knife at the Fury, taking Megaera full in the heart. There was a huge implosion, which knocked Glen from his feet. When we looked up, Megaera was gone.

Rising slowly, I staggered over to check on Decland. He and Jason were groaning like men do when they get so much as the smallest scratch.

"Damn, that hurt," Jason muttered, rubbing at his shoulder.

"You okay, baby?" I asked, seeing Jason was okay.

"Yes," he grunted, wincing in pain. "I'll be right as rain once I heal." He reached out and touched my face. "You saved me."

"I love you," I blurted, tears filling my eyes. "What was I

supposed to do?"

He smiled and looked past me, seeing the others make their way toward us.

"Everybody alright?" Glen asked, fretting at his siblings.

Jason smiled, the first such look I'd seen from him. "Just a normal Tuesday night," he gasped, rising to his feet. "Slaying demons and such."

"I knew what you were thinking at the end," Sierra said, nodding at me with excitement. "Light the bomb and WHAM, killed a bitch! Did you see what happened, Glen?"

"Yes, I was standing right there," the eldest brother said, chuckling at his sister.

Jeanna honked her truck's horn at us from the back of the church. "If ya'll are done congratulating yourselves, we've got folks to rescue."

Sierra looked over. "Granny and Pappy?"

Jeanna smiled. "They're fine." Jeanna paused a moment. "Proud of you, girl, proud of you all."

"Well, we'd best go lend a hand," Glen said, nodding at his brother.

"Come along when you're ready," Jason said, reloading his shotgun. "Come on, Double C."

Decland looked at me and stroked my face as the trio of siblings walked off. "You okay, love?"

"I'm alright," I answered, wiping away my tears. "But—do you have any more ex-girlfriends I should know about? If I'm gonna marry you, I need to know about that shit."

DRAGON CROWN BOOKS

❖ ❖ ❖

"Hell Hath No Fury" by Michael K. Falciani appears here for the first time.

Samuel Post Davis

The Hermit
of Treasure Peaks

In 1858, a couple of ragged and vermin-inhabited prospectors, wandering about one of the spurs of the Sierra, discovered gold, an article for which they had been assiduously searching for some months. Immediately on fixing their hungry optics to the fragment of auriferous rock, they gave a shout of delight, drove down a stake, fixed a notice of location, and announced the birth of a new town, calling the same Treasure Peaks.

When the place was dubbed Treasure Peaks, even the visionary minds of the two unkempt gold-hunters did not for a moment imagine that the mountainside would ever be graced by any more than one, or perhaps two, miners' cabins. They were not selfish men, and the next time they visited the town of Forks Flat, they proclaimed their golden discovery at the first public bar of the place.

The idle population of Forks Flat was not slow in availing itself of the traveling facilities which led to Treasure Peaks. The trail up the mountainside was a rugged and tedious one, and took the better part of two days to traverse; yet, inside of six months, a passable wagon road was worn to the camp, and the place witnessed all the scenes of life and activity incidental to the birth of a new city.

When Treasure Peaks contained about a thousand inhabitants, the little town began to swell with importance. The mining prospects were, indeed, flattering, and the quartz ledges in the hills were rapidly being developed. Besides, they were productive, and the deeper the workers went the richer and wider grew the veins. New cabins went up every day, the prospect-holes became shafts, the bucket and windlass gave way to the donkey-engine, people poured in from all directions, and the village child began to assume the airs of the municipal man.

In the midst of the bustle of business and moneymaking, the inhabitants of the Peaks did not forget that they had a rival—a small one, it was true in the shape of the town of Forks Flat, and to wipe out the Flat from all commercial and geographical recognition was their sole aim. Joe Beggs, a man whose opinions had the advantage of considerable weight as he ran a first-class blue-chip faro game—insisted on a newspaper:

"What we want for this growing camp is a first-class newspaper, that can properly set forth the interests of this mountain metropolis."

One of the crowd suggested that a man named Lightner, in San Francisco, was the party wanted.

"Has he got the classical education necessary to run a newspaper in in a town like Treasure Peaks? Is he a man of elevated thought and vigorous expression? Is he a man that's well read—one that we can refer gambling disputes to with a guarantee of a proper rendering of the points?"

The party who had suggested the name of Lightner vouched for the thorough capacity of the man, and by the next day, three thousand dollars were raised, as a bonus, to induce him to come. Lightner was sent for, and in about a month the citizens of the Peaks began to look for the advent of the printing office.

One sultry afternoon, a horseman came up the grade at a brisk pace to announce that the printing establishment was on the way, and would arrive in a few hours. This intelligence caused an extraordinary commotion in the camp, and as soon as the first flush of excitement was over, preparations commenced for giving the new editor a fitting reception—something which would glorify the Peaks forever, and correspondingly humiliate the commercial pride of Forks Flat.

It was just at nightfall when John Lightner, with two loaded freight wagons, came in view at a bend of the grade, half a mile below town. The sighting of the team from the top of the hill was signalized by the explosion of an anvil—a mode of firing salutes much in vogue at that period. In an instant more, an American flag was hoisted to the top of the pole, while on a neighboring eminence the welcoming bonfires were lighted, and there was a general rush to the foot of the main street.

When the teams halted, steaming and panting, at the town level, the journalist was considerably astonished to find a delegation of citizens drawn up to receive him. It had been agreed that Joe Beggs, the leading faro-dealer in the town, should deliver the address of welcome; and for the first time since attaining his majority, the man of notable nerve and coolness was in a state of excitement which required a stiff horn of brandy, taken every fifteen minutes, to allay. When Lightner got down over the wheel, however, Beggs advanced, and with half-lifted hat, grasped him warmly by the hand, cleared his throat for the first oratorical effort of his life, and, after a slight pause, began :

MR. LIGHTNER: *In behalf of the citizens of this growing commercial metropolis and mining center, I bid you thrice welcome to Treasure Peaks. [Here he threw his weight on the other leg.] I assure you that the fact of my being the first man to be afforded the opportunity of welcoming a writer of your brains and ability to our midst causes my breast to swell with a pride which would be impossible for me to conceal, even if I so desired. It is the happiest moment of my checkered and eventful existence, and I will not efface it from the tablets of my memory to my dying day.*

At this point, the speaker, whose remarks had fully realized the most sanguine expectations of his friends, looked about him in a dazed way, and it was quite evident, to those who knew him best that his stock of English had given out. Nothing daunted, however, he plunged boldly into the more congenial and familiar parlance of his profession, and struck out as follows :

You will find the journalistic layout in this section a bang-up game to buck at, and with a man of your heft in the lookout chair, we can call the turn on the whole coast. We boys propose to play you open-up from the start, and chip up our subscriptions to the last cove in the camp, and to the full limit of the game. As long as you don't ring in a brace deal, and keep clean cases, you can bet heavy on the square-up support of this camp, and don't you forget it.

Three rousing cheers greeted Beggs' closing words, and one of his admirers critically remarked :

"He made some awful wild play at the start, but called the

turn beautiful at the close."

Lightner thanked them cordially in a few quiet, well-turned remarks, and introduced his wife, who had remained on the elevated seat of the freight wagon, curiously contemplating the lionizing of her husband. She heard the three cheers given in her honor, saw the waving hats and bristling hands of welcome, and wished, more than at any other time in her life, that she had a thick veil to cover her beauty and blushes. Then came a fusillade of small arms, as a sort of gunpowder supplement to the cheering, and the boom of another anvil shook the air. A moment later, her hand was grasped by the supple fingers of Beggs, who hastened to extend his apologies for the incompleteness of the preparations for the reception, and the utter poverty of their execution.

After having made the speech and chatted with the first respectable woman ever seen at the Peaks, Beggs seriously considered the propriety of securing a municipal charter for the town, and getting elected mayor. When the reception was over, and the ruddy light of the bonfires had ceased to gild the rough crags lying behind the Peaks, the crowd dispersed, and for the rest of the night the public sentiment could be summed up in a remark of Beggs :

"Now we'll make them Forks Flat fellers sick."

It took some weeks to set the little printing office on its legs, and the constant presence of squads of inquisitive visitors did not materially facilitate matters. Over a hundred men came in to suggest a name, and such names! *The Tidal Wave, The Mountain Thunderbolt, The Mining Blast, The Sierra Snow Slide, The Voice of Truth, The Forks Flat Crusher,* and *The Treasure Peaks Howitzer* were a few proposed. The excitement incidental to the baptism of the new journal ran so high that one man was shot dead in his tracks, in a street debate over it.

The editor finally announced *The Treasure Peaks Standard*, and the first issue was hailed with a general outlay of enthusiasm, liquor and gunpowder. The proprietor of the leading saloon purchased the first copy, damp from the press, for twenty dollars, and put it proudly on exhibition in his cabinet of curiosities. The leading article, dilating upon the prospects of the town, its growing industries and inexhaustible resources, was voted "just the business" by everybody. Subscriptions and advertising poured in, and Lightner came to the conclusion that he had reached a spot where a small fortune awaited him.

Time showed that the editor had, indeed, wielded a prophetic pen. Treasure Peaks progressed with a steady development, and the founders of the city began to regret that they had not built on some spot where there was more room, instead of being huddled up in the confines of a mountain, with a precipice below and a wall of rock behind them. Claims increased in value, corner lots advanced, the saloons were crowded, and the gambling halls resounded with strains of music and revelry, while the abodes of vice and the resorts of commercial industry literally made money "hand over fist."

The *Standard* was a weekly, and Lightner and his wife did the work, both setting type, and each assisting the other in the odd jobs which are found in a printing office. As business increased, Lightner concluded that his wife was overtasking herself, and finally the following was inserted in the paper :

WANTED. A good, steady compositor, to whom the highest wages will be paid. Apply at this office immediately.

Next day, a young man called and said he had come to answer the advertisement.

"I've been keeping cases at Beggs'," he said, frankly. "I could get nothing else to do, except mining, and my health won't stand it."

He said his name was Houghson, and he was from Maine. He was set to work at once, and proved to be a rapid, careful compositor, and just the man for the place.

There was no longer any necessity for Mrs. Lightner, working as a typesetter, yet, after a few days, she came down and took a case by the side of Houghson. Presently, Houghson changed his slouched attire for new clothes, and manifested a decided interest in clean shirts.

One day, Mrs. Lightner left a composing stick half full, and when she returned from dinner, noticed that the balance of the type had been set. Next day Houghson found some wildflowers on his case. The new compositor assisted Mrs. Lightner whenever she "pied" a line, or fell into any vexatious troubles with the type. She needed assistance quite often, and Lightner was delighted with the thrifty ways and accommodating spirit of his new employee. On one occasion, in correcting Mrs. Lightner's type, their hands touched, but she made no effort to withdraw hers, and they lingered in contact. The woman's eyes met Houghson's, and in her confusion, she "pied" a line, and the type, rattling upon the floor, caused her husband to look up. He saw, however, nothing but two people absorbed in their work.

Soon after, the new compositor resolved on a desperate venture. He was setting some reprint, and a fresh piece of copy began with the words "I love you." He set them in his stick, and held it where she could see it. She gazed at it steadily a few seconds, and bit her lip with an angered expression, as if she considered such a liberty unwarrantable. Lightner went out a moment after, and Houghson took advantage of the opportunity afforded to make an explanation and apology, saying that the words he had set were in his copy.

"Then you did not mean it seriously?" she said. "No."

The anger which Mrs. Lightner had assumed a few moments before now changed to genuine discomfiture. Houghson saw that the point so daringly won had been lost by sheer cowardice. She noticed his troubled face, and a few minutes later, they exchanged smiles which spoke louder than the type.

It was a day or so before they began to renew their conversation, and then they did so by touching, successively, the boxes containing the letters, thus spelling words and sentences quite rapidly. Houghson grew bolder every day, and finally, using their system of dumb signals within a few feet of the unsuspecting husband, they talked without reserve; their expressions of affection, born of a finger-touch upon piles of inanimate type, leaving no trace.

One night, the woman contrived to have Houghson invited to the house. After accepting, Houghson gave her to understand that she must search the right pocket of his overcoat for a letter, when he came. That evening he called, and, taking off his coat, handed it to his employer, who was assisting him. He passed it to his wife, instructing her to hang it up, and, the instant his back was turned, the letter was extracted and another put in its place. Houghson smiled in the husband's honest face at the idea of making a letter carrier of him, and Lightner smiled cordially in return.

After that, Houghson spent his evenings quite frequently at Lightner's—the husband pressing him to come, and the wife professing she considered him a bore. They exchanged letters daily—each seeming to be endeavoring to outdo the other in expressions of affection; and all this time the woman treated her lover so coldly in the presence of her husband that on one occasion he took her to task for it.

"If you don't like the man, you should at least remember that he is a gentleman, and treat him with politeness."

"I can't endure his ways," was the reply, and the subject dropped.

The crisis in events was bound to come, sooner or later, and it came in due time.

One night, Lightner was standing on a knoll in the rear of the printing office. It was an evening sweet with the delicious atmosphere which characterizes the mountains, and the sweet scents of the pines loaded the breeze with a fragrance so suggestive of woods. and glens that one could almost see the splendid scenery with closed eyes. He watched the rush of busy life beneath him. The roar of machinery, the clamor of the stamp-mills, and the cheery songs of the men blended grandly together. As the doors of the furnaces were opened, at intervals, the glow of the fires penetrated the dark recesses of the foliage beyond, and lit up the bleak rocks with mellow reflections. Lightner's mind reverted to the business of the past year, while he considered the prospects of the future; and when he thought of his cheerful though humble home and devoted wife, he was indeed a happy man.

As he sat gazing upon the works below, he fancied that the glare upon the pines and rocks suddenly grew more pronounced. A moment later, the shouts of fire rang out; it was the first time that cry had ever been raised in the Peaks, and the camp was a scene of confusion at once.

The main mine of the place was burning; and there being nothing to check the rush of the flames, and no water facilities to speak of, the whole line or works went, one after the other. All night the pillars of fire shot upward from the shafts—as the underground workings communicated with each other—and these pillars rose above the tallest crags, while the thick, dun smoke shut out the sky. Below, the mines were filled with men perishing in the flames that swept from drift to drift, or suffocated long before in the sulfurous gases that on such occasions find their way to the remotest corners.

In the morning, the flames were flaring from the shafts. The town had escaped, but every vestige of the mining industry had been swept away. It would not pay to rebuild. There was no longer any reason to conceal a fact, well known to the insiders, that the vein had "pinched out." Treasure Peaks was already a thing of the past, and the exodus began. The grade was filled with men and horses, leaving the stricken-town as fast as possible. They did not even remain to take out the dead from the lower levels.

"Why should we dig 'em up from the ground to bury 'em again?"

No one could answer such a question, and the subject was not agitated. Business men did not sell out, they simply vacated the premises—finding, in many instances, that it was cheaper to leave provisions and merchandise than to remove them, something not at all uncommon in those days. Stores were gutted, and barrels of liquor rolled out for the mob. The streets were filled with howling drunkards, most of them singing snatches of the wild refrains which were born of the rush and riot of '49. Thus the town passed out of existence, with the inhabitants singing, fighting, drinking, and drowning their troubles in a delirium of revelry.

The night after the fire, Lightner's wife advised him to go down to the office and look after affairs. As he left, she remarked that she was indisposed, and would go to bed early, but he need not hurry back.

Half an hour later, as Lightner was sitting in his murky office, he thought he heard the clatter of hoofs, and went to the door; as he did so, he saw two figures disappear over the grade, but thought no more of it.

By midnight, he had put things to rights about the place, determining to move away with the rest in a day or two. As he went home he thought of the brave little woman who had faced the trials and privations of the past two years, and all for him. He entered the room where she was sleeping, but did not light the candle, for fear of waking her. He sat for half an hour beside the bed, filled with gloomy reflections and miserable forebodings. Then he bent over the pillow where he knew her head lay, and tried to kiss her cheek. He found nothing, and his hands wandered nervously over the bedclothes a moment. Rushing to the window, he tore aside the curtain, and let the moonlight stream in. The bed was empty.

Three days later, a man wandered aimlessly about the streets of the deserted city. It was Lightner, gone mad from the events of the past week, and the sole surviving inhabitant of the dead camp. He roamed about the streets all the forenoon, and then drifted back to his little office. Sitting down at his desk, as he had before a thousand times done, he wrote:

CHEERING PROSPECTS —Treasure Peaks was never on a more substantial basis than at present. Its population is constantly increasing; buildings are going up at a rate which bespeaks a population, by next fall, of double that which we can boast of at present. The strike in the Lone Pine, yesterday, is one of immense importance, and more will be said of it in our next issue.

He hung this on the hook, and went out to "rustle" for more items; going from one empty store to another, and returning in an hour or so to scribble his impressions on paper. He moved about all day and returned home at night, wholly oblivious of the fact that he was the only inhabitant of the dead and desolate city.

Occasionally, the Indians would pay the Peaks a visit, but seldom, as the dreariness of the place was to them more lonely than the unexplored forest. These savages, who never harm a demented man, brought Lightner provisions, and treated him with great respect. He usually alluded to their visits as the arrival of New York capitalists seeking investments in mining property.

There was an old hall at the Peaks, which had been occasionally used for theatrical performances by local talent. Not infrequently, Lightner would repair to this building, and, taking a front seat in the dress-circle, sit for a couple of hours under the supposition that a play was in progress. Here, indeed, was the "beggarly array of empty benches." The moon, shining through the gaps of dismantled windows, threw but an indifferent light upon the stage and over the interior of the building, and occasionally Lightner would allude, in his paper, to the fact that it was a pity that the leading place of amusement in that city was not better lighted. He was always very guarded in his comments, however, as he seemed to fear that, unless he remained on good terms with the manager, he might lose his advertising patronage. Sometimes he would hang about the empty box office for days, with a bill which he was anxious to collect.

On one occasion, he delivered a lecture in the theatre, on the "Life of Charlemagne," and roared and gesticulated for an hour and a half, by the light of a tallow candle, to absolute emptiness, weaving his mad oratory to the irresponsive air, and trying vainly to call down the applause of the silent gallery.

On the Fourth of July, he decorated his office with evergreens; pulled out an old American flag, which he hoisted early in the morning; read the Declaration of Independence to a band of Washoe Indians; marched them up and down the main street, and wanted to get gloriously drunk, but lacked the spirituous auxiliaries.

During the next few months, the town shrank away like a withered vegetable. The buildings twisted and warped with the summer's heat, and the dry rot set in. Here and there, patches of grass could be seen in the streets, a sort of verdigris collecting upon the town. Day after day, the signs and awnings were shaken by the mountain winds, and fell to the ground alongside the sinking buildings. Vines and weeds began to mantle and choke the charred and blackened ruins of the hoisting works, and cover the grim wrecks of machinery.

In the midst of all this, the demented editor prolonged his solitary existence, subsisting on the scanty allowance which the Indians furnished him, and occasionally issuing the *Standard*, printing it on odd bits of paper, and distributing it by throwing it into the yawning doorways. Its circulation was generally about a dozen copies, and it came out as the humor seized him.

When not at work on his journal, he was digging among the ruins for the body of his wife, whom he firmly believed had been burned in the fire. One day he found some bones, probably belonging to a miner, and believing them to be the remains of his lost helpmate, he buried them in a little knoll back of his office, and began to plant flowers there, watering the spot daily. These flowers soon completely engaged his attention, and, one day, seeing them through the open window, he wrote:

The flowers are coming up close by our door again. All hail! As, in our wild and uncertain struggle for wealth, we toil in the lower levels, let us not forget the priceless treasures of the upper earth. The gold of the mine is not half so bright as the yellow buttercups that fleck the sod above it. The cold crystals, the gleaming pyrites, and the many-colored traceries of wealth and beauty that blend in the soulless rocks, that make poor compare with the vines and grasses which, a hundred feet above, tell us of God's

*divine sympathy and Nature's exhaustless bounty. The
gold and silver lasts forever because neither have lived.
The flowers spring up and die because they are immortal.
Does not the spirit of the rose, upon the hill yonder, live
and breathe as a man lives and breathes? Does it not feel
every movement and change of the air which surrounds it,
and die as the blast smites it? Does not the spiritual
essence of its fragrance haunt the earth, while its seed is
quickened for another spring? Let every man have his
share, for the treasures of nature are illimitable.*

In the fall, he imagined that he was nominated for Congress, and for about six weeks he conducted a vigorous political campaign. He went on a canvassing tour through the mountains, and whenever he struck an Indian camp he made a speech—a rousing and ringing Republican oration—which was generally listened to with marked attention by groups of stolid savages.

On Election Day, he distributed his tickets through the saloons, laying a pile on each dusty counter, and covering them with small stones to hold them in place.

In a day or so, he imagined himself elected, and thanked the solitudes about him as follows :

*It is with a feeling of no inconsiderable pride that the
editor of the* Standard *is able to announce that he has
been chosen by the people of Nevada as their
Congressional representative. We did not seek the office,
and, in accepting it, we but bend to the royal will of the
popular majority, who were determined to do us honor, in
return for our labors in behalf of the growing country
during the past four years. Our record as a pioneer, a
journalist, and a citizen we feel proud of, and shall make
it our endeavor to retain the confidence of our*

constituents in the future as we have in the past.

That night, he packed a small black valise, and determined to set out for Washington on the early stage. He went behind the office, and stood for half an hour by the grave which he supposed to be that of his wife, and then turned sadly back to the dingy old printing shop. Sitting down to his desk, he seized a scrap of paper and began to write. He wrote slowly for about half an hour, and then, throwing away the manuscript, wrote again. Then he carefully read his copy, and hung it on the hook. "Julia," said he, "set that up in leaded minion, and then we'll go home."

He looked over toward the case where his wife had so often worked, and his dimming eyes tried to pierce the gloom. Folding his arms upon the table, he laid his head down upon them with a sigh of weariness, and was soon asleep.

Three years later, a man and a woman came up the grade on horseback and entered the deserted town. They walked where the ruins of the hoisting works crumbled beneath masses of waving grass, and inert machinery lay in the close embrace of creeping vines. The pair rode through the flowers and weeds in the main street, and neared the office of the *Standard*. The woman's quick eye caught sight of the grave at the top of the knoll, and she walked up to it. On the headboard she saw the inscription cut deeply into the wood:

JULIA LIGHTNER,
MY BELOVED WIFE.
Died April 16th.

The two looked in each other's faces, when the man remarked:

"The day of the fire."

They walked through the office, passed the cases, thick with spiders' webs, the rusty press and the pied masses of type. They saw something bowed over the editorial table. It was a human figure, half skeleton, half mummy, over which clung some ragged remnants of clothes.

"My husband!" said the woman.

A horrible shiver came over the man, and the woman, ashy pale, clung to him for protection, as if she expected the figure would rise up and confront them.

Presently, Houghson walked up closer, and seeing a sheet of paper upon the hook, took it off, shook the dust free, and, with some difficulty, read as follows :

HOME. Love is a sleep, in which a man dreams of joy which rise before him in the air, in endless architecture which the imagination never tires of rearing upon the clouds. He awakes, is at home, and the unsubstantial castles of his dreams become as solid masonry, when he views the cheerful hearth, hears the prattle of his children, and presses the responsive lips of his faithful wife. This is the glad consummation of all his hopes, and all other joys which wealth and power and satiated ambition tempts us with, pale before the splendor of such a sun as this whose fire the grave itself quenches not, and whose light pierces the shadows of eternity.

As he read, Houghson had moved toward the light which came through the broken window, and his back was turned away from the woman whose affections he had won. Suddenly, the crash of a pistol's report caused him to leap back as if the ball had pierced him.

As he turned, the woman fell to the floor at the skeleton's feet, the blood which streamed from her mouth mingling with a bubbling froth which swelled from her nostrils. She made no motion after a fall, except to inflate her chest once or twice.

Houghson gazed, transfixed, upon the corpse, for a few minutes, incapable of motion. The sun had set, and the scene was shrouded in the gathering shadows. He made a step to approach the body, met the fixed gaze of the eyes, and, recoiling, reeled through the open door. The two horses were close at hand; one he liberated and the other he mounted. He turned one more look at the office, and paused, as if he would go back; and then, wheeling his horse about, dashed through the crumbling and rotting city at a pace which made the frail houses tremble as he passed, and in the misty twilight disappeared down the lonely grade.

"The Hermit of Treasure Peaks" is taken from Samuel Post Davis' collection of short stories, published in 1886.

Mark Twain

A Bloody Massacre
at Empire City

From Abram Curry, who arrived here yesterday afternoon from Carson, we have learned the following particulars concerning a bloody massacre which was committed in Ormsby County night before last. It seems that during the past six months, a man named P. Hopkins, or Philip Hopkins, has been residing with his family in the old log house just at the edge of the great pine forest which lies between Empire City and

Dutch Nick's.

The family consisted of nine children—five girls and four boys—the oldest of the group, Mary, being nineteen years old, and the youngest, Tommy, about a year and a half. Twice in the past two months, Mrs. Hopkins, while visiting in Carson, expressed fears concerning the sanity of her husband, remarking that of late he had been subject to fits of violence, and that during the prevalence of one of these he had threatened to take her life.

It was Mrs. Hopkins' misfortune to be given to exaggeration, however, and but little attention was paid to what she said. About 10 o'clock on Monday evening, Hopkins dashed into Carson on horseback, with his throat cut from ear to ear, and bearing in his hand a reeking scalp from which the warm, smoking blood was still dripping, and fell in a dying condition in front of the Magnolia Saloon. Hopkins expired in the course of five minutes, without speaking. The long red hair of the scalp he bore marked it as that of Mrs. Hopkins.

A number of citizens, headed by Sheriff Gasherie, mounted at once and rode down to Hopkins' house, where a ghastly scene met their gaze. The scalpless corpse of Mrs. Hopkins lay across the threshold, with her head split open and her right hand almost severed from the wrist. Near her lay the ax with which the murderous deed had been committed. In one of the bedrooms six of the children were found, one in bed and the others scattered about the floor.

They were all dead.

Their brains had evidently been dashed out with a club, and every mark about them seemed to have been made with a blunt instrument. The children must have struggled hard for their lives, as articles of clothing and broken furniture were strewn about the room in the utmost confusion. Julia and Emma, aged respectively fourteen and seventeen, were found in the kitchen, bruised and insensible, but it is thought their recovery is possible.

The eldest girl, Mary, must have taken refuge, in her terror, in the garret, as her body was found there, frightfully mutilated, and the knife with which her wounds had been inflicted still sticking in her side.

The two girls, Julia and Emma, who had recovered sufficiently to be able to talk yesterday morning, state that their father knocked them down with a billet of wood and stamped on them. They think they were the first attacked. They further state that Hopkins had shown evidence of derangement all day, but had exhibited no violence. He flew into a passion and attempted to murder them because they advised him to go to bed and compose his mind.

Curry says Hopkins was about 42 years of age, and a native of Western Pennsylvania; he was always affable and polite, and until very recently we had never heard of his ill-treating his family. He had been a heavy owner in the best mines of Virginia and Gold Hill, but when the San Francisco papers exposed the game of cooking dividends in order to bolster up our stocks he grew afraid and sold out, and invested to an immense amount in the Spring Valley Water Company of San Francisco. He was advised to do this by a relative of his, one of the editors of the *San Francisco Bulletin*, who had suffered pecuniarily by the dividend-cooking system as applied to the Daney Mining Company recently.

Hopkins had not long ceased to own in the various claims on the Comstock lead, however, when several dividends were cooked on his newly acquired property, their water totally dried up, and Spring Valley stock went down to nothing. It is presumed that this misfortune drove him mad and resulted in his killing himself and the greater portion of his family.

The newspapers of San Francisco permitted this water

company to go on borrowing money and cooking dividends, under cover of which cunning financiers crept out of the tottering concern, leaving the crash to come upon poor and unsuspecting stockholders, without offering to expose the villainy at work. We hope the fearful massacre detailed above may prove the saddest result of their silence.

"A Bloody Massacre at Empire City," appeared as a news story in the Virginia City Territorial Enterprise on Ocober. 28, 1863. It was written as satire, but several other newspapers picked it up and printed it as fact. Twain subsequently apologized to those who took it at face value.

Jeadene Solberg

Union Hotel

We found ourselves in a unique situation, caring for our friends' cats at a historically rich and captivating location in Dayton. This place was not just any residence; it was a beautifully reconstructed old hotel that held a regal charm, yet had an intriguing air of mystery surrounding it. It was impossible to ignore the whispers of restless spirits that lingered, creating an atmosphere that was both exhilarating and deeply unsettling.

One evening, as the sun set and darkness began to creep

through the dimly lit hallways, I emerged from the bathroom upstairs. Just as I reached for the doorknob and walked through to the main living room, I felt an overwhelming wave of darkness wash over me, wrapping around me like an icy shroud. It was as if fear itself had taken on a physical form, pressing me against the wall. My heart raced uncontrollably as I instinctively moved toward the bedroom, the sound of my pounding pulse drowning out any logical thought.

Upon entering, I quickly shut the door behind me, my breath hitching in my throat. My partner, trying to lighten the mood with a teasing smirk, asked, "Are you scared much?" and followed it up with a haunting reminder: "You know that the spirit can come right through the door."

Despite her lighthearted demeanor, I felt an intense wave of fear wash over me as I dove into bed, pulling the covers tight around myself. In that moment, I confronted a deep-seated terror that wrapped around my insides, making me feel vulnerable and exposed. I wasn't just scared; I was grappling with a profound, primal fear that shook me to my core.

Note: The spirits of their home, which we call "Our Mansion," have come to an understanding; they cannot scare me any longer, and we are at peace with each other's presence. We have also moved right down the street from "Our Mansion."

"Union Hotel" by Jeadene Solberg appears here for the first time.

Angela Laverghetta

Danse Macabre

July 1993

B ark scraped against Del's shoulder blades as Marko pushed her harder against the tree, his hand dragging over her slip dress. His flannel, tied at the waist, pushed into her stomach like a fist, and the smell of stale cigarettes overwhelmed the fresh night air. Her body trembled, and for a brief moment she wasn't sure whether she wanted to pull him closer or push him away.

Marko's cracked lips scratched up Del's shoulder and into the curve of her neck. Her head fell back against the trunk, her eyes staring up into the dark void of the tree canopy. When she'd walked to the park, the half-moon overhead had lighted her way well enough. But now the surrounding shadows appeared blacker. Deeper somehow. She searched for the moon above her, not finding it.

The clink of metal chains in the darkness pulled Del's gaze over Marko's shoulder toward the playground, a darker shadow among shadows. She could barely make out two swings shifting in the breeze, twisting away from each other like enemies.

Movement flickered at the corner of her eye.

Del twisted her head toward it. Was there someone there? What if her mother came home early and found her gone? What would she do? Would she come to the park looking for her? Del could imagine the lecture she'd get, and her mother definitely wouldn't wait until they got home. She'd yell right in front of Marko. Del nearly died of mortification at the thought. But there was nothing there when she looked. She was being ridiculous. It was much more likely that her mother would pick up an extra shift. Coming home early meant losing money, not gaining it.

Del shivered, her heart pounding as Marko pulled down one of her spaghetti straps and skimmed his way back up to grab her bra strap, too. His lips slammed down upon hers, and he groaned like a dying animal.

Earlier in the evening, a rush of energy had flooded her when she'd lifted the phone from its cradle and punched Marko's numbers with shaky fingers. She was ready for this. She wanted this.

Her stomach clenched. But was she really going to do *this*? In a park? At night? Up against a tree? The tightness in her stomach spread outward, and suddenly she couldn't seem to catch her breath. With a jerk, she slipped under Marko's arm, gulping the night air like water.

"What gives?" Marko asked.

Del couldn't answer. She didn't know. She just needed a second. A moment to think. She stumbled toward the playground. "You wanna swing?" she said over her shoulder.

When he didn't respond, she stopped and turned around. In the darkness, she could make out the sharp glint in his eyes. "Should've known better. You're just a kid."

Del met Marko not long after she had moved to Nevada. She hated everything about her new home. First it wasn't L.A. Stike one. Second, the dry air made her nose bleed. Strike two. And third, there was fuck all to do. Strike three. She wanted to hate her mom for dragging her over the mountains to this cesspool of sad casinos and sagebrush, but it didn't take a genius to realize rent was way cheaper here for a single mom and her teenage kid.

Five days a week, sometimes six or even seven if her mom could add overtime shifts, Del woke up in the afternoon to her mom already having left for work at one of those sad casinos. Del couldn't remember which. Maybe the one with the Irish name? Not that it mattered, they were all the same. Her junior year of high school wouldn't start for another month and a half, and Del wasn't allowed to leave the apartment alone. Ever.

Her mother still seemed to think they still lived in a big city and not B.F.E..

Her boredom level had reached critical mass when she couldn't take it any longer. She'd pilfered a bunch of ones from her mom's tips, found the address for a movie theater—correction, the only movie theater—in the phone book and found the closest bus stop.

The bus dropped her off in the south of town between a casino and a theme-roomed sex hotel. Classy. She had to walk the rest of the way to the theater. It wasn't hard to find. The large, faded tan dome rose from the skyline like a dead camel hump. Reno was all grossness AND way lame. Maybe she'd grow to love it... not!

There was only one couple at the outside ticket counter, and they took their tickets and entered just as Del walked up. The guy behind the glass watched her approach, a knockoff Billy Idol with bleached hair curling tightly against the sides of his head and rising into a cloud of curls in front. Del was wearing an old flannel open over her tank top, and Ticket Guy's eyes noticeably lingered on her chest before making their way up to her face.

Del's cheeks heated. She tried to ignore it as she smiled. He was way too old for her. Definitely out of high school. But truthfully, she hadn't met anyone since moving, and it was really nice to be noticed, even if ogling her was a pretty skeezy thing to do.

"*Sleepless in Seattle?*" Ticket Guy asked.

"What?"

"The chick flick. Isn't that what you're here to see?"

Del didn't know what she was going to watch, but she had a feeling that if she wanted Ticket Guy to keep looking at her, it wouldn't be the chick flick. "No. I don't watch 'em." It wasn't really a lie. She didn't watch a lot of movies, chick flicks or otherwise.

Ticket Guy snorted, but he kept looking at her, his lips curling into a lopsided smile. "What? You here to see *Body Bags*?"

Body Bags sounded like a horror movie. If Del didn't watch many movies, she watched ZERO that were meant to terrify people. But Ticket Guy continued to watch her, his dark eyes intense and interested. So she cocked her hip and leaned close to the counter, pushing the crumpled ones through the glass cutout. "Yeah, so what if I am?"

"Well, aren't you all that and a bag of chips?" The low tone of Ticket Guy's voice slid over her like oil, and her stomach flipped. He pushed her ticket back through the hole. "What's your name?"

"Del." Her full name was Delphine, but no one ever needed to know that.

"Marko," Ticket Guy replied with a flick of his head.

Body Bags scared the shit out of her, and she turned every light on when she got back home. Before her mother left the next day, she shook Del awake and ranted about the power bill and how money did not grow on trees.

Still, Del started going to the cinema as many days as she could get away with. Sometimes Marko would be at the ticket counter, and sometimes he'd be inside slinging popcorn or checking stubs. His eyes would find her every time she arrived, and her entire body tingled. When Del asked how old he was, Marko told her 25, and Del told him she was almost 18. A lie. Sometimes Marko would take a break during his shift and sneak into the theater she was in. They'd make out in the back row.

"You're not like other girls," he told her when she'd been going to the theater for two weeks. He handed her an old receipt with his number scrawled on the back. "Call me sometime, and we can hang out when I'm not working." And even though Del was pretty sure she was just like everyone else, she smiled and said she would.

Nausea roiled through Del's stomach when Marko turned to leave. She rushed to his side, latching onto his arm. She couldn't let him go. He was the only person she knew if she didn't count Margaret in the unit downstairs. And Del definitely didn't count that cranky old woman who banged on the door if Del forgot to move her load of laundry from the washer to the dryer. If Marko left, she'd be all alone, and she didn't just mean tonight in the park. "Wait," she pleaded. Marko paused, but when he looked down at her, there was a shutter over his gaze. He seemed to look straight through her, leaving a gaping hole behind. Del gripped his arm harder. "It's just... I thought I saw something... what if someone was watching?"

Marko stiffened and glanced around with what seemed like

glee. "Maybe it was a ghost." He smiled, his white teeth almost sharp in the shadows. When he looked back down at Del, she could see his attention had returned. She was forgiven. She thought she'd feel joy, but the gleam in his eyes sat between her shoulder blades like an ice cube.

Ghosts weren't real. The movement she thought she'd seen could've been anything. Anything real. But all the horror movies she forced herself to watch so she would have something to talk about with Marko rushed into her mind, and she desperately wanted to turn on a light. Ghosts weren't real, she repeated to herself.

Marko pulled her up hard against his chest, and she yelped in surprise. The gleam in his eyes brightened. "Isn't that why you picked this park?" His fingers dug into her back.

Del had chosen the park merely because it was within walking distance of her apartment. What was he talking about?

"All the dead bodies. It's exhilarating." Marko pulled in a breath through his nose as if the air held a banquet of delicious scents and not asphalt and dirt.

Shock seized her, locking her muscles from moving. Bodies? What did he mean by bodies?

Before she could ask him, he dropped his lips against hers, sucking at her mouth, stealing her breath. Del felt a flash of pain and tasted blood on his tongue. "Wait," she whispered against his mouth. "Wait," she said louder as she finally found the strength to pull her head to the side.

"What?" Marko snapped, and the violence in his tone rang in the night. "What?" he said, his tone softer, and Del wondered if she'd imagined how angry he'd sounded a moment earlier. She wiped at her lip, her fingers coming away with a dark smudge of blood.

"Bodies? Who are they... why are they...?" Del stumbled over her questions.

Marko laughed, and the sound bounced off every tree. "You really didn't know when you picked here, did you?"

Del shook her head.

Marko raised a hand to push a strand of her hair back behind her ear. "Some hospital for whackjobs used to be here, and they buried a bunch of them in the yard. Friend of my cousin said he found a bone once." Marko dropped his hand from her ear to her breast and squeezed. "Now where were we?"

Del tried to pull away, but Marko's arm held her tight, and the hand on her breast squeezed harder. She winced against the pain but didn't tell him it hurt. She didn't want him to think she was a child again.

Something called out in the distance. Del couldn't tell if it was a bird or a person. And another flicker of movement danced in her periphery. Tendrils of cold raced down her scalp. What if it really was a ghost?

Distracted, she didn't realize what Marko was doing until he was wrapping a leg behind her knees, and they were both falling to the hard ground. His heavy weight landed on her, pushing the air from her lungs. He'd placed an arm behind her head, possibly to protect it, but it still bounced against the dirt. Pain exploded through her brain. She blinked her eyes to clear them, only to see Marko's feral expression above her. She shifted, trying to move away. "What? This is why you called me, right?"

She *had* called him. She'd met him here, at night, in the dark, and all alone. This is what she had wanted. To have him see her and want her.

Marko forced his knee between her legs, and his hand slipped under her dress, scraping along her thigh. Del opened her mouth to say "stop," but Marko silenced her with his own, his teeth hitting hers as he pushed his tongue past her sore lip.

Her heart slammed against her ribs, threatening to break free.

She had wanted.

"Had" wanted.

Past tense.

Now she wanted to leave. She tried to drag herself out from under him, the skin on her elbows ripping as she used them for leverage. Marko pawed at her underwear. She struggled harder. "No," she yelled, finding her voice. She pushed at his chest with all her strength. Marko remained a solid, immovable mass.

Del squeezed her eyes shut.

Wind whistled past her ears, freezing the tears on her cheeks.

Stop. Stop. Stop.

The pawing hands and the weight on her chest and between her legs disappeared. Silence, thick and complete, settled over her. She couldn't even hear her heart pounding in her ears. She pulled a harsh, shuddering breath into her lungs.

Slowly, she opened her eyes.

The park was empty. Marko was gone.

"Marko?" His name came out hoarse and weak. Del sat up, pushing her dress down and brushing the dirt from her scraped elbows with a wince. "Marko?" She called louder.

A scream, long and low, rang in the distance, but Del couldn't tell from which direction it came.

She scrambled to her feet. "Marko?" she yelled again.

His name hung like a white cloud before her face before dissipating, and she flung her arms around her body as a sudden chill settled heavy enough her teeth chattered.

A streak of movement. An unintelligible hiss of words.

Del spun in a circle, finding nothing. Fear threatened to pull her back down to the ground, where she could pull herself into a ball and hope it all went away. Only the violent shaking of her body against the cold kept her upright. The plotlines of every horror movie raced through her brain, and she whimpered. She was literally going to die just like one of those stupid girls.

The words came again. Clearer. Louder. "It's not worth it."

"Wha—wha—what is—isn't?" Del asked through her clacking teeth. It was crazy to respond to disembodied voices, but what did it matter? She knew how this story ended.

She turned once more.

And found a face inches from her own.

The scream that echoed in the night was Del's own.

Void-dark eyes sunken deep within a translucent skull held Del rigid with fear. Lips, rotted and thin, pulled away from broken and missing teeth in a rictus smile, and tendrils of hair lay lank against its cheek. "The notice of a man." The skull cackled, its words dragging against Del's nerves like nails on a chalkboard.

The face disappeared, and the barest sound of music wafted in the air.

"Marko?" Del cried, spinning around to look in all directions. This had to be a joke. A prank.

A few feet away, the skull returned, this time with its whole body. It shimmered, wavering in and out of existence, draped in a soiled gown. An overwhelming smell of sweat and rot slicked the air. Del heaved, her hand flying up to block her nose from inhaling more.

The ghostly woman cocked her head to the side. "Do you want him back?"

It took Del a moment to process the words. Pressure inside her head created dark spots in her vision. Did the ghost have Marko? Oh god, was that even possible? Did she believe in ghosts now? But what else could the thing in front of her possibly be? Those screams. Marko.

Del opened her mouth to say yes. Of course, she wanted him back.

But couldn't.

The memory, fresh and searing, of Marko above her filled her mind, his weight suffocating, his hands under her dress, pulling on her panties... Del's gut twisted. She'd said "no." She'd said "no," and he hadn't stopped. Marko wouldn't have stopped. Her body heaved again, and it had nothing to do with awful smells.

Why? Why had she wanted his notice so badly? Why did she think coming here was a good idea? She wished desperately she could start the night over, unplug the phone, and watch reruns of that old dorky show *The Waltons*.

"What will you do to him?" Del whispered. Part of her didn't want to know the answer, but a small, shocking part of her, the part that wanted to gnash her teeth and scream with rage, hoped it hurt.

The ghost twirled, her gown rising into a bell around her to reveal pale, dirt-covered feet. "Just dance. We're wonderful dancers." The ghost stretched out an arm, skin flayed and hanging, showing bone beneath, and pointed off into the night.

Following the ghost's direction, Del could just make out other spectral forms twisting and bending in unnatural ways; between them, they yanked and pulled on a dark and solid form.

The next scream Del heard definitely came from the direction of the disturbing dance. She twitched when it cut off sharply.

A fearful, but almost giddy laugh bubbled up into her throat.

"Now run along," the ghost said, swinging her arm in the opposite direction and toward the park exit.

A warm droplet of blood swelled on Del's lip from where Marko had split it earlier, and she licked it away. She took a step toward home, but turned for a moment, her gaze searched for the dance but not finding it again. The ghost who'd spoken to her was gone, too. Del stopped shivering.

Under the moonlight, she walked home, never looking back.

Two days later, Del was torn between never wanting to

think about Marko again and needing to know if she'd imagined the whole thing. She rode the bus and walked to the theater. Marko wasn't at the ticket counter. She purchased a ticket for a random movie set to run soon. She stepped into the popcorn-scented lobby. Marko wasn't checking stubs. Or slinging popcorn. Before Del could head into the theater hallway, someone called out her name.

Her heart pounded, and her hands fisted, slamming against her thigh. She slowly turned around, her teeth bared. But it wasn't Marko, it was one of his co-workers, a dark-haired, dark-eyed teenager. She didn't remember his name.

"You're Del, right?" he asked.

Del nodded, her jaw clenched.

"Have you seen Marko? He was a no-show yesterday and today."

She watched New Guy's gaze roam over her, possibly wondering what Marko had admired about her. His eyes lingered on everything but her eyes, and he lifted a lip like a dog scenting a bitch in heat.

Del's heart calmed, and her own lips lifted to show her teeth, more a snarl than a smile, but New Guy responded, leaning in towards her. "You're his girl, right?" New Guy ran a tongue over his lips.

"Marko isn't seeing me anymore," she said, letting her voice lure him in like a siren song. "Maybe you'd like to join me sometime for a dance?"

She didn't wait for his answer but tossed her hair over her shoulder and walked down the theater hallway. New Guy stumbled after her.

"Danse Macabre" by Angela Laverghetta appears here for the first time.

A Frightful Death

Between 3 and 4 o'clock yesterday afternoon, a frightful accident happened at the Manhattan mill, by which a man named Hugh Lewis met with an appalling death.

It was part of Lewis' duty to oil the machinery in the amalgamating room, and about 3 o'clock, he went under the platform upon which the pans stand for the purpose of oiling the running gear. The platform is some four feet above the ground; and the timbers supporting the platform, and the various parts of the propelling machinery, so fill the space as to require care in moving about.

It is believed that fully half an hour elapsed after Lewis went under the platform before he was missed and found. Alderman Love came into the room and inquired about Lewis, to whom he was about to give some instructions, and at the same time, he observed that one of the settlers had stopped revolving. He sent a man under the platform to ascertain the cause, who returned and reported that the belt had slipped or been thrown off the drum, and that he heard a dragging and pounding noise.

Mr. Love gave the alarm and caused the engine to be stopped, for he had a foreboding that an accident had happened to Lewis.

As soon as the engine had stopped, several workmen with lighted candles made their way rapidly under the platform to the counter shaft which drives the machinery attached to the pans and settlers, where they beheld an appalling spectacle. Lewis, who was a tall man, quite six feet high, was literally wound round the shaft, except his legs. His right arm was crushed and around the shaft; his right leg was broken and the flesh torn from it, and his right foot was broken and mangled.

The lower part of his body was bare, for his pantaloons had been torn and whipped off, as well as his boots, by the revolutions of the shaft, which are at the rate of fifty per minute. His body was so firmly bound to the shaft by his jumper and shirt that the men were obliged to use knives to cut them in pieces before they could extricate it.

When taken off, he was warm, but his neck was broken and his heart was still, and he had been dead for some time.

We went into the place this morning where the frightful accident occurred, and saw the pieces of his clothing, his boots, and his oil can lying there. The vacant space is greater around this part of the shaft than elsewhere under the platform. The shaft is four inches in diameter, is a trifle less than two feet from the ground floor, and about two feet and a half from timbers in front of and behind it, and nearly on the same level.

His body must have revolved in this place, his foot striking against the ground and the timbers at each revolution, for nearly half an hour. The instant the accident happened, the unfortunate must have been engaged in oiling the shaft, near which there is a collar containing several set screws which project from an inch-and-a-quarter to an inch-and-a-half, and it is supposed that his jumper, which he wore outside of his pantaloons, caught on one of these screws, and that finding his clothing caught, he threw his right arm over the shaft round which his clothing and body were wound.

His death was undoubtedly instantaneous.

—*Carson Daily Appeal*, March 5, 1870

Bill Brown

Getting Ahead

A lfred Caldwell III wasn't well, and his millions of dollars weren't going to save him. He had spent his life amassing a sizeable fortune, and he had all he wanted. All, except for one thing: a wife to share the rest of his life with. A wife who would ease his pain. A wife who would help him find happiness and laughter even through his pain. The doctors gave him up to two more years to live—while taking his money—as they struggled to keep the cash flowing, and he wanted to learn to smile again. The right woman would do that.

He found a woman who in the beginning was perfect and seemed loving. She did take care of his needs at first without any negative comments, but that had slowly changed. She met his needs for sex twice a week well enough, but now she was less caring and became more apathetic when he wanted that passionate encounter. Now she was making it more of a duty she would rather not perform.

"Oh, again already?" or "Hurry up will you? I've got drinks with the girls later." There was no encouragement or tenderness.

She was more like an expensive sex doll that didn't want to be there.

He was approaching 70 years of age, he wasn't happy with his trophy wife, and he had begun to express his disappointment. Often she said nothing, just offering a sly grin that said, "You finally figured that out, did you?"

His memory was fading on many things, but not about how he had first met her. She was introduced by a millionaire friend he had confided in. He wanted a little encouragement and tenderness even if it was all just a show. Was that too much to ask? His friend arranged the introduction and told him she was looking for an old pot of money to marry but would play the good wife to enjoy the bucks.

And that is exactly what he had. He could guarantee an incredible life after he was gone. Then she could have all the men she wanted with his money. She could buy mansions, travel the world and even keep her own stable of young studs if she wanted.

At first, Alfred thought they hit it off quite well. He told her he knew she wanted security and wasn't going to shed too many tears when he died. He just wanted the company and the feeling of happiness, however fake it would be. His message? Play this right, and the world is yours.

"Ally," short for Allison had said, "No one wants to die alone, Alfred. But I am not that kind of girl. Let's just date a few times and see if we both might be happy."

That was music to the sick old man's ears, and he loved music. In the beginning, it was everything he had hoped for and even more. Those dates turned out to be fun and happy, or at least he thought so. They were followed by flights around the world with shopping at the best stores in Paris, London, and even on Rodeo Drive in Los Angeles. Finally, they were married with a huge stunning ceremony in her favorite city, Rio.

As a gift for her, Alfred presented her with a new version of his will promising everything would go to her, except for a small share reserved for his sister. He told his sister she would have received more if she hadn't been dead set against the marriage from the beginning, knowing Ally for what she was: an actress, albeit a good one.

As his health continued to decline, Ally played her role perfectly as she waited for her husband to die, hoping for sooner rather than later but never revealing her impatience.

Then, one afternoon, things began to change.

Ally took her Lamborghini to the dealership for its usual checkup and immediately saw what she thought was the most beautiful man in the world. He was tall, tanned and very muscular with wavy black hair and not a hint of gray: a color she was tired of seeing. His smile revealed blazing white, perfect teeth. He spoke fluent Italian, and his English carried an accent she loved. He was in his 20s, and therefore much younger, but he doted on her with that killer smile hinting at something more. She guessed that she was his mark just like Alfred had been hers, but she didn't care. If the old man would just hurry up and die, she could get on with living the life she wanted. He'd already lived longer than she had planned, but she had to hold on for the big money. She could always wish he was dead, though, and her new friend was one way to distract herself in the meantime.

But that friend, Antonio, was beginning to lose patience. His changing attitude didn't go unnoticed, as Ally began to worry that he would find another rich older woman and offer *her* his "manly gifts" as he called them. She began to take longer trips away from home with "the girls"—her cover for meeting up with Antonio. Alfred couldn't stray too far from his bed now, anyway, but he was just taking so long to die. Ally had made sure that any nurse near him was much older and if possible, unattractive and disagreeable.

Alfred had become wise to what was going on, but he tolerated his situation because there were times when Ally almost seemed like the Ally of old. He knew deep down she was still trying to play that role in the hope inheriting his wealth, but he chose to ignore his intuition, hoping for what seemed impossible.

Then came his latest visit to his doctors, who had been treating him with an experimental "cocktail" of new drugs.

"Alfred," the lead physician said, smiling, "believe it or not, these new wonder drugs have bought you some more time."

Shocked, Alfred could barely speak, "How... how... how long?"

The doctor looked very pleased with his team's work and creative use of experimental medicine.

"Two, possibly three years. But we are only beginning to understand the true power of what is happening. The drugs are working together in ways we hadn't expected. Your generosity in providing full funding for our research may help prolong thousands of lives. We'll be keeping in frequent contact and learning more as we go. You can expect us to stop in every few days for testing and updates."

"Thank you, doctor. Thank you very much for the good news and the good work. I don't mind being a guinea pig at all. I will certainly express my appreciation in a more tangible way."

"Thank you Alfred, and please remember it was a team effort."

As he departed, the physician closed the door to the bedroom suite behind him... still smiling.

Alfred felt as though he had a new lease on life. With the new medicines working so well, who knew what might happen at the end of the two or three years the doctor had mentioned? He might even have more years to live beyond that. Of course, he couldn't be sure.

One thing he *was* sure of, though: He knew Ally would make his life a living hell trying to shorten it. So it was time to offer her a generous settlement and part ways with her. But first, he would answer the pain she had inflicted on him by dishing out some of his own.

Ally arrived home later that evening from her latest tryst with Antonio, eager to see how much closer the old man had moved to death. "It won't be long now," she kept telling herself —dismissing his recent improvement in color and increase in energy. She chalked that up to a condemned man's last desperate attempts to hold on to what she considered a miserable life.

"Ally! Sweetheart! Great news!"

"Oh, what's that Alfred?" She had long ago stopped using terms of affection like "sweetheart" or even "honey." Now, all she could summon was a feeble attempt to sound interested.

"You know that drug cocktail the doctors came up with?"

"Yes." Now she was more interested, fearing what for her would be the worst news.

"It's working, darling. The doctors have given me at least two more years and maybe longer—much longer if the drugs keep working. Isn't that wonderful?" Alfred smiled, playing his role as well as he could.

Ally felt as though she had been hit squarely in the gut. She gasped as she fell back against the nearest wall.

This wouldn't work at all.

This wasn't the plan.

Alfred's smile twisted into a sly grin as he watched her try to feign happiness at his great news.

"We might even be able to take short trips again, sweetheart. Can you imagine?" Alfred poured it on, payback for all the lies he had been told. All the hurt he had endured.

"Why yes, Alfred." Ally suppressed a cough, trying to hide the shock in her voice. "That's great news, Alfred." She tried to think... *What should I do? This can't be happening.*

Alfred, pleased with the effect as he drove the knife in deeper, decided to deliver the coup de grace with a final twist. Ally wasn't the only game-player in the room now.

"Don't worry, sweetheart." His voice dripped with sarcasm, "I know who you really are, and I know what you've been doing. Sorry to throw a wrench in your plans, but I won't make you suffer. We'll call the game a draw, and you'll have a few million to play with in what's left of your miserable life. But you won't have it all, Ally. You won't have it all..." Alfred knew Ally was a stickler for planning, and he had just ruined the plan she'd been counting on most. He felt almost as good as when the doctors had extended his death date.

"I'm tired now, dear." He leaned his head back on his pillow. "Time to rest while you go to your room and plan your graceful well-paid exit."

Still reeling from the news, she walked slowly from the master suite to her own. Watching her through eye slits, Alfred couldn't stop smiling. Tomorrow, he would chart a new course and begin his hunt for someone who cared, again.

Ally was crying on the phone as she broke the news to Antonio—who responded by reminding her she would be getting a great settlement, probably more than she could spend before she grew to Alfred's age.

But Ally would have none of it. "I *always* win," she reminded him, "and this time will be no different." She had her own plan on how to handle the rejuvenated old man, and she would soon put that plan in motion.

Antonio told her he didn't want to hear any more and he would be there for her regardless of what happened. He wasn't about to give up on the millions that could still come their way but this was a side of Ally he hadn't seen before—at least not this clearly. He would have to be careful in the future. He briefly toyed with the idea of finding someone else, but the money was too close.

The next morning, the household help prepared Alfred's breakfast, but Ally intercepted the woman taking the tray, saying she had to talk to Alfred. Waiting until the woman left, she produced a vial from a pocket in her robe and poured several clear liquid drops into his already-sweetened coffeepot. Pulling the top of her robe apart to expose her braless breasts, she knocked first and then entered.

Alfred had expected an attempt to worm her way back into his life, but the sight of her nearly nude chest still made him take a breath. He remembered many nights of pleasure as he fought to resist the idea of tapping into his renewed energy and giving in to her wiles.

"Alfred, darling." Ally brought that seductive smile of hers out of hiding as she bounced a little, adding some more spice to his morning coffee. "I have been thinking. Maybe you're right. Maybe it is time. You did promise a generous settlement, and you've never lied to me—that I know of. I'm happy you're better. I have treated you terribly, and there's no excuse for it. I won't try to apologize, because you wouldn't believe it. I think parting as friends is the best for both of us."

She smiled and turned to leave. As she did, Alfred felt a twinge of pain in his chest but thought it was only gas. He finished his coffee and poured some more. It was sweeter than normal, and he liked that. He might even finish the whole pot, something he never did. As Ally closed the door, she heard him say, "Hmmm, good coffee..." Her smile broadened: *You have no idea how good that coffee is, old man.*

A few minutes later, the pain in Alfred's chest was back—only worse, and this time he knew it wasn't gas. His left arm began to go numb. Fear gripped him. Could it be a heart attack? No, his doctors told him his heart was the least of his worries. Still, the pain was increasing second by second until he finally called out for help. He tried to reach for his cell phone on his ornate nightstand, but his arms would barely respond. Then he knew what had happened: The bitch had decided to go for all his money, and it was working.

The door to his bedroom opened, and Ally strolled in a devilish grin on her face.

"You... you poisoned me?" His mouth struggled to form the words.

"It was too easy, old man. Too easy. And now I will have everything and you will just be a memory and—a bad one at that. Tell me. Is it getting tough to breathe now? Do you feel your lungs shutting down? Oh, I am enjoying this. It's been such a long time." Her voice seethed with hatred. "Do you know what I am going to do? I am going to have a death mask made for my dresser, so I can loathe you every morning and night. And you can see Antonio and I make love better than you ever could. You don't have long now."

"You haven't won," Alfred hit his hand against his chest near his heart. "This is only a body... I will see you again..." Alfred's hand dropped as he coughed with a choking sound and collapsed back against his pillow.

""Ta-ta." Ally's voice dripped with hatred and satisfaction. She found his doctor's phone number on his nightstand and broke into tears when he picked up: "Doctor, it's Alfred!" she wailed. "I think he's dead. He screamed in pain. His chest. Hurry, please hurry!"

"I don't understand. He was getting so much better." The doctor looked at Alfred's bare chest where she had opened his bedclothes, trying to make it look like she had done her best to save him.

"So it was a heart attack?" Ally sniffled as the tears began again.

"Yes, as far as I can tell. We can order a formal autopsy if you want, but all the physical remains show that was the case. But... so strange. I thought he had a new lease on life."

"If you're satisfied, Doctor, that's fine. I hate to think of all the scars and things. I want him to be as handsome as possible when he goes to our crypt."

"Yes, well, did he leave any instructions for—?"

"He told me how happy he was with you. I want you to know that the research you did with the new drugs has to continue. Just let me know what you need, and I'll make it happen—plus a generous allowance for you and the team."

The doctor heard what he wanted to hear.

"I'll fill out the death certificate, Mrs. Caldwell, and I'll notify the funeral home to get here immediately."

At the funeral home, Ally followed through with her promise and ordered a death cast of Alfred's head so she could verbally taunt and abuse it at her whim. Antonio thought it was bizarre, but her body and her money kept him quiet. Still, he hated that thing being on the dresser, staring at them when they made love. He felt as though he was being watched and, on more than one occasion, he could have sworn the expression on the head changed ever so slightly. But then Ally was a bit wild, so it could have just been her thrashing on top and the dim light of the candles in the room.

One night when they were in the throes of passion, Antonio thought he saw the head smiling at him: not a slight movement but a full-toothed grin. The mouth opened almost as if it were laughing.

That was enough. Instead of spending the night Antonio

hurriedly got dressed, apologized, and said in the future if they were going to make love, it would have to be at his place, not hers. Not with a grinning dead man laughing at him.

Ally laughed it off, telling him he was imagining things. But Antonio wasn't backing down. When they were having sex, his goosebumps rose right along with... other things. It was too much.

As she opened the front door, Ally told him she would think about it. But inside, she dismissed his worries.

She wasn't angry. Antonio's imagination could open up more nights for her to explore other men—other men to taunt her late husband with. She brushed her hair, preparing to turn in for the night, when she thought she saw a shape in the mirror across the room. Spinning around, she could have sworn she heard faint deep laughter.

Oh no, she thought, *Antonio is getting to me now. There are no such things as ghosts. Alfred is dead. Dead.*

She walked across the room, examining the mirror to see if it was dirty and casting a reflection in the shape of a human. But no. It was clean. She turned around to go back and gasped. Alfred's death mask, which normally was positioned to look at the bed, was turned around, looking toward *her.*

That's not possible. I must have turned it around by accident. Yes, that's it. An accident. She went back to the head, intending to turn it back to the bed, but decided instead to do it in the morning. That was enough fear for one night.

Ally slept soundly without dreaming. She had been afraid of nightmares and was happy to spend a peaceful night. Confident her mind had been playing tricks on her the night before, she decided to move the head back toward the bed. It was daylight, and the automated curtains had risen, letting in brilliant sunshine. She had just put on her robe and was starting toward her dresser when she cried out and gasped for air.

Alfred's head had turned back toward the bed.

No... no this isn't possible. I must have had a dream after all. That's it. I was dreaming the whole thing. I did have a nightmare.

Breathing a sigh of relief, she summoned her courage and went to taunt the head again. She intended to perform her morning ritual of laughing at it while telling her dead husband he was a lousy lover... but what was this? Next to the head was a large knife, the kind she thought they called a butcher's blade. She knew she hadn't put it there, and Antonio would never have done so, as frightened as he was. Resisting the urge to run from the room, she picked up the knife, intending to mutilate the death mask, but the sound of heavy footsteps approaching from down the hall stopped her. Then there was the sound of deep laughter. It kept building until it stopped just outside the bedroom door.

"Alllly. Allly." The voice drifted threateningly through the door. "I told you I would see you again. It's me, darling. It's me. I've come back for you, my loving wife. We can spend eternity together." She heard a loud, demonic laugh as the bedroom door handle began to turn and creak—something it never did. With a trembling hand, she held the knife up, its blade pointed toward the door.

"Oh, that's not for you, my love." The voice grew louder. "It's for me!" As the door burst open, she heard the laughter again. Only this time, it didn't stop. She screamed and fainted, falling to the floor. Now she couldn't hear the laughter... but no one could have heard her screams either.

Four days later, after not hearing from Ally, Antonio decided to go to the stately mansion on Reno's Millionaires' Row. When his key didn't work, he knocked repeatedly, then pounded on the door. Hearing no answer, he began walking around the huge home, peering in the windows. Finally, with no neighbors nearby, he called the local police for a welfare check.

Going back to his car, he sat there sipping water until they arrived, followed by a locksmith.

Receiving no answers to their knocks or pleas over their patrol car loudspeaker, the officers gave the go-ahead for the locksmith to do his thing. But nothing he tried worked either; just as he was about to give up, though, the door slowly creaked open by itself.

The officers quickly backed away, pulling their service weapons, and motioned Antonio and the locksmith to the side. Knowing self-opening doors were not good business, they slowly made their way to either side of the door frame, each clearing their field of fire before going in. Once inside, they separated, with each taking a different room.

Antonio and the locksmith could hear shouts of: "Living room clear!" "Kitchen clear!" as the officers searched the ground floor.

Satisfied, they motioned for Antonio and the locksmith to enter and stay near the door in case they were needed. Then the cops made their way up the stairs. They advanced slowly toward the end of the hall; huge, ornate oak doors adorned with gold hinges and doorknobs awaited them there. But they were methodical, quietly nodding to each other as they cleared one room at a time.

When they finally reached the master suite, they stationed themselves on opposite sides of the doors and silently counted to three before finally bursting through into the room.

At first they saw no one. The bed was made. Everything seemed in its place until they saw a pair of legs on the floor extending beyond the end of the far side of the huge bed. One officer quickly moved to the body, while the other cleared the bathroom and the walk-in closet.

"Oh my God, look at this!" The officer nearest the body holstered his gun and backed up, suppressing vomit.

The other man moved quickly when he saw the body—a headless body without any sign of blood. He looked around the room but saw no signs of a struggle or other remains. It was as though a super-hot blade had cut off the head, cauterizing the wound as it went. He bent down to touch the leg, thinking it might be a dummy, but the flesh was all too real. He turned around, holding back his lunch.

His eyes were met with the sight of Alfred's death mask head on the dresser. Next it to it was another head. It was the same dullish gray color as the man's, but this one faced the wall behind the dresser. Slipping his thin evidence gloves on, the officer touched the head to turn it around. He quickly pulled his hands back, his fingers burning from an intense blast of heat.

"What the hell is this?" The two men backed up, staring in disbelief at the head.

They saw a woman whose face was frozen in a moment of absolute terror. Her eyes were wide and pulled back, her eyebrows raised and twisted in panic. Her mouth was wide open, revealing her tongue in an expression that made it seem as if she was desperately trying to scream. Whoever this was had not only seen something terrifying, but soul-shattering.

The officer stripped off his gloves and dropped them, seeing the pinkish hue of his burned figures.

"Let's get the hell out of here. This is way over our heads. Let the coroner handle this."

As they left, they both stopped, listening to something like a soft murmuring. But they could hear words...

"Welcome, my love. I told you you would see me again... Welcome to Hell..."

DRAGON CROWN BOOKS

"Getting Ahead" by Bill Brown appears here for the first time.

Sharon Marie Provost

The Collector

Adelaide had been a collector of the weird and the macabre for as long as she could remember. Her newest obsession fit in the with the rest of her collection perfectly.

Tintype and daguerreotype photos had always fascinated her. But when she began to explore antique memento mori, she found a ghoulish Victorian tradition that combined these two interests into one glorious *pièce de resistance*.

Children posed in family portraits on tintypes.

Dead children posed to look as if they were still alive.

The first time she saw one, she couldn't believe what she was seeing. It looked like any other portrait of the time: a family sitting together ramrod-straight, dressed in their finest, with not even the barest trace of a smile. Their eyes looking dead to the world, probably in concentration as they tried not to move during the long exposure time.

Except this one was different. One of the family member's eyes truly were dead to the world.

Glassy and vacant.

The pose of the little girl in ringlets was a little askew. A rosy tint had been added to her cheeks on the tintype, imbuing life that was no longer there. Adelaide had run up to the proprietor of the antiquities shop to inquire about her dark suspicion. The woman had referred her to a book that discussed the tradition.

Post-mortem photography had been practiced all over the world, but had become especially common in Victorian England with the creation of cheaper daguerreotype images. The earliest examples were photos of lost loved ones in their coffins with flowers surrounding them.

Over time, the practice became more involved and sentimental. The loved ones, especially children, were posed for their "last sleep" in their beds, babies cradled in their mother's arms, or children with toys piled around them who had seemingly fallen asleep playing.

Then it evolved to full family portraits with the child held in a parent's arms, tucked in between siblings, or propped up in a chair. Sometimes, that rose-colored tint was added to the cheeks or eyes were painted right on the tintype. These photos were then put on display in the home or in family albums.

As an introverted loner, Adelaide rarely had visitors, especially since she lived in the town of Goldfield, with its tiny population of 150 hearty souls. She was therefore unconcerned about dedicating her living room to her personal museum of oddities and the macabre. Who would ever see it other than her?

Besides, as a "living" ghost town itself, Goldfield boasted several popular destinations for paranormal enthusiasts—most notably the Goldfield Hotel and the Goldfield High School. Her home just catered to the morbid side of life... specifically, the end of it.

Adelaide had reserved the wall visible when she entered her living room from the back hallway for the main attraction of her collection. There she had placed a framed wall hanging she had hand embroidered depicting a skull, other bones, an hourglass, and wilting flowers surrounding the words "memento mori."

That marker was bookended by two framed hair wreaths. The wreaths had been painstakingly created by two families over several generations with clippings of hair from deceased family members.

Adelaide had also set aside two lighted oak curio cabinets that protected her Victorian memento mori objects behind glass. One held pieces of mourning jewelry: rings, brooches, and lockets that contained bits of hair, bone, or even teeth from dead loved ones. The other cabinet was half full and held objects like wax death masks that were created after death to preserve a family member's likeness.

She had finally found the perfect items to fill the top two shelves.

After that fateful day in the shop, Adelaide had begun an exhaustive search through every antique shop she visited and scoured the internet trying to find pristine works of post-mortem photography depicting children.

Her first purchase after that had been a photo of a couple in one final embrace sharing the same coffin, with their infant daughter cradled in their arms. She had bought the photo at an estate sale and found out the family had been victims of a smallpox epidemic.

Before long, Adelaide found other photos as well. One

showed a little girl propped up in a velvet armchair with her dollies placed around her and one tucked upright in her arm. A little babe "fast asleep" after a long day playing. Another showed a newborn cradled by his stoic mother.

An era beset by so many epidemics of contagious disease produced a number of tragic examples, such as one depicting a little girl and her father sitting beside the lifeless bodies of the mother and another child. A last portrait to document a family that would never be together again.

Her latest find showed an infant boy braced in an armchair draped in black fabric. One leg had been tucked underneath his other outstretched leg. His right arm had been laid in his lap, while the other had been placed on the arm of the chair. He was clothed in a long, lacy dressing gown. The infant stared off into oblivion. A beautiful photograph taken to memorialize a beloved lost child, probably the only one ever taken of him.

But Adelaide's "Fantastical Collection of the Weird and the Macabre," as she had come to call it, extended to other items as well. She had antique medical equipment, such as Civil War-era saws for amputations; an orbitoclast and hammer for lobotomies; old medicine bottles that had once contained belladonna, cocaine, and opium; quackery bottles for anti-aging and cure-alls; a scarificator for blood-letting; a cupping set; a plague doctor mask; a barbaric tooth key for tooth extractions; and an old electrotherapy machine.

She had taken a class a few years back and made a few taxidermied animals: an owl, a skunk, and an opossum she had found as roadkill on a trip once. It hadn't been easy to keep the unfortunate creature fresh enough for preservation on the three-day drive home with the air conditioning out in her car. *But where there's a will, there's a way.*

She had the bleached skull of an old burro that had died out in the desert and sat around, picked over by scavengers until the sun turned the bones bright white. She even still had the poster-size shadow box collection of pinned insects she had made in grade school for her science project.

With maturity and some artistic flair, she had recently created more sophisticated bug and small animal skeletal displays under glass domes using dried flowers, bits of wood, sand, and rocks.

A terrarium of the dead.

She'd even sold a few of those each year during Goldfield Days, the annual summertime festival celebrating the town's rich mining history. She set up a table in front of her house along the main road through town. Plenty of visitors always came from Tonopah and up from Beatty for the event, along with tourists driving down Highway 95 to Sin City, only two-and-a-half hours away.

She'd bought her current home in the property auction that was part of the event. It was over a hundred years old and had seen better days, but it suited her just fine.

Adelaide's odd personality was well-known in the area. It was hard to hide anything in a small-town, much less a flair for the weird. People were nosy and stared in her window when they walked or drove past. The mailman hand-delivered items that could have been left on the porch, just to peek inside. Word of her collection spread throughout the area, among locals and tourists alike.

One day, she began to get knocks at her door from people politely requesting a tour of her "museum." She wasn't sure how they'd come to call it a museum, but she couldn't help but puff out her chest a little at the description. At first, she took them through her collection in small groups for free.

As her notoriety grew, Adelaide began to offer organized

tours for a small donation. She'd even put out a little sandwich board listing dates and times the museum was open.

Before long, The Fantastic Museum of the Weird and the Macabre was listed on the *Travel Nevada* webpage as a sight to be seen in the Las Vegas area, along with Beatty, the Valley of Fire, the Hoover Dam, Area 51, and the Extraterrestrial Highway. She'd made a name for herself.

From the first time Adelaide took a person through her home, she started each tour with a translation of the Latin term memento mori.

She'd adopt a serious tone as she explained, "Memento mori means 'remember that you must die.' I'm sure you must consider that an awfully morbid idea. It might even sound a touch threatening. But I assure you it means just the opposite. The purpose of the phrase was to remind people to enjoy life. You shouldn't be afraid of death but instead make use of the time you have, while remaining aware that one day you will leave your earthly form. You must remember that all of us have been dying since the very moment we were born. It is inevitable. It must come. There's no way to avoid it, so we must treasure and make the most of every single moment."

Adelaide usually received applause after that little speech. She finally felt like she'd found her purpose in life. Her calling. If she could make even just one person understand the preciousness of life, then she'd have made an actual difference in the world.

People thought she was cool now, even if just a touch weird. That didn't mean she failed to hear the whispers and snickers behind her back: jokes about the old maid who was so odd she couldn't find a husband. Or the people who gossiped that maybe her husband, the one she'd never had in reality, lay back in their bed, taxidermied.

But far more people were supportive than cruel. Besides, she profited from the admission paid by each one of those vile ones, $5 a head now.

Adelaide had even been approached by a couple of paranormal teams who inquired about the possibility of doing an investigation of her museum. They speculated that spirits could be attached to those memento mori items crafted with body parts from deceased people. And of course, they worried about the tormented souls of those who had received lobotomies or lost limbs via the medical equipment she had in her possession.

She'd rented her house to three different teams: Only one had turned out to be professional; the other two caused her problems.

The first one turned out to be a group of amateurs calling themselves a team. They'd left Adelaide's home dirty, invaded her private space outside the museum, despite the signs and rope barriers she'd put up, and even stolen one of her apothecary bottles.

She'd contemplated never renting it out again, but the leader of the second team had made such an impassioned plea that she'd relented. That group had been the legitimate one and had actually come up with details that fit the history of some of the items in her collection.

The third team was the one that made Adelaide decide to end private rentals. They had broken a priceless death mask when supposedly using it as a trigger object. They'd also insisted her home was infested with demonic energies after holding Ouija board sessions... something she had expressly forbidden.

She'd been approached several more times over the years—the most insistent being the last team. When she denied them the last time, they'd warned her about the dangers she might face from vengeful spirits who didn't appreciate her putting their pain on display. Adelaide didn't believe in any of that, so she blocked their calls and emails.

One day, a couple years after the official opening of the museum, Adelaide received a visit from a renowned psychic. It was the height of summer travel season, so she'd been busy hosting tours all morning for travelers passing through town on their way to Vegas. The psychic had paid extra to take the tour alone, which Adelaide happily accepted, as she was tired and rundown from the oppressive late-summer heat.

The psychic asked if Adelaide would let her do a small psychic investigation, and she wanted Adelaide to confirm or debunk her impressions if she knew the real history.

Adelaide didn't know if she believed in true psychic ability or not. But she'd been impressed and startled by the accuracy of some of the info from that paranormal team, so she was excited to see what might happen this time.

The woman looked totally normal. Adelaide didn't know what she had expected to see, but she couldn't put aside images of those old gypsy fortune tellers always depicted in movies.

"Thank you so much for having me here, Adelaide. Excuse me, may I call you that?"

"Yes, of course."

"I'm Elaine. So what are your ground rules? Anything off limits? May I touch items?"

"I ask that you don't lift up any fragile items like the death masks. Otherwise, you are free to gently touch any item you like. How does this all work? Am I supposed to tell you anything in advance? Do I need to leave the room?"

"It is all up to you. This is your place. Some people are uncomfortable around this kind of thing because of religious beliefs. Others are fascinated. I like to explore a room without any prior information to bias my experiences. Then I'll tell you my impressions."

Adelaide chose to sit in a chair in the back corner of the room and let Elaine begin her work uninterrupted.

"Adelaide, when I touched this hair wreath, I saw you—but not as you are now. It was you as a child. You were sitting with someone I felt was your... grandmother, and she was adding in some short gray hair. Does that make sense to you?"

Adelaide's eyes widened, and she nodded. She'd never told anyone that one of the hair wreaths belonged to her own family. It had been a tradition passed down for six generations. Adelaide had been the last person to add hair from her own mother who passed a little over a decade ago.

The psychic continued examining the collection, focusing on any items she felt drawn to. Adelaide could verify the backgrounds of many, but with some of the items, she had no idea of their history.

Adelaide had enjoyed Elaine's company so much that she invited her to have tea, and Elaine gladly accepted.

"This probably sounds stupid, but I have no experience with psychic abilities. Were you born with your talent, or is this something you cultivated?" Adelaide asked, her cheeks blushing with embarrassment.

"Don't worry, dear. I get asked that question all the time. The ability has been passed down through the women in my family for generations. But yes, it is also a skill that must be cultivated. My impressions are just that, impressions—flashes of images in my head and words or phrases that just float through. I must concentrate to understand the connections—one cannot always be made, though—sometimes I can only express what I saw.

"That is why a thorough reading can only be done as part of a cohesive meeting of the minds. Sometimes if I am investigating a historical place or if I've been asked to investigate a paranormal experience, I work with a historian. I pass along what I sense to a recorder. We then work together to piece together what it all means."

"I didn't realize that, but it makes sense. It sounds like you take your ability very seriously."

"I truly do, especially when I am doing a psychic reading for someone. They are my sounding board then. They are as much a part of the process as I am. No psychic works in a vacuum, not if they are legitimate. I ask no questions of the person before we start. After I get my initial impressions, I ask only what they are seeking to learn. I process any further information I receive, and then we discuss it. Sometimes we can't make heads or tails of it in the moment, but usually it is very helpful."

"Why do you think they can't figure it out sometimes?"

"Self-reflection is an important part of the process. Sometimes a person wants to know something about their future or about themselves, but they aren't ready to hear it. I do have to say, though, that on those rare occasions when that happens, I've always had my clients contact me a few weeks or months later and tell me that they figured it out."

"That's so fascinating. I have one more question if you don't mind."

"Of course! You were kind enough to open your home to me. It's the least I can do. Fire away."

"Well, it's actually two. You've really piqued my interest. Do you ever sense stuff about people when you aren't trying to do a reading: Like you are walking through the store and make eye contact with someone or accidentally brush against a person's arm? It's probably my naivete, but you always see that in movies."

Elaine giggled.

"Let me guess, you were expecting a woman in a long skirt down to my ankles, wrists adorned with jingly bracelets, and a red scarf tied in my hair. Am I close?"

"Don't forget the wart on your nose." Adelaide snorted as she laughed at her own joke. "Excuse me. You got me. I may have watched *Thinner* by Stephen King a few too many times."

"I forgive you. But your question isn't that far off base.

Sometimes I get very strong impressions from those in severe pain or who are in great peril. When I am totally relaxed, as I am when I am out doing everyday tasks, I am the most open to receive. So yes, it does happen sometimes."

"Do you tell them? I imagine it would be kind of awkward to approach someone in that situation. And you mentioned peril, which kind of leads to that other question I had. Do you ever not tell someone if you sense something bad? If you sense danger around them, is it even possible to change what you see, like with a warning? Or do you hide information you sense that might upset a person?"

"That's a loaded question. I can't just give you a pat answer. First, like I told you before, I receive impressions. So, I might sense peril surrounding a person but not have any specific details I can provide to help them avoid it. If they didn't ask for my help, don't know me from Adam, and I can't actually help them avoid it—I feel like I am doing them a disservice by making them fret. Does that make sense?"

"Yes, of course. But..."

"If I feel like I have enough details to make a difference, and if I feel like they might be open to receive it, I have tried to pass it along. Unfortunately, it usually doesn't go far. People don't like strangers butting into their business—even well-meaning strangers."

"I hate how closed off people have become. This world is a darker place with everyone isolating themselves."

"Now if a person has approached me for a reading, I always pass along everything I sense. It is my duty. Sometimes that includes information that people are not ready to or didn't want to hear. That has angered some people, but they came to me for answers. I promised to deliver what I could feel, not what they wanted to hear."

"That's very honorable of you."

"It's good for my heart and integrity to do what's right, not always good for my Yelp rating or pocketbook." Elaine smiled and shrugged. "But that isn't why I do this, so it doesn't matter. My realty job is what pays the bills."

Adelaide reached out and squeezed Elaine's hand. "You're a good woman. I really enjoyed your company today. You're free to come back whenever you'd like, even if it is just for a social call. Although I don't imagine you come to Goldfield very often."

Elaine began to squeeze Adelaide's hand harder. Her eyes widened. She was holding her breath and then let it out in a rush as her eyes turned up to meet Adelaide's worried frown.

"What? What's wrong? Are you okay, Elaine?"

"Yes... um... yes, I am."

"Talk to me."

"I'm still processing. Give me a moment."

Adelaide sat there, biting her lower lip as she waited for Elaine to speak. She began wringing her hands in her lap, a nervous tic she'd thought she had finally broken herself of a few years ago. She was staring at the old lathe board peeking through the peeling paint in the hallway when she felt Elaine's soft hand on her arm.

"Adelaide, I need to tell you something."

"Just tell me. I'm nervous as a cat in a room full of rocking chairs."

"I don't have much detail, but I'll tell you what I know. But first, do you know of anyone who might be angry at you? Who might want to get revenge?"

"No, of course not. *You* are the first person I've visited socially with in over 25 years. I'm a loner. A total outcast from society until everybody got interested in seeing my collection. Why do you ask?"

"I have the strongest feeling of someone trying to get back at you, and, in the process, you are hurt. Possibly even..." Elaine's last word was intelligible as her voiced dropped low and trailed off.

"What was that last word you said? You spoke so quietly I didn't make it out."

"Killed."

Adelaide gasped. "How is that possible? You must be mistaken. Who would want to hurt me?"

"I don't know. I really wish I did. I am wracking my brain, but I just don't have any other details to give you. I don't know how soon or why or who. I can't even give you any details about what will happen. Just that it happens here." Elaine had wrapped both her hands around Adelaide's clenched hands and gave a comforting squeeze. "Sometimes more will come to me if I just let it stew in my brain. I'll call you if I figure it out."

"Thank you, Elaine. I really appreciate it."

"I hate to leave you after laying all this on you, but I really must get started on the drive back toward Las Vegas. I have a red-eye out tonight. Just promise me you will be careful."

"I will. Please keep in touch."

Adelaide couldn't get what Elaine had said out of her mind. She vowed to herself to be careful and stay watchful.

But of what?

The next two months passed quietly. Elaine had contacted Adelaide to make sure it was okay to write a blog about her experiences at Adelaide's house. Adelaide happily agreed.

The museum received many phone calls after the blog appeared from people wanting to make reservations for tours and schedule private rentals. Adelaide told them what she told everybody, "The museum is open Tuesday through Friday from 10 a.m. till 3 p.m. and on Saturdays from noon to 4 p.m. I don't take reservations. It is first come, first served. I don't offer the museum for private rentals."

As late fall arrived with the drop in temperatures, shorter days, and the kids back in school, the tourist traffic through southern Nevada slowed. Those who chose to visit Vegas were flying in rather than making road trips. Adelaide reduced her schedule to winter hours, closing during the week and operating only on Friday and Saturday.

On a Thursday morning just before noon, she drove the two-and-a-half hours out to Las Vegas to do some shopping at stores that weren't available any closer. While she was out, she received several frantic phone calls from Elaine, who left messages on her outdated answering machine. Adelaide had never opted to buy a cell phone with voicemail.

"Adelaide, *please* call me back as soon as you get home. It is an emergency... *life or death*. I figured something out."

An hour later, she left another, "Adelaide, I'm really worried about you. Where are you? Call me back."

Thirty minutes later, "Adelaide! Are you home yet? It's Elaine. Please answer. Never mind... I'm in Vegas again visiting my cousin. I'm leaving there now and coming to check on you. It's just about 6, so I'll see you about 8:30."

Adelaide arrived home at 8:05 p.m. and found her front door unlocked. She could have sworn she'd locked it, but she wasn't too concerned in quiet little Goldfield. She took her purchases to her bedroom in the back and left them on the bed.

As she walked out of the room, she heard a noise in the spare bedroom. The door had been closed when she'd passed it a moment ago. She peered down the hall, listening, and heard a quiet, rhythmic creak... almost rocking. When she turned into the doorway, she saw a woman who looked strangely familiar looking down adoringly at a baby cradled in her arms. She was sitting in Adelaide's antique rocking chair. Both of them were deathly pale.

The woman whipped her face up to stare at Adelaide, anger flashing in her eyes. "GET OUT!!!"

Adelaide was so startled she didn't even stop to ask the woman what she was doing in her house. She turned to run and caught her foot on a loose floorboard, tripping and falling to the ground on her arthritic hips. She struggled to get up as she heard footsteps rushing across the floor toward her. She rolled to the door and pulled it shut as she saw the woman's skirts swish past the door.

She heard a woman's voice through the door, "Keep your prying eyes off my precious baby. He was only two days old, you nosy parker."

Was?

What could the woman have meant by that? Why was she here? Nobody used "nosy parker" anymore.

Adelaide had climbed to her feet and hobbled down the hallway to the phone hanging on the kitchen wall when she encountered another sight that startled her. There was the still form of an infant sitting in her antique velvet armchair near the Memento Mori section of the museum.

She couldn't take her eyes off the baby. Was it breathing? It was dressed so oddly... a lace-covered long gown, almost like a christening gown. Then it struck her why the sight was so disarming. Why the woman and child in the back seemed familiar.

They all looked just like people from her Victorian post-mortem photos. As her pulse raced in time with her mind, she found herself gasping for breath. With each second, the vice-like pressure on her chest increased. She grabbed her chest with one hand and leaned on the wall with her other outstretched hand.

She jumped when she heard a deep man's voice bellow, "Where is my leg? Doc, what did you do? Did you take my leg?"

The spirits, all of them, were mad at her. They had come to get revenge. She'd never meant any disrespect. She thought it was touching how people in Victorian times dealt with grief and mourning. She didn't want history to be forgotten. Her museum had never been about making money... other than enough to maintain the property and safety of the relics.

She heard a knock on the front door turn into pounding. A voice—a woman—was yelling her name and telling her to open the door. Adelaide took slow, halting steps toward the door. She slumped against it and slid to the floor as the pain in her chest became unbearable.

Adelaide was shoved aside as someone turned the handle and threw themselves bodily against the door to push it open. As Elaine slid through the crack of the door, she saw a man with one leg come limping into the room on crutches.

"Who the fuck are you?" Elaine screamed at him.

"Oh fuck, Samantha! Get out of the house now. Someone's here."

"What?" screamed a woman's voice from the back of the house.

"Help me move her now, or so help me, I will hurt you myself," Elaine demanded.

The man came forward and helped pull Adelaide into the center of the room. She was pale, her breathing shallow, and she was barely conscious. Then the man rushed over to grab the "reborn doll" he'd left in the chair. A woman in white makeup came down the hall with a real infant in her arms.

"We need to bail, Charles. Fuck her! Leave the bitch. If she'd just let us come back, none of this would have happened," the woman spat in Adelaide's direction.

"We were just trying to scare her. We didn't mean to..."

"Just get out!" Elaine shouted.

The two people slipped out the front door and headed

quickly toward a car parked in the darkness across the street.

Elaine held Adelaide's hand and tried to comfort her. "Everything is going to be okay. Just hold on for me. I called 911. I tried to get here in time. I'm so sorry."

"Ghosts... sorry."

"Shhh! You didn't do anything wrong. I will make sure those assholes pay."

The police arrived about two minutes later and called for Care Flight. Adelaide was rushed to the hospital, but she never regained consciousness. She'd suffered a major heart attack from the stress and fright of the experience.

The police investigation found the break-in had been perpetrated by the so-called paranormal team that had harassed Adelaide for years about wanting to rent her place again.

The headline in *The Tonopah Times-Bonanza and Goldfield News* read "Vengeful Ghost Hunters Scare Grisly Collector to Death."

"The Collector" by Sharon Marie Provost appears here for the first time.

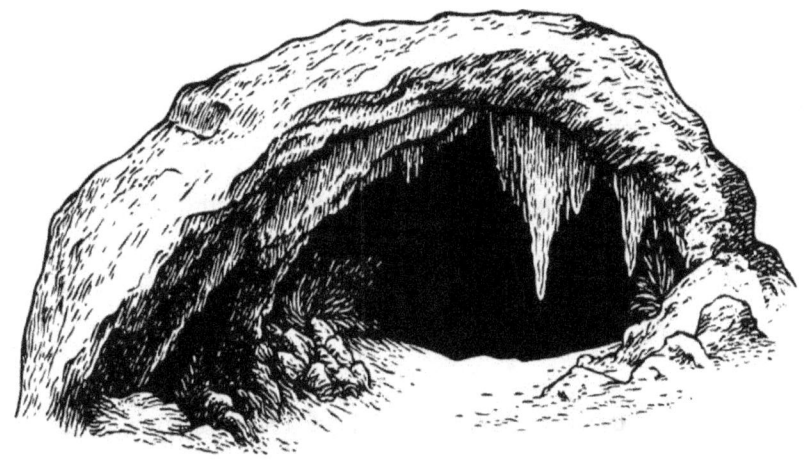

Richard Moreno

The Cave of Wonders

In Jack Gilbert's dream, the cave's walls are covered with delicate, spaghetti-like tubes and in various spots are massive, smooth, clam-shaped plates seemingly growing from the rock face. In other places, the walls are covered with a substance that resembles white sea coral. Thick, tapered stone icicles hang from the ceiling while similarly shaped shafts grow from the floor. Sometimes they merge to form giant, magnificently decorated pillars. As he slowly walks through the cave, he steps around smaller, round sea cucumber-like rock formations also growing from the ground.

Despite being far underground, the cave isn't dark. Soft light comes from somewhere—he isn't sure of its source—and bathes the entire passageway, which seems to go on for miles. He continues to walk through the huge corridor, which must be at least 30 feet high in some places, noticing the various kinds of rock formations in the cave. Each is more magnificent than the last. Over there is a pair of white and caramel-colored stone wings, while over there are thick pillars that resemble melted, dripping white chocolate. Some of the hanging rocks are jagged like teeth, while others are smoother and more rounded, almost organic in appearance. He passes several small pools of water and hears water dripping. This cave is alive and still growing.

He has visited many caves in Nevada before, but this one is surely the grandest and most decorated he has ever seen. It is truly a cave of wonders.

"Where you headed this early in the morning, Jack?" Raj Agarwal asked.

"I ran into this old timer who told me about this amazing vertical cave that's supposed to be somewhere in the mountains northwest of Pioche. Like all those old cavers, he was pretty proprietary about exactly where it was located, but I managed to get a few things out of him that give me a good idea where it's located," Jack responded. "I'm thinking about trying to find it so we can go back later to check it out."

"Sounds great," Raj said. "Let me know what you find."

Jack caught the climbing bug when he was in his teens. During his freshman year in high school, his class took a field trip to a Las Vegas indoor rock-climbing gym and, after scaling up and down the concrete surface like Spider-Man, he was hooked. He almost missed the bus back to school because he was trying to scamper up the wall just one more time. By the time he was in college, he had discovered the thrill of climbing down rather than up—he'd begun regularly cave rappelling, usually with his roommate, caving partner, and best friend, Raj Agarwal.

In Jack's mind, nothing was quite as exhilarating as hauling his climbing gear to some remote hole in the ground and then, after securing his rope, dropping into the darkness below. He lived for the anticipation of the rappel, the adrenaline rush during the descent, and, once at the bottom, the satisfied feeling of discovery.

Over the years, he'd studied Nevada's caves, learned how they were formed, and how the often otherworldly rock formations in them were created. The two had honed their spelunking skills in places like Leviathan Cave in the Worthington Mountains near Rachel, Nevada, and Pinnacle Cave on Mt. Potasi in southern Nevada. But, occasionally, Jack would go off on his own, following the whispered leads from other cavers—who are notoriously tight-lipped about their discoveries and favorite spots—in order to seek out new places to explore. Raj hated wasting time on what he called, "snipe hunts," so he didn't mind if Jack did the reconnaissance work. Jack, on the other hand, loved the search.

"I'm going to the gym, man," Raj said. "Have fun and let me know what you find."

Jack nodded as he packed up his gear, including several flashlights. Based on the information he wrangled from the old man, this cave, which was supposedly one of the deepest the man had ever seen, was most likely in the Bancroft Range. From his previous trips to that part of the state, he knew it was riddled with abandoned mine shafts, Native American petroglyphs, and caves. In fact, not too far to the northeast was Lehman Caves, probably the most famous of Nevada's subterranean passages, that was part of Great Basin National Park.

After stowing his gear in his green Toyota Tacoma, Jack headed north of Las Vegas on U.S. 93. It was still early enough in the morning that he would reach the tiny hamlet of Alamo by 8:30. He had packed a cooler with bottles of water, a couple of turkey sandwiches, and carrots sticks because there wasn't much in terms of places to eat in Alamo—mostly a couple of truck stops that served things like fried chicken, plank fries, and prepared salads.

About ten miles past Alamo, at Crystal Springs, he turned off

U.S. 93 and onto State Route 318. If U.S. 93 was lightly traveled, S.R. 318 was a virtual ghost road. Other than the occasional trucker heading to or from Ely, or the handful of people who called Lund, Nevada their home, there wasn't much traffic on the highway. According to the old man, the cave he was looking for was about 75 miles north of Crystal Springs via an unmarked mining road. Jack set his trip odometer so he could keep track of the miles.

As the miles raced by, Jack took in the landscape. For much of the drive, the highway traversed a long, wide valley whose dusty, beige openness was only interrupted by gnarled clumps of sagebrush and the occasional Joshua tree. Paralleling the valley on each side were mountains, stretching north to south. Jack remembered reading somewhere that on a topographical map Nevada's mountain ranges resemble strings of giant caterpillars marching toward Mexico.

Jack saw the odometer reading was nearing the point where he should look for the mining road. At almost exactly 75 miles, he spied the route. There was no sign indicating it was the place, but, somehow, he knew. He slowed and turned right onto a rocky, dusty trail that looked like no one had traveled on it for a very long time. The road crossed the east side of the valley from the paved state highway, then climbed into the range.

The truck bounced over the rippled, washboarded road. The vibrating, teeth-chattering drive was only broken for short periods when the road crossed a semi-sandy dry wash. Jack was thankful he had outfitted the Toyota with slightly larger tires with aggressive tread because it seemed to make the trip slightly less unpleasant. The bone-jarring journey continued for about 40 miles before climbing into the mountains.

Jack slowed when he saw a small clearing at the entrance to what appeared to be a canyon. He stopped the truck, climbed out of the vehicle, and walked for about a hundred yards. It certainly looked like the place described by the old man. Since the canyon was too narrow for his vehicle, he grabbed his ropes and backpack, and started to walk.

He tried to recall if the old man had mentioned anything else that might give him a clue that he was heading the right way. And there it was. A burned tree near the canyon entrance. Now he remembered. The old man said look for a burned tree and then keep climbing onto the rocks above the tree until you reach a pair of 10-foot round boulders. Behind, should be a smooth stone shelf and a stone bridge. The cave would be located near the arch.

Jack followed the instructions and stopped. The old man had been right. In the rocks in front of him was a 12-foot-long rock arch and behind that was a rock overhang that partially covered an opening in the ground. He walked to the edge of the hole, which appeared to be about 10 feet across. Because of the overhang, the opening was dark, too dark to see much beyond a foot or two in the natural light.

Taking off his backpack, Jack grabbed a large flashlight and shined it into the hole. He could make out the shapes of stalactites and columns. This was a cave that appeared to be worth exploring, he thought to himself. He decided to take a quick look with his GoPro camera, but wait until he returned with Raj before doing anything too daring or dangerous. He knew it was stupid to rappel into a strange cave without backup.

After securing the GoPro to a rope (and tying the other end around his waist), Jack synchronized the camera with his cellphone so he could see what it was recording. With one hand, he slowly lowered it into the cave, trying hard to keep it from spinning too much, while looking at the image on his cellphone.

The light module on the camera illuminated the cave so he could see more of what was down there. While shadows jumped around with each movement of the camera on the rope, he could still see some of the cave's features. Off to one side was a massive column made of hardened calcium carbonate that was profusely decorated with layers of smooth flowstone and jagged, teethlike spirals. In one corner were several pairs of cave shields or plates that typically form when calcium-rich water under hydrostatic pressure flows through cracks in a ceiling or wall. These were the largest he had ever seen—even bigger than the giant Parachute Formation in Lehman Caves at Nevada's Great Basin National Park.

As the camera continued to descend, Jack began to get excited. This had to be one of the most decorated caves he had ever seen. Everywhere the camera faced he could see a fantasyland of formations. He ached to grab his helmet, strap on his harness, secure a rope, and rappel into the hole to see it for himself. But he knew better.

The camera finally came to rest on the cavern floor. Jack estimated it was about 125 feet to the bottom. As for the size of the cave, the camera's small light was too limited to provide an answer. But what he could tell was that the cave was something special, and he needed to explore it more. Now he understood why the old man had been so stingy with the details.

Following several minutes of carefully moving the camera to face different directions in order to see what he could see, Jack gingerly pulled it from the cave. He made mental notes of the details about the drive. After returning to the mouth of the canyon, he pulled a red nylon ribbon from his pack and tied it around the blackened tree. This would be his claim, much like the old-time miners who staked their mining claims a century ago.

Jack returned to his truck and began the journey home. He had so much to tell Raj.

The first time Jack and Raj tried to return to the cave of wonders, they encountered a sudden downpour that made driving to the site impossible. Within a few miles on the dirt road, it had become a river of boulders, thick mud, and debris. Despite having a high-clearance vehicle, it quickly became apparent that to continue was to invite disaster. Plus, rappelling was out of the question under such conditions.

The second time Jack and Raj attempted to find the cave, one of the tires on Raj's Jeep had a flat about ten miles from Alamo. When they tried to replace it with the spare, they found that it, too, was flat. They abandoned the journey after having no luck hitching a ride, walking to Alamo, and waiting for the tires to be repaired. The only thing they came away with from the trip was a story to share with their girlfriends when they got home.

About a month later, they tried again. This time, the drive had—finally—gone well and they made it to the mouth of the canyon without incident. As they climbed out of Jack's truck, they saw the burned tree.

"The ribbon's gone," Jack said immediately. "Someone must have stolen it."

Looking at the ground, they did not see fresh tire tracks or footprints or anything indicating anyone had been there recently.

"No problem. I can remember the way from here," Jack told Raj as he headed into the rocks.

The two entered and began the climb leading to the two big boulders. They walked around the large round stones and immediately saw the stone archway. But as they crossed the smooth stone shelf and headed toward the rock shelter, Jack became confused. There was no cave opening in the ground.

"What the hell?" he said to Raj. "There was a cave right here. I don't understand."

Frantically, he stamped his feet on the hard, stone floor beneath the rock overhang. It wasn't like there had been a rockslide that might have covered the cave entrance. It just wasn't there anymore.

Jack pulled his cell phone from his pocket to look at the video he had taken of the cave. The jerky footage was still saved on his phone. The magnificent column, the incredible cave formations, and the rest could still be viewed.

"Perhaps this is the wrong place. It's not unusual that one place looks just like another out here," Raj said.

"No, no, this is it. I know this is where I came. You saw the video," Jack said. "There can't be another canyon with a burnt tree and the two boulders, and all the rest. No, this is the place. I just don't understand where it went. What happened to the damned cave?"

The two spent several hours hiking around the hills searching for a cave opening. Jack felt disoriented. His instincts told him he was in the correct location, but the fact remained there was no cave at this location. Finally, Raj suggested they head home. Jack was reluctant to give up the hunt, but acquiesced when it became clear they weren't going to find anything that day.

As they drove back to Las Vegas, Jack was silent for most of the trip. None of this made any sense. He had followed the directions exactly as he did before, when he found the cave the first time. Did he forget some small detail? What the hell was going on?

Despite traveling to the same location in the Bancroft Mountains at least a dozen more times over the next few years, Jack couldn't relocate the cavern. Raj had begged off after joining Jack for several more, always unsuccessful, searches, deciding that they were simply never going to find it again—if it even existed. When he wasn't brooding about making another trip out to the spot, Jack was rewatching the video. He just knew it was out there, waiting for him to come visit again. The cave was real, and it was there—even if no one else believed him.

In the five years since Jack had first seen the cave of wonders, his girlfriend, Amanda, had dumped him, and he was no longer rooming with Raj, who had grown tired of Jack's obsession with the cave. Given his disinterest in nearly everything not cave-related, it was a miracle that he still held on to his job at the sporting goods store. Jack's apartment was littered with topo maps and satellite images he had downloaded from the internet. He'd even tried looking for the old man who had told him about the cave. He'd met the man at a local speleological society club meeting, but no one could remember ever seeing anyone matching his description. As Jack left the meeting, where he'd pestered everyone about the old man, he could hear the whispering behind his back.

There was also the dream. Nearly every night, he dreamed about the cave, his mind filling in the blank spaces on the video. In his mind, he'd begun calling it his Cave of Wonders. He knew it was out there, and he just had to find it again.

It was five years to the day since Jack found the cave that he decided to try again. If he didn't find it this time, he decided he was finally going to let it go and reclaim his life. He would retrace his steps from the first time, even to the point of packing the same type of turkey sandwiches and brand of water bottles. He turned off on State Route 318 and watched the odometer tick off exactly 75 miles. He took a right on the dirt road and drove for another 40 miles to the clearing.

He parked, saw the burned tree, and then made the hike up the hill to the two boulders. As he rounded one, he saw the stone shelf and the stone arch and rock overhang across the way. There was also something else. As he crossed the shelf, he saw what he'd been seeking for the past half-decade. It was an opening in the ground.

It was the goddamned cave.

Jack walked to the hole and felt cool air coming from its

depths. It was real. This time, he was going all the way. Screw everyone who doubted him. He was going to explore the cave alone. But just to be safe, he decided to leave a message for Raj, who he knew was working that Saturday.

"Buddy, you're not going to believe this, but I found it! It's real, and it's right in front of me. I'm texting you my GPS coordinates just, you know, in case anything happens. I am so stoked to have finally found it again! Anyway, talk to you soon, man."

With that task completed, he secured his ropes, slipped into his harness, and strapped on his helmet, which had a bright LED light. He tied another, larger flashlight to his belt, and slipped his cell phone into a side pocket. Satisfied that he was good to go, Jack walked cautiously to the edge of the opening, backed into the hole, and slowly began his descent.

Raj didn't listen to his phone messages until he returned home from his job at the bank. He saw that Jack had called—probably to ramble on again about some new theory he had about that damned cave. After listening to his other two messages, he reluctantly decided to hear what Jack had to say. When the message ended, Raj wasn't sure what to think. Jack had become so weird about the cave, yet now he was saying he had found it? He listened again to the message. Jack sounded happy and so... normal. He hadn't sounded that way in such a long time.

He tried to call Jack but was routed to voicemail. He figured he'd just wait until he heard again from Jack and maybe the two of them could go check out the cave together. It could be like old times.

The following day, Raj attempted to telephone Jack several times, but each time his calls went directly to voicemail. He stopped by his old roommate's apartment, but it was clear no one was there. On the second day after receiving Jack's call, and hearing nothing else, Raj called 911.

Throughout the next week, the story about the missing caver somewhere in eastern Nevada made all the television news channels in Las Vegas and southern Utah. The local newspaper took to calling Jack the "Clark County Caveman" in its headlines. The Clark County Sheriff's Office called in the Search and Rescue Unit, but, in spite of having the GPS coordinates, drones, and on-the-ground search parties, there was little trace of Jack. The authorities had found his green Toyota in the clearing near the canyon with the burned tree, but nothing else and no cave. One TV station sent a helicopter out to the area, but all it came back with was B-roll video for its stories about the now-infamous caveman.

About ten days after Jack disappeared, Raj was sitting at home, thinking about his friend. "What the fuck, dude? Where the hell did you go?" he asked himself. He wished Jack had invited him to go along, but deep down, he knew he would have declined. He picked up his cell phone absentmindedly and noticed a message that hadn't been there before.

"Raj, you've got to see this place," an excited Jack said on the recorded message. "It is so fucking cool. There is so much to see! I think I could stay here forever."

Then tears filled Raj's eyes, and he began to sob.

"The Cave of Wonders" by Richard Moreno appears here for the first time.

George Wharton James

The Ghost Who Suckled Her Child

An Indian woman died, leaving a little child and her husband. The latter spent the accustomed four days and nights watching at her grave without food or drink.

On the fourth night, the grave suddenly opened, and the woman stepped out before him. "Give me my child," said she. The man said not a word but went quickly and brought the little child.

The woman did not speak but took the child and suckled it. Then holding it close in her arms, she began to walk slowly away. The man followed her, but he did not speak. On, on they went, through forest and meadow, up hill and down dale.

By and by, the man made a movement as though he would take hold of her to stop her. But the woman warded him off with a wave of her hand. "Touch me not," she said. "If you touch me, you must die too!" She stood and suckled the child once more, then laid him gently in her husband's arms. "Go home," she said, and faded from his sight.

Home he went with the child, full of awe and fear.

A few days afterwards, the child died, though there was nothing the matter with it. The man, however, lived to be very old.

"The Ghost Who Suckled Her Child" was contained in a letter by Mrs. W.W. Price to George Wharton James and was included in his 1921 book, The Lake of the Sky.

The Origin of Lake Tahoe

The natives in the vicinity of Lake Tahoe ascribe its origin to a great natural convulsion. There was a time, they say, when their tribe possessed the whole Earth, and were strong, numerous, and rich; but a day came in which a people rose up stronger than they, and defeated and enslaved them.

Afterward, the Great Spirit sent an immense wave across the continent from the sea, and this wave engulfed both the oppressors and the oppressed, all but a small remnant. Then the taskmasters made the remaining people raise up a great temple, so that they, of the ruling caste, should have refuge in case of another flood, and on top of this temple, the masters worshipped a column of perpetual fire.

Half a moon had not elapsed, however, when the Earth was again troubled, this time with strong convulsions and thunderings, upon which the masters took refuge in their great tower, closing the people out.

The poor fled to the Humboldt River, and getting into canoes, paddled for their life from the awful sight behind them. For the land was tossing like a troubled sea, and casting up fire, smoke, and ashes. The flames went up to the very heaven and melted many stars, so that they rained down in molten metal upon the Earth, forming the ore that the white men seek. The Sierra was mounded up from the bottom of the Earth, while the place where the great fort stood, leaving only the dome exposed above the waters of Lake Tahoe.

The inmates of the temple-towers clung to its dome to save themselves from drowning, but the Great Spirit walked upon the waters in his wrath and took the oppressors like pebbles and threw them far into the recesses of a great cavern on the east side of the lake—called to this day the Spirit Lodge—where the waters shut them in.

There they must remain until the last great volcanic burning, which is to overthrow the whole Earth, shall again set them free. In the depths of their cavern prison, them may still be heard, wailing and moaning, when the snow melts and the waters swell in the lake.

—*Nevada State Journal*
November 13, 1875

Dan De Quille

A Haunted Mine

For some years past, there have been observed by the miners working in the old upper levels f the Yellow Jacket Mine, Gold Hill, Nev., various phenomena apparently of a supernatural character. Recently, these unaccountable disturbances have been renewed in a startling manner.

Few miners like to own to having been frightened by anything of a ghostly nature. The majority prefer quietly leaving a mine to acknowledging themselves frightened by unnatural sights and sounds. For this reason little has heretofore been made public in regard to the doings of the spooks and goblins in the old upper workings of the Jacket.

Miners are credited with being as thoroughly saturated with

superstitious notions and fears as are sailors. Taking into consideration the scenes of labor of the two classes, miners have much greater reason for being overcome at times by superstitious fears than have sailors. While the labors of the latter are at all times performed out under the free vault of heaven, in the midst of the open waters of the broad ocean, and much of the time in the broad light of day, the business of the former carries him into subterranean depths where reigns a perpetual darkness surpassing that of the land "beyond the ocean-stream" where Cimmerians dwell.

In the Old World, there has always existed a belief in gnomes, goblins, kobolds and other supernatural beings peculiar to mines—subterranean bogies—all of a more or less unwholesome nature. In Germany, the kobolds are particularly abundant and audacious in the drifts and galleries of the old mines.

Paracelsus states that "in Germany, they do usually walk in little coats, some two feet long."

Magnus asserts that there are no fewer than six kinds of subterranean goblins, "some bigger, some less," all of which are seen in and about mines.

Munster says: "Some of these are noxious; some again do no harm."

Georgius Agricala speaks of the most notable of these being... a very ancient tribe of subterranean imps, as the Greek kobalos is the German kobold.

Agricola says that "both the getuli and the cobali are clothed after the manner of metal-men, and will many times imitate their works."

Although stories of these goblins of the mines have been brought to the Comstock by miners from Freiberg, Altenberg, Clausthal and other mining regions in Germany, with similar stories from the mines of Cornwall, our miners have never encountered any such sprites in the lower levels here, nor seen any trace of their works.

If our miners fear anything at all, it is the spirits of the dead—the regular old-fashioned churchyard ghosts. But even of these, very little has heretofore been heard. Occasionally a story has been started of some strange sounds having been heard in some one of the mines, but nothing more than vague accounts of any sound heard could be obtained.

Now, however, we have something definite in regard to the strange sights and sounds in the Jacket. On Thursday night, November 10th, W. P. Bennett, who is employed in that mine, had an experience so startling that it gave him a fit of sickness from which he has not fully recovered at this writing.

Mr. Bennett is well known to many persons in San Francisco, as well as in this part of Nevada, and in many of the mountain towns of California. He was, for a number of years, in the employ of Wells, Fargo & Co., and in the old staging days had charge, as superintendent, of all their horses and coaches, and was much of the time travelling to and fro over their routes. He is a very truthful man, a Pacific Coast pioneer, and a man who throughout his life has feared

"No evil thing that walks by night
In fog or fire, by lake or moorish fen,
Blue meager hag, or stubborn unlaid ghost
That breaks his magic chains at curfew time,
No goblin or sward faery of the mine."

He says that never until last week did he see or hear anything that he could not account for.

He is now employed in the Yellow Jacket Mine as powder man. He has charge of and distributes to the miners the powder they require in blasting. He has been at work in the mine over four years. During that time, he has frequently been in the mine alone and passed through all parts of it without a thought of seeing or hearing anything of a ghostly nature.

He knew of men leaving the mine on account of things they had heard or seen, but paid very little attention to the mysterious talk about them which he occasionally heard among the miners, further than to say that he would very much like to see or hear some of the things they spoke of.

But now he wants no more of it. He says he has "got his dose," and will never get over it till his life is ended.

Last Thursday night, he spoke to Pete Langan, the foreman, of some shovels he had seen up on the 1,000 level, and said he would go up and get them. He was told to do so. He went up to the old deserted level, and ascended to the first floor above the track floor. He went out across this floor to a station, and, taking up two shovels, returned with them to descend to the track floor. He was carrying a lantern, and when he had got on the ladder that led to the track floor, and was moving down with his lantern below the hole in the floor, but his head still through it, he was startled at hearing heavy footsteps coming tramping over the planks directly toward him.

He began to descend the ladder as rapidly as possible, and while he did so heard the steps immediately over his head at the hole he had just left. He pushed on down the ladder a short distance till he reached an ore chute that leads down from the floor on which the footsteps were heard.

Halting at the chute, he looked up it, but saw nothing. He knew that no men were working on the level, but it came into his head that Pete Langan might possibly have followed him up to that part of the mine, though the thought then struck him that Pete could not have come up without a light, and would not be tramping about in the dark.

Although feeling very shaky and uncertain, Mr. Bennett

mustered courage to call out: "Who's there ? Anybody up there?"

Instantly he heard begin above, on the floor, from the hole through which he had just descended, a heavy tramping as of two men coming forward toward the ladder-way. As he stood on the ladder, he held his lantern in his left hand, and under the same arm the two shovels, tightly pressed against his side.

Suddenly, from behind, the shovels were violently thrust forward and sent flying a distance of two sets of timbers (about twelve feet), when they struck against the wall and went down the ladder-way, landing at a point distant nearly thirty feet from where they started.

"Up to this time," says Mr. Bennett, "I was not very badly frightened, but when I felt the thrust from behind, and saw the shovels flying ahead of me, I felt, through my whole system, a chilling, sickening shock. For a moment I was almost paralyzed; then in fear of something worse (the tramping on the floor above still continuing), I descended the ladder as swiftly as possible.

"When I reached the floor below, in my excitement, I took a wrong turn. I got off into a strange drift, and did not discover my error until I came to where was caved down in it a large pile of dirt. I dreaded going back under the ladder, the way from the floors above, but managed to creep round behind the ladder, and then came to the drift that I should have taken at first.

"There lay my two shovels, but for a time I was afraid to touch them, not knowing what might happen at the moment of my laying hands on them. However, I plucked up the courage to lay hold of the tools, and soon got down to the 1,100 level, nothing occurring to alarm me.

"When I got down among the men, I asked for Pete Langan, and was told he had been up on the surface during my trip to the 1,000 level. I was so sick that I was obliged to quit work. The men all saw that something had happened to me and wanted to know whether I had seen or heard anything. I gave them no answer further than to say that I had been overtaken by a sudden fit of illness. They were not satisfied, and that evening at suppertime, I told them what had occurred up on the 1,000 level. Then I learned from them of strange things that had happened to others in the old upper levels."

It appears that the 900 level is that on which supernatural manifestations are of most frequent occurrence. It is said that three men have been killed on that level and that one man was buried under a big cave, and that his body has not yet been recovered.

At the time of the great fire in the Jacket, which broke out on the morning of April 7, 1869, forty-five men lost their lives. The bodies of three of these were never recovered, and it has always been thought that they were walled in when bulkheads were built to confine the fire to certain limits, as afterward, when the fire had exhausted itself, some bits of bone were found in that section.

Quite a number of men have left the mine at different times on account of strange happenings on the 900 level. The fact that these men were giving up steady work at $4 a day shows that they were pretty thoroughly frightened. At times, men have been startled by cries and shrieks as of someone being pressed to death under timbers, but most of them have been alarmed by footsteps above and around them, such as were heard by Mr. Bennett.

The men who heard these sounds were not always alone. Men working in crosscuts would hear footsteps out in the main drift, as of someone on patrol marching up and down along the floorboards. At first, under the impression that it was the foreman promenading in the drift, some of the men went out to investigate, but could never see anyone, the sound of footsteps ceasing when they came into the drift, though it had been distinctly heard a moment before. With the return of the men to their work, the sound of footsteps tramping and grinding along the sandy footboards of the track board would again be heard, or perhaps the groanings and cries would begin.

The disturbances in the 1,000 level have been much less frequent than above on the 900 and the levels above that. But about a month ago, a miner named Bruce, who was at work on the 1,000 level, suddenly threw up his job. Being pressed for a reason, he at first said he was ill, but finally told a friend that he had seen a thing which he took to be a warning for him to leave the mine. He would not say what he had seen, but said it meant his death if he remained in the mine.

Fear of being laughed at prevents many from telling the cause of their fright. About two years ago, a miner who was at work on the 200 level heard footsteps in the main drift, and told the man who was at work with him in the face of a crosscut that he would look out and see who was there. Taking a candle, he went out, but in a few moments came rushing back with his hair on end and trembling in every joint.

He said that when he got out to the main drift, two shoes with no person in them came tramping along before him on the foot walk. He was so badly frightened that he would not stir an inch from his partner during the remainder of the shift, and when it was ended, left the mine, never to enter it again.

Mr. Bennett says that although he formerly went by himself through all parts of the mine without a thought of fear, no money would now hire him to again go alone into the old drifts and chambers of the 1,000 level. He says he has all his life laughed at the stories told of the pranks and spooks and the tricks of spiritualists, but the push he got when his shovels were sent flying was a thing that he cannot get over.

As Mr. Bennett has always been known as one utterly fearless as regards supernatural things, his experience has had a great effect upon the men working in the mine. There are at present about twenty men at work on the 1,200 level. Formerly, at change of shift, when these men reached the 1,100 level, they would make a rush for the shaft to get on the first cage going up; now, however, they move along as they pass the opening leading up to the 1,000 level, many sidelong glances are case toward it, and there is some quick stepping among the men who bring up the rear.

In writing an account of these old haunted levels, it would not have been difficult to have invented some startling things, but I have preferred relating just what is reported by Mr. Bennett and the miners themselves. Without comment or any attempt at explanation, I give the story of this supposed to be haunted mine, leaving all to draw their own conclusions.

"A Haunted Mine" by Dan De Quille is reprinted from an article in the San Francisco Examiner *dated November 27, 1887.*

Stephen H. Provost

Six Weeks to Eternity

"It's too hot to have the top down. Did you forget I'm bald?"

"A little color might do you good. You're so pale."

"Can I help it if I'm Swedish?"

"You're not Swedish. Your parents are. You've never been there in your life."

"Still..."

"If it bothers you that much, maybe you should have worn a hat."

"And have it blow away into the desert?"

"Stop being an old fuddy-duddy. Just enjoy the ride. Feel the wind in your hair... oh."

"That was deliberate."

"No one said you had to come along. I didn't want you here. You invited yourself."

"I'm your husband."

"In six weeks, you won't be."

"We'll see about that. Let's just put the top up, honey."

"Don't call me that."

"What do you want me to call you then?"

"Lorraine. Like everyone else does. Lorraine *Carr*."

"Your parents don't call you that, *Mildred Caravelo*. Or Magnusson. If you were going to shorten your last name, at least you could shorten the one on your marriage license. Mine."

"You would have preferred Lorraine Mag? You can't put something like that on a marquee. The studio wouldn't stand for it. Anyway, I'm changing it back, *legally*, after we're divorced."

"To Carr or Caravello?"

"*That* is none of your business, *Gustav*."

"It doesn't matter. You're not changing your name back anyway, because we're not getting divorced. *Millie*."

The Duesenberg screeched to a halt on the dirt shoulder of Highway 6, tossing stones up into the undercarriage and off the rear bumper.

"Hey! Easy on the wheels! I paid good money for this buggy."

"Yes, Gustav, the money I made from *Don Juan's Delilah*. I'm keeping the Doozy. Here's where you get off."

"Death Valley? Really?"

"Really. I'd say you look like death warmed over, but that would be a compliment. You *need* to be warmed over, bubby boy, and there's no better place to heat up than the good ol' Mojave

Desert. Right?"

Gus rolled his eyes. "I should be the one divorcing you."

"So why don't you then?"

"Because I'm not letting you off that easy, baby cakes. You're stuck with me. Go ahead and leave me here. I'll walk to Reno if I have to."

Lorraine burst out laughing. "You better start walking then, bub. It's 300 miles to Reno, and if you don't get a move on, you'll be divorced by the time you get there." She kept it in park and gunned the gas for emphasis, then shifted into gear.

Gus cupped his hands on both sides of his mouth as the Doozy lunched forward, then pulled back onto the road. "Don't forget to double-clutch her," he said, smiling.

"Who's been driving since we left L.A.? Right after you showed up out of nowhere and demanded that I take you along?"

"And who taught you to drive in the first place?" Gus called after her. He smiled and waved as she pulled away onto the nearly deserted highway.

Looking back in her rearview mirror, Lorraine saw her husband swallowed up in the waves of heat rising from the shimmering mirage on the road.

It felt great to finally be rid of him.

Lorraine turned heads when she rolled into Reno. She'd been determined to keep a low profile, but it went against her nature. She was a starlet, and she craved attention—so much so that she occasionally went to unusual lengths in seeking it out.

She'd once sat on top of a flagpole as a publicity stunt. She'd heard about a casting call for a movie called *King Kong* at RKO, where she happened to be under contract. She'd heard through the grapevine about the movie's big scene: a giant ape carried a beautiful girl up to the top of the Empire State Building. She thought she'd prove herself suited to the role with that flagpole stunt.

She hadn't gotten the part, and later learned that the scene in question was filmed using miniature models and animation.

That hadn't stopped her, though. She'd gone on to get her big break in *Don Juan and Delilah* after hamming it up in a church play about Samson and the biblical femme fatale—and making sure to invite a well-connected producer who also happened to admire her derriere.

That film had been the first in a series of bawdy romances that were just "clean" enough to avoid violating the Hays Code. And all of them were built around her: *Delilah's Dalliance*, *Delilah's Eyes*, *Delilah's Diary*, *Delilah's Destiny*, and so forth.

She *was* Delilah Jones, even more than she was Lorraine Carr—and certainly more than she was Mildred Caravelo Magnusson. She became so closely associated with the part that RKO turned down an overture from a young up-and-comer named Joan Fontaine to replace her.

But Lorraine knew that age wasn't her friend, so she'd made it her business to stay in shape and had continued to indulge in publicity stunts to stay relevant. She hadn't done any more flagpole sitting, but she had entered a marathon dance contest and married Gustav in a gazebo built specifically for their nuptials under the Hollywood sign.

Chasing headlines had become second nature to her, so she hadn't considered the ramifications of rolling into Reno in her Doozy.

Driving a Duesenberg into the center of town was simply not compatible with keeping a low profile. Only a few hundred Model Js had ever been made, and at $15,000 a pop, not just anybody could afford one. Almost everyone *couldn't*.

Lorraine might have taken a Ford or a Hudson, and she might have chosen to pass her six-week waiting period at "divorce destinations" in Verdi or Washoe. But as with everything else, she demanded the best, which meant staying at the Riverside Hotel in the heart of Reno.

She realized her mistake too late.

Then she started envisioning how everything would explode in the press, which would bombard her with the kind of headlines she *didn't* want: "Delilah Searching for New Don Juan," and "Lorraine Carr Drove Husband Crazy."

She registered at the Riverside under her maiden name, but she knew it probably wouldn't matter. The press would see through that thin façade and realize that Mildred Caravelo was really Lorraine Carr. And once they did, they wouldn't want to hear her side; they'd just want to make up juicy stories built on assumptions—assumptions bolstered by some uncomfortable truths.

Yes, she'd cheated on Gus with her *Don Juan* co-star, Vincent Barradino. And yes, she'd had Gus put in an asylum—temporarily—to deflect the blame. But he *was* a danger to her, especially when he got jealous, and he was a drunk who had blacked out in the middle of a conversation. Argument. Fight. It wasn't her fault he'd threatened to kill her if she left him—right before the blackout incident. And all that was old news anyway. At least they weren't writing about the real reason she was in Reno: not for a secret rendezvous, but to get a divorce. How they could have missed that was a mystery, but she was thankful for little favors.

Still, for the first time in a very long while, she wished she could be anonymous. She began avoiding the main streets whenever she went out, ducking around corners to avoid reporters she felt sure were following her. But that wasn't the worst of it: She swore she saw Gus peering out at her from the Riverside elevator just as it was closing.

She tried to shake it off, telling herself he couldn't have gotten here so fast. She'd only been in Reno a couple of days.

Unless someone had given him a ride.

Of course that had to be it... if it was him. But she told herself it wasn't... until she saw him again, or thought she did. This time, he was in a taxicab sitting in front of the Riverside as she stepped out onto the sidewalk for the short walk to her attorney's office. The Riverside had been built as a haven for divorce-seekers, so it was natural that a number of attorneys had set up shop nearby.

Lorraine had taken the precaution of buying a new outfit, a red wig, and a sun hat, but the moment she started down Virginia Street, the cab pulled out and began following her. She tried to quicken her pace without being obvious, but the cab seemed to be pacing her.

Sure enough, there was Gus smiling out at her from the back seat, looking happy and healthy, just like he'd never been stuck out in Death Valley. The sun hadn't touched that Swedish complexion of his, and he looked as if he hadn't missed a meal. How had he recognized her? She'd gone to such great lengths to conceal her identity.

Once she reached the north end of the bridge, she walked to the nearest intersection and swiftly rounded the corner.

The cab didn't follow, and she breathed a sigh of relief.

She told herself she must have been mistaken, that Gus just *couldn't* have been here: It must have been someone who bore a resemblance to him. An uncanny resemblance, but just a resemblance.

When she reached the offices of Kittinger and Associates, she stepped inside briskly, as if she were entering some sort of safe haven. Gus couldn't follow her in here, and this was the beginning of the end for their marriage.

"May I help you, dear?" said the woman at the reception desk, standing and extending her hand. She looked to be in her

50s, with graying hair coaxed by hot curlers into stiff waves and spirals that framed her mildly wrinkled face. She wore a gray pantsuit, which seemed jarringly out of place on one of her gender. "Kit Kittinger at your service."

"*You're* Kit Kittinger?"

The woman chuckled. "I get that a lot."

"I thought it was Kit... like in Kit Carson."

Kit shrugged. "It's a man's world. Having a name that *could* belong to someone of the male persuasion helps me keep up with the Joneses, if you know what I mean."

Lorraine wasn't sure about having a woman represent her. Women were nurses and schoolmarms and secretaries, not lawyers. But she supposed that, if she could command top billing in Hollywood, a woman could do the same at a law firm. She'd just have to get used to it.

"I don't see any associates," she remarked.

"Well... I don't have any," Kit confessed, "unless you count Felix and Felina." She pointed to an orange cat curled up on top of a bookcase and a tuxedo kitten grooming itself furiously at their feet. "I confess, it's another way to sound a little more impressive. There *will* be associates, when my practice grows. As of now, they're just positions I haven't staffed, waiting to be filled at the appropriate time... speaking of time, do you have an appointment?"

"I do. I'm Mildred Magnusson. I'm here to get rid of a man."

"Most of my clients are," Kit chuckled. "I can tell you're wearing a wig, Mrs. Magnusson, which is understandable. There's quite the stigma attached to being a divorcee. But you don't need it with me."

"All right." Lorraine removed her hat and took off the wig, waiting to see the lawyer's reaction.

She didn't have to wait long at all.

"Ah," Kit said, her face brightening. "Now I understand, Miss Carr. I'm a big fan. I didn't realize that was your stage name, though."

"Would you buy a ticket to see Mildred Magnusson?"

"Well..."

"I guess it's the same as you presenting yourself as an assumed-to-be man with phantom associates."

"Yes, I suppose it is. So... you're seeking a divorce."

"I'd rather have an annulment, but yes, a divorce will do. What do I need to do?"

"I'll just need some information. Do you have your marriage certificate?"

Lorraine had come prepared. She reached into her purse and produced the requested document.

"Ah, yes... let me see. Your spouse's name is Gustav Horatio Magnusson, and you were married six years ago in Santa Monica, California. Is he still a resident of California?"

"Yes."

"Well, this shouldn't be too difficult. I'll just need his specific address and date of birth for us to move forward. How does that sound?"

"Just peachy, Miss Kit. I'm staying at the Riverside until this mess is done with."

"Fine. We'll have you divorced in no time—well, six weeks. I'll be in touch if there are any problems. It was a pleasure meeting you."

"I assure you, Miss Kit, the pleasure was all mine."

As she walked out and closed the office door behind her, Lorraine ran smack into someone walking by in the corridor.

"Surprise!" said Gus. "Fancy meeting you here."

"What the...?"

Gus leaned in close, like he was going to plant a kiss on her lips, and she recoiled.

He frowned.

"Is that any way to treat your *husband*?" he said, indignant.

"Six weeks," she spat. "That's all the time you have. After that, I'll be free of you, you pathetic oaf."

"Six weeks to eternity, sweetheart," Gus said, grinning. "Now let me set you straight about one thing: You are *not* going to divorce me."

Lorraine took a step backward and stood up straighter. "And I suppose you're going to stop me?"

"Oh, no, Millie baby. You don't get it. I won't have to."

Lorraine tried not to let Gus get to her. He always acted this way; nothing new there. But she couldn't help wonder why he'd been so sure of himself—and whether he knew something she didn't. Or, worse, was he threatening her? Was he going to keep her from divorcing him by somehow ruining her career? He had plenty of dirt on her, that was for sure. But what if he'd meant something worse? What if he'd been threatening her? She couldn't divorce him if she was dead.

No, it wasn't possible. Even he couldn't stoop that low. Could he?

But it wasn't that. When the phone rang the next day in her hotel room and the switchboard operator put the caller through, she was surprised and a little worried to hear Kit's voice on the other end. "I'm afraid I have bad news," she said.

Lorraine tried not to let the concern she felt register in her voice. "What is it?" she said stiffly.

"The address you gave me for your husband..."

"Yes, it's the home we share. I haven't been there much lately; I've been staying with friends most of the time. I just go back now and then because I keep most of my clothes there."

"Whose name is the house in?" Kit asked.

"*His*." Lorraine hadn't been happy about that, but as Kit had said, it was a man's world.

"Not according to the records I looked up. Your name's on the deed. Could he have turned over ownership to you without you knowing? Maybe he planned to surprise you in an attempt to reconcile."

Lorraine laughed into the receiver. "That cheapskate? He'd *never* do that. He wants *everything* in his name."

"Well...," Kit said. "Be that as it may, I'll need to get his current address from you before we can proceed."

"But... that is *his* current address."

"Clearly it's not."

Then something occurred to Lorraine. He'd tried to come with her to Reno, then he'd followed her. He'd seen her just yesterday. What if he'd relocated to Nevada?

"I bumped into him as I was walking out of your office yesterday," Lorraine blurted out.

"Do you think he's stalking you?" Kit asked.

"Oh, I'm *sure* of it," Lorraine said. "Maybe he's living *here* now, but I have no idea where. He doesn't have any relatives that I know of in the area."

Kit's tone brightened a little. "Still, that gives me something to go on. I'll check the divorce ranches and motels to see if he's checked in anywhere, and I'll run a title check, just in case he's holding property here you don't know about. We'll get to the bottom of this. It just may take us a little longer than six weeks."

"Of *course* it will," Lorraine said, exasperated. "I'm sorry. None of this is your fault."

Kit's voice was sympathetic. "I understand. I run into this sort of thing a lot. We'll get it figured out. But if you see him again, try to get him to invite you to wherever it is he's staying. If you get his address, you can pass it along to me."

"Got it!"

Lorraine hung up the phone, feeling a little better, but still wondering what the hell Gus was up to.

You'll Always Be at Home in Our
DOG HOUSE
Opening
WEDNESDAY
Reno's New Popular-Priced Center of Entertainment
Dancing, Floor Show — Continuous Performance
130 North Center Street

Lorraine took Kit's advice and asked Gus if he wanted to meet up with her, but it didn't go as planned. He suggested her room at the Riverside, but she told him there was no way in hell she was going to do that. When she suggested his, he said, "Let's meet at this club I heard about. Then we can go to my place after."

Now she was stuck. He hadn't given her his address, so she'd have to spend an entire evening with him just to find out where he lived. And she didn't know how she was going to get away once he had her there, wherever it turned out to be. She only hoped the club he was talking about was a good one.

It turned out to be... interesting, at least.

The Dog House on North Center Street featured a cabaret and dance floor, advertising itself as the "Divorcee's Haven." That was a good sign: Maybe Gus had finally gotten the message and accepted that they were splitsville. Then again, Gus was still Gus. The place didn't have a cover charge, and its "big floor show" advertised "beautiful girls" for him to leer at. That didn't necessarily mean he was on the prowl for someone new; he'd spent most of their marriage leering at girls, beautiful and otherwise.

She arrived at the club fashionably late, hoping he wouldn't show, even though that would mean not getting his address. The man seriously made her skin crawl like a snake in a swamp... which described him pretty accurately.

Not to be outdone, he arrived even later than she did, sauntering in like he owned the place, dressed in a white jacket offset by a black-and-gray striped tie. She'd been dancing with a tall gentleman dressed like a cowboy—not uncommon for folks around here—who called himself Dexter Bradley and had been kind enough to buy her a Manhattan. Gus strode right up to them and cut in, but instead of standing up to the cad, Dexter just gave her a dirty look and called her an "uppity broad" when she stopped dancing. Then he strode off to the bar in search of greener pastures.

No skin off Lorraine's nose. She hadn't come here for new blood. She'd had her fill of men, period; she just hadn't been about to turn down a drink in exchange for a whirl on the parquet.

"Whaddya think of the place?" Gus asked her, as though he owned it or something.

"Meh. I suppose it's okay for a backwater town like this, but it's a dive compared to Ciro's."

"You would say that," Gus sneered. "All you care about is hobnobbing with those phony-baloney bigshots. I'm surprised you ain't gotten into Errol Flynn's pants. Everyone else has."

Lorraine rolled her eyes. "You know I'm more of a Tyrone Power kinda girl... or I would be if I was a cheating snake-in-the-grass like you."

"We could ask Vinnie Barradino about that if you want."

She winced.

"Let's not."

"Can I help you?" A large man in a ten-gallon hat stepped in front of Gus and stood staring at her.

"Hey, watch it, cowboy!" Gus said, but Lorraine knew he wouldn't do anything about it. He talked a big game, but his fists were as useless as a couple of dinner rolls—of which his belly betrayed he'd had a few too many over the years.

The cowboy ignored him, and Lorraine took a mental note. She needed to learn to do that herself, but somehow, he always managed to get under her skin.

"I'm fine," Lorraine said, exasperated, then softened her tone. "Thank you, though, for checking..."

"Hoss Carrington, ma'am. I'm just here to make sure nothing gets out of hand."

Oh. He was the bouncer. Maybe he'd escort Gus out.

But Hoss was still ignoring Gus and fixing his gaze on her. "Sorry to have bothered you," he said. "But the cops have come been slammin' us for drunk and disorderlies, and as much as we want to keep the juice a-flowin', we don't need them coming down on us. I'm sure you understand."

She looked around for Gus, hoping to blame him, but he had taken the opportunity to disappear into the crowd.

Lorraine flashed her best Hollywood smile. "I'm perfectly fine, really. Do I sound drunk to you?"

"Well, no," Hoss admitted. "It's just that..."

"It's just that what? Let me guess: You recognized me and wanted my autograph. That's it, isn't it? Well, sure, hon, if you hand me a pen and a napkin, I'd be glad to oblige. All I ask is that you keep mum about me being here, and that you overlook whatever infraction you think you saw me commit." She pursed her lips in a mock kiss. "I promise to be a good little girl." It was her signature line from *Don Juan's Delilah*, the one that had made Vincent Barradino and half of America fall in love with her.

The bouncer's eyes widened. "You're not... no way."

Lorraine winked at him as she reached into her purse and grabbed a twenty, slipping it discretely into his hand and closing it. "Our secret, big boy." That was another of her famous lines. It never failed to do the trick.

Hoss nodded, handing her a napkin and a pen. "I don't want you to give yourself away," he whispered. "So just sign it for me in the ladies' room; maybe include a nice little note along with it, eh?" He tried to wink back at her, but he'd never gotten the hang of it, so it wound up being more of a half-scowl.

"Sure, sugar. And thanks again. Ta-ta!"

Lorraine walked into the ladies' room, wondering where Gus had gotten to. Not that she cared. He could stay away forever as far as she was concerned. She'd find another way to get his address for Kit.

"Boo!"

She just about jumped out of her skin as she looked up to see a very strange looking woman peeking in at her over the stall door. But it wasn't a woman. It was Gus, *dressed* like a woman. He looked atrocious: worse than Cary Grant crossdressing in *Bringing Up Baby*. That was saying something, but at least Cary was attractive as a man, which was more than she could say for Gus.

"Get out of here now!" she hissed under her breath. "You can't be in here!"

"Seen it all before, babydoll."

Her eyes bugged out as she opened her mouth and glared at him. "Well, you're never seeing it again!" she seethed. "We're getting a divorce!"

"No, we're not," he teased in a sing-song voice. "But if you really want an address, you can tell your lawyer I live at 1313 Mockingbird Lane."

"How did you know I wanted...?" Lorraine started. "Where is that, anyway?"

"Hell if I know. I just made it up. They don't care what

address they get, as long as they have one. And you win, dollface. I'll be in court whenever they set the date. This is getting old. We'll see if they grant you a divorce when the time comes. I'm willing to bet you they won't."

Lorraine pulled up her skirt and opened the stall door forcefully outward, hoping to cold-cock Gus, but he managed to step effortlessly out of the way in the nick of time.

"They won't have any choice," she nearly shouted, then spat in his face. "And if for some ridiculous reason they don't, I'll make being married to me a living hell until they do!"

Gus guffawed. "It already is," he said. "But I ain't lettin' you go."

Kit was skeptical about the address Lorraine gave her, but she put it down on the paperwork anyway.

They couldn't find Gus at that address to serve him. They couldn't find the address itself. So Kit petitioned the court with a request to serve him by printing an announcement in the *Gazette*. The request was granted, and the court date was set for April 1.

Lorraine had breathed a sigh of relief at that. Gus never read the newspaper, which meant he wouldn't show up, and she'd get the divorce without even having to see his Neanderthal face.

Except it didn't work out that way.

Gus *did* show up in court, inexplicably dressed once again like a woman—or someone trying to dress like some grotesque excuse for a woman. He'd crafted a wig out of a floor mop and tied the strands up in "curlers" made out of cardboard toilet-paper rolls. He wore a hard plastic green "dress" shaped like a waterpot, with the spout sticking out in front of him at his waist.

Lorraine did a double-take and almost ran out of the courtroom. The publicity would be horrible! Word had gotten out that "Delilah" was to appear in court that morning, and a small group of reporters and photographers had already gathered outside. Lorraine was sure Gus had leaked the date and time of their court proceeding to the press. It was just like him to dress like a buffoon to hog the attention.

Mercifully, however, the press had been too busy focusing their attention on her. *She* was the famous one, after all...

Everyone rose as the judge called the court to order.

"What's the next case on the docket?"

Kit rose and announced, "Mrs. Mildred Magnusson is seeking a divorce from Gustav Magnusson under Nevada law," she said.

"Is the defendant present?"

Gus just sat there grinning. He didn't say a word.

"Is the defendant present?" the judge repeated.

Again, no answer.

"Very well," he said finally. "Let me see the paperwork."

He took out his reading glasses and started looking the documents over, pausing occasionally to let out a "hmm," or an "uh-huh," before folding them again in front of him.

"Well," he said finally, "everything seems to be in order, except..." He paused and looked directly at Lorraine. You wouldn't happen to be the actress known professionally as Lorraine Carr?" he asked.

Lorraine blanched. She hadn't wanted her name in any court transcript.

"Uh... yes, your honor."

"I see," he said. "Then I'm afraid I can't grant you this divorce. You see, I follow the newspapers, and I distinctly remember a front-page report about Lorraine Carr's husband being found dead under suspicious circumstances six months ago."

"Wha...?" Lorraine stammered.

Then it all started to come back to her.

She shot a fierce glance over her shoulder at Gus, who was

nodding underneath his mop-top, toilet-roll hairdo, smiling like a lion who'd eaten a whole pet shop full of canaries.

She stood up and pushed her way past Kit.

"Order," the judge said, pounding his gavel once.

She ignored him and flew over to where Gus was sitting. Actually, hovering now. "I killed you!" she shouted. "You're supposed to be dead!"

"So you finally remember," Gus said, slow-clapping in front of her. "I have to hand it to you babydoll, you're such a good actress you actually convinced yourself it never happened—that we've been living together all this time in marital bliss. Or should I say, a marital *mess*. But it was all in your mind, really. I've been perfectly happy these past six months without you, even if it is a little *hot* down here."

The bailiff stepped up behind Lorraine and grabbed hold of her arms as the judge, who was now standing, called out from the bench: "Mildred Magnusson, I'm locking you up for contempt of this court. You will remain in custody until such time as it is determined whether a murder charge may be brought against you. This court is dismissed."

Everyone started filing out, the reporters writing furiously on their notepads.

Gus was waiting for her at the door, though no one else could see him. He was, after all, an apparition.

"I told you, you couldn't divorce me," he whispered. Then, with a laugh, he added, "See you in hell!"

"Six Weeks to Eternity" by Stephen H. Provost appears here for the first time.

Sandie La Nae

Haunted Painting

In 2006, our paranormal investigative team went into the historic St. Charles Hotel in Carson City. Built in 1862, it holds the esteemed honor of being the only Nevada hotel that has never closed its doors. Linda, the caretaker, was happy we were investigating, as much paranormal activity was going on.

While exploring a second-floor hallway, we came upon a painting that I knew right off was haunted. At the time, the picture was in an ugly frame and hung on a wall near an outside entrance. About 24 by 18 inches, painted in dark, drab hues, it depicted forested mountains in the background, and a very dark river in the foreground. Even the sky was a dull blue. The picture was very depressing and drab.

There was no signature on the painting, nor on the back of the canvas or frame. No one knew where it came from. It had just "always been there." Linda stated that many renters did not like this portrait and felt uncomfortable near it. I could see a black, ribbon-like creature wavering in and out of the trees, and it was easy to feel the extreme negative energy embedded in the canvas.

A week after the investigation, Linda contacted me, saying the painted had disappeared. This hotel had a few longtime residents, and she had asked each if they had moved it to their rooms. Nope. She spent several days (and, ultimately, years) searching for the picture, but it was nowhere to be found.

Four years later, Linda called with a surprise for me. I hurried to the hotel. Inside a small conference room, to which only she had access, was the missing painting. It was leaning against an old dresser stored within—but minus its frame.

Linda stated, "Just this morning, as I walked down the hallway, through the viewing window I noticed something different in the conference room. Unlocking the door and turning on the lights, I was astonished to see the painting!"

We decided to leave it in that dark room.

Sometime later, a tenant named John who was renovating that room to create a small museum hung the painting on one wall. While positioning it on the nail, he said, the portrait felt very cold. The silver bracelet he was wearing at the time became icy, forcing John to quickly remove it. Reddened skin marked where the bracelet had been situated on his wrist. He called that afternoon, relaying what happened and asked for help.

On October 18, 2011, I brought my cameras and filmed the twenty-minute process of binding the painting's spirit within, hindering negative energy from harming anyone. The room turned very warm while I was performing the ritual, and I heard many knocks and loud raps on the walls. Photos taken during the session captured anomalies like black orbs on the walls. Later, when viewing the video, I heard numerous "hmmphs" and "tsks" on the audio.

A few weeks passed. John called again, asking for help after curiosity-seekers—who he let touch the picture—became dizzy and sick. He'd also heard strange sounds like scratching and moaning coming from the conference room.

Once again, returning to the hotel, I again bound the entity in the canvas.

A week later, John called again, shouting, "Come and get your damn painting!"

When we arrived at the hotel, Linda pleaded with us to "Please get that thing out of there!"

Loud noises were resounding in the little room. Residents and renters were frightened.

Packing it carefully up in two plastic bags and a large flat box, I put the painting in the trunk of my car, telling it to LEAVE ME ALONE—I did NOT want to get me into an accident. But upon leaving the hotel, that's what nearly happened: A big delivery truck turned right in front of me onto the street where I was driving. How the driver failed to see me was baffling, as no cars, trees or buildings were in his line of view. I stopped quickly, cussed out the painting, and drove home.

Very slowly.

In my back yard, I have two sheds, side by side, and I set the picture in one of them. When I let others view it from time to time, they asked why I didn't keep it in the house or at least in the garage.

When I relayed the story of the painting, they understood.

My daughter had many of her things in the same shed, and when she was moving out on her own, friends and family helped retrieve her items from inside. I discovered that afternoon that the painting was missing. A bit panicked, I asked her if it had been moved, accidentally, with her belongings. She looked, but could find no painting among the boxes and crates. I was a bit frantic then: The picture had hurt people when they touched it and made them sick when they came near it. I hoped that, wherever the painting had gone, it would return.

A few days later, some boxes in the other shed needed to be moved out. One stack of them was sitting away from the wall about 4 inches. That was strange, as the other stacks on either side were tight up against the wall.

When I moved that pile of boxes away, the large flat box with the painting inside showed itself. How it had gotten into the other shed and behind a stack of boxes was puzzling, as both sheds are closed with padlocks—and I have the only keys. No helpers moving my daughter's things had been in this other shed, since none of her items were stored there.

To this day, I look in the shed once a month to make sure the painting is safe and secure... and that it hasn't moved on its own, as it has been proven to do.

If I'd been chosen to safeguard that painting, then I would be sure to keep that energy within protected.

"Haunted Painting" by Sandie La Nae appears here for the first time.

I.C. Coggin

The Serpent of Wonder

The story of a sea serpent comes from so many sources and from people of undoubted veracity that it cannot be doubted that there is living in the Atlantic Ocean a serpent of monstrous size. But it remains for California, with its remains of gigantic monsters scattered all over its surface where the animal life attained its greatest perfection, to have a serpent now living within its borders much larger than any described by so many witnesses.

It was my fortune to be one of the earliest settlers on the west short of Lake Tahoe—from June, 1861, to 1869. I located a meadow and was engaged in cutting wild hay for the market on the Placerville road.

In the fall of 1865, in the month of November, I took my gun and, accompanied by a very intelligent setter dog, started out for a hunt for grouse along the shore and in the creek bottoms emptying into the lake.

My attention was called to a very curious state of things happening around me. First, a flock of quail and other birds were flying out of the canyon, uttering cries of alarm; next came some rabbits and coyotes, and soon three deer came running at full speed. Last of all, an old bear with one cub came along. All passed close to me, and all running at their best.

All this did not occupy much time, and I began to wonder what was up. My dog kept looking up the canyon and was evidently alarmed, and I began to feel shaky myself.

All at once, the dog set up a howl and started for home, eight miles away, running as fast as a dog could run, and going under the cabin, stayed there two days and nights. No amount of coaxing could get him to come out sooner, and never after would the dog go in the direction of the lake.

I began to feel that some unknown danger was near, and looking about me, saw a spruce tree with very thick limbs, standing near a very large pine.

I climbed up about 60 feet from the ground and began to look up the canyon.

I had not long to wait. I heard a sound as if the dead limbs of trees—willows and alders—that grew in the canyon were being broken and crushed. Soon, the monster appeared, slowly making his way in the direction where I was hidden in the treetop, and passed on to the lake within 50 feet of where I was. And as His Snakeship got by, and I partly recovered from my fright, I began to look him over and estimate his immense size.

After his head had passed my tree about 70 feet, he halted and reared his head in the air 50 feet or more, and I was thankful that the large pine hid me from his sight. I dared to breathe again as he lowered his head to the ground and moved on.

His monstrous head was about 14 feet wide, and the large eyes seemed to be about 8 inches in diameter, and shining jet black, and seemed to project more than half this size from the head. The neck was about 10 feet, and the body in the largest portion must have been 20 feet in diameter.

I had a chance to measure his length, for when he halted, his tail reached a fallen tree, and I afterward measured the distance from the tree where I was hidden to the fallen tree, and it measured 510 feet, and as 70 or 80 feet had passed me, it made his length about 600 feet.

The skin was black on the back, turning to a reddish yellow on the side and belly, and must have been very hard and tough, as small trees 2 and 3 inches in diameter were crushed and broken without any effect on his tough hide. Even boulders 500 or 600 pounds in weight, lying on the surface of the ground, were pushed out of the way. His Snakeship slowly made his way to the lake, glided in and swam toward the foot.

This serpent has been seen by several of the old settlers at the lake since that time, but it was generally agreed that it would be useless to tell the world the story, knowing that it would not be believed. I will give a few names of the early settlers who have seen His Snakeship at different times since I first saw him:

William Pomin, now living in San Francisco; John McKinney, Ben McCoy, and Bill McMasters, all at that time living on Sugar Pine Point; Homer Burton, now living in Sacramento; Captain Howland of the old steamer Governor Blaisdell; Tony and Burk, fishermen living near Friday's Station; Rube Sexton, now at the lake, and several others [who] could not be named.

I know many will doubt this story, but sooner or later His Snakeship will be seen by so many that all doubt will be removed.

I was induced to write this description by reading an article in *The Call* of last Sunday, stating that there was a living mastodon in Alaska and that it had been seen by the natives. Believing that I have seen a more wonderful sight and, as in time my story is sure to be verified, I venture to give this to the public.

This account originally appeared in the San Francisco Call *newspaper on November 21, 1897.*

Whistling in the Wind

(Originally published as "A Ghost Story")

A few miles out of town stands a two-story frame cottage, its blinds hanging from broken hinges and the paint scaling off the clapboards.

The house was one of the prettiest in the vicinity until it got the reputation of being haunted. About two years ago, the family which then occupied it, consisting of a man named Hawkes, his wife and two children, moved out, and soon after, Edward Williams moved in. He was a matter-of-fact individual, who attended to his own business.

One day, he called on Henry B. Rule and said there was something wrong with the house. On stormy nights, he said, or when there was a high wind, a voice would go wailing through the upper part of the house, making sleep impossible and causing his wife fear. He had ascended the stairs and the sound would cease, only to be repeated when he would return to the first floor.

Mr. Rule made a thorough investigation, but could find nothing, and a few days after, Hawkes gave up his lease.

Nothing was said to the next tenant, but it was not a month before he inquired if anything had ever happened in the house. When asked to give his reasons for the inquiry, he said that his wife complained she heard strange noises in the garret. He was assured that nothing of any account had occurred there, but on pretense of repairing the roof, the agent called and gave the garret another thorough overhauling. Within a week, the house was vacant.

One day, about two weeks ago, a man called at the office of Henry Rule in [the] Nevada Bank Building, and said he had heard that the place was haunted. Scenting a prospective tenant, Mr. Rule pooh-poohed the statement, but was informed that the inquirer was studying the problem of spiritualism and would rent the premises on any terms Rule might fix for one week. He was installed for one week, rent-free, his countenance wearing a peculiar smile.

At the expiration of a week, he appeared at Rule's office.

"Have you found the ghost?" was the peculiar inquiry.

"I have," was the reply, "and here it is."

So saying, the man pulled from his pocket a child's whistle, one of the round tin specimens, with a hole in the center.

"This," he said, "had been fastened in a knothole, and was directly opposite the broken pane of glass. When the wind blew hard, it caused a draft, and the wild shrieks your tenants heard were the natural result."

—Reno Evening Gazette
March 27, 1897

Hallow'een Jinks

If any town in Nevada times are better—if there is a community in the state where people have a better time—if in the "battle-born" region, to the square inch, there are more pretty girls or money than in Yerington, we would like to know where.

While the older folks on Hallow'een were stuffing themselves with pinenuts from the Walker river, large red apples from Webster's orchard, sweet and hard cider from Nordyke and tons of pumpkin pie and turkey, the young folks were splitting the air and homes into pieces with tick-tack and songs.

Twenty young girls led by Miss Shirley Holland, dressed in black komonas and high white caps haunted three automobiles until within a mile of Wabuska. After capturing the new engine of the Nevada Copper Belt railroad and lighting it with small incandescents hidden by hideous pumpkin and squash heads, they cast a spell over the engineer and until all the oil was used up rode up and down the two miles of track.

The farmers in the vicinity—different from days of old—are now convinced that their night of terror was occasioned by neither a spooky promotion nor a phantom ship, but a real engine of a real live railroad.

— *Yerington Times*,
November 6, 1909

Sarah Winnemucca

The People-Eaters

Among the traditions of our people is one of a small tribe of barbarians who used to live along the Humboldt River. It was many hundred years ago. They used to waylay my people and kill and eat them. They would dig large holes in our trails at night, and if any of our people travelled at night, which they did, for they were afraid of these barbarous people, they would oftentimes fall into these holes.

That tribe would even eat their own dead, yes, they would even come and dig up our dead after they were buried, and would carry them off and eat them. Now and then they would come and make war on my people. They would fight, and as fast as they killed one another on either side, the women would carry off those who were killed.

My people say they were very brave. When they were fighting, they would jump up in the air after the arrows that went over their heads, and shoot the same arrows back again. My people took some of them into their families, but they could not make them like themselves. So at last they made war on them.

Their number was about 2,600. The war lasted some three years.

My people killed them in great numbers, and what few were left went into the thick bush. My people set the bush on fire. Then they went to work and made tule or bulrush boats, and went into Humboldt Lake. They could not live there very long without fire: They were nearly starving.

My people were watching them all round the lake, and would kill them as fast as they would come on land. At last, one night, they all landed on the east side of the lake and went into a cave near the mountains. It was a most horrible place, for my people watched at the mouth of the cave, and would kill them as they came out to get water. My people would ask them if they would be like us, and not eat people like coyotes or beasts. They talked the same language, but they would not give up.

At last, my people were tired, and they went to work and gathered wood, and began to fill up the mouth of the cave. Then the poor fools began to pull the wood inside till the cave was full. At last my people set it on fire; at the same time they cried out to them, "Will you give up and be like men, and not eat people like beasts? Say quick [and] we will put out the fire."

No answer came from them.

My people said they thought the cave must be very deep or far into the mountain. They had never seen the cave nor known it was there until then. They called out to them as loud as they could, "Will you give up ? Say so, or you will all die."

But no answer came.

Then they all left the place. In ten days, some went back to see if the fire had gone out. They went back to my third or fifth great-grandfather and told him they must all be dead, there was such a horrible smell.

This tribe was called people eaters, and after my people had killed them all, the people round us called us *Say-do-carah*. It means "conqueror"; it also means "enemy." (I do not know how we came by the name of Piutes. It is not an Indian word. I think it is misinterpreted. Sometimes we are called Pine-nut eaters, for we are the only tribe that lives in the country where Pine-nuts grow.)

My people say that the tribe we exterminated had reddish hair. I have some of their hair, which has been handed down from father to son. I have a dress which has been in our family a great many years, trimmed with this reddish hair... It is called the mourning dress, and no one has such a dress but my family.

28 years later...

The report of James H. Hart: In 1911, I heard David Pugh of Lovelock tell of an old Indian cave some 20 miles south of Lovelock. He said that it was full of bat guano in which he had dug down four feet. When a boy he had learnt from the Indians where the cave was. There had then been fires in it for there was much smoke on the walls.

Realizing that, if the cave was as large as described, the guano might be of value, I arranged with Pugh to file a mineral location upon it and ship out the guano. This we did, working from the fall of 1911 to the spring of 1912.

We drove a small tunnel into the mouth of the cave, or rather to one side of it, the natural opening being too small to work through. We took out about five carloads of guano, which were shipped to the Hawaiian Fertilizer Company of San Francisco.

We soon began to discover Indian relics, and notified Dr. J.C. Merriam of the University of California, who took the matter up with the University of Nevada and the Nevada Historical Society. We also wrote to the Smithsonian Institution, but they advised that they had no funds for collecting, receiving only donations.

After some of the best specimens had been destroyed, we received word from the State Historical Society that, in conjunction with the University of California, they would send an investigator. This was Mr. Loud. We gave him all possible facilities for collecting. Many objects had been destroyed by the weather, and others had been taken away. I recall many boas or ropes of fine feathers. As these lay strewn about in the open end of the cave in the way of the workmen, they were irreparably damaged. Some of these boas were found perfectly preserved.

All the Indian objects began to appear about 4 feet below the surface of the guano. In the south end of the cave, "about 20 feet deep," we unearthed some skeletons.

In the north-central part of the cave, about 4 feet deep, was a striking looking body of a man "6 feet, 6 inches tall." His body was mummified and his hair distinctly red. There was a grass rope about his neck with a knot under the left ear. The rope was about 8 feet long. The feet were bound together from the ankle to above the knees with stout rope. The mummification was complete except for a part of the abdomen.

The other mummies all had red hair—I think there were either four or five. Those that appeared to be women were small, something like a Japanese woman in height.

This was not altogether due to the shrinking of the bodies in mummifying, because the man was "a giant." The women had on moccasins which reached clear to the knees; the buckskin was beaded with shells. Two of them had on a kind of buckskin coat (gown) that came down to the knees.

These bodies were from the deep south end of the cave.

There were no bats in the cave when we went there to work.

Besides David Pugh, there worked in the cave Samuel Pugh, Hanson, Cummings, and perhaps one or two others. We screened the guano through a three-quarter-inch mesh, discarding everything that did not go through the screen. Probably all objects that passed through the mesh were shipped away with the guano.

After we got through working the cave, one George Stautts worked on what was left in the cave for a while.

He probably shipped out about a carload of guano.

"The People-Eaters" by Sarah Winnemucca is an excerpt from her book Life Among the Piutes, *first published in 1883.*

DRAGON CROWN BOOKS

Janice Oberding

Séance

Retired detective John Copley carefully placed the notebook and photos back into the large manila envelope.

"By God, Frank, you're right! If I didn't know that he was in the old cemetery, I'd swear Garrett was out there and up to his old tricks."

Detective Frank Waring shifted uncomfortably on the sofa that he knew to be older than he was. He had hoped that Copley, having cracked the case that finally brought serial killer Walter Garrett to justice, would offer him some insight.

But Copley didn't.

"A copycat?" Waring finally asked.

"Either that or Garrett's been resurrected." Copley chuckled at the thought. "You know Frank, his was one of the few executions I actually took pleasure in witnessing, the way he slaughtered those people—."

He slapped his hand down on the table so fiercely that the coffee cups rattled. "You've got to stop this killer, Frank. Vegas isn't ready for another Walter Garrett."

Promising to do just that, Waring shook Copley's hand, then stepped out the front door and into the scorching desert heat. Even as he did so, the killer claimed yet another victim.

Myra felt like a smiling zombie serving comped cocktails to people who perched in the rows of slot machines at the hotel/casino where she worked. A locals' place, so the tokes weren't as good as those she could have made working on the Strip. But locals were so much easier to deal with than tourists who expected the moon and the stars—this was Las Vegas after all.

It was a living, and not her life. Myra's life centered on ghost hunting; by night, she and her team, the Vegas Three, sought out ghosts. Myra and Geneva were neighbors who'd become friends. As the friendship deepened they'd discovered that they were both fascinated with the paranormal. On a lark, they'd joined Lou in his effort to form a ghost hunting team. In the beginning, they'd made contact with Liberace, Elvis, and a few tourists who'd added to the city's dark statistics with their suicides. Lately it was different.

And Myra was convinced it had all begun after Geneva conducted a pre-investigation séance at the old murder house out on Boulder Highway.

A self-professed medium who exaggerated her abilities, Geneva called the spirits forth, spoke to them a moment and then quickly closed the séance. Assuring the team that at least one evil spirit had broken forth, Geneva suggested the place be spiritually cleansed before they came for the next investigation.

Lou, who was surlier than usual, called it all nonsense, saying, "Maybe we should forget this séance stuff altogether."

"Evil was there with us, I know it." Geneva countered.

"It's the old murder house, what do you expect?" Lou smirked

It was mid-September, and the heat still hung across the valley like heavy showroom drapery. The Vegas Three were meeting in the basement of Lou's house. A cave-like room, the only good thing about the basement was that it was private and it was cold enough to offer respite from the hellish autumn heat. They'd recently concluded another investigation of the murder house, and were discussing their findings.

Myra studied her laptop. "We've been told that two people were killed in the house, but..."

"There were more than two." Geneva broke in.

If looks could kill, Geneva would have been a ghost by the look Lou shot her.

Geneva smiled. "Didn't we get at least four voices on your E.V.P., Myra?"

Myra nodded silently.

"And at least five people spoke to me," Geneva added.

"Who was killed there again?" Myra asked.

"Two women, their bodies were discovered in the kitchen," Lou replied.

"All this murder stuff is so negative." Myra shuddered.

"How do you suppose people become ghosts?" Geneva laughed.

"You don't have to be murdered to become a ghost!" Myra countered.

Lou held his recorder to his ear.

"Listen!" he said. "Someone just said, 'You've set the devil free.'"

Myra scooted close to Lou.

"I heard it," she said. "Is it a man or a woman?"

Geneva smirked. "It's a woman. And that is the same thing she told me."

"Maybe we ought to go back for another investigation," Lou said.

"Not me!" Myra said. "I didn't feel good the whole time I was in the place. It's evil. No, thank you."

"You're right," Geneva said. "The place is permeated by evil. I think we should investigate—but from a distance."

"Did we get the victims' or the killer's name?" Myra asked.

"As you remember, we were told the story of the murders in that house has been going around Vegas since before the mob ran the town," Lou said. "We don't even know if any of it is true."

"It is true," Geneva said. "Murder did take place in that house, and the victims spoke to me."

"We never settled on a timeline. When exactly did these killings take place?" Myra asked.

Lou laughed. "You sound like an old TV detective show. If we're just looking for murder victims, we could have gone out to Lake Mead, had a nice barbecue and then done an investigation."

"I take my work more seriously than that!" Geneva responded. "This calls for an in-depth investigation—from a distance."

"Agreed. I've got to be on the floor at 8, so I'll leave you to it," Myra said.

John Copley couldn't sleep. The air-conditioning unit was on its last legs, and the question of Walter Garrett raced through his mind. How on God's green earth had a copycat killer got every horrendous detail right? Some had never been made public. Did Frank Waring have what it took to stop this new monster before he terrorized the city all over again? Copley, who was halfway through his 50s, was limited by various infirmities. With his arthritis, burned-out knee joints, and easily upset stomach, just how much help could he offer the young detective?

None, he told himself. Little did he know the odds were changing in his favor as he drifted off to a fitful sleep.

Those who work in the casinos worship the Goddess Lady Luck. And it's all about tokes; a good first toke signals a profitable day ahead, while a smaller one means a grueling unrewarding day. On this morning, Myra prayed for luck, wiped her tray, and strode through her section, eager to make her first toke of the day.

An old man was waving to her from the far side of her section.

Definitely not a large toke, she told herself, making her way to him. *On a slow day, beggars can't be choosers.*

"What can I get you?" she asked.

"Would you please bring me a cup of coffee—Myra?" he asked, studying her name badge.

"Certainly," she smiled.

At least twenty years separated them, but this was the start of a friendship neither of them could ever have imagined: the retired homicide detective and the ghost-hunting cocktail waitress.

Soon John Copley was a regular at the row of slots, and soon they were discussing their cases: Myra and her ghosts, Copley and his killers. It might have seemed bizarre to the rest of the world, but this was Las Vegas with a reality all its own.

One afternoon, Myra stopped in the row of slots and invited Copley to that evening's meeting of the Vegas Three.

"You could tell us about what to look for when chasing the ghosts of killers," she explained.

He had nothing better to do. And to Myra's surprise, he agreed. That night, he sat in Lou's basement with the others, his arthritis screaming, as thunder roared across the sky and rain deluged the valley. Geneva was especially impressed with Copley and the stories he told. Lou, however, was bored with him.

"How many investigations have you done at the old Boulder Highway murder house?" Copley asked.

"Three," Geneva responded. "Why?"

Copley smiled at Myra across the room. "Just so you know, that was a whorehouse back in the fifties. It was run by the grandfather of the worst serial killer this town's ever known."

"Was anyone murdered there?" Myra asked.

"Not that I'm aware of," Copley responded.

Geneva was not about to let this slight to her mediumship abilities go unchallenged. "I felt murder all around me in that place."

"Maybe you were feeling the ghost of Walter Garrett." Copley shrugged.

"Who?" she asked.

"The serial killer—his grandfather Nathan Garrett ran the whorehouse. Rumor was, he'd beat any woman who dared to cross him. And by 'cross him,' I mean any woman who wanted to get out of the business. Garrett spent a lot of time there with the old man after his parents stepped into the wrong mob hit."

"The place seems to have a really violent past," Lou said, flipping his recorder on.

"Here, listen to this," he said to Copley, handing him the recorder.

"You've set the devil free—do you hear it?" he asked.

Copley nodded. "I don't know much about ghosts. For that matter, I'm not sure I put much stock in such things. Best advice—stay away from that old house."

"The owner is a friend and she says we can go in there

anytime we want," Lou said.

Copley stared at Lou. Clearly both men had formed a strong dislike for the other.

"Just because you can, doesn't mean you should," he said.

That night after they'd all left, Lou opened himself a beer and eased back into his recliner. His headaches were getting worse. And sitting at the computer screen all night wasn't helping. He needed to take some time off. But first, he decided, the Vegas Three needed a new direction; he would call for a team hiatus. This was his team, and he would make the decisions whether they liked it or not. And if they left the team, he didn't care. Although he might not be the best looking man in a town where looks were secondary only to money, he could be persuasive and charming—just like Ted Bundy, but look what happened to him.

Lou still couldn't imagine why Myra had brought that old man to the meeting. He might have known some history, but he hadn't added anything to the discussion. Lou downed the beer and made a plan; he would postpone further meetings until he had it all sorted out. While they might have seen this as a vacation of sorts, Myra and Geneva were eager to investigate the unknown and formed a stronger friendship.

At lunch, Frank Waring slid into the booth with John Copley, Myra and Geneva.

Orders placed and introductions made, Copley said, "I know this will sound crazy, Frank. It did to me at first—but the more I think about it..."

Waring laughed. "Is this some sorta Halloween joke, John?"

"I wish it were," Copley said. Turning to Geneva he added, "Will you explain it to him?"

"How much do you know about the paranormal?" she asked.

"I'm not into gobblygook," Waring responded, diving into his double bacon burger.

"Close minded much?" Myra said.

Geneva sighed. "Okay, I'm just gonna say it. John tells us that someone is killing people in the same way a dead serial killer did over thirty years ago."

Waring wiped his napkin across his mouth. "It's been all over the news," he said.

"Yes, but not every single detail. Look, I'm not into coincidence. Don't you think it's odd that the killings started two nights after we investigated the old murder house?"

"Not a bit," Waring said, reaching for a French fry.

"How would someone know every grisly detail?" Myra asked.

"So you're trying to tell me that the ghostly Walter Garrett is killing people?"

"In a manner of speaking—yes we are."

Waring stared at Copley. "What the hell is this?"

"All I ask is that you listen to them, Frank."

"We believe this is a form of possession," Geneva continued, unperturbed. "We disturbed something in that house during our first investigation. Consequently, the demonic spirit of Walter Garrett may be possessing someone and leading this person to kill."

Waring stood, opened his wallet and placed a twenty-dollar bill on the table.

"I don't have time for this nonsense, John. And I'm surprised that you'd buy into such crap."

Geneva stared at Waring intently. "There have been three killings—the victim always has long hair, which the killer shaves off. The large toe and the little toe are cut off of each foot. That's not public information and yet—"

"You told them, John?"

"We gathered that knowledge through our E.V.P., and John confirmed." Geneva said haughtily.

Waring turned to Copley. "You've lost your damn mind," he said, before hurrying for the door.

Things change fast in Las Vegas. What is new and exciting one day is imploded to make room for the newer and more exciting the next. So it was with Frank Waring's assessment of John Copley and the Vegas Three. After a fifth victim turned up in a parked car at one of the city's newest hotel/casinos, he was willing to listen to anything that might help stop the killer, even what Copley's weird friends had to say.

A week later, Myra, Geneva, and Waring met at Copley's stucco house not so very far from where Tony Spilotro once lived. That fact was lost on everyone but Copley, who took a certain amount of pride in living in close proximity to the mob's notorious hitman.

While Waring and the two women attempted to make themselves comfortable on his lumpy old sofa, Copley poured ice tea into old casino glasses.

"We've not narrowed it down to any suspects," he said to Waring, handing him a glass.

"I thought you said it was the ghost of Walter Garrett," Waring said.

"A spirit," Myra corrected. "A demonic spirit that is possessing a living person and guiding him to kill."

"They're gonna laugh me off the force," Waring said.

"You certainly won't be making an arrest, but you can stop these killings," Copley said.

"Is that good enough for you?" Geneva asked.

Waring looked at her. She would have been a very attractive woman if only her hair wasn't purple.

"I want to stop these killings," he responded.

"We may have a way to do just that," Geneva said.

"Let's suppose you are right, God forbid. How do you suggest I go about it?" he asked.

"Something like an exorcism," Geneva said. "We will command the evil to leave the body."

Waring laughed. "And just like that the killings will stop?"

"Yes!" Myra said.

Against his better judgement, Waring agreed to let them help him.

Several candles illuminated Lou's basement. Being the control freak that he was, Lou could not have imagined that Myra and Geneva would abandon the team. And they hadn't. Not wanting to lose them until he found replacements, he allowed himself to relent and let Geneva do the séance. He'd even agreed to allow John Copley and Frank Waring to attend.

They sat at the small table awaiting Geneva's instructions. She looked from one to the other. If only she hadn't boasted about her abilities to conduct a séance. This was only her fourth séance in her entire life. The paranormal was full of frauds and fakes. She was just another one. What if these people were to discover the lies she told about her successes with the spirit world? She trembled at the thought and began.

"Since there are five of us, we won't hold hands like a traditional séance. I am the medium, but if you are sensing anything, please by all means speak up. This is the only way we will get at the truth."

"The truth?" Lou asked.

She shrugged her shoulders. "Well Lou, do we want to know the truth about the old murder house or not?"

"Frankly, I don't care one way or the other. I'd rather find a new place to investigate and be done with that place," he replied.

For all her bravado, Geneva was feeling out of sorts. Something wasn't right. And she couldn't shake the feeling that this séance would not end well. She could claim a migraine and call it off. But she and Myra had promised Frank Waring and John Copley some answers concerning the murders.

"Okay," she said, "we'll begin. We are believers in the power of love and of light and of the spirit world; we've come together tonight to invite the spirits to join us. Although our questions for you may border on the negative, we ask that you come of your own volition and with positivity and good intent." She looked around the table. All eyes were on her—especially those of Frank Waring, who, oddly enough, found himself smitten with this crazy lady.

"Firstly, we would like to know if there is any truth to murders being committed at the old place on Boulder Highway," she said.

"Yeah," Lou added with a chuckle. "We're sick of the place, and if you tell us the truth, we can investigate another one."

"Someone is saying that there were no murders there. But that an evil person was affiliated with it," Geneva said.

"Could that be Walter Garrett?" Myra asked.

"Yes!" said a snarling voice.

"And who might you be?" Geneva asked.

"Walter Garrett!"

"You are Walter Garrett, and you admit you are evil?" Geneva asked calmly.

Ignoring her question, Garrett laughed. "Isn't that why they sent me to the gas chamber, Detective Copley?"

Copley stared into the darkness. "You were a murderous animal that needed to be put down," he responded.

"Maybe I should possess you, Detective Copley," Garrett said. "Let's see what I can get you to do."

Geneva had never been involved in such a séance. Everyone

at the table was hearing this disembodied voice. Hoping to control it, she said, "There will be none of that! I want you to leave whoever it is you are possessing."

"I'm not possessing anyone!"

"And you've led this person to kill five women," Geneva said, ignoring Garrett's denial.

The basement walls shook, and an intense howling filled the room.

"No! That's a lie. You can't blame me for those deaths."

"Then who?" Copley demanded.

"You're the detective, you figure it out," Garrett said.

"I'll be a son of a bitch!" Waring shouted, pointing to Lou across the table.

Ghostly forms were taking shape around Lou, who was crying out in agony.

Geneva had lost control of the séance to this dark and negative entity calling itself Walter Garrett. These people she called friends were in danger because of her lies. And she couldn't help them. All she wanted was to be back at her studio apartment with her cat and her knitting.

"Please tell us who you are and how we can help you," she sighed, feigning calmness.

The ghostly forms spoke in unison. "He stole our dreams, and our hopes. He slaughtered us."

"I-I didn't want to. I was possessed—he made me do it," Lou cried.

"Shut your lyin' pie hole," Walter Garrett shouted, causing the table to rattle.

The ghostly women spoke. "Lou is a liar! He was not directed to kill us. He was a demon holding his evilness in check—until he acted of his own volition."

Unaware that Geneva silently trembled in fear, Waring had suddenly become a believer in the paranormal.

"If Walter Garrett didn't direct him, how did Lou know to cut off the toes and shave the heads?" he asked.

"Our E.V.P. Then, too, there is the Dark Web," Myra replied. "Anything you want to know, I'm told."

"Nooo, it wasn't me. He made me do it," Lou cried as the ghostly women's talons tore at his flesh. "You're hurting me for something I didn't do."

Suddenly Myra's chair began to rise from the floor.

"Put me down!" she screamed.

Conley was on his feet. "Damnit Garrett! Stop picking on women."

Geneva couldn't let her friend be hurt. "Stop it! I command you to bring that chair slowly back down."

To her surprise, the chair slowly came to rest on the floor. Maybe she wasn't such a fraud after all. Conley pulled Myra from the chair and hugged her tightly. To her amazement it felt good to be held by this old man.

Black smoke rose from the table as a foul stench encircled them. "Time's up. All the living better leave this place at once!" Walter Garrett said.

Held firmly by the ghostly women, Lou squirmed in his chair.

"You will feel the pain you inflicted upon us."

Geneva cried, "I demand that all negative spirits leave our circle at once."

Walter Garrett's booming laughter shook the basement. "You called us forth, and now you have no control over us."

Lou had become a blackened skeleton, writhing in pain as blood spilled from its gaping mouth and hollow eye sockets.

"Leave unless you want to suffer the same fate!" the ghostly women cried out to them.

Promising herself to never conduct another séance, Geneva

mumbled, "You've ripped the flesh from his body! He—he's no longer human."

"He never was. He's a demon, escaped from hell. Go!"

"I must close the séance, first," Geneva whispered.

"No time for that. Go!" the ghostly women commanded.

Waring grabbed Geneva's hand, pulling her from the table. The four of them scrambled out of the basement, which was already engulfed in flames.

They stood across the street by Waring's car, watching the house crumble in the fire. In the distance, they heard the squeal of fire trucks and sirens.

"Do you believe this will be the end of these killings?" Waring asked Copley.

"Yes, Frank, I do," Copley replied. "In the meantime, we'd better get out of here before someone asks us more questions than we care to answer."

"Séance" by Janice Oberding appears here for the first time.

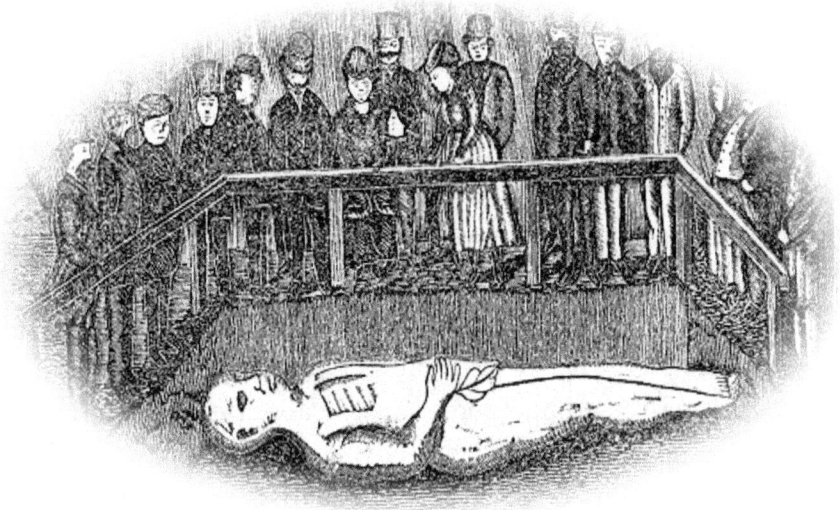

Mark Twain

A Ghost's Tale

I took a large room, far up Broadway, in a huge old building whose upper stories had been wholly unoccupied for years until I came. The place had long been given up to dust and cobwebs, to solitude and silence. I seemed groping among the tombs and invading the privacy of the dead, that first night I climbed up to my quarters. For the first time in my life a superstitious dread came over me; and as I turned a dark angle of the stairway and an invisible cobweb swung its slazy woof in my face and clung there, I shuddered as one who had encountered a phantom.

I was glad enough when I reached my room and locked out the mold and the darkness. A cheery fire was burning in the grate, and I sat down before it with a comforting sense of relief. For two hours I sat there, thinking of bygone times; recalling old scenes, and summoning half-forgotten faces out of the mists of the past;

listening, in fancy, to voices that long ago grew silent for all time, and to once familiar songs that nobody sings now. And as my reverie softened down to a sadder and sadder pathos, the shrieking of the winds outside softened to a wail, the angry beating of the rain against the panes diminished to a tranquil patter, and one by one the noises in the street subsided, until the hurrying footsteps of the last belated straggler died away in the distance and left no sound behind.

The fire had burned low. A sense of loneliness crept over me. I arose and undressed, moving on tiptoe about the room, doing stealthily what I had to do, as if I were environed by sleeping enemies whose slumbers it would be fatal to break. I covered up in bed, and lay listening to the rain and wind and the faint creaking of distant shutters, till they lulled me to sleep.

I slept profoundly, but how long I do not know. All at once I found myself awake, and filled with a shuddering expectancy. All was still. All but my own heart—I could hear it beat. Presently the bedclothes began to slip away slowly toward the foot of the bed, as if someone were pulling them! I could not stir; I could not speak. Still the blankets slipped deliberately away, till my breast was uncovered. Then, with a great effort, I seized them and drew them over my head. I waited, listened, waited. Once more that steady pull began, and once more I lay torpid a century of dragging seconds till my breast was naked again. At last I roused my energies and snatched the covers back to their place and held them with a strong grip. I waited. By and by I felt a faint tug, and took a fresh grip. The tug strengthened to a steady strain—it grew stronger and stronger. My hold parted, and for the third time the blankets slid away. I groaned. An answering groan came from the foot of the bed! Beaded drops of sweat stood upon my forehead. I was more dead than alive. Presently I heard a heavy footstep in my room—the step of an elephant, it seemed to me— it was not like anything human. But it was moving from me—

there was relief in that. I heard it approach the door—pass out without moving bolt or lock—and wander away among the dismal corridors, straining the floors and joists till they creaked again as it passed—and then silence reigned once more.

When my excitement had calmed, I said to myself, "This is a dream—simply a hideous dream." And so I lay thinking it over until I convinced myself that it was a dream, and then a comforting laugh relaxed my lips and I was happy again. I got up and struck a light; and when I found that the locks and bolts were just as I had left them, another soothing laugh welled in my heart and rippled from my lips. I took my pipe and lit it, and was just sitting down before the fire, when down went the pipe out of my nerveless fingers, the blood forsook my cheeks, and my placid breathing was cut short with a gasp! In the ashes on the hearth, side by side with my own bare footprint, was another, so vast that in comparison mine was but an infant's! Then I *had* had a visitor, and the elephant tread was explained.

I put out the light and returned to bed, palsied with fear. I lay a long time, peering into the darkness, and listening. Then I heard a grating noise overhead, like the dragging of a heavy body across the floor; then the throwing down of the body, and the shaking of my windows in response to the concussion. In distant parts of the building I heard the muffled slamming of doors. I heard, at intervals, stealthy footsteps creeping in and out among the corridors, and up and down the stairs. Sometimes these noises approached my door, hesitated, and went away again. I heard the clanking of chains faintly, in remote passages, and listened while the clanking grew nearer—while it wearily climbed the stairways, marking each move by the loose surplus of chain that fell with an accented rattle upon each succeeding step as the goblin that bore it advanced. I heard muttered sentences; half-uttered screams that seemed smothered violently; and the swish of invisible garments, the rush of invisible wings. Then I became conscious that my chamber was invaded—that I was not alone. I heard sighs and breathings about my bed, and mysterious whisperings. Three little spheres of soft phosphorescent light appeared on the ceiling directly over my head, clung and glowed there a moment, and then dropped —two of them upon my face and one upon the pillow. They, spattered, liquidly, and felt warm. Intuition told me they had— turned to gouts of blood as they fell—I needed no light to satisfy myself of that. Then I saw pallid faces, dimly luminous, and white uplifted hands, floating bodiless in the air—floating a moment and then disappearing. The whispering ceased, and the voices and the sounds, and a solemn stillness followed. I waited and listened. I felt that I must have light or die. I was weak with fear. I slowly raised myself toward a sitting posture, and my face came in contact with a clammy hand! All strength went from me apparently, and I fell back like a stricken invalid. Then I heard the rustle of a garment; it seemed to pass to the door and go out.

When everything was still once more, I crept out of bed, sick and feeble, and lit the gas with a hand that trembled as if it were aged with a hundred years. The light brought some little cheer to my spirits. I sat down and fell into a dreamy contemplation of that great footprint in the ashes. By and by its outlines began to waver and grow dim. I glanced up and the broad gas-flame was slowly wilting away. In the same moment I heard that elephantine tread again. I noted its approach, nearer and nearer, along the musty halls, and dimmer and dimmer the light waned. The tread reached my very door and paused—the light had dwindled to a sickly blue, and all things about me lay in a spectral twilight. The door did not open, and yet I felt a faint gust of air fan my cheek, and presently was conscious of a huge, cloudy presence before me. I watched it with fascinated eyes. A pale glow stole over the Thing; gradually its cloudy folds took shape—an arm appeared, then legs, then a body, and last a great sad face looked out of the vapor. Stripped of its filmy housings, naked, muscular and comely, the majestic Cardiff Giant loomed above me!

All my misery vanished—for a child might know that no harm could come with that benignant countenance. My cheerful spirits returned at once, and in sympathy with them the gas flamed up brightly again. Never a lonely outcast was so glad to welcome company as I was to greet the friendly giant. I said:

"Why, is it nobody but you? Do you know, I have been scared to death for the last two or three hours? I am most honestly glad to see you. I wish I had a chair—Here, here, don't try to sit down in that thing—"

But it was too late. He was in it before I could stop him and down he went—I never saw a chair shivered so in my life.

"Stop, stop, you'll ruin ev—"

Too late again. There was another crash, and another chair was resolved into its original elements.

"Confound it, haven't you got any judgment at all? Do you want to ruin all the furniture on the place? Here, here, you petrified fool—"

But it was no use. Before I could arrest him, he had sat down on the bed, and it was a melancholy ruin.

"Now what sort of a way is that to do? First you come lumbering about the place bringing a legion of vagabond goblins along with you to worry me to death, and then when I overlook an indelicacy of costume which would not be tolerated anywhere by cultivated people except in a respectable theater, and not even there if the nudity were of your sex, you repay me by wrecking all the furniture you can find to sit down on. And why will you? You damage yourself as much as you do me. You have broken off the end of your spinal column, and littered up the floor with chips of your hams till the place looks like a marble yard. You ought to be ashamed of yourself—you are big enough to know better."

"Well, I will not break any more furniture. But what am I to do? I have not had a chance to sit down for a century." And the tears came into his eyes.

"Poor devil," I said, "I should not have been so harsh with you. And you are an orphan, too, no doubt. But sit down on the floor here—nothing else can stand your weight—and besides, we cannot be sociable with you away up there above me; I want you down where I can perch on this high counting-house stool and gossip with you face to face."

So he sat down on the floor and lit a pipe which I gave him, threw one of my red blankets over his shoulders, inverted my sitz-bath on his head, helmet fashion, and made himself picturesque and comfortable. Then he crossed his ankles, while I renewed the fire, and exposed the flat, honeycombed bottoms of his prodigious feet to the grateful warmth.

"What is the matter with the bottom of your feet and the back of your legs, that they are gouged up so?"

"Infernal chilblains—I caught them clear up to the back of my head, roosting out there under Newell's farm. But I love the place; I love it as one loves his old home. There is no peace for me like the peace I feel when I am there."

We talked along for half an hour, and then I noticed that he looked tired, and spoke of it.

"Tired?" he said. "Well, I should think so. And now I will tell you all about it, since you have treated me so well. I am the spirit of the Petrified Man that lies across the street there in the museum. I am the ghost of the Cardiff Giant. I can have no rest, no peace, till they have given that poor body burial again. Now what was the most natural thing for me to do, to make men satisfy this wish? Terrify them into it! haunt the place where the body lay! So I haunted the museum night after night. I even got other spirits to help me. But it did no good, for nobody ever came to the museum at midnight. Then it occurred to me to come over the way and haunt this place a little. I felt that if I ever got a hearing I must succeed, for I had the most efficient company that perdition could furnish. Night after night we have shivered around through these mildewed halls, dragging chains, groaning, whispering, tramping up and down stairs, till, to tell you the truth, I am almost worn out. But when I saw a light in your room tonight I roused my energies again and went at it with a deal of the old freshness. But I am tired out—entirely fagged out. Give me, I beseech you, give me some hope!" I lit off my perch in a burst of excitement, and exclaimed:

"This transcends everything! everything that ever did occur! Why you poor blundering old fossil, you have had all your trouble for nothing—you have been haunting a plaster cast of yourself—the real Cardiff Giant is in Albany!—[A fact. The original fraud was ingeniously and fraudfully duplicated, and exhibited in New York as the "only genuine" Cardiff Giant (to the unspeakable disgust of the owners of the real colossus) at the very same time that the latter was drawing crowds at a museum is Albany,]—Confound it, don't you know your own remains?"

I never saw such an eloquent look of shame, of pitiable humiliation, overspread a countenance before.

The Petrified Man rose slowly to his feet, and said:

"Honestly, is that true?"

"As true as I am sitting here."

He took the pipe from his mouth and laid it on the mantel, then stood irresolute a moment (unconsciously, from old habit, thrusting his hands where his pantaloons pockets should have been, and meditatively dropping his chin on his breast); and finally said:

"Well, I never felt so absurd before. The Petrified Man has sold everybody else, and now the mean fraud has ended by selling its own ghost! My son, if there is any charity left in your heart for a poor friendless phantom like me, don't let this get out. Think how you would feel if you had made such an ass of yourself."

I heard his stately tramp die away, step by step down the stairs and out into the deserted street, and felt sorry that he was gone, poor fellow—and sorrier still that he had carried off my red blanket and my bathtub.

"A Ghost's Tale," also known as "A Ghost Story," by Mark Twain, was first published in 1870. Although it takes place in New York, it is the spiritual successor to "The Petrified Man," written in Nevada and contained in Volume 1 of this work.

Jeadene Solberg

Delta Saloon

During a Virginia City Paranormal Conference in the spring of 2018, I had the opportunity to lead a tour of about six or seven investigators at the Delta Saloon in Virginia City, specifically in the chapel. Out of nowhere, I suddenly felt an overwhelming dizziness and decided to step outside, not wanting to disrupt the investigation for my fellow participants.

Once outside, I experienced a strange sensation, as though something had entered my energy space and taken over my feelings. An intense anger washed over me, and I felt an unbearable heat inside, making me want to tear off my clothes and my necklace of crystals. Images of my grown children began flooding my mind, their faces appearing as if they were submerged underwater. I struggled to breathe and felt an impulsive need to be alone. I don't remember pushing anyone away, but I later learned that I even pushed my partner aside.

This unsettling episode lasted 15 to 20 minutes, and my friends quickly noticed my erratic behavior. They reached out to some more experienced investigators for assistance. I genuinely felt like I had lost control of myself. One of the investigators rushed to my side and tried to give me a comforting hug, but I instinctively wanted to push him away. From what I've been told, I was taken outside and sat on the ground in an effort to help ground me and reconnect with myself.

It took two or three seasoned investigators to help me regain my sense of normalcy. Afterward, I felt incredibly drained and confused for several days. The only unusual thing I can recall from that time was having a conversation with a participant about religion, where I shared that my beliefs didn't align with traditional views. Usually, I'm a very grounded and protected person, so it's bewildering to me that this happened. To this day, I can't help but wonder, "Why did this happen to me at that particular moment?"

"Delta Saloon" by Jeadene Solberg appears here for the first time.

Restless Spirit

(Originally published as "Haunted")

The house on Buel Street formerly occupied by Kate Miller, the woman stabbed two weeks ago, is haunted. The disembodied spirit of the late occupant has returned and, according to the stories told, is acting in a lively manner for one who is supposed to be dead.

A woman living next door became so frightened at the racket the ghost was kicking up that she has vacated the house owned by her and gone further down the street.

A well-known spiritualist in town intends [on] interviewing the spirit, and hold[ing] a seance in the haunted house. If such a meeting takes place, there will be a lively time for some parties.

"Rest, perturbed spirit, rest."

—*Eureka Daily Sentinel*
September 14, 1876

Sharon Marie Provost

Forty Miles From Hell

T he Forty-Mile Desert became the most dreaded and difficult segment of the California Trail back in the 1800s. The barren, dry stretch of alkali flats and wasteland just outside of Fallon that stretched between the Humboldt River and Truckee or Carson Rivers—depending on which route emigrants chose—took the lives of approximately 1,000 people and 10,000 animals in just two decades.

The creation of the car and a paved road traversing it made passing through it safe. These days, it is no longer perilous. Or at least it shouldn't be.

Jacob drove to the Trinity rest stop at the Highway 95 junction on I-80, between Fernley and Lovelock, then pulled into one of the parking spots. His trailer, hitched to the back, carried his all-terrain vehicle. Jacob unloaded the ATV and strapped his camera bag to the rack on the back, along with a cooler containing a liter bottle of water and some sandwiches.

He intended to spend the day exploring the Forty-Mile Desert, hoping to finding some old livestock bones, gravesites, or valuables left behind by emigrants fleeing for their lives from the incessant heat and thirst.

Being a professional photographer, he knew he could also get some amazing photos of the desert with the mountainous backdrop just before sunset. The midday sun in August created beautiful, undulating heat waves that rose off the striking white patches of alkali, mesmerizing and disorienting at the same time.

He rode the ATV out of the parking lot and across Highway 95 to head out into the desert toward Lovelock. Not being tech-savvy, he was searching the area bordered by 95 on one side and Interstate 80 on another, which gave him reference points he could use to find his way back.

Even knowing the history of the desert, Jacob found himself quickly overheating. It was barely 10 a.m., and the sun beat down on him relentlessly, already soaring past 90 degrees. He had finished his water and lunch by noon; if he drove into Lovelock to cool off for a few hours, he could still return in time for sunset.

The cerulean blue sky had developed large, white puffy clouds. Jacob had just come across a vast swath of the bleached alkali flats peppered with small desert scrub bushes and sagebrush. Even with his sunglasses on, he strained to see through the heat waves and blinding sunlight reflecting off the flats.

He put a filter on his camera and caught some stunning images of the stark landscape, with those billowy clouds in the background. He couldn't help but wish for the drastically cooler temperature and menacing gray skies that came with a summer thunderstorm. But being the tallest object in a vast, flat plain didn't mix well with lightning, and he didn't relish the prospect of the alkali flats being turned into a thick muck—from whence he might never be extracted.

Excited by the fantastic photos he had obtained, Jacob continued to explore, determined to find artifacts or remains from the past. As he crested a small rise, he found the skeleton of a cow, still covered in some dried, leathered hide left behind by scavengers. While not a specimen from the 1800s as he'd hoped, it was still an awesome find. He could see it now... a photographic exhibition of "Life and Death in the Desert West."

He explored further, photographing a large Great Basin rattlesnake as it slithered off the rock where it had been sunning itself and vanished into a hole in the ground. A few seconds later, a kangaroo mouse skittered out from under a rock and darted into its burrow. The relentless beating of the sun seemed to be chasing away even the hardiest souls who called this infernal environment home.

Jacob couldn't bear the heat any longer. He returned the camera to its bag and turned the ATV back toward his truck. His parched mouth stuck together when he tried to swallow behind chapped, sunburnt lips, and his skin burned as the salty beads of perspiration streaked their way across his face.

At first, he felt a little cooler as the air rushed across his sweat-soaked clothes. But that perspiration soon dried, leaving only the harsh, hot air. Jacob revved the engine and pushed the ATV to its limit as he blazed across the desert. He couldn't see either highway yet, but he felt sure he must be getting close to one or both of them. Possibly just beyond that sandy rise.

At his current velocity, he miscalculated the height of the hill he was approaching and didn't consider what it might be like on the other side. The ATV raced up the sandy hill at blistering speed and launched into the air awkwardly when the ground disappeared beneath it.

"Arrggh! Fuck!"

Jacob hadn't been an avid bike rider or skateboarder as a youth. Balance had never been his strongpoint. In the slow-motion seconds that followed, he tried to reassure himself that a four-wheeler would land safely on the uneven ground six feet below him.

It'll be okay. I'll just lean forward, and it'll land just fine.

He stretched his body forward over the handlebars, trying to distribute his weight evenly over the ATV. But when it crashed to the ground, he was catapulted forward over the front of it.

He landed hard.

"Oooommphh!"

His lungs expelled the air in them in a rush a mere second

before the ATV flipped and landed on top of him. The engine sputtered, and silence once more fell over the desert landscape.

Jacob's fingers twitched as a blue-belly lizard ran across them. At first, his only sense was the sound of his own ragged breathing. As he regained full consciousness, the blinding pain in his pelvis became his whole world. His eyes burned when he opened them as salty sweat swept sand into them. He reached up and rubbed his hand across his face.

"Damn it!"

How long have I been out? My skin feels like it's on fire.

He tried to sit up and cried out in pain.

"Ahhhh!"

He was pinned under the ATV, which lay across his pelvis and legs. He reached up and unzipped the camera bag, removing his cell phone. He died 911 and pressed SEND. "No signal" flashed across the screen.

"Fuck, fuck, fuck!"

He held the phone out every direction, including straight above him, but he couldn't find even one bar of signal.

"Piece of shit! What good are you in an emergency?"

He threw the phone out into the desert as he contemplated his next move. He used all his strength to push up on the heavy ATV, trying to wiggle his body out from underneath it.

A bolt of white-hot pain shot through his entire groin area, making him lightheaded. He was relieved to find he could wriggle his feet and toes: at least he didn't have a spinal injury.

He unzipped the front pouch on his camera bag all the way, and the contents spilled out onto his chest and across the desert floor.

"Eureka!"

He picked up the small bottle of Tylenol and popped off the top, downing the pills left inside.

I'll worry about my liver when I get out of this mess.

As he shuffled through the rest of the contents lying on the sand, his hand shot up in triumph.

"Will wonders never cease?"

Grasped in his hand was a small bag of Area 52 Magic Pluto Mushroom gummies.

"Don't mind if I do," he said as he shoved three into his mouth.

Screw the two-a-day dosing.

Twenty minutes later, Jacob knew he was orbiting Mars—either that, or dehydration had made a few gummies far more potent than he'd imagined possible. Either way, he knew he needed to get out from under the ATV.

Jacob pushed up with one hand and used the other to wiggle his legs out from underneath it. The pain shot through his body in waves, but his fuzzy mind felt it more distantly than before—so distantly that, before he knew it, he was leaning on the ATV and using his arms to push himself up.

He climbed to his feet, but only stood for a fraction of a second.

Then he felt a crunch of bone in his pelvis and crumpled to the ground again.

He cackled wildly.

Guess I got my first broken bone. Shitty timing though.

Jacob managed to sit up and look around. His head was spinning, though, and he couldn't focus on which direction he needed to go. In his tumble, he'd become completely disoriented: He didn't know which direction he'd come from or where he'd been going, and he couldn't find any landmarks.

A far-distant shimmering vision beckoned him; it was the only thing he could focus on.

I'll just go cool off in that lake, and then I'll feel better. There's bound to be other people over there.

Jacob crawled toward it. He didn't even feel the sand scraping his burned skin raw. He used his hands to drag himself forward until they were bleeding, but he never got any closer to the refreshing pool of water.

It remained *just* beyond his grasp, even as it became more tantalizing to his warped senses. He began to hallucinate half-naked girls dancing around the edge of a pool. He heard the blond with double-Ds yelp in surprise as she splashed into the water at the end of the slide.

But as his body temperature rose to dangerous levels, he finally began to sense the full weight of the situation. He felt like he'd been lit on fire... or left in that firepit he saw in the sand to roast like the pig on the spit over there by the Tahitian dancers.

I could have sworn it was a lake, but then there were those bimbos at the pool. Did I go to Hawaii?

Get your head on straight, Jake! There's no dancers. The only pig roasting is you.

Jacob managed to crawl behind a sandhill that was partially shaded by the direction of the sun. He leaned against it as he peered into the distance, hoping to see cars zipping along one of the highways.

But there was nothing!

He turned toward the sandy hill and dug into it, creating a hollow just big enough to hide his body from the ruthless ball of fire in the sky.

When he awoke hours later, Jacob wasn't sure if he had been asleep or lapsed into unconsciousness. He was just grateful that he'd awoken at all. The lobster-red, blistered skin on his body felt devoid of all moisture. Now he knew how that poor cow back there must have felt.

His mind was flooded with a plethora of what-ifs. Why had he stopped to take that stupid picture? Why hadn't he brought more water? If he'd just turned around sooner...

The sun was dipping toward the horizon, creating the most beautiful red, pink, and orange bands across the sky. He couldn't see his ATV in the distance—not that he knew which way to look.

What a sunset! That's why I came out here: to take photos just like this. And now I don't even know where my camera is. Why didn't I stay at the crash site and see if I could restart that worthless ATV? A fucking POOL? Instead, I went after a pool of water surrounded by busty girls in the Forty-Mile Desert. I'm a fucking FOOL!

Jacob lay in his den and waited for the last vestiges of sunlight to disappear from the sky and the wonders of starlight to appear. Once again, he regretted having lost his camera. Stargazing opportunities like this in the vast open spaces around Nevada were phenomenal.

But this one was an opportunity lost.

When Jacob crawled out, his whole body hurt, not just his fractured pelvis. Stiffness had set in, and muscle cramps caused by his severe electrolyte imbalance had begun in earnest. He rolled into a ball as his abdominal muscles tensed into fiery knots.

His squinted his eyes shut as the tear ducts cramped: They were trying to squeeze out tears, but there was no moisture left. A few moments later, as he lay there panting, he blinked at the unexpected sight.

Moving beams of light speeding past in the distance.

There were cars!

The highway was not as far away as he'd feared.

I can do it!

Jacob ignored the burning of his skin as he pulled himself

NEVADA NIGHTMARES, VOL. 2

across the sharp rocks, gravel, and sand. The cramps returned, but he pushed the pain away as he first slithered hand-over-fist, then clambered to his knees to crawl, slow and awkward as a baby, toward the highway—the bones in his pelvis grinding and popping with each movement. It was just a couple thousand feet away now...

Jacob's strength gave out and he collapsed to the ground.

The pain had become unbearable.

His fingernails had broken below the quick—some had been pulled off completely. His weathered hands had split open. Somewhere along the way, he'd lost both shoes and had worn holes through his socks.

Catching his breath, he resumed his torturous slither. He rocked back and forth, using his shoulders and hips to propel himself forward inch-by-inch. He remembered laughing at the performers he'd seen on that documentary about the old sideshows and their performers.

How did that freak show performer, The Human Torso, do this every day? I'm such a jerk for laughing at him!

He could see headlights approaching as he neared the edge of the road. He just had to climb a small hill, only about two feet, and he'd be visible to the oncoming driver.

As he reached the edge of the cracked blacktop, he felt a surge of energy—his body's last drop of adrenaline—pushing himself up onto his knees and flinging himself on the road.

He saw the woman point at him and then...

Bette never saw the man crawl out onto the road. She still had two more hours to drive that night, and she'd cranked the radio up, trying to stay awake. She bopped along to the music and poked her finger out into the air in front of her as she sang the last line to "You Got It" by Roy Orbison.

The VW Bus thumped and shuddered as she drove along the road.

I really need to get those shocks checked out. 'Course the roads out here do leave something to be desired.

She stopped at the Trinity Rest Stop to run to the restroom before continuing up the highway. She couldn't wait to pitch camp out in the Black Rock Desert. She wanted some time to commune with nature out there before she returned in a few weeks for Burning Man.

Jacob sputtered and choked on the blood that gurgled in his throat as he fought to breathe with a punctured lung. He saw the woman's taillights disappearing in the distance as he closed his eyes. A few more shallow breaths, and then he lay still, pondering his own life and death, just forty miles from hell.

❖   ❖   ❖

"Forty Miles from Hell" by Sharon Marie Provost appears here for the first time.

Stephen H. Provost

Gil and Fred's

Exotic Misadventure

Fred couldn't take his eyes off the scantily clad redhead as he boarded the bus. She was standing at the top of the steps beside the driver's seat, which gave him the best possible view of her long, shapely legs.

"This is gonna be good!" he whispered to Gil, who was walking just ahead of him as they passed her.

"Damn right it is." Fred turned halfway around and nearly stumbled over the seat protruding into the narrow walkway. He hadn't thought the woman could hear him.

"You're in for one helluva ride, cutie," she said.

Despite his determination to maintain his skater dude-meets-Rico Suave vibe, Fred was at a loss for words.

"Bruh, I think she digs you," Gil said, elbowing him in the side.

"Shut up," Fred whispered. "You wanna ruin it?"

"Hell yeah. I want some of that action."

The two of them found a seat near the front of the converted school bus.

"Dude, they expect us to sit in these lame-ass seats?" Gil griped. "This shit was built for little kids."

"Just chill and enjoy the view, bro. It wasn't like there was room to get seats to ourself."

He had a point: The bus was full up, and all the passengers were men.

"Wonder how many of these loverboys have bitches back home?" Fred snarked.

"Two fer sure, right bruh?"

Fred broke up. "What happens in Vegas stays in Vegas, right?"

"Right ON!" Gil tried to high-five his friend, but the seat was so cramped his arms were pinned in.

"Well, we WON'T be staying in Vegas, baby!" the woman at the front of the bus quipped, staring straight at the two of them.

Fred had been so fixated on her legs before, he hadn't noticed her breasts seemed ready to fall out of her bikini top, which was tied in the middle like a Dallas Cowboys cheerleader.

"Why not?" Gil piped up.

"Because, sugar, they don't have brothels in Vegas. You did sign up for the Brothel Bonanza Tour, didn't you?" She leaned forward and wagged a finger at him, parting her lips ever so slightly and leaving them there.

"Hell yeah!" Fred shouted. "Bring on the babes!"

The woman laughed. "Well you're the eager beaver, aren't you?"

Fred chuckled. "She said 'beaver,'" he whispered to Gil.

"Yeah," Gil snickered back.

The woman shook her head but smiled broadly, then stood up straight and clasped her hands together in front of her.

"On behalf of the Good Time Girls, I'd like to welcome you to the Brothel Bonanza Tour. My name's Kortney, and I'll be your guide for the next three days as we visit some of the most famous—and infamous brothels in Nevada. We'll be spending the night at some of them. But I have to warn you, Nevada's a rough place, so I hope you're packin' your pistols and brought along some form of protection."

This elicited a round of whoops and hell yeahs from the assembled pool of testosterone.

"Mustang Ranch, here we come!" Fred shouted.

"We won't be going quite that far north," Kortney said. "But I'm sure you'll be more than satisfied with the stops we have on our itinerary."

"Fine with me," groused a middle-aged guy in an Indiana Jones hat sitting directly behind Fred and Gil. "The guy who sold me the ticket said it was a 'luxury expedition.' I'll need a knee replacement after a few hours on this old tin can."

"Serves him right," Fred whispered. "Only a jerkoff would be dumb enough to buy a ticket at one of those lame tour kiosks."

"Shut up, dickweed," Gil hissed. "Lay off the guy. He's probably got oldtimer syndrome. Besides, you saw the friggin' bus and signed us up anyway. Who's the real jerkoff, jerkoff?"

"Hey, it's a hot pink bus with 'Good Time Girls' on the side. It had a number and said, 'for a good time call.' So I called."

Gil managed to dislodge his hand from halfway under his ass cheek (it was better than being under Fred's, which was the only other option in their cramped space), and swatted his friend upside the back of the head. "You woulda called a number in a stall at Hooters if you had the chance."

"F-off."

As though in answer to Indiana Jones' objection, Kortney raised a hand and announced, "Your complimentary cocktails will be served as soon as we get underway. Get ready to have a *good time*, guys!"

There was a whooshing sound as the accordion door expanded to seal off the entrance. The bus started rumbling and lurched forward, rolling down the ramp and out of the parking garage onto Las Vegas Boulevard.

"I don't know how we're supposed to drink on this garbage scow," Indiana Jones mumbled.

"What's a garbage scowl?" Gil asked.

"Hell if I know," Fred said. "But I guess that makes him the garbage."

They busted up laughing together, then said "Whoa!" together as they leaned hard to the side for the left turn onto Charleston Boulevard. From there, it was west to U.S. 95, which they took north out of Sin City.

"Huh. I thought we were goin' to Pahrump," Fred said.

"Her rump?"

"No, jackass, PAH-rump. Where they got that old radio show *Coast to Coast AM* with the Art Bell dude." He deepened his voice to imitate the host's: "Live from the Kingdom of Nye in the High Desert of the Great American Southwest."

"Oh, yeah. The remote viewing dude. Those shows were a trip. All that shit about alien abductions and chupacabras."

"You know why he set up shop out there, right, in Pahrump,

I mean?"

Gil nodded. "The chupacabras."

"Yeah, and jackelopes," Fred snarked. "Not quite, numbnuts. The chupacabras are all down in Mexico and Arizona. He was in Pahrump for the brothels. Had to be. Why else would anyone go to Pahrump?"

Gil nodded. "Point."

But if they were headed up 95, they obviously weren't going to Pahrump. Fred looked out the window and noticed they were heading out of Vegas now.

"There's a Big Boy in Indian Springs," Gil remarked.

"Hell with that," Fred replied. "There's way too many big boys on this bus already."

"It's a diner."

"Stupid name for a diner. I'm thinkin' Big Girl would be a lot better. You know, like that Queen song. Ohhhhhhhh," he warbled, then segued into the first verse of "Fat Bottomed Girls," and Gil joined right in.

Pretty soon, the whole bus was rocking out.

It was right about the time they got to the part about the naughty nanny that the Good Time Girls finally broke out the booze. Another woman, who must have been seated at the back of the bus, sashayed down the aisle with a tray in her hands.

How anyone could sashay down the aisle in a converted school bus was lost on everyone seated on either side, but somehow, this woman accomplished it. She was another redhead, every bit as attractive as Kortney, but with eyes like Zooey Deschanel and hips like Jessica Rabbit. She wore a name tag that read Shekinah and a smile that looked permanently plastered on.

Impossibly balanced on the tray she carried were thirty shot bottles—one for each passenger—with labels that read "The Black Death."

"I thought they'd at least give us some Jack or a keg," Fred piped up, seemingly oblivious to the fact that there was no room on the bus for a six-pack, let alone a keg.

Gil was squinting as he shook his head, and was suddenly looking very green. Fred began searching frantically but in vain for a barf bag, then pressed up hard against the side of the bus. Gil's carsick projectile vomiting was legendary.

Shekinah reached across him and handed Fred a bottle of Black Death.

"What's in this?" Fred asked.

"Black licorice Schnapps with more of a kick," Shekinah teased. "I'll leave a bottle for your friend too. Get him to try it. It actually soothes the stomach."

"Party on!" Fred hooted, his eyes superglued to her cleavage.

He handed one bottle to Gil, who shook his head and passed it back. Fred shrugged and downed it himself. A moment later, he was out.

He woke up at the Amargosa junction, where the bus was pulling off the road, rumbling onto a parking lot in an otherwise barren stretch of desert.

Gil, who hadn't fallen asleep, was shaking him excitedly. "Wake up, dude!" he said, pointing.

Fred blinked and rubbed his eyes.

The sun was setting, sending a blood-red glow across the hills to the west that seeped down onto the flatland that surrounded them.

"Rise and shine, sleepyheads," Kortney sang. It seemed that everyone else in the bus had been sleeping, too—with the exception of Gil. They had pulled up at the Area 51 Alien Travel Center, a convenience store that looked a little like an Old West saloon, but painted puke-green: the alleged color of alien life forms, if old comic books and B movies were to be believed. None of the sex-starved male hominids on board were looking at the store, though. Their eyes were glued to the building next door, set back a little from the other, an elongated ranch-style structure painted southwestern pink. Several doors appeared at regular intervals along its length, giving it the appearance of a sleazy motel. But only half that description was correct: Motel, no, but definitely sleazy. A sign out front identified it as the Alien Cathouse Brothel.

"Everybody out," Kortney said as the bus door opened, and everyone inside began falling over one another to get there.

"Potty break," Shekinah added. "Be back at the bus in five."

Everyone stopped in their tracks. "Five *minutes*?" a short, obese man in a white tank top said. "That's barely enough time for a..."

"Wham bam, thank you, ma'am," chortled a tattooed goth twenty-something wearing steel gauges wider than the rest of his ears.

"I'm sorry," Kortney drawled, feigning exaggerated remorse. "We won't have time to explore the amenities here. Just head to the little boys' room, do your business, and return to your seats pronto. Shekinah and I will have a surprise for you when you get back!"

The passengers' faces brightened, and they started clamoring for the exits again, their minds captivated by X-rated speculations about what the Good Time Girls' surprise might be. They tumbled out of the bus into the sunlight, set off on a wobbling sprint across the parking lot, and returned to find Kortney and Shekinah loading a large case of something onto the bus.

"What's in there?" Gil asked.

Shekinah turned to him and smiled. "More Black Death, cutie pie. It's your reward for being such good, patient little boys."

Gil turned up his nose. "Don't you have any other flavors?" he asked.

"Sorry, sweetheart, but I'll see what we can do when we stop for gas."

Everyone piled back into the bus, their disappointment at missing out on the Alien Cathouse tempered by the new supply of booze.

"How can you drink that stuff?" Gil asked Fred as they settled into their seats again.

Fred didn't answer. He just put the bottle to his lips and downed the contents in one swig, then sighed contentedly. "Nectar of the gods!" he declared—and within seconds, he was out like a light again.

Fred awoke with a start to find Gil leaning across him, looking out the window. It was after dark, and the bus had stopped. He rubbed his eyes.

"Get offa me!"

"Chill, dude. Just tryin' to see where we are."

"Fine. Fine. Just don't go gettin' all bromantic on me. So, whaddya see? Where are we? A truck stop or somethin'?"

"Do you *see* any trucks out there?" Gil asked.

"Nah, just some airplane sittin' out in the middle of nowhere."

"Plus some sign, but there ain't no lights on it, so I can't quite read it," Gil added.

Fred squinted. "I think it says 'Angel's... I can't make out the second word. Whatever it is, you're right: It ain't no truck stop."

"And if it is, strange things are afoot at the Flying J."

Shekinah came walking up the aisle with a bag, inviting the passengers to discard their empty bottles of Black Death. Fred tossed his in and looked at Bill. "Didn't you drink yours?" he asked.

"Nah, man. You know I hate licorice, and I didn't think you wanted me pukin' all over ya."

"Thanks for that."

"Don't mention it." He handed the bottle to Fred. "You have it. No sense in it going to waste."

Fred took the proffered bottle and slipped it into his pocket for later.

As he did so, he heard Kortney snap her fingers at the front of the bus. "If I can have your attention, we've arrived at our first destination. For those of you who've been catching some shuteye, we're a couple of miles north of Beatty, at the Angel's Ladies Brothel."

"We missed Beatty?" Gil lamented. "I heard there was a righteous candy store there."

"Relax, dude. I bet we'll find some tootsies to roll in there. We're gonna Skor tonight!" Fred chortled.

Gil looked out the window again. "Dude, it's dead out there. I don't see no lights or nothin'."

"O, ye of little fate..."

"Isn't it faith?"

"Whatever. Don't you know they hide these places back from the road so you can't see 'em. Makes 'em harder for the coppers to find."

"Oh, ah..."

Kortney blew a kiss at Fred to get his attention, then curved her finger and beckoned him to follow her off the bus. Gil was right behind, and then came everyone else, ducking in the aisle under the bus's low ceiling before heading down the steps and out into the warm southern Nevada night air.

Everyone gathered around her on a patch of dirt in front of the plane. "See that aeronautical marvel there?" she cooed. "It's the *star* attraction. Back in the seventies, when this place was called the Star Club, they held a contest to see who could jump out of that plane and land on a mattress. The winner got a roll in the hay with one of Fran's babes. But when the plane crash-landed where you see it today, they turned it into a billboard for the brothel."

Shekinah moved from one person to another, handing out more shot bottles of Black Death.

"Um, don't they have anything else?" Gil whined as Fred downed his drink.

"Who doesn't like black licorice?" Fred scolded.

"I don't."

"You could at least try it."

Gil glared at him. Fred was pushy and used to getting his way. He wouldn't persuade you to do what he wanted. He'd just wear you down until you gave in.

"No, *thank you*," Gil hissed.

Fred grabbed Gil's bottle and downed it, too. "Man, you should feel the buzz!" he said.

Gil tried to ignore him.

Kortney was speaking again. "We have a little surprise for you tonight," she said. "We've fixed up the old plane, and we're gonna re-create that little stunt tonight. We're gonna take three of you lucky cuties up in the air, and if any of you can hit that mattress over there"—she pointed to a white mattress sitting on the ground a few yards away—"you'll spend the entire night with one of Angel's Ladies."

"Whoa!" Fred shouted, pumping a fist in the air.

"No way!" Gil exclaimed at virtually the same time.

Fred turned and looked at him like he was crazy. "Dude, did you hear what she said? An entire night? Do you know how much most suckers pay for an hour?"

"I heard. I also heard her say the plane *crashed*..."

Kortney was talking again. "Before anyone freaks out, let me assure you that everyone in the plane when it crashed survived, and we've taken every precaution to make sure it's in good working order."

"You hear that?" Fred slapped his friend on the shoulder. "Man, you gotta loosen up. We're out here to have fun, bro."

Gil pulled away, then lunged forward, shaking Fred by the shoulders. "Look around you. There ain't no brothel here, just a couple of abandoned buildings. It doesn't look like anyone's been here in years. And that plane looks like it belongs on the scrap heap. It's all tagged up and everything. There ain't even a runway... or a propeller!"

Gil pushed Fred.

Fred pushed him back.

While they kept going back and forth like that, three of the guys in the circle had answered Kortney's call for volunteers and were headed toward the plane.

"Damn!" Fred groused. "You made me miss it!"

"Dumbass," Gil mumbled. "It won't get off the ground. They don't even have a pilot."

But as he watched, he saw Kortney climb into the cockpit, and a moment later, the engine—as if by some kind of miracle—started up. It didn't sound particularly safe or dependable. A single *thunk* was followed by a *double-thunk*, and then, slowly, the engine began to rumble. The plane started to shake.

"Just a bit of turbulence, sir," Fred cackled.

Gil placed a hand on his shoulder. "Dude, how toxic is that Black Death shit?"

Fred ignored him. His eyes were fixed on the plane as it started to move and, somehow, pick up speed as it flattened rabbitbrush plants and tumbleweeds, its wheels sending stones spinning and sputtering into the air. Gil ducked and shielded his eyes, but one struck him in the forehead anyway. "Ouch! Mother...."

"Look! It's flying!" Fred shouted, oblivious to his friend's discomfort.

And so it was.

Somehow, impossibly, the plane was in the air, teetering this way and that as though it might plummet back to Earth at any moment, but staying aloft despite it all.

Everyone else on the ground was looking upward, standing in a perfect circle and craning their necks to see the spectacle above them. It looked like a sabbat of the possessed, awaiting the coming of the antichrist. But without any illumination save a sliver of moon mostly hidden by clouds, the aircraft seemed to have been swallowed up by the gargantuan maw of the night sky.

Then it happened.

Something came hurtling down at them, like a meteorite flung out of the sky by an invisible giant. A scream of terror flooded their ears, then was silenced abruptly, without an echo, as though with the slamming of a door. Simultaneously, the *something* that had been hurled down from the heavens landed with a sickening splat and crunch on the hard earth, just a few feet from the mattress.

"Woohoo!" Fred howled, even though he must have known that the object was one of the men he had boarded the bus with back in Vegas. Others howled their approval as well, like a bunch of drunken tailgaters whose team had just scored a touchdown.

Gil was dumbstruck.

Then it happened... again.

This time, the body missed the mattress badly, impaling itself on a large, pointed rock sticking up out of the ground.

"Let the bodies hit the floor!" Fred shouted, and the others joined in the chorus as the inevitable third man came screaming down... landing squarely in the middle of the mattress. The splat this time was a muffled thud, but the unfortunate "winner" of the competition was no less dead for the meager cushion.

Fred shouted, "We have a winnah!"

Gil sat down on the ground and looked away from the gruesome spectacle.

"What's wrong, bruh?" Fred asked him. "Those losers got what was comin' to 'em. Less competition for us, eh?" He slapped Gil on the back, eliciting a sound that came out like a gasping belch.

A few moments later, the plane descended from the sky and landed smoothly on the rough ground, coming to a stop exactly where it had been before.

Kortney stepped out of the cockpit and, despite her high heels, glided across the stony earth and came to stand at the center of the circle. "I'm afraid our winner didn't survive to collect his prize," she said through pouty lips. "So I'm sorry to say we'll have to leave Angel's Ladies behind us without allowing any of our tourists to inspect their wares. But never fear: We have another stop ahead of us tonight, and our friend who was so despondent about missing the candy shop in Beatty..." She fixed her gaze directly on Gil, smiling and running her tongue over her upper teeth. "...I have good news for you. We'll be heading back through Beatty to our next destination, and we'll be happy to stop there for you to fill up on some of those luscious confections."

Kortney got off the bus first at EddieWorld in Beatty, which was just a few minutes back down the road from Angel's Ladies. "Gas stop," she announced, and flagged down a man in blue coveralls who'd been standing out front. EddieWorld was an oversized convenience store that was part gift shop, part confectionary. If you had a hankerin' for nuts or candy, there was a good chance you could find it there.

"I gotta pee," Fred lamented, and a couple of other passengers muttered something in agreement, but Shekinah stood there in the doorway, blocking the exit. "Just hold it, honey," she said. "The restroom's out of order."

"How do you know?" the goth guy asked.

"Because I do."

Shekinah gave them all the kind of warning glance that the Rock gave bad guys in the movies, and somehow, it was even scarier coming from her. No one else said anything. It was clear she wasn't going to budge, and no one wanted to piss her off.

Outside, Kortney was talking with the guy in blue.

"Hey, sexy," she said. "You got the stuff for me?"

He nodded vigorously like a puppy dog eager to please his master. It wouldn't have been surprising to see him start panting, sitting up on his haunches, and rolling over.

Gil scowled. It sounded like Kortney was doing a drug deal right out there in the open—and not even bothering to lower her voice.

The man nodded and kissed her solicitously on the cheek, then used his debit card to activate the gas pump and disappeared behind the store. He re-emerged a few minutes later carrying a large polka-dotted box wrapped neatly in a red bow. "Don't say nothin' to Eddie," he said. "He don't know shit about this."

"And he doesn't need to," Kortney soothed, "as long as you're a good little boy."

The man smiled and nodded, looking like a bobble-headed clown on the dashboard of a 4-by-4.

Kortney took the box with her and brought it with her back to the bus.

"What's that?" Gil asked.

"You'll find out," she said teasingly, "after our next stop. I promise you won't have long to wait."

That next stop wasn't far away. The bus chugged its way through Beatty but got off U.S. 95 to continue west on Nevada 374. Only a couple of miles farther on, it turned right onto a gravel road that took them past some sculptures that looked like ghosts standing outside a small structure. In the darkness, no one could tell if they were actually ghosts or not... but they weren't moving, which seemed like a good sign.

The bus kept going into what looked like a literal ghost town: The decaying buildings loomed over them like phantoms in their own right, daring them to pass. Kortney seemed unaffected by them, steering the bus onward as the spirits of the dead who had once lived there cast disapproving glances at them from on high. The desert wind whirled in a serpentine dance in one vacant window of the old three-story bank building and out the next, as though taunting the passengers below with forbidden secrets. What had once happened here in this place, and why was it deserted now?

It seemed to cast a spell on everyone in the bus.

"Bro, I think there's ghosts here," Fred said. It wasn't cold, but his teeth were chattering.

"Get a grip, dude," Gil said. "It's just the wind."

"Noooo, man. I think I saw a witch behind that bush over there."

Gil looked where he was pointing and saw a movement in the sagebrush.

"Chupacabra!" Fred exclaimed.

The long-eared rabbit bounded out and across the road, directly in front of the bus. Kortney made no attempt to brake, and the passengers were jarred momentarily by a thump under the right front wheel. Gil saw the rabbit's head fly off to the side and into the darkness, leaving a dark spot on the road behind him that would have been bright red in the sunlight.

"Aw, poor Bugs!" Fred shook his head. "I guess it's wabbit season!" He threw his head back and laughed.

"Duck season!" Gil said.

"Wabbit season!"

"Duck season!"

"Wabbit season!"

"Wabbit season!"

"Duck... aw dammit! You always get me."

The bus hit something and came to a jarring stop. "Oopsie," Kortney said. "Well, boys, we're here."

The impact had brought down a section of chain-link fence around what looked like an old railroad depot.

"Now," Kortney said, standing up and facing the passengers. "If I can direct your attention to your right, you'll see we have arrived at the historic Rhyolite Depot, also known as the Ghost Casino. But it's not just a casino, it's a brothel, too... which is, of course, why we're here, boys."

There was some whooping and hollering from some cowboys at the back of the bus, along with scattered exclamations of "Finally!" and "About time!"

"You mean the girls here are ghosts?" Gil asked.

"Of course not," Shekinah tsked. "They just need a little coaxing to come out and play. You see, the gals upstairs have certain... tastes. They need to see how much of a man you are before they offer up their services. Now, they will provide those services one hundred percent free of charge—if, that is, you prove yourselves worthy."

"Free? Hell, yeah!" Fred yelled.

"Hold on there a second, little missy," one of the cowboys objected. "Your flier said this was a package tour, with everything included."

"Except," Shekinah said, holding up a copy of the contract and insurance waiver everyone had signed, "for any premium upgrades. And this is definitely a premium upgrade—which you are getting for free anyway." Her voice dropped to a growl. "So what's your point?"

The cowboy put both hands up, palms out in front of him in a sign of surrender. "Nothin' at all, ma'am. Nothin' at all."

Fred snickered and leaned over to whisper in Gil's ear. "What a douche."

"Yeah," Gil agreed, "a real dork."

"Now," Kortney said, "are you man enough for the girls of the Ghost Casino? Do I have any volunteers?"

Every hand on the bus shot up.

Kortney perused the lot of them slowly, then pointed, one at a time: "You... and you... and... you!"

The goth and the two cowboys came forward. "All you have to do is lie right there on the ground in front of the depot, and the girls will come out and attend to you," she said.

The three of them clambered off the bus and lay down obediently on the dusty earth where Kortney indicated, side by side. "Oh," she said, "and one more thing: We'll need to tie you up."

Fred whistled. "Oohoo! Gimme a B. Gimme a D. Gimme an S. Gimme an M!"

"You wanna watch?" Gil said. "Sicko."

Kortney overheard him. "Oh, but you *have* to watch," she said. "Otherwise, you won't get any goodies." She held up the box with the bow on it. "And we went back to the candy store at Beatty just for you."

Gil turned beet-red and watched as Shekinah took a sturdy rope and bound each of the volunteers, hand and foot, then stepped back.

"What's interesting about this place," Kortney said, "is that, at one time, there was a railroad line exactly where our three volunteers are lying." She went around the bus, passing out pieces of candy as she spoke. Gil took one with the rest of them and bit into it... and was disgusted to find that it tasted like black licorice. He swallowed it quickly to get the putrid taste out of his mouth, but a few moments later, the nausea had passed and was replaced by a sort of giddy euphoria.

"Whoa! That stuff is righteous!" he said.

"Told you, man!" Fred said, keeping his eyes fixed on the

NEVADA NIGHTMARES, VOL. 2

three men lying in the dirt below their bus window.

"Where's the girls?" Gil hooted "We want the girls!"

The rest of the passengers took up the chant: "We want the girls! We want the girls! We want the girls!"

They broke off at the sound of a distant whistle.

"Here they come now," Kortney said in a low voice, almost as if she were talking to herself.

A second whistle sounded, louder this time, and Gil noticed for the first time that the volunteers appeared to be lying across a pair of rails—rails he was sure hadn't been there before. "This Black Death is some crazy-ass shit!" Fred shouted.

"You're telling me!"

The whistle sounded a third time, still louder, and a rumbling shook the ground where the bus was parked. The wind picked up, and there was a sudden whoosh as a train roared past them, the force of it nearly knocking the bus sideways. Then, a moment later, it was gone, and so were the rails that had carried it past them. The only thing that remained were the scattered, splattered remains of the three men who had volunteered.

"Whoowee! Now that's what I call a show!" Gil yowled.

"Damn straight," Fred agreed, high-fiving him.

"Gentleman," Kortney said, "if you'll please give it up for the girls of the Ghost Casino!"

The passengers burst into a raucous round of applause as the bus started again and Shekinah strolled up and down the center aisle, passing out more candy to the eager passengers.

Each of them took a large handful and shoveled it into their mouths.

Before long, they were all passed out.

Shekinah slapped Gil hard across the face, and he awoke with a start. The bus was empty and sat in front of a large, abandoned three-story building with a sign over the doorway that read "Goldfield Hotel."

"Where'd everyone go?" he asked, his voice slurred.

"They're all inside, waiting to go into the brothel," Shekinah said. "How do you feel?"

"Like shit," he said

Shekinah clicked the button on her walkie-talkie and whispered into it, "He's having a reaction. His body's rejecting the serum. If we try to take him in with the others, he might ruin everything."

Static cackled over the speaker.

"Everything's spinning around," Gil moaned.

Shekinah put a hand on his shoulder. "Just close your eyes, baby. You'll feel better in no time." She pulled the switchblade out and jabbed it deep into the side of his neck, and drew it slowly across his throat, producing a gush of blood that flowed down over his chest. He gagged on it and sputtered, convulsing for a moment before he fell still. "He'll miss the fun, but it doesn't matter," Shekinah said under her breath. "They'll all end up in the same place anyway." She stood up and nearly jumped when she saw Fred standing behind her, looming over her.

He smiled a goofy smile. "Righteous!" he said. "Now, where's the girls?"

Shekinah caught up to Kortney in the hotel basement, where she was directing a line of men through a door that led to an underground passage. She stood there at the entrance, handing each of them a shot bottle of Black Death as they went by.

"Liquid courage!" one of them shouted, raising the bottle in a toast as he moved past her.

The hotel, like the depot and the Angel's Ladies brothel, was deserted. But the men didn't seem to notice... or care.

"This," Kortney was saying, "is the passageway the hotel's

wealthy male guests have always used to sneak away from their wives and under the street to the Goldfield brothel. It doesn't look like it now, but in its prime, this place was the most happenin' place in Nevada. It was Vegas before Vegas was Vegas. Everyone who was anyone showed up here to watch prizefights, mine for gold, and gamble it away at the Northern Saloon. It's pretty quiet these days, and the brothel at the end of this tunnel is the only one still standing. The girls there are ready to show you a really hot time."

Fred elbowed his way past the others and ran to the head of the line. He'd missed out at Angel's Ladies and the Ghost Casino. He wasn't about to be left out of the fun this time. A little voice tickling at the back of his brain tried to remind him that the men who'd been at the front of the line in Beatty and Rhyolite weren't around anymore, that they'd met their end in gruesome fashion, the promises of sinful bliss in the arms of a sweet painted lady forever unfulfilled. But *that* wouldn't happen to *him*. He was different. Those were losers, unworthy of tasting the apple of enlightenment bursting forth from the forbidden tree. The inner voice of his own ego, amplified by the effects of the Black Death, drowned out that other voice as he rushed forward headlong toward his destination.

Within moments, he stood on the threshold, staring at a pink door emblazoned with the symbol of serpents crawling out from between two full red lips. The doorway glowed bright red around the edges, and Fred could hear the sound of moaning coming from the other side.

"Excellent!" he yelled, grabbing the door handle and throwing it open.

He barely caught himself before he realized he was standing on the precipice of a drop into something that looked like volcanic molten lava. But there were *men* down there. They were the ones moaning, but not in ecstasy but in pure misery and anguish.

"Dude!" he gasped, his eyes wide. "This is a totally deep hole."

He squinted his eyes for a better look, heedless of the steam and hot coals rising toward him.

"Is this a sex dungeon? Any babes down there?"

He reached into his pocket and took out the shot bottle Kortney had given him on the way in. He heard footsteps closing in from behind him, running toward him, but he was here first, and no one was going to deny him. Just before the writhing mass of male lust slammed into him from behind, he took a flying leap forward.

"I won!" he cried. "Bodacious!"

From somewhere far below, a voice drifted up to his burning ears: "No one has ever won."

"Gil and Fred's Exotic Misadventure" by Stephen H. Provost appears here for the first time.

A Tangled Tragedy

About 10½ o'clock a.m. to-day, a terrible accident occurred at the Sunderland Mill, lower Gold Hill, whereby an estimable lady resident of this town was so badly injured that death was the result.

On the lower floor of the mill stands a barrel into which flows a small stream of hot condensed water from the stream, through a pipe. Through a side door nearby, the neighbors have always been allowed free access and permission to supply themselves with water for washing and other purposes. A few feet from this barrel, and about a foot and a half from the floor, the end of the counter shaft which runs the pans on the floor above, projects some ten inches beyond a pulley, and a slot or score is cut along one side of it, for the key which fastens this pulley onto the shaft.

At the time mentioned, Edward Burke, who keeps a boarding house on Main Street, came in for water, followed by Mrs. Bridget Curran, who also lives nearby in a little cottage opposite the Crown Point office.

She stood just behind him, waiting while he dipped water from the barrel, when suddenly, above the loud din of the batteries and machinery, he heard her cry out, and immediately turning, saw the unfortunate woman caught by her steel hoop skirt and underclothing wound tightly around the projecting end of the shaft, and being carried around, with each revolution her head beating upon the floor.

He made a desperate attempt to tear her skirts loose, but could not. He then succeeded in attracting the attention of the superintendent of the mill, who was upon the floor above, and who immediately sprang to the rescue.

Finding it impossible to tear the skirts free from the shaft, Mr. Gray ran to the engine room and soon stopped the mill. Even then they could only get the skirts free from the shaft by cutting them off with a hatchet.

The poor woman was insensible, and remained in that condition up to the time of her death, which ensued two hours afterward.

Dr. Hall, who happened nearby at the time of the accident, came at once and rendered all possible assistance. She was taken to her cottage.

None of her bones were broken, but both hands were badly lacerated, the right one nearly torn off, her head badly contused from striking the floor in the several revolutions she made around the fatal shaft. Concussion of the brain was doubtless the immediate cause of her death.

Mrs. Curran was about 45 years of age, and her husband works in the Yellow Jacket Mine. She was the mother of Johnny Curran, the well-known messenger boy of the Yellow Jacket office, and one of her sons was killed in the shaft of that mine about two years ago.

— *Gold Hill Daily News*,
December 1, 1869

Megan Russ

Yellow Jacket

It is a bright day in Virginia City. The crisp desert air carries a few flurries from the late snow. The crystals sparkle in the bright spring sun, a rainbow of hope in the silver city.

Children toss snowballs back and forth across the road. Their mothers watch from within the parlors of their grand homes. They chat and knit close to roaring fires.

Despite the early hour, a few men push into the saloons farther down C Street.

The noise from the Crystal Bar, opened two years prior in the Douglass Building, echoes onto the boardwalk as James steps through the swinging doors.

He turns and kicks snow from his boots. Brushing flakes from his duster, he spins to face the sparsely populated tables. A wench slides over to him, a serving tray tucked under her arm.

"Food, drink, or entertainment?" Her voice is like silk as she slides a smooth hand up his chest.

James slaps her hand away, and she huffs, placing her hand on her hip.

"I'll take a drink and food over there," he grunts and points to an empty table near the front window.

"Three bits," the woman says through pursed lips. She holds out her hand.

He drops the coins into her palm and heads for the table.

James hangs his duster and hat on the chair. His brown eyes scan the saloon for his patron, but no one matches the description of the man he is meant to meet. James huffs and sits back in his chair, crossing his arms over his chest and glaring at any passersby who dares look his way.

Down the road, two men step out of the surveyor's office. They pull top hats onto their graying hair and laugh. One claps the other on his shoulder and heads for a mansion up the hill. The other tucks a pack of papers under his arm.

Damon Limin pulls at the strands of his mustache as he sneers at the piles of snow blown up against the fine-wood side of the appraiser's office building. He pulls his fine silk coat tighter over his vest and steps out onto the boardwalk.

He whistles as he strolls down the lane and tips his hat to ladies along the boardwalk. A few swoon and fan themselves as he passes. Men narrow their eyes and wrap their arms around their women's waists, pulling them closer.

The Douglass Building, later to be rebuilt and rechristened the Old Washoe Club, greets him as the sun rises higher in the pale blue sky.

Piano music and jovial voices fill the smoky air. Clean coats and dusty jackets alike sit amid the dim interior. The smell of tobacco and hemp assaults his nose and causes the man to sneeze. The eyes of those closest to the door turn to take in the newcomer.

A few scoff and roll their eyes. Turning away from him without a word.

In the corner, another man stands and straightens his white shirt.

James adjusts his shirt and holds his chin high as the banker steps over to him. Damon holds out his hand to James. The young man takes it and holds firm as he shakes it. The lack of calluses on the banker's hand rankles James, but he waves for the man to sit.

"Mr. Comston, pleased to meet you," Damon says.

"Please, James. Mr. Comston is my father," James says, waving to the table for the pair to sit. He gestures for the serving girl to bring something for Damon and returns to his seat.

"How was the trip?" the banker asks as he places papers on the table in front of him.

"Long, and I am eager to return. I'm only here to get the numbers," James says, tapping the table between them with a dusty fingernail. "Why you couldn't telegraph these to my father is beyond me," he adds with a wave of his other hand. "Instead, I have to come to this speck of nowhere."

The banker chuckles and shakes his head as he pulls the papers from the waterproof satchel. Sliding the sheets across the table, he pulls out an ink pen and places it beside the contracts.

"As I am sure Mr. Comston explained before your departure, I need an authorized signature on all of these." The smarmy man's face twists into a jovial grin as James glares from the papers up to him.

"Is there something wrong with the post?" James asks as he reads the contracts and proposals.

"Of course not, but Mr. Comston insisted that he wanted a representative here to inspect the mine before we continue to dig. I assured him everything was going perfectly, but after that collapse up in Ely, no one blames the lode owners for wanting to be cautious," Damon says, rubbing his hands together.

"Yes, well, my father could have had a local partner do all of that," James growls, waving a hand dismissively as he focuses on the pages.

"We can take the carriage out to the mine as soon as you are agreeable," the banker says with a curt nod.

James glances up at him from the papers. The well-dressed man is one of the wealthiest on the mountain and owns two of the most profitable silver mines in the area. James knows it will not do to upset his father's business partners, nor their patrons.

He signs the papers and slides them over to the banker without complaint. Damon folds them into his satchel and finishes his drink.

"Tell me about my father's mine."

"Ah, the Yellow Jacket has been one of our best producers for years now," Damon says, patting the table beside his snifter of whiskey. "This new vein indicates another couple of years of profit, and we are sure to find more as we go. We have shafts planned for other possible spots in the Yellow Jacket as well."

"I didn't realize that was the name of the mine." James shudders and takes the final swig of his drink.

"Got something against it? I didn't name it. I'm pretty sure the company don't care who likes it."

"Company?"

"The Yellow Jacket Silver Mining Company. They employ more than just your mine's people. They are the owners of your mine. Owners can name their mines whatever they wish."

"Named for the yellow coats the miners wear then?" James asks, a hopeful smile on his face.

Damon's lips pull into a thin line. "Have something

against the insect?"

"They are terrible, useless creatures," James snaps.

A few ladies enjoying their breakfast nearby glare in their direction. Damon waves and smiles at them. One waves back, while the other pulls her friend's attention back to their food.

"Well, then, you will not want to stay in the silver city for long. Perhaps a room over in Gold Hill will be better than this. One of the self-proclaimed witches up the hill cultivates hives of the blighters," Damon says with a laugh.

"A witch!" James' shout causes the music to stop, with a whine from the piano. Damon flinches and holds up his hands to the familiar faces of the Crystal Bar. "Why would you allow a hag to live here? Why would someone keep such creatures?" he says with a grimace.

The pianist glares at the men before returning to her music. This time, an increase of whispers and pointed fingers in James' direction accompanies the soft keys.

"Is there a problem?" The bartender asks as he and one of his bouncers come over to check on James and Damon.

"No, Arty, I was just telling Mr. Comston to avoid Clare's. He ain't a fan of the yellow jackets," Damon says, placating the glowering brutes.

"Yer in the desert, son. Buzzers be the least o' yer concern. Giant snakes that could swallow a man, crows so big they can carry off a child, or those giants causing problems up north. A few bugs ain't nothin'. Hell, the ghost upstairs be worse," the bartender laughs as he turns and marches to the front.

"He's joking, right?" James asks.

Damon stares after the bartender and shakes his head. "About the giants, yeah, the tribes hunted them to extinction a while back," the banker says as he stands and gestures for James to follow.

The young man's mouth hangs open as Damon makes it

to the door and pulls on his top hat.

"Well, Mr. Comston, are you coming?" the banker asks with a grin on his smug face.

"Such superstitions are not civilized," James says as he pulls his coat over his shoulders and pulls his hat on as they emerge onto the sunbathed boardwalk.

"Superstitions?" Damon asks as he deftly avoids a pile of melted slush.

Damon looks over his shoulder at the young man with a raised eyebrow. He smirks as James splashes into the puddle with a grimace. The easterner shakes the muddy mess from his boots with a cry of disgust.

"Witches, ghosts, monsters. What do you take me for, a child?" James says as he catches up to Damon.

The banker shakes his head. "Welcome to the Wild West, boy. Where the tales we tell children at night are more than your grandma's bedtime story."

"What is that supposed to mean?" James says as he grabs Damon's shoulder and spins him.

The young man flinches away when the banker's eyes flash white for a moment. He blinks away the vision as Damon cocks his head at him. James attributes the color to the snow and blinding streets.

Who scatters white dust in the streets?

"There is more than silver in these hills, Mr. Comston. I suggest you make your trip brief," Damon says, turning to continue toward the stagecoach stop.

"I thought we were going to the mine?" James asks as they approach the booking office.

The clerk waves the pair through when Damon shows the man a badge.

"We are, but as I said, with your opinion of Miss Clare and her bugs, Gold Hill might be a better place for you to stay.

NEVADA NIGHTMARES, VOL. 2

The coach can take us to the trail from there. I can point out the mine along the way," Damon says as he climbs into the stagecoach opposite an elderly couple.

"Is it close to the stage station?"

"Right off the road, in fact." Damon says with a nod. "It is perfect for the wagons that haul lumber to the site or take out stone."

"Tell me more about the mine and find," James says, pushing the superstitions of the westerners from his mind.

I shift. My nest is tight and secure. It is not yet time to awaken.

The world above is warming. But my time is yet to come.

When I burrowed away from the world, it was quiet. Everything was covered in ice. There was no place for me anymore. I slept and waited for the warmth to return.

It is almost time. I should sleep more...

What is that insistent racket?

"I must stay until the shaft opens. I need to be able to give an accurate report to my father upon my return," James says as he and Damon exit the Yellow Jacket Mine.

The banker's eyes widen as he turns to James.

The young man is brushing dust off his shoulder and squinting into the bright sun. He grimaces at the white grains that sprinkle from his coat. The easterner pulls a cigarette case from his pocket and offers Damon a stick.

"Thank you, but no," the man says, holding up a hand between them. "You plan on staying?" Damon asks.

"Oh yes, I must see the shaft open. My father will want to know how it goes."

"We can send you a telegram once the shaft is open and

give you both an accurate account. By the time you get back home, you will probably be arriving at the same time as the news," Damon says as he waves toward the coach.

"No, I will stay—ah!" James cries out as a buzzing insect zips toward his face.

The cigarette drops to the dirt, the cherry popping out into the dry brush. Damon cries out and stomps on the smoldering grass.

James screams, spinning around while a handful of yellow and black wasps flutter around his head.

Damon gets the fire stanched and grabs James' coat. He pulls him forward.

"Come now, we must be too close to their nest. They will leave you alone," Damon says as he heads for the coach.

"Horrible creatures," James shouts as he swats one from the air.

The thin insect slams into the ground and rolls dazed, its mandibles and legs flailing as it tries to right itself. James growls and lifts a boot.

"No! Don't!" Damon yells, but it is too late.

James' boot slams into the yellow jacket and crushes it into the dirt. The young man sneers at the ground as he grinds the leather heel into the innocent creature.

Damon's mouth falls open as he stares at the dirt-scuffed boot.

"What have you done?" Damon growls as he shoves James toward the carriage. "Get in! Now!"

"What? It was a stupid yellow jacket," James says as he is shoved through the door of the stagecoach. "They were trying to sting me."

"A yellow jacket of Yellow Jacket Mine!" Damon snaps as he slams the door closed and the driver heads for Gold Hill.

"Is this part of that stupid superstition?" James asks with

a wave of his hand.

Damon lunges across the small space in the coach. The banker's hand grabs James' collar and pulls him inches from the huffing man. He growls in the young man's face, a sneer on his mouth.

"Superstition keeps us alive out here, boy." Spittle flies from his lips and lands on James' cheeks. The young man flinches. "If you cannot understand you are in the West, then it is time for you to go home."

Damon releases James and sits back in his seat with a huff. The banker straightens his coat and keeps his eyes on the window of the cab. James' mouth falls open as he watches the older man's stoic demeanor return.

"It was self-defense," James grumbles.

Damon's shoulders stiffen, and he takes a deep breath.

"Yellow jackets don't sting until they bite. They have to land on you to do that. You were not in danger." His eyes flash white in the diffused light as he looks at James.

The easterner sits up straighter and glares at the man across from him.

James does his best to keep the stutter out of his voice. "I'm not leaving."

"Then I would avoid the mine unless necessary," Damon says, turning to the window once more.

James crosses his arms and glares at the banker. "It is my mine."

The older man laughs. "Your father is an investor. The find belongs to the Yellow Jacket Mining Company. The mine belongs to the mountain. And to those who have lived here long before us." Damon's voice is a growl, and he keeps his gaze on the passing sagebrush.

Miss Clare bends to scoop the loose grains of sand in

her knobby hands. Her fingers shake as the dust sifts through her grasp, leaving the curled yellow and black body.

Tears drip onto her palm around the corpse.

Yellow jackets buzz around her head, bobbing angrily up and down beside her shoulders. Clicking their little mandibles.

"I know, my dears," Clare says as she turns her cloudy gaze toward the dissipating dust cloud on the road. "I will make sure he pays the price for his insolence."

The witch closes her hand around the wasp's body. She ignores the ache in her joints as she white-knuckles the creature.

Her eyes roll up into her head. As a chant escapes the old woman's lips. The voice is not Clare's, sounding like a loud buzz and clacking that form human words.

When the words end, the swarm of angry yellow jackets drops to the ground, bodies curling inward as they go still. Clare falls to her knees, blood dripping from her eyes. She blinks and gasps for air, as her vision refuses to focus as much as it used to.

"Wh-what have you done?" A voice cracks behind her.

Clare looks over her shoulder at the miners standing in the shaft entrance.

"I suggest you find a new mine." The witch croaks before limping away into the sagebrush.

"Crazy ol' hag," Baxter grunts as he pushes past those in front. "Like I'll give up this job. They're paying twice as much as up in Virginia City," he says as he and a few others head for the stage station.

What has happened?
My blood boils; my scales itch. I need to get out. I
need to see the sun.

I shift. Gravel showers me as I move and press against the roof of my nest. My heart pounds, my mind races, and I cannot focus.

I screech, and more rocks rain onto my scales.

I have to get out. I have to feed. I must...

I cannot focus as my claws scrabble at the stone and I pull myself upward.

There was a purpose once. I had a goal before. Now there is just rage.

I have to get out!

Six miners quit overnight. With no notice. Despite the extra pay, no one else takes on the jobs.

James sends word home once a week. His father has grown tired of waiting for a return on his investment. In his last telegram, he orders James to join the miners and get the new shaft open.

When the easterner goes to the mining office the next morning, and applies, the owners of the Yellow Jacket Mine grin behind their soft hands. They give him his permit and safety gear and instruct him to report to the foreman.

On the same day, James joins the mud team of the Yellow Jacket Mine. The miners kindly welcome him into their union. The workers are so used to men coming and going, it is nothing new for them to have men quit suddenly, or show up uneducated on the mine.

Baxter is welcoming and teaches the newcomer the ropes. The mining veteran takes the stranger under his wing and teaches him what it means to haul the rocks away from the mine entrance.

It means a sore back.

James' calluses from riding horses are not enough to protect his hands. His fine clothing causes sweat to pour down his spine, and his boots rub at his feet the more he walks.

When James drops onto his bed in the boarding house room, his lower back is burning. His blister-covered hands shake as he lifts them to look at the seeping pink circles. He drops back onto the cot and glares at the ceiling.

"At least I'm only working until the mine hires more people," James sighs as his hands land on his chest.

Heavy eyelids drift closed as the hard work takes its toll.

A clicking noise awakens James, and he sits up. He glances toward the second-story window as the sound continues, over and over, like pebbles clattering against the glass. He stands and pulls the curtain aside.

"By the Lord!" he shouts and stumbles away from the window.

Slamming their hard exoskeletons into the glass, a swarm of yellow jackets clatters against the window in an attempt to get to the gawking man. James screams as one slams into the pane and a loud snap fills the air. A crack spiders out from the center, and the swarm frantically aims for the break.

James scrambles to get to his door while keeping his eyes on the bugs. He yanks open his door and slams it shut the moment he is in the hallway.

Five minutes later, he is standing behind Mr. Hamon. The landlord looks over his shoulder at James with a raised eyebrow. The easterner wrings his hands as he prays.

Mr. Hamon opens the door and looks around James' room. The old man huffs and turns with his hands on his hips. He chews on the ends of his beard as he tries to decide what to do with the daft young man.

"There ain't any bugs in yer room," the landlord says, waving a hand at the room.

"They were coming in through the window," James says, stepping closer to his door.

"Well, tha' tends to happen when ya leave it open," Hamon says as he tosses his hand up with a shake of his head. He moves and closes the window with a huff. "Whateve' was flyin' aroun' ain't in here now," he says, stomping past James.

"I didn't open the window," James says to himself as he stares into the yellow jacket-free room. "They broke through it." He slides a hand over the intact pane.

The world is knocking.

With each rock I loosen, I pull myself toward the surface.

I cannot focus on anything but digging myself out. I need to get out.

The sound from above tells me the world is helping to free me. My claws frantically scrape at the stones, burying my trail.

Everything burns and aches for the sun, for the air. I want to feel the wind on my scales. After an eon hiding from the cold, I need the heat of the world above.

I need to feel. I need to kill.

The world is loud. They are desperate for me to reach them.

James stomps down the road toward the surveyor's office, his miner's hard hat clutched in his fist. White dust sparkles in the air behind him with each heavy step.

He yanks open the door with a fierce grimace on his face. The secretary looks up and stands. She straightens her rumpled skirt. James takes a breath and lets it out slowly to calm himself before he takes his anger out on a woman.

"Sir, can I help you?"

"I need to speak with Mr. Limin or Mr. Salt," James says through gritted teeth.

"Well, Mr. Limin is at the bank, sir," she says. "But Mr. Salt is available."

She leads James to the office door. Knocking softly, she opens the door and waves him in.

"James, for you, Mr. Salt," she says. She smiles at him as she returns to her desk.

James' eyes twitch at her use of his first name.

"Mr. Comston." The surveyor stands and holds out his hand to James. He ignores the grit on James' hand and waves for him to have a seat. "What brings you to the office in the middle of the day?"

James grits his teeth so hard his jaw aches. "Have you managed to find any new miners for the Yellow Jacket Mine?"

Mr. Salt's mouth pulls into a thin line as he settles into his chair. He shuffles a few papers on his desk before sitting back and meeting James' gaze.

"Unfortunately, no workers have come into town or applied from the other mines," Salt says, shaking his head.

James waves a dust-covered hand toward the window. "When I came to this hole in the ground two months ago, you could throw a rock and hit a miner looking for work."

"That was two months ago, Mr. Comston. There have been three finds since then. It happens here in the spring." The surveyor taps his clean fingers on the desk.

"There have to be more workers!" James shouts, slamming his hands down on the polished dark wood.

Mr. Salt's eyes narrow at the mine worker across his desk. He takes a deep breath.

"More stages will be coming tomorrow. Perhaps new miners will be available by the end of the week."

James grinds his teeth together as he stands and leans

over the desk toward the surveyor. Mr. Salt's mouth twists into a thin grin.

"Find more miners for the Yellow Jacket Mine. We need to get this shaft open. Pay them whatever you need to." James growls out each word.

"You don't have that authorization, Mr. Comston," the man says, straightening his suit. "I will do what I can to find more workers for the Yellow Jacket." Mr. Salt stands as he speaks and waves James toward the door.

"Now, if you will excuse me, James. I have other meetings."

James glares at the man but follows him to the door.

"Find us more workers," James growls.

"I will do what I can, Mr. Comston," the surveyor says as he all but pushes James out the door.

James blinks as he steps onto the boardwalk outside the building. He glares up at the spring desert sun.

"Mr. Comston, shouldn't you be at the mine?" A familiar voice pulls James from his staring contest with the pale blue sky.

He looks over to see Damon coming toward the office building. The miner turns and crosses his arms over his chest, and glares at the banker.

"There was an accident," James growls. "I came to find out about more workers."

"An accident?" Damon's voice rises as he steps up to James. "What happened? Do we need to get the digger teams out to the Yellow Jacket?"

"No, nothing so serious. A cart tipped over and dumped a load. They were cleaning it up when I left."

"A cart tipped? Was anyone hurt?"

"No." James shrugs and shakes his head, his eyes narrowing. "I was almost hit by one of the larger rocks, but no one was hurt. We need more help."

Damon sighs and places a hand over his heart, his gaze falling to the snow piled against the shady side of the building. His eyes flash white before he looks back at James. He takes a deep breath.

"Well, I am sure the surveyors are working hard on finding more workers in the mine," Damon says, patting James' dusty shoulder. "I will try to persuade Mr. Salt to hire a few new workers, next stage."

"That will not be for days," James says through gritted teeth, his fists clenched at his sides.

"That cannot be helped, Mr. Comston. Two more days won't make a difference for the mine or the investors."

"I want to go home!" James shouts.

His outburst attracts the attention of men and women on the other side of the boardwalk. He presses a finger into Damon's chest, leaving a pale streak against the man's dark coat. The ladies cover their mouths as their eyes widen. Their husbands pull them along, away from the public drama: It is not unheard of for an argument to turn into a gunfight in Virginia City.

Damon glares down at the silver dust on his black silk. His mouth twists into a grimace as he brushes the sparkling white powder from his lapel.

"Then go home, Mr. Comston. No one is making you stay here," Damon says as he adjusts his top hat and steps around the miner. He holds his head high.

James glares after him. His fingers itch to move toward his pistol. He imagines for a moment shooting the stuck-up banker in the back, but shakes the thought away.

He stomps toward the stagecoach stop to catch a coach to Gold Hill.

He stumbles as a door swings open and a small form steps

out onto the boardwalk. James and the old woman tumble to the ground in a heap. A shout comes from the other side of the door and, a moment later, hands are helping the woman from the ground.

James looks up to see the shopkeeper dusting off Clare. The witch smiles at the young woman as they fix her petticoats. No one pays the miner any mind as he pushes himself from the ground.

"Watch where you're going, old woman," James snaps, spitting on the boardwalk.

Both women stare at him with wide eyes. The shopkeeper keeps her hands on Clare's shoulders as the old woman turns to look up at the glowering worker. She puts her hands on her hips and cocks her head at the man. Her cloudy eyes take him in with more clarity than such eyes should have.

"Sir, I did look prior to opening the door. It is not my fault you are in too much of a hurry to pay attention for yourself," Clare says, pursing her wrinkled lips.

"Listen here, woman. You need to watch where you're stepping around here," James growls, looming over her.

The shopkeeper pulls the witch closer to her. At the same time, a man slightly older than the young woman steps out the door, a Winchester resting against his shoulder. He steps between the pair of women and the fuming miner.

"Move along, sir. We ain't want no trouble," the shop owner says, putting his free hand on the stock of his rifle.

James sneers at the man, his hand moving toward his pistol. The young woman gasps at the same time Clare huffs.

James' fingers close around the pistol, and pain flares through his palm. He yanks his hand away from the gun and stares at the wriggling yellow creature clamped onto his flesh. The yellow jacket opens its mandibles and chomps onto him again.

James screams and thrashes his hand. The yellow jacket is flung off and buzzes into the air between the locals and the miner. The easterner rushes away from the agitated creature.

Clare holds out her hand as the couple watches. The snapping, zigzagging yellow jacket slides onto her palm and nibbles at the bit of flesh in its jaws.

"Y'all have any family in the Yellow Jacket mine?" she asks, turning cloudy eyes to the shop owners. The couple shake their heads. "Good."

Clare turns without another word and heads up the hill toward her cottage.

I can taste the air. There is a hum to it now. I am close.

My claws pull stone after stone, but some stones are thick, and I have to dig through.

How long have I been at this?

I cannot bring myself to care. All that matters is escaping this darkness, this cold.

I need to get out!

James looks up from his newspaper as the serving maid sets a cup of coffee and his breakfast in front of him. He grimaces at the wet scrambled eggs and greasy bacon. He folds his newspaper and sets it beside his plate.

The date glares up at him. Mocking him. His finger taps the "7" as he wonders how many more weeks he will have to be here. The useless banker and fat surveyor had promised new workers at the beginning of April. One week later, and still nothing.

He picks at his food until the whistle calls for the miners to report to the station. The sun has yet to rise as he joins the flood of workers heading to the stage stop.

James crosses his arms and glares after the stage once workers of the Yellow Jacket Mine have climbed off. The horses kick up dust and disappear around the corner of the canyon into the dark.

"Come on, James," Baxter calls from the entrance.

The young man huffs and spins in the mud. He stomps toward the flickering lights of the mine. Candles and lamps are lit on hats, and they duck into the tight interior.

James crouches as he walks through the mine. He keeps his eyes on the dark iron of the cart tracks until the shaft opens up and the lift heads down into the dark.

Three at a time the workers climb into the large metal buckets and are lowered into the mine. The next three climb onto the next bucket as it appears. James climbs on beside Baxter and Orion.

I can hear the knocking like the world is on the other side of this rock.

When I breathe, I taste the sun in the air. The warmth of the stones beneath my claws tells me I am almost there.

The world is waiting for me.

It is knocking back.

The time has come.

James hums along with the other miners as he slams his pick into the rock. The clangs of metal on stone creates a beat to the wordless sound of the workers. The staccatos echo through the shaft and out through the entrance of the mine as the sun rises.

James pauses as his pick plunges into the stone. He stops. The foreman had prepared him for this eventuality. He lifts his hand without pulling the pick out of the stone. There is a risk of water, gas, oil, or stagnant air if he removes the pick. His fingers close around the rope beside the ceiling.

He pulls the rope, and down the shaft, a bell rings.

Others around him come to a stop and the mine falls silent.

A few moments later, the foreman appears and crouches down the tunnel to join James. He stares at the pick. The older miner closes his hand around the handle and wiggles it.

"Hmmm, everyone back to the buckets. We'll get this checked out. Any luck, we get a new shaft." There are some cheers as they all move back along the tunnel to the open area of the central shaft.

Two experienced miners move to where James' pick extends from the rock.

One pauses as he sees the pick shudder.

A claw has opened the stone for me. Not my own claw. Long, smooth, hard enough to puncture rock.

One of my people survives?

Impossible. The ice would have killed all my children. None could have survived. This is something else. A poor excuse for a powerful claw.

I push against it. It invades my space, my stone. The fake claw shifts, but not enough.

Then the imitation is pulled from the stones before me and light spills in. My eyes burn after an eon in the dark. It is what I desire, but it hurts.

I stab my claw through the stone. The rocks crumble away and expose a tunnel. Light fills my space and blinds me.

A high-pitched noise fills my ears. The sound is like claws in my head.

I lash out, and my claws hit something solid, but not as hard as rock. Something hot showers against me and covers my unblinking eyes in a red film.

I can see movement in the flickering light.

Pain flares through my side as one of the shadows lunges toward me and hits me with a fake claw. I slash out, and the shadow is no more. More of the hot liquid showers me.

Something clicks inside me as the smell of blood and flesh fills my nose for the first time in an age. As another shadow lunges toward me in the bright red haze, I spring.

James screams and yanks at the chains, hoping that the young man up top will turn on the buckets.

"Help!"

Shouts fill the tunnel as some of the miners climb the chains. Others run down the other tunnels to hide in the darkness.

In the light of the lanterns, the scales of a giant fill the tunnel.

Black eyes spin to focus on James through the chaos. He can feel its eyes on him. The thing is looking over the bodies of his friends to him.

A few miners crawl through the puddles of blood toward the buckets. James shakes his head, grabs the chains in his shaking hands and climbs upward.

The yellow and black scaled creature scuttles through the tunnel. Its mandibles tear at the flesh of the miners. Its loud chomping and clicking echoes off the stone along with the sobs and cries of those bleeding out on the ground.

Long clawed legs skitter along the earth. The sharp ends plunge through the bodies and stone alike.

The massive insect continues toward the central shaft; buckets clank and shake as miners scramble up.

James pulls himself over the edge of the ground floor and

rolls onto the muddy floor. Others rush past the carts, knocking ore loose from the top. The stones clang against the iron tracks, echoing down the shaft.

A screech comes from the darkness below.

James cries out as the sound of clattering comes from the mine.

He peeks over the edge to see three of the lanterns crash to the lower tunnel. The oil spills out into the mud, spreading the fire through the mine. Flames illuminate the giant insect from below.

The yellow and black monster tears men from the chain as they climb for safety. They vanish into the flames with screams that pierce James' ears. With each clang of the creature's massive body against the buckets, it gets closer to the top.

"We can't let it get out!" James shouts as he helps Baxter over the edge.

"I saw Rob hit it before it killed him. If it can bleed, it can die!" Baxter shouts over the discordant clanging of the chain as it swings wildly.

"Mike, help us!" James shouts as he throws a pick to the chubby miner managing to pull himself out of the shaft.

The man grabs the pick from the ground and stares down at the hole. He shakes his head and drops the pick. Mike turns to run.

A long black leg erupts over the lip of the stone, flashing in the flickering light as the man rushes away from the edge. The claws come down and burst through his back and out his front.

Red splatters across the rocks and cart.

Mike gawks at the hard shell like a pipe through his middle before slumping over the appendage as the giant yellow jacket pulls itself over the edge. The leg slides from his body with a loud slopping noise. The miner's corpse crashes to the ground with a smack and splash of blood.

James and Baxter shout as they charge the monster together.

The giant bug clacks its mandibles and snaps toward the two men. It slashes at the humans with its long sharp claws. Exoskeleton bounces off metal and wood as they deflect and swing again. The creature screeches as the men force it back over the edge.

Smoke billows from the mine below. The wasp thrashes as the men aim their weapons. It swings at them, and they duck. Rocks shatter and shower down on the miners and beast.

James swings, and his pick lodges into the monster just behind its first arms. The thing screams in pain and, in a blur, the leg slams into James' side.

The miner cries out as he flies backward. James hits a beam of wood along the tunnel and crumbles to the ground with a groan.

A loud screech fills the air as Baxter slams his pick into the beast's chest. He yanks his pick out and rolls away as it swings at him. The monster pulls away into the gloom of the smoke.

The men cough as the creature retreats into the glowing haze.

"We did it!" Baxter shouts, swinging his pick over his head.

"Did we?" James asks as he gasps for air a few feet away.

Baxter turns to face his wounded friend. "Yeah, it's gone. Stupid bug can burn in that hell it opened," the big man says with a cough.

He crouches and steps toward James. The young man pushes himself up the wood at his back, continuing to lean against the beam for support.

"We need to get out of here," James says, covering his face with his scarf.

The glow from below flickers as Baxter joins James and pulls his arm over his shoulder. Baxter helps James off the wall and toward the tunnel. The exit from this smoky hell is just around the corner.

The light at the end of the tunnel is just a few hundred yards away.

A screech splits the air as the miners' legs are swept from beneath them. The pair tumble to the ground and roll away from each other.

How dare they do this to me!

I have finally escaped the darkness, and they try to drive me back down?

This creature, the thing wiggling like a worm on the ground, is my prey. I will destroy it.

The other one swings another fake claw at me. I pull away quicker this time. It will not touch me again. It is a pest, a speck of dust between me and my goal.

I swing. My claw is a blur and hardly pauses in its arc. I loom over the aggressive thing and hiss. My scales rattle, and atrophied wings slide against each other. The sound alone is enough to cause the rocks to shutter.

The earth knows I have awakened.

"Baxter!" James screams as he pushes himself up.

The monster is towering over Baxter in the cramped tunnel. The sound from the creature echoes through the smoke and haze. Small pebbles shower down on James and bounce off the monstrous insect's hard body.

The giant yellow jacket bows in a blur and chomps down on Baxter's head with its powerful mandibles.

The man's skull bursts in a shower of gray, red and white chunks.

James gags but swallows the bile rising in his throat. He steels himself and turns to grab a pick off the ground.

"No!" James shouts and slams his pick into the wood above his head.

The beast turns to face him and hisses at him.

"You will not leave here!" James cries out as he smashes the metal into the beam again.

The wood shifts, and more rocks rain down on the only living creatures left in the smoke-filled mine.

"And neither will I." He moves to strike the pick again.

James gasps as a claw bursts through his chest. Blood spills from his lips and down his front.

The young man feels his arms weaken as the monster lifts him from his feet. With all the strength his failing body has, he swings.

With a crack that splits the air like a gunshot, the beam slips loose.

The monster turns James to face it as rocks shower down on them. James smiles as the yellow jacket turns its head to regard him with eyes that reflect the glow from below.

The tunnel collapses, and the earth itself presses down, forcing the creature into the flames below.

With a screech, both James and the Queen vanish into the smoke.

The Yellow Jacket Mine was lost to a fire on April 7, 1869. The mine can still be seen in Gold Hill from the road or the train from Virginia City. "Yellow Jacket" by Megan Russ, appears here for the first time.

John A. "Snowshoe" Thompson

The Howl of the Wild

I was never frightened but once during my travels in the mountains. That was in the winter of 1857. I was crossing Hope Valley when I came to a place where six great wolves— big timber wolves— were at work in the snow, digging out the carcass of some animal.

Now, in my childhood in Norway, I had heard so many tales about the ferocity of wolves that I feared them more than any other wild animal. To my eyes, those before me looked to have hair on them a foot long. They were great, gaunt, shaggy fellows.

My course lay near them.

I knew I must show a bold front. All my life, I had heard that the wolf—savage and cruel as he is—seldom has the courage to attack anything that does not run at his approach. I might easily run away from bears, but these were customers of a different kind. There was nothing of them but bones, sinews, and hair. They could skim over the snow like birds.

As I approached, the wolves left the carcass, and in single file came out a distance of about twenty-five yards toward my line of march. The leader of the pack then wheeled and sat down on his haunches. When the next one came up, he did the same thing, and so on, until all were seated in line. They acted just like trained soldiers. I pledge you my word, I thought the devil was in them!

There they sat, every eye and every sharp nose turned toward me as I approached. In the Old Country, I had heard of "man wolves," and these acted as if of that supernatural kind. To look at them gave me cold chills, and I had a queer feeling about the roots of my hair. What most frightened me was the confidence they displayed, and the regular order in which they moved. But I dared not show the least sign of fear, so on I went.

Just as I was opposite them, and but 25 or 30 yards away, the leader of the pack threw back his head and uttered a prolonged howl.

All the others in the pack did the same. "Ya-hoo! Ya hoo, woo-oo!" cried all together. A more doleful and terrific sound I haven't heard. I thought it meant my death. The awful cry rang across the silent valley, was echoed by the hills, and re-echoed far away among the surrounding mountains.

Every moment, I expected to see the whole pack dash at me. I would just then have given all I possessed to have had my revolver in my hand. However, I did not alter my gait nor change my line of march. I passed the file of wolves as a general moves along in front of his soldiers. The ugly brutes uttered but their first fearful howl. When they saw that their war cry did not cause me to alter my course, nor make me run, they feared to come after me, so let me pass.

They sat still and watched me hungrily for some time, but when I was far away, I saw them all turn around and go back to the carcass. Had I turned back, or tried to run away, when they marched out to meet me, I am confident the whole pack would have been upon me in a moment.

They all looked it.

My show of courage intimidated them and kept them back.

"The Howl of the Wild" is Snowshoe Thompson's verbatim account of the incident described, as reproduced in Dan De Quille's telling of his life.

DRAGON CROWN BOOKS

B.B. Arbogast

Viktor Tilman

As a miner, nothing about him was remarkable. He had denim-blue eyes, stood 5 feet, 10 inches tall, weighed about 175 pounds, and sported a dusty canvas hat over his short brown hair. Yet as a ghost appearing before me, clad in the cotton serge work shirt and worn jeans he must have died in, one thing stood out. His gloves had razors stitched into the fingertips!

My name is Jimmy. I'm what some people consider "sensitive." I'm perceptive—frontier folks would have called me ghost-wise. Fifteen years ago, I visited The Washoe Club for the first time, and I'd recently returned to offer tours. Today, after I'd finished another ghost tour, the miner seemed insistent.

Fading in and out of view, he told me his story in a deep voice that echoed as if from a mineshaft. "As I approached my twentieth year, I perceived a strange aspect of my nature. Unlike most men of my acquaintance, who were entranced by the honied scent of a woman's perfume, I was drawn by the reek of death. I yearned to experience the sticky-sweet scent of nectar that is life's blood."

The story you are about to read was told to me by the ghost of Viktor Tilman. He was tired of the tour guides of The Washoe Club calling him "Steve" or a daemon and wanted to set the record straight.

⌘ ⌘ ⌘

I first encountered the lovely Mrs. Theresa Walker at the funeral rites for her late husband, with whom I had toiled in the mines. He was an esteemed gentleman who was faithful to his honorable wife. I offered Theresa my handkerchief, which she used to blot her tears.

Being from Ohio and a recent arrival in town, my circle of friends was limited; thus, when William Walker extended the hand of friendship, my heart filled with joy. William departed this earthly realm just as the soil of Virginia City began its thaw. The labor of digging his eternal resting place proved most grueling indeed. On this occasion, it occurred to me that I should align my lusty pursuits—murder of the fairer sex—with the cadence of the seasons.

Theresa was a vision of beauty, having ringlets of raven black hair that, though bound high upon her head, I imagined would cascade elegantly over her shoulders when she let it down. Her enormous hazel eyes, fringed with lush lashes, held intelligence and kindness, and her smile bore an air of melancholy and shyness. Reserved and ladylike, she was a model wife. The demanding life in Virginia City cast a shadow poised to rob her of her youth far too soon.

"I shall return this handkerchief to you, having laundered it with due care, so that it may appear as if newly fashioned," she said. "I am most grateful, kind sir."

"It is with the utmost delight, dear Madam," I replied.

"To what address should I return it?" she asked.

"I lodge within The Washoe Club," I replied. "A chamber there is mine for the season."

"Very well, I shall call upon you when it is prepared," she said.

Within a fortnight, I had received word of dear Theresa's impending visit. Garbed in mourning attire as befitted her station, she called via a saloon employee, and we convened just outside. I entwined my arm with hers to stroll along C Street. After an exchange of pleasantries, I escorted her to her dwelling on K Street and prepared to take my leave.

"Might I beg the honor of calling upon you before too long?" I asked.

"Why, I would be pleased to see you," she answered with a faint smile.

Then I pressed her, "Tell me—how long do you think you will carry the sorrow of losing my dear friend?"

"Oh, I reckon I will mourn him 'til my dying day; but I will put aside these mourning clothes soon enough."

I pressed her delicate hand to my cheek and took my leave.

Theresa awakened an emotion within me that I have never known. I returned to my lodgings at The Washoe Club. Who did I find waiting for me? My ghostly minx of a friend, Winifred.

"Who was it you kept company with?" she asked. There was a forced lightness in her voice, which I found disturbing.

"That was the Widow Walker, Madame Theresa," I said.

"So then, why were the two of you linked arm in arm?"

"Well now, that is how you walk a lady when the street is

all uneven," I said.

"Somethin' is different about your face," Winifred remarked.

"Different, how?"

"I cannot say. Your smile was affected when you looked at her. Tender. You do not smile like that at me. And your eyes were glossy. With me, it is... different. Almost like you are lookin' right *through* me," Winifred replied with a pout.

I let out a mirthful chuckle. "Of *course*, I look through you, you whimsical girl. You are a specter. Madame Theresa... err... The Widow Walker is solid and brimming with vitality, even though her husband is so recently departed."

"Did you take the life of her husband?" Winifred did not mince her words.

"Nah, he met his end in an accident at the mine. I nearly did so myself. William was my good friend."

"So now you are courtin' his widow?" Winifred probed.

She misunderstood my intentions. That was good. Such misunderstanding would serve me well, for others in the town would likely make the same assumption. But for Winifred's sake, I explained my thinking.

"No, I am not of a mind to wed her, though I will say she has got a fine little ring finger I would not mind callin' mine."

"I do not follow," Winifred said. "Speak plainer."

"I just had me a thought... It came to me at William's funeral. The ground is finally soft from the thaw. Means I can lay the Widow Walker to rest." A grin spread across my face as I looked upon my ghostly companion.

Winifred giggled wickedly as her smile grew.

"Just got to work up a plan," I told her. "But it has got to be handled mighty careful."

"How will you silence her screams?" Winifred asked.

"I believe the most persuasive approach might involve

striking her about the head with some implement. I have been thinkin' about a way to craft some toys for my amusement," I said.

"Toys?" Winifred's countenance brightened with curiosity.

"I anticipate employing a straight-edge razor."

"Just one?" Winifred asked.

I laughed, for the delight in her inquiry stirred my own spirits. I wanted to share the plan that had percolated through my imagination.

"My scheme calls for a quick throat slit," I answered.

"Why, where lies the merriment in that?" Winifred asked.

"What would you recommend?"

"Make some gloves with razors worked into them," she said. "Razors? Within gloves? A trick like that is bound to get spotted easy."

"Go to more than one tanner. Instruct one to make a set of gloves. Then, acquire another set from a different fellow. But where would you get the razors? A blacksmith, maybe?" Winifred was brainstorming. Wind stirred about my chamber as the otherworldly child glided restlessly before my bed.

"I may obtain a straight-edge razor from my barber in Virginia City. Then there's a barber in Gold Hill, and a tanner as well. I can hire a horse to go the three-mile journey, so I do not miss no work."

"Best not gather up all you need in one go. If things turn sour and folks find out Widow Walker met with foul play, you do not want the sheriff pointin' a finger your way."

"Are you certain that you are only six years old?" I asked.

"I been watchin' men coming and going round here for years. I heard whispers." She chuckled. "How 'bout we play a round of hide-and-seek now?" So, we engaged in her favorite pastime for a spell before I needed to retire for the evening.

I was filled with anticipation to act on my plan. The next day, I went to the tanner to have gloves fashioned, "before the winter rush." He appreciated my patronage.

A few days later, I found myself a horse and rode over to Gold Hill, where I purchased a razor and commissioned a second pair of gloves.

As time went by, I did my best to become better acquainted with Theresa. I called on her every other day after work. I drew her closer to me. After several weeks of courtship, she began to confide in me that although she had cherished her late husband, her heart yearned for children, but he had not shared such a desire.

"What are your sentiments regarding children, Viktor?" she asked me.

I was nearing twenty years old. It was time to contemplate the prospect of a family. My answer to her was simple, "Well, first I desire your hand," I replied.

Theresa beamed with pleasure. "You wish for my hand? To marry me?" she breathed.

I gulped. Despite her beauty and cheerful humor, I had no real desire to wed—but I did yearn for her hand. I just nodded in implied agreement.

Another month of courting Theresa went by quickly. I began to question my intentions.

My ghostly little friend was adamant. "You said you was going to kill her, not marry her." She pouted. "You need to get another razor, do you not?" Winifred smiled up at me. Those rose petal lips and wide eyes made the ghost seem so sweet and innocent, yet the thoughts she entertained, and her manner of speech, belied her childlike visage.

When preparations were complete, I had obtained three pairs of gloves and six razors. The ground had long since hardened and was now beginning to thaw again. The time to carry out my plans had arrived.

One fine evening, I was delighted to meet the lovely Theresa at The Washoe Club. I had obtained tickets to the Opera House for a splendid performance there, and we had agreed to meet in the tavern below my abode. The price of admission took a sizable fraction of my weekly earnings, although we miners were paid well for our labor. While I remember many details about that night, the identity of the performers escapes me, for my thoughts were entirely consumed by my scheme. There was a chill in the air that night, so my new gloves were not out of place.

Theresa wore a fine gown. Her corset had her bosom pushed up so you could see a fair bit over the top of her bodice. Enticing... I was consumed with an urge to plunge my razor into those luscious breasts that seemed to be presented for my attention and admiration. But I had to bide my time.

Following the performance, I escorted my enchanting Theresa down K Street. As we got closer to her home, I still had second thoughts. Little Winifred's voice echoed in my head from our discussion the night before. "Now is the time. No second chances—go on, take her hand!"

I led Theresa to within a block of her house. Releasing her delicate hand, I pretended to retie my bootlace. In the dark, she was unable to see me switch my gloves to the ones I had cunningly crafted with razor edges fitted onto the index, middle, and ring fingers.

I rose in a flash, planting the three razors of my left hand into her long, graceful neck while the three razors from my right hand plunged deep into her breast.

Her penetrating cry momentarily pierced the night before the gurgle of her essence silenced it. The smell of iron in her blood stormed my senses in a wave. I cleaved through Theresa's neck with my right hand, uniting the previous wounds that had spurted forth fresh crimson.

An extremely sharp knife I had acquired long before served to sever her left hand from her body. Using the ample fabric of her gown, I shrouded her head and throat and then walked with her draped over my shoulder to the nearby cemetery.

On a recent break from work, I had dug a hole just outside the cemetery wall, into which I now unceremoniously dropped dear Theresa's remains. Her delicate digits, however, went into my pocket.

After refilling the hole and mopping away any blood I could see from my body and my clothing, I trudged up the steep incline to The Washoe Club.

A radiant Winifred greeted me. Her ghostly presence was such that it rendered her almost opaque, so bright did her light shine. "Tilman, did you accomplish it?" She was breathless with eagerness.

I pulled Theresa's hand from my pocket. "Indeed. I have officially claimed fair Theresa's hand," I replied.

I cleansed my beloved's hand in the basin beside my bed and carried the dirty water outside to dump it. The guests had long since departed the saloon.

Gently, I wrapped Theresa's hand in the very handkerchief she had borrowed at her late husband's burial and placed the small bundle into the storage trunk at the foot of my bed.

I waited for the authorities to find Theresa's body. I awaited a knock from the sheriff. Nothing. Theresa had not been well known.

After taking Theresa's life, I continued to work in the mines, but I found I had an insatiable thirst for blood. I craved another life to extinguish.

In the bar on the train to Gold Hill, I encountered Isabelle. Her light-brown hair poured over her shoulders and skin like ivory. Clearly single, Isabelle did not appear to have any menfolk looking after her. She was a "lady of the night" and lived above the grandest tavern in Gold Hill.

Isabelle wished for a breath of fresh air that evening, and I, fresh lifeblood. We were a well-suited pair. I didn't need to feign courtship with Isabelle as I had endured with Theresa.

After hours, I guided Isabelle around the rear of the tavern's bar. With my three-pronged right glove, I made a swift slash to her throat. I was consumed by a passionate desire to remove her gown, and, since she could not scream, I stripped Isabelle of her garments.

Upon plunging my blades into her tender abdomen, an unusual relief washed over me. As I pulled my cutlery upward to her ribs, a long, measured exhale came directly from her lungs, rather than her lips. The soft, high-pitched whimper Isabelle emitted upon her departure took me back to the sound of rabbits I had hunted as a youth.

No burial rites were required for Isabelle. I discarded her in the recesses of a mine we had sealed. This time, I did not use my knife to take her hand. Instead, I excised her foot at the ankle. I tucked her dainty black boot into my pocket and spent the night at a hotel in Gold Hill.

In the wee hours of the morning, I braved the frigid three-mile walk back up to Virginia City. As I climbed the stairs to my room, Winifred appeared on the landing.

"And where have you been all night?" she asked.

I put my finger on my lips. "Hush. Come," I whispered. She followed me to my room.

I pulled out the boot, with Isabelle's foot still inside. The blood had dried, and I had cleaned the gore from the boot directly after doing the deed.

Winifred grinned an evil little smirk. "Who was she?"

"No one special. Her name was Isabelle," I answered. "I am captivated by the smell of fresh blood from young women. What is better?"

Winifred started jumping up and down on my bed. How she did that without going through it, I did not understand. She could walk through walls but did not fall through the floor, or chairs, or beds. She did not know why, either. "There are random rules for being a ghost," she told me one day. "But I do not know what they are. I am confined to this building, but I do not have to stay where I died within it."

Just over a fortnight later, I felt my bizarre craving again.

Layla was an unexpected treasure. She agreed to come to my room for a price. She was a beauty, with luscious lips, big brown eyes, and full, chocolate hair that ran over her shoulders like a gently falling waterfall. Her hips were roomy, and her waist was tiny.

The striped dress she wore was usually reserved for higher-class women, but little imperfections in her seams showed that, although she was an adequate seamstress, she was not a professional. Loose black lace along the neckline was tempting to tear off for strangulation. But that was not why I tore it off.

Instead, I tied Layla to the bed with her lace. She did that willingly, believing it to be a perversion of mine. It was not.

I donned my gloves. When she realized what I was going to do to her, she clawed at the headboard above my bed. Alas, by then it was too late.

Metal from my razor-tipped gloves reflected the moonlight. The flecks of light with each scratch, stab, and twist, along with the seductive smell, the warmth, and the wet crimson of blood, were mesmerizing. Entranced, I slashed.

I do not recall if Layla screamed. She must have. I did not bother to cut her throat first, nor attempt to muzzle her in any way. Once she passed away, I paused.

Out of thin air, Winifred showed herself and peered into

Layla's dead, staring eyes.

"Curious, she appears like she is alive," Winifred said.

"You say that, even with the deep trenches I dug into her from navel to neck?" I asked.

"Just her eyes look alive. And you have blood on your chin."

I wiped my chin. "What shall I do with her?" I asked.

The weather was just barely getting warm during the day. It was downright blistering cold at night.

"I do not believe the ground is *completely* frozen," said Winifred. She directed my attention to the corner of the room where a sack of old mail sat in a ball.

After separating Layla's right hand at the wrist and her right foot at the ankle, I stuffed the remaining parts of her body into the sack. I worked quickly so that her body was still pliable. Afterward, I cleaned off my prizes before dropping them into my storage trunk. Parched, I broke for a drink.

Sweaty and out of breath, I nearly knocked Lena over in the hallway.

"Well, aren't you the dapper scoundrel?" she said with a wink, before passing by me to go downstairs to the saloon. I nodded cordially and followed her down the stairs. While finishing my beer, I observed the appreciative gazes of my fellow patrons upon the figure of lovely Lena, attired in a well-appointed blue gown.

I then returned to the third floor and resumed cleaning my room. After adding Layla's frock to the sack with her remains, I stuffed my mining tools into it as well. When Winifred gave me the "all clear," I hoisted the sack over my shoulder, went back downstairs, and headed past two arguing drunks lingering by the bar.

Exiting the saloon, I made my way straight up to the end of B Street and then even farther up past A Street before I found earth soft enough to dig a shallow grave for Layla.

When I returned to my chamber, I saw the fingernail marks and two pretty painted fingernails she left behind. I pried the fingernails free from the wood and threw them in the trash.

Winifred watched me. She looked so pleased. "Tilman," she said, "I do believe you are my hero!" She batted her eyes and held her hands together over her heart.

I had to laugh. She was behaving coquettishly, but I am fairly certain she had no idea what she was doing. She was, in fact, stirring my desire for kinship of a more innocent variety.

"Tilman, do you realize you're halfway there?" Winifred said with a grin.

"Yes. I just need to find the right woman, with an 'M' name," I replied.

I first noticed young Mary hiding behind her father's shoulder. She was a beauty with coal-black hair and icy blue eyes. She made my heart skip a beat. Having completed her education that very day, regardless, she was not allowed to date boys unless they had her father's approval.

Mary was a sweet Catholic girl. One day, I saw her walk past the schoolyard without her father as escort. Fresh from the barber, I took a chance; I walked over to her.

"How do you do? I am Viktor Tilman," I said.

"A pleasure to meet you," Mary giggled and nodded her head slightly, before two other girls her age magically materialized by her side. "This is Abigail." A tiny girl with straight blonde hair and blue eyes nodded. "And this is Nanette." Nanette had wavy blonde hair and dark brown eyes and was slightly shorter than Mary.

I nodded hello to both newcomers.

"How ever did your clothes get so soiled?" Mary asked.

"I work in the mines," I answered.

To that, Mary replied, "Father does not like miners. He says they are dirty, no-good, get-rich-quick men."

"We get dirty at work, for sure. Your father is not wrong. But I am a good miner and saving my money so that someday, I can buy land and do some prospecting of my own."

In truth, I had no real plan. Live another day, I reckoned.

I said, "If my prospecting comes through, I will get rich."

Mary smiled shyly. "Well, you clean up real nice." Her girlfriends giggled and elbowed each other. I heard the tiny blonde whisper, "He is charming, soiled garments or no." Mary blushed. The soft pink that rose in her cheeks touched off a deeper shade on her lips, which she licked before she spoke. "If you wash and dress proper, I can tell Father you are callin' on me."

I could not believe my luck. A glint flashed in her eyes like I had seen in Winifred's. Maybe her shyness was an act.

"How about if I call on Friday, tomorrow, at half past six?" I said. "Where shall I call?"

Her friends giggled and led her away. "Twenty-four M Street," she called over her shoulder.

"Twenty-four M Street it is." Somehow, I needed to make a good impression on Mary's father. I had to talk with Winifred. Pulling Mary away from her protective father's gaze would prove difficult.

I loved a challenge.

When I arrived in my room, Winifred was nowhere to be found. I called her name, but she did not come. Instead, she yelled, "Come find me, Tilman! It would please me to play hide-and-seek!"

I went to each room on my floor. The other residents must have thought I was out of my right mind as I knocked on their doors. "Have you seen my friend, Winifred?" I asked. "She is about this tall." I held my hand up to my waist. "She is six years old, wearing a white dress and has long, auburn curls and big, expressive eyes."

The first resident shook his head, "No."

Doc occupied the largest room on the floor. "No, I have not seen her today," he said. "I have seen her once or twice. Has she spoken to you?"

"Yes. We are playing hide-and-seek."

"Well then, if I tell you her whereabouts, that would be cheating, would it not?"

"I do not know. I just cannot find her, and she wants me to look for her," I said.

"Have you tried Lena's room?" Doc asked.

"Not yet." I walked down the hallway and tapped on Lena's door. "Lena! Have you seen Winifred?"

"I am with someone, Viktor," Lena said politely.

"My apologies," I replied and continued on my search. Not finding the imp, I returned to my room.

Out popped Winifred from the wall of my room. I should have known.

"Hello, Tilman!" she cried.

"Hello, Winifred. I met a young lady today. Mary, her name is."

"That is perfect. But why are you telling me?"

"Help me devise a means to pry her away from her overprotective father's grasp," I said.

"Hee hee," giggled Winifred. "Is he really overprotective or just protective enough? She *is* his little girl." She tilted her head to the side.

"Good point. I want to lure her here, to her death. But I should like to see the beauty of her youthful face every day thereafter."

"Oh... You will need to borrow the ax from our fire brigade."

"Yes. That will be perfect. How do I convince her to come to me without a chaperone?"

"Silly, silly Tilman." Winifred shook her head, wearing a sad expression on her face. "She is young, you say. Does she have girlfriends?"

"Yes. Two were by her side today, Abigail and Nanette."

"Perfect! You shall slay all three in one day!"

"But the ground has not yet thawed," I said.

Winifred sighed, seemingly impatient with me.

"You need only to figure out what to do with the rest of Mary. Her young friends may fit in there." She pointed to my storage chest. It already housed Theresa's left hand, Isabelle's left foot, and the right hand and foot from Layla. There would be room to add Mary's head and the headless bodies of her little friends, Abigail and Nanette.

Winifred was a genius!

At half past six the next evening, I called on Mary and was welcomed into her home on M Street by her mother. Notably, her father frowned upon my entrance and did not shake my hand in greeting.

Anxiously, I fingered the note I had in my pocket. The ax I had borrowed was in my room at The Washoe Club. Somehow, I had to persuade Mary and her friends to slip out quietly after dark.

Mary's mother and father sat on their sofa in the parlor, while Mary and I sat on the courting chair in the foyer in their clear view.

From our chair, I heard the faint lilt of Mary's mother's voice scolding her husband for his rudeness. "You need to be gentler and more realistic. Miners earn good money for hard labor. Better she be courted by a miner than a gambler or a drunkard."

After we exchanged pleasantries for an hour or so, I was surprised when Mary's mother called out, "Mr. Tilman, would you care to return next week for dinner with us?"

"Thank you. I would be honored," I said.

Secretly, I pressed my note into Mary's hand, which read: "Tonight—midnight. Come to The Washoe Club, third floor, back room. Bring your friends. We can talk. You can meet my little friend, Winifred. She is not permitted to leave The Washoe Club. But she would be pleased to meet you and play hide-and-seek."

"Good night, Mary."

Mary held the note close to her bodice and scanned it, nodding.

"Good night, Viktor!" Mary called. "I will see you soon," she whispered.

"Good night!" I called to Mary's parents. I skipped away from the house, jubilant that my plan was going to work.

A few minutes after midnight, Mary, accompanied by Abigail and Nanette, knocked on my bedroom door.

"Come in," I addressed all three girls. "Welcome."

Mary walked right in, followed by Abigail. Nanette lingered in the hallway. "Friends, I've taken on the strangest feeling," she said.

"You and your 'strange feelings,'" Abigail said dismissively. "Quickly now, come inside before someone sees us." Nanette crept into the room but did not shut the door.

"Viktor, where is your little friend?" Mary asked.

Winifred appeared behind Nanette and sauntered past her into the room.

"You must be Tilman's friends. I am Winifred."

"Viktor," Mary said. Her icy blue eyes were like growing storm clouds. "She... I can see *through* her."

Abigail and Nanette drifted farther into the room.

Winifred smiled at the three girls. "Welcome," she said.

The door shut behind them.

Abigail elbowed Nanette. The two girls were so preoccupied with the appearance of Winifred and the door slamming that they failed to witness Mary's demise. The points of my razors came through from behind her throat, surprising the beautiful girl. Her mouth dropped open, and blood drooled out. Her big blue eyes looked like two full moons in her bewildered face.

I wanted to preserve her like that. The shock. The surprise. She did not look to be in pain. I knew I had picked the right face to keep!

Mary dropped onto my bed with a plunk. I stabbed Abigail quickly before she could run. Then I slashed Nanette across her chest before putting my claws through her brown eyes.

Using the borrowed ax, I cut off Abigail and Nanette's heads. Then I decapitated pretty Mary and cleaned the blood from the stump of her neck and around her mouth with tender affection.

Blood had splattered all over the walls of my room. I undressed Abigail and Nanette without much care before hacking their bodies into pieces small enough to fit into my storage chest. I gathered their clothes and Mary's. Winifred kept watch and let me know when there was no one around.

I put the girls' dresses into the tavern's fire and watched the flames lick up, consuming their bright colors. The smell of the blaze was not as seductive as the perfume of fresh lifeblood.

In a moth-eaten quilt, I wrapped Mary's body—without her head—snuck it outside and gently placed it into a wheelbarrow. With her friends' heads added to Mary's quilted body, I rolled the wheelbarrow a short distance and dumped its contents into the depths of the mining pit. I returned to my room and placed Mary's head and cut-up parts of Abigail and Nanette into my storage trunk. (The usual contents of my trunk had long ago been dumped on my floor.) I knew I must act quickly, for the dawn would soon strip the darkness from all I had done. I washed off the ax and returned it to the firehouse. My strength felt renewed; it was almost as if shedding blood gave me more life.

I had, of course, washed the gore from my hands and face.

Still, there were splatter marks on the walls of my room. I did not care to wash them off. I was much taken with the new appointments.

When 5 o'clock in the morning came, I went to work wearing fresh clothing. Down in the mine, I stayed the length of twelve hours, after which I came up and scrubbed off the grit. With a sense of joy and calm, I climbed the stairs at The Washoe Club. As usual, Winifred was waiting for me.

Outside, I heard men yelling.

"Tilman, you seem very pleased," she said. "I am glad. Shall we play hide-and-seek?"

"In a minute, Winifred," I said, while putting on my special gloves. "There is a commotion outside."

"It would please me if you would stay here and play with me," Winifred said. She gave me the biggest smile I have ever seen on her lovely porcelain face. Her eyes were warm. "Close your eyes. Start counting. No peeking!" she said.

"One, two, three, four..." I counted up to thirty, while Winifred hid. "Ready or not, here I come!" I shouted. I walked around my room and looked under my bed. I went to the hallway. Doc's door was open. I glanced in, but no Winifred. I could hear that Lena was with someone.

Finally, I looked down the hall to the dark staircase. The railing was broken.

I thought I heard Winifred giggle.

There was a cold chill—a breeze.

Presently, I was being pressed toward the stairwell by an unseen force.

"Winifred? Is that you?" I cried out while something pushed me harder across the wooden planks. It felt as if I were thrown down the stairs by the forceful hand of a full-grown man.

The last thing I heard was Winifred.

"It would please me to be friends—forever."

I tumbled down the dark stairwell and awoke in the Red Room—my permanent home.

It occurred to me that the miner, Viktor Tilman, had never been caught by the authorities, even though his victims' first initials told the authorities exactly who had committed these six grisly murders. But he had been stopped.

❖ ❖ ❖

"Viktor Tilman" by B.B. Arbogast appears here for the first time.

Ellie Mage

Campfire Ghost Story

"The cabin in the woods had been abandoned for years, but one night, a candle burned in the window."

"And no one was there to see it. The end!" Patrick interrupted, rolling his eyes.

Sabrina sighed inwardly, feeling the familiar weight of irritation at her children's bickering. The campfire crackled hot between them, throwing dancing yellow shadows across their faces. She pressed her fingers gently against her temple, wishing they could make it through just one night without arguing.

"Stop it, Patty! That's not how it goes," Jaclyn snapped, her face dirt-streaked from the day's adventures. "You told your stupid ghost story. It's my turn."

Patrick didn't back down. "Yeah, but everyone knows your story already. Every twenty years the witch emerges and—"

"That's not even right! You're making stuff up!" Jaclyn shot up so abruptly her chair toppled backward, kicking up dust.

"Jaclyn!" Sabrina's sharp voice sliced through their argument. She stood and moved into the firelight between them, silently demanding calm. Both children fell quiet, recognizing her stern look. She softened, helping Jaclyn right her fallen chair, then sank back into her own seat.

She took a deep breath, composing herself. "Okay. Jaclyn, it's your turn."

As Jaclyn started over, Sabrina watched her daughter's expressions and gestures grow more animated. Patrick's skeptical eye rolls soon faded into genuine interest, and Sabrina felt a quiet warmth in her chest at this rare moment of peace. Even Chris joined in from his hammock, deepening the children's delight with his ominous additions.

Patrick's humorous witch impersonation drew laughter from everyone, including Sabrina, whose exhaustion temporarily lifted in the glow of shared amusement. Still, she knew bedtime couldn't come soon enough.

"Alright, you two," she yawned, stretching. "Bedtime."

Despite their protests, Sabrina stood firm, and with a reluctant sigh and exaggerated yawns, the kids retreated to their tent.

Chris joined her beside the dying fire, chuckling softly. "Nicely handled. I almost sent them off to the witch myself."

"I miss the days when they just ran around," Sabrina murmured, staring at the glowing embers. "Their constant arguing wears me out."

"Yeah," Chris agreed quietly. "It's exhausting."

"Yet, somehow, I still love them to death," she said softly, smiling as she met his gaze.

They sat and chatted for another half an hour as the fire died down, alternating between reminiscing about when the children were younger and dreaming of the adventures they'd have once grown.

Most of the campground was dark and quiet as they finally made their way to their tent, though a few scattered fires still glowed. Muffled voices from other campers drifted through the trees, punctuated occasionally by bursts of laughter.

Sabrina awoke suddenly in the pitch darkness, her heart already thumping hard in her chest. The rustling outside had wrenched her from sleep—a low, urgent whispering punctuated by stifled sounds, something muffled and desperate. She strained to listen, anxiety knotting in her stomach. Had she just heard, "No! Sto—" or had she imagined it?

Her breath caught painfully in her throat. She fumbled nervously for the flashlight, her fingers trembling so much she almost dropped it. The zipper of their tent felt stiff, resisting her shaky hands as she finally tugged it open and stepped out. Her flashlight cut a narrow, wavering beam through the darkness, landing on the kids' tent. Her breath hitched sharply as she saw it—the flap hanging wide open, a dark void that seemed to mock her unease.

"Patrick? Jaclyn?" she whispered urgently, her voice barely audible even to herself. No answer.

Her pulse drummed loudly in her ears as she approached the tent, each step producing an unnervingly loud crunch on the gravel beneath her feet. Peering inside, she gasped—one sleeping bag was empty, a crumpled heap, while the other concealed a mess of auburn hair. Sabrina's stomach twisted. Where was the other child?

She forced herself to breathe. *They're probably just at the bathroom.* But the rationalization felt thin, fragile against the creeping dread.

Sabrina hurried toward the bathroom, her light cutting a shaky path through the blackness. She found it eerily vacant, the fluorescents buzzing overhead, oppressive and unnerving. As she sat, she thought of their story from earlier and suppressed an involuntary shiver.

"Hehehe." A tiny chuckle echoed faintly, making her blood run cold. She froze, every muscle tense. Had she imagined that? No—again it came, louder, clearer, undeniably real.

She flushed quickly, heart racing as she rushed to the sink, desperate for something ordinary, something safe. As she splashed cold water on her face, another deep-voiced chuckle echoed, louder, closer, chilling her to the bone. Sabrina jerked her head up, eyes wide.

In the mirror, her reflection stared back, pale and frightened—and then shifted. Beside her stood Patrick and Jaclyn, skin deathly pale and soaked in blood, their eyes wide, terrified. Blood poured silently from their mouths, streaking down their chins and pooling grotesquely onto the floor. The dark red liquid was splattered on the walls behind them.

She screamed and spun around, heart nearly bursting from her chest.

The room behind her was empty, sterile. The walls clean and pale. No blood, no children. She looked again at the mirror, only her terrified face staring back.

"God!" she whispered, her voice ragged. "You're losing it. Get a grip."

The walk back felt endless, her flashlight trembling so badly she nearly stumbled.

"Sebbie? Is that you?" Chris whispered urgently, the sound startling her again. His sleepy voice now oddly menacing.

"Yeah, it's me," she said shakily, fighting tears of relief as Chris poked his head out. "Just the bathroom. Stupid ghost stories." Her laugh was brittle, forced.

"You sound terrified." He looked at her with a furrowed brow.

"No, I'm fine," she lied weakly, grateful as he drew her into a comforting hug. His warmth calmed her racing heart, yet shame crept in, embarrassment replacing her terror.

"You sure?" he questioned in a gentle voice.

She nodded, eyes stinging slightly. "I'm fine, really. Just being silly."

They slipped into their sleeping bag together, Chris' reassuring presence easing her nerves. She curled into him, trying desperately to shake off the lingering chill.

"You know," he murmured playfully, brushing his lips softly against her ear, "we have some time before morning. Maybe a distraction?"

She nodded, forcing a smile, determined to convince herself. She was safe. Her children were safe. It was just a story. But deep down, as Chris' lips traced her neck and shoulder, the chilling image of blood-soaked faces lingered, haunting her thoughts.

Sabrina awoke slowly, greeted by the gentle warmth of sunlight filtering through the tent fabric. She stretched leisurely, enjoying the peaceful morning calm. The air smelled pleasantly of pine, mingled with the faint scent of last night's campfire. She smiled, wrapping her arms around Chris' warm, sturdy frame.

"Morning," he murmured sleepily, pulling her closer.

"Morning," she replied, content. "We should probably get up before the kids begin their next reign of terror."

Chris chuckled softly. "Five more minutes."

She laughed and relaxed into him, savoring the rare quiet. But slowly, a subtle tension crept into her chest. The morning quiet lacked something—a quality she couldn't quite place.

With a dramatic yawn, Sabrina slipped from Chris'

embrace and stepped out of their tent. Her legs and lower back objected as she stretched, eyes closed against the sun's rays. Kinks loosened, she spread her arms wide and opened her eyes. Her smile faded and her stomach twisted uneasily. The spot where the kids' tent had been was empty. Not just empty—the area appeared untouched, as if their tent had never been there.

Confused, she turned in a slow circle, unease blooming steadily inside her. The campsite looked pristine, carefully arranged—for two. No scattered toys, no towels drying on branches, no shoes carelessly tossed aside. Her heartbeat quickened as dread began to sink in.

"Chris?" Her voice wavered slightly, betraying her growing anxiety.

Chris groaned as he emerged from the tent, rubbing his eyes but smiling warmly. "What's up, Sebbie?"

"Where are the kids?" Her voice cracked slightly. "Their tent—it's gone."

Chris frowned, looking confused, then laughed softly. "You mean they packed up and left early? Fantastic!"

Her breath froze. "Chris, stop joking. *Our* kids. Patrick and Jaclyn."

Chris' expression shifted immediately from amusement to concern. "Sabrina, are you okay? We don't have any kids." His voice was gentle, eyes sincere.

Head spinning, Sabrina backed away, eyes darting frantically to their SUV. She rushed toward it, hoping desperately to find some sign of the children—evidence of their existence, anything. She yanked open the door, staring helplessly into the immaculate interior. There were no toys, no crumbs, no indication that children had ever been there. Only a neatly folded emergency blanket tucked under the passenger seat.

A cold, disembodied chuckle drifted through the air, making her spin around sharply, her skin prickling with fear.

"Chris?" she whispered shakily, watching him approach with caution.

"Hey, Sebbie," he said softly, reaching gently for her hand. "You're scaring me a little. Let's sit down and talk, okay?"

"No!" She pulled away, heart hammering wildly as the haunting laughter echoed louder, mocking her panic.

Chris quickly caught up and gently grabbed her by both arms, his eyes filled with genuine worry. "Sabrina, please, stop. Look at me—I'd know if we had kids. What's happening? Talk to me."

"I don't have time for this, Chris! I have to find them!" She struggled weakly, sobbing now. "Please, if this is a trick, stop. I'm freaking out here."

Chris wrapped his arms around her gently, pulling her into a comforting hug. "Baby, listen to me. I think you might be having a breakdown. Please, let's just breathe and figure this out together. I love you. I'm worried about you."

The voice returned, a haunting, pleasure-filled moan edged with malice. *They're gone.*

Chris' voice suddenly shifted, still gentle yet oddly unsettling. "Sebbie, you never wanted them anyway. You won't miss them." His hold tightened, painfully firm. "It's okay, let's talk. Just you and me."

"No," Sabrina whispered desperately. "This isn't right! I have to find the kids!" She shoved away from him with all her strength, turning and bolting toward the woods.

"Patrick! Jaclyn!" she shouted frantically.

The voice followed her, chillingly clear. *Not here. They were never here.*

She ran past abandoned campsites, decay surrounding her, the sky darkening unnaturally fast. The bathrooms had vanished, replaced by a decrepit cabin looming ominously ahead.

Her chest tightened painfully as the cabin's door slowly creaked open, revealing nothing but a consuming black void.

Sabrina opened her mouth to scream for help but found she couldn't.

Her heart, which had been beating rapidly despite her lack of breath, suddenly caught, as though grasped and squeezed. She felt it stop like a sharp pain in her chest, but she couldn't reach up to grasp at it. She couldn't move at all.

There was a moment of calm.

Then came the pain.

Her body convulsed where it stood as she felt the mysterious presence rip into her. Her tank top shredded against her, exposing scratches across her chest and torso. Blood oozed, soaking into the shredded shirt. Unable to make a sound, she screamed inwardly, stuck in the prison of her brain, witnessing every sensation, yet unable to stop it.

She wanted to reach out to protect herself. To run. To take just one breath and relieve the burning in her lungs.

No, no, no! she thought, but soon, even thoughts blurred into madness.

With her last bits of awareness fracturing, she felt a pull, strong and vicious, toward the door of the house. Her body flew.

The last images to flit through her mind were of Jaclyn and Patrick. Then, with an explosion of pain that radiated through her being, she crossed the threshold of the door and all went dark.

Nothing remained where she had stood, only a few tattered scraps of bloodied fabric drifting lazily down to settle on the shadowed forest floor.

The door swung gently shut, silence settling back over the woods.

The cabin had been abandoned for years, but now a single candle burned ominously in the window.

The morning after their night of campfire stories, Jaclyn and Patrick sat at the picnic table, wrapping their hands around mugs of hot chocolate. Chris emerged from the tent, stooping as he climbed through the nylon flap.

"Morning, kids." He called in a low voice, wary of nearby campers.

"Hey, Dad! We made you and Mom coffee." Jaclyn said with a smile on her face.

"Oh yeah? You guys are awesome! Where is your mom anyway?"

Both children shrugged.

"She head off to the bathroom or something?" Chris picked up the French press and poured the black liquid into a blue speckled camping mug. With a yawn, he began to add powdered creamer and sugar.

"No, we've been out here for a while. We thought she was still sleeping." Patrick began opening up a package of Hostess donuts.

"Nope, she's not in there. She must have gotten up before me." Chris sipped at his coffee and let out a satisfied "mmm."

"Huh," Jaclyn mused, "She probably went for one of her early morning walks."

"Probably." Chris shrugged.

The three let the issue go while they enjoyed their warm, early morning beverages and sugar pills. She would pop back into camp, eventually.

"Campfire Ghost Story" by Ellie Mage appears here for the first time.

George Wharton James

The Legend of the Two Brothers

Once long ago in Paiuti-land, Nevada, there lived two brothers. The older was a hunter and brought home much game. His wife, whose name was Duck, used to cook this for him, but she was very stingy to the younger brother, and often times he was hungry.

When he begged her for food, she scolded him and drove him out of the campoodie, saying, "Got none for you."

One day when the older brother was off hunting, Duck was cleaning some fish. She had been very cross to Little Brother, refusing to give him any food, and he was terribly hungry. Presently he came creeping up behind her and when he saw all the fish he became very angry. He took up a big club, and, before Duck could turn around, he hit her on the head and killed her.

Paying no attention to her dead body, he cooked and ate all the fish he wanted and then lay down in the sunshine on a big rock and went fast asleep.

By and by, his Hunter Brother came home. Of course, when he found his wife dead, he was filled with great anger at his young brother, though his anger was lessened when he thought of his wife's cruelty.

He shook him very roughly and said, "I don't like you anymore! I'm going away. You can stay here by yourself!" But Little Brother begged, "Don't be angry! Don't be angry! Let's go far away! I will help you all the time! Don't be angry!"

Gradually, he persuaded the Hunter Brother to forgive him and they started off together toward the "Big Water"—Lake Tahoe. On the way, the Hunter Brother taught the Little Brother how to shoot with a bow and arrow. By the time they reached the spot now known as Lakeside, both their belts were filled with squirrels they had shot. At dusk, they built a good fire and, when there were plenty of glowing coals, Hunter Brother dug a long hole, and, filling it with embers, laid the squirrels in a row on the coals covering them all up with earth.

He was tired and lay down by the fire to rest till the squirrels should be cooked. With his head resting on his arms, the warmth of the fire soothing him, he soon fell fast, fast asleep. Little Brother sat by the fire and as the night grew darker, he grew hungrier and hungrier. He tried to waken his brother, but the latter seemed almost like one dead, and he could not rouse him.

At last he made up his mind he would eat by himself. Going to the improvised oven, he began to dig up the squirrels, counting them as they came to light. One was missing. Little Brother was troubled. "How can that be? My brother had so many, I had so many!"—counting on his fingers, "One gone!" And he forgot how hungry he was as he dug for the missing squirrel.

All at once, he came upon a bigger hole adjoining the cooking hole. While he stood wondering what to do, out popped a great big spider.

"I'll catch you!" cried the spider.

"No, you won't!" said the boy, and up he jumped and away he ran, followed by the spider.

They raced over stock and stone, dodging about trees and stumbling over fallen logs for a long time.

At last, Little Brother could run no more. The spider grabbed him and carried him back to his hole, where he killed him.

It was almost daybreak when Hunter Brother awoke. He called his brother to bring more wood, for the fire was almost out. Getting no answer, he went to look at the cooking squirrels. Greatly surprised to see them lying there all uncovered, he, too, counted them. Discovering one gone, he thought his brother must have eaten it and was about to eat one himself when he saw the old spider stick his head out of the hole.

Each made a spring, but the Hunter Brother was the quicker and killed the wicked spider with his knife.

Carefully, he now went into the spider's hole. There, stretched out on the ground, lay Little Brother dead! Taking him up in his arms, he carried him outside. Now this Hunter Brother was a medicine-man of great power, so he lay down with Little Brother and breathed into his mouth, and in a few minutes he came back to life and was all right.

The Hunter Brother was very happy to have his Little Brother alive again. He built up the fire and while they sat eating their long-delayed meal Little Brother told all that had happened to him. The sun was not quite above the horizon before the meal was finished, and soon Hunter Brother was anxious to be moving on, so they took their way along the lake shore. On their way they talked and laughed one with another and seemed to agree very well, until they had gone around the lake and reached where

Tahoe City now is.

Here they quarreled, and the Hunter Brother left Little Brother to return and go up the Big Mountain Tallac—where he had heard there were many squirrels. After his departure, Little Brother decided to follow him and get him to make friends again. So he trudged along the lake shore until he came to Emerald Bay.

There, lying on the log at the edge of the lake, lay a water-baby. It was asleep with its head resting on its arms and its beautiful, sunshine-golden-hair was spread over it.

"Oh," said Little Brother, "I'll get that beautiful sunshine-hair as a present for my brother!"

So he crept very softly down on the log, thinking to kill the water-baby before it awoke. But he was not successful in this, for the creature opened its eyes as he laid his hand on its hair, and a furious fight ensued. Sometimes it seemed as though Little Brother would be killed, but finally he was able to scalp the poor water-baby and get possession of the beautiful sunshine-golden-hair. Everyone can see where this fight occurred. The red hill near Emerald Bay stands as a memorial of the struggle, for its color is caused by the blood of the slain water-baby.

Tucking his prize in his hunting shirt and hugging it close, Little Brother now went on, murmuring to himself, "Oh, my brother will like this, my brother will like this beautiful golden-sunshine-hair!"

But suddenly, as he was climbing upward, he noticed the water lapping at his heels, and when he turned to see whence it came, he found that the big lake behind him was rapidly rising, and even as he stood wondering, it arose above his ankles. Then he remembered what he had heard of revengeful water-babies, but frightened though he was, he could not bear to throw away his prize.

However, he knew he must do something, so he plucked out a few hairs from the scalp and threw them into the ascending waves. For a minute, the water ceased to rise and he sped onward, but before long he felt the water at his heels again, and knew that once more he must gain a short respite by throwing out a few of the golden-sunshine-hairs.

And ever and again he had to do this until at last he spied his brother ahead of him. "Ah, brother," he cried, drawing the scalp from his blouse, "see what a beautiful present I have for you!" But when his brother turned toward him, he saw only the angry, rising waters, and rushing forward, he snatched the beautiful sunshine-golden-hair and cast it back into the waters, crying, "How you dare meddle with water-babies? Don't you know water surely come up and get you?"

And poor Little Brother felt very sad; but the danger he had been in seemed to have endeared him once more to Hunter Brother, and they stood arm-in-arm and watched the waters recede. But there were hollows in the land, and when the waters went back, they held the water and so were formed that chain of lakes on the other side of Tallac and Emerald Bay, the Velmas, Kalmia, Cascade, and others.

"The Legend of the Two Brothers" by George Wharton James was included in his 1921 book, The Lake of the Sky.

The Legendary Snake of Pyramid Lake

For many years, there has been a story current amongst the miners and prospectors of Nevada, of a monster snake in Pyramid Lake, Humboldt County, Nevada. But none of them had ever seen the amphibious monster, and only related the story as an Indian legend.

Every Indian in the region firmly believed in this snake, and you could no more get one of them to go near the lake than you could get him to rush into a burning pile of sagebrush. Some, more venturesome than others, had approached the lake and obtained a glimpse of the monster while he was sporting in the waters. But all firmly believed in its existence, and by common consent, gave the lake as wide a berth as possible.

Some time ago, a prospector, who had a half-scientific education, strayed away into the mountains, and finally arrived upon the shores of this lake, and from the appearance and taste of the water, he came to the conclusion that it contained borate of soda. Upon his return to his home, he organized a company for the purpose of erecting works upon the lakeshore and engaging in the manufacture of borax.

But the company, before putting much money into the enterprise, determined to send an agent to the lake to explore it, and to thoroughly test its waters. They selected a man by the name of Spence, who resides, we believe, at Cisco, furnished him with a boat, assistants, and the necessary equipments to accomplish the object in view.

Accordingly, on the 25th of September, 1869, Mr. Spence departed on his journey, and soon reached the lake.

When some miles away, he met an old Indian who endeavored to persuade him from going near the lake by telling him that he would surely be destroyed by the snake, which, according to the Indian, possessed the power of drawing everything into its mouth that came within a mile of its head. Mr. Spence did not believe in ghosts, neither did he believe in sea serpents, but he did believe in performing the task set for him. Therefore, he pushed on and reached the lakeshore on the evening of the 28th of September, and made his camp beside a clear spring that he was lucky enough to discover.

The next day he devoted to taking observations along the shore and making tests of the water. On the morning of the 30th, he launched his boat upon the lake, and determined to row across it. The lake was some 10 or 12 miles wide, and perhaps 20 miles long. Its waters were as smooth as a mirror, for a dead calm had existed ever since they had reached the lake.

The trip across the lake was begun, and as the voyageurs looked down into the clear water, they wondered why there was no fish to be seen. They also wondered why they had seen no ducks nor waterfowl upon its surface. They had rowed for more than an hour, and had got some eight miles from the shore, when Mr. Spence discovered what appeared to him to be an immense serpent. It was lying on the surface of the lake, apparently asleep, for it was not moving.

After a consultation with his companions, it was finally resolved to approach His Serpentship still nearer. They accordingly moved forward, and each moment, the snake grew in proportions.

Stopping when within a hundred yards of the monster, they took a good survey of it. As near as they could judge, it was about 300 feet long, and in the thickest part was probably three feet in diameter. Its scales appeared to be black and white, with a tendency to copper color.

The appearance of the monster was anything but inviting, and a lengthy consultation ensued, whether to back out or go on. Mr. Spence argued that it was no more dangerous to go forward and touch the monster than to approach as close as they had already. The result was that they determined to go forward, and a few more strokes of the oar brought the boat alongside the snake.

Then Mr. Spence discovered it was not a monster serpent, but an agglomeration of millions of worms, of a species never before seen by him. They had fastened upon one another until they presented the appearance of a monster snake. Mr. Spence believes that whenever there is a calm in the waters of the this lake for several days, these worms agglomerate together, but the moment a breeze springs up, and the surface of the water is agitated, the worms separate.

We leave the explanation of this singular phenomenon to scientific men, and hope the Academy of Sciences will place themselves in communication with Mr. Spence, and get a fuller account of his trip than we have been able to give.

— *The Elko Independent*
(*San Francisco Call*)
October 20, 1869

About the Editors

Sharon Marie Provost is an award-winning author who specializes in horror, thrillers, and speculative fiction. Beginning her career in late 2023, she has published a novella, two short story collections, and three collaborative collections of short stories with her husband. Her first novel, *Dark Arts: Love Me Tinder*, was published in 2024. It has received acclaim for its detailed and chilling story of a serial killer who turns his victims into works of art. In 2025, her *Shadow's Gate* received the Imadjinn Award for Best Short Story Collection, and she published two collaborative novels with Stephen H. Provost: *Azrael's Assassin: Testament in Blood* and *Evermore: Dark Soulmates*. Sharon is the chief operating officer of Dragon Crown Books. She has lived in Carson City since 1987.

Stephen H. Provost is a former reporter and columnist with more than 30 years of experience at daily newspapers. Over the past 11 years, he has written or co-authored more than

60 books. In addition to six novels and three novellas, he has produced an extensive collection of nonfiction works on topics ranging from Nevada's pioneer days to the history of retail in the United States. He has written more than 20 books on U.S. history in the 20th century focusing on highways, towns, and culture. Stephen is the founder and publisher of Dragon Crown Books. He lives in Carson City.

About the Authors

B. B. Arbogast is a retired software and database developer making her second career as an author. She has an interest in myth, the occult, and the macabre, and she releases that part of her imagination in her writing. She wrote her first two picture books in German while learning the language when she worked briefly as an au pair in Germany. She writes for a variety of audiences ranging from early middle-grade to adult in multiple genres, including magical realism and horror. Her short story "Zeetageia Finds Her Voice" was included in *The ACES Anthology 2024*. She lives in Reno with her husband and her dogs. You can find her online at http://bbarbogast.com.

Bill Brown is a retired Emmy award-winning journalist with more than 40 years in the business. Since leaving broadcast journalism, he has become a full-time author, writing and publishing nearly 20 novels. He has been named Reno's Favorite Author, an annual award presented by the *Reno Gazette-Journal*, and has been a top five finalist on other occasions. His books are available at https://www.billbrownnovels.com/.

I.C. Coggin (fl. late 19th century) of San Francisco was a cornetist, and, beginning in 1883, manager of the Golden Gate

Park Band. His account of an encounter with a giant serpent at Lake Tahoe is included here.

Samuel Post Davis (1850-1918) was a journalist, humorist, and author in the Sagebrush School, which also included Mark Twain and Dan De Quille. As a journalist, he wrote for the *Chronicle* in Virginia City beginning in 1875 and served as the editor of the *Morning Appeal* in Carson City beginning in late 1879. The author also had a career in politics, serving as deputy secretary of state in 1895 and two terms as Nevada state controller. He published a book of his short stories in 1886 and *History of Nevada* in 1913.

Dan De Quille (1829-1898) was a reporter for the *Territorial Enterprise* in Virginia City for more than three decades, where he was a contemporary and colleague of Mark Twain. He wrote the definitive history of silver mining on the Comstock, *The Big Bonanza*, and like Twain, was known for his humorous "quaints" or tall tales that would appear in print from time to time.

Michael K. Falciani is a multiple award-winning author and native of upstate New York who lives in Carson City. His honors include the Imadjinn Awards for Best Fantasy Novel (*The Raven and the Grow: The Gray Throne*) and Best Steampunk Novel (*Dwarves of Rahm: Omens of War*), as well as the ACES High Award for best Northern Nevada Short Story ("The Shadow's Edge"). His books are available at https://www.amazon.com/stores/Michael-K.-Falciani/author/B087WM4PN7.

George Wharton James (1858-1923) was a British-born

Methodist minister who served parishes in Nevada and California. A journalist, editor, photographer, and lecturer, he wrote more than 40 books, as well as a number of pamphlets on the Southwest. His works include a book on Lake Tahoe, *The Lake of the Sky*, published in 1915, as well as books on the Colorado desert, the California missions, the Grand Canyon, New Mexico, and Native American basket making.

Sandie La Nae is a spirit sensitive, remote viewer, psychic and author who lives in Carson City. To date, she has written 35 books on an array of topics, including history, the paranormal, minerals, poetry, and a textbook for a ghost-hunting class. She is the co-author of the "Weird..." history and trivia book series on Nevada towns and places with the Nevada Historical Society's "Special Works" historian, Arline La Ferry. Her books are available at https://www.sandiespsychicstones.com/cc_2012/books/books.html.

Angela Laverghetta is a Northern Nevada based fantasy author. Almost all her writings take place locally, including her debut modern fantasy novel *The Buried Knight* published in 2023, and its sequel, *The Hidden Druid*, released at the end of 2024. Other published works include a novella previously published by a small press and two short stories both for The ACES Anthology in 2023 and 2024. This is her first entry in the horror genre. Her books are available on Amazon and at https://angelalaverghettabooks.com/

Ellie Mage is fascinated by the breadth of human experience, delving deeply into what it means to feel, think, and exist. Drawn to the captivating shadows of dark urban fantasy, she uses the fantastic and supernatural to explore the boundaries of perception and the depths of our reality. Also writing as Laura Magee and Liz Miller, she navigates the spectrum of human experiences; Laura explores mysteries and supernatural realms, while Liz embraces the softer, warmer side of relationships. Through Ellie Mage, she invites readers to step into darker possibilities, to question their realities, and to find the truths hidden in the shadows. Ellie hails from Reno, Nevada. You can find her Liz Miller books at https://www.amazon.com/stores/Liz-Miller/author/B0F9TWQGMB.

Richard Moreno, recipient of the Nevada Writers Hall of Fame Silver Pen Award in 2007, served as publisher of *Nevada Magazine* from 1991 to 2006. His historical works include *Frontier Fake News*, *A Short History of Reno*, and *The Roadside History of Nevada*, among more than 20 titles. Dragon Crown Books has published his short stories in *The ACES Anthology 2023* and *2024*. He currently lives in Washington state. You can find his books at https://www.amazon.com/stores/Richard-Moreno/author/B001JP3UC0.

Janice Oberding is the author of more than 50 books of fiction and non-fiction in a variety of genres including the paranormal, history, true crime, and the Western short story series *A Virginia City Mystery*. Her other works include *The Big Book of Nevada Ghost Stories*, *Murders Mysteries and Misdemeanors of Hollywood and Los Angeles*, and *Haunted Las Vegas*. A Reno resident, Janice lectures on a variety of topics and is well known for her investigations into the paranormal. You can find her books at https://www.amazon.com/stores/author/B001JP8S6I/.

Megan Russ is the author of a dozen novels and short story collections focusing on dark fantasy and horror. After growing up in the Mojave Desert of Southern California, she settled in the Great Basin of Northern Nevada—a journey that has given her a unique perspective on life. This haunting desert inspired her first short story collection, focusing on more obscure desert history and features. You can read about these desert themed horror stories in *Shadows of the Great Basin*. You can find her books on Amazon or her website at https://meganrussauthorbooks.com/.

Jeadene Solberg is an in-house collections specialist by day at USAC, a nonprofit based at the University of Nevada, Reno. By night, she is one of the founders of Northern Nevada Ghost Hunters—a thriving nonprofit paranormal tour company she co-launched in 2005. A passionate energy reader, Jeadene works with crystals and helps others understand their own energy fields. She's also a devoted mom of four, proud Grammie of seven, and serves on the board of a local wildlife sanctuary for senior animals. A resident of Dayton, she spends much of her free time researching Virginia City's Comstock and the Gold Rush era, bringing the past to life through storytelling, exploration, and a heartfelt connection to the spirits of history.

John A. "Snowshoe" Thompson (1827-1876), born in Norway as Jon Torsteinsson Rue, delivered mail between Placerville, California, and Nevada—Genoa and, later, Virginia City—for two decades beginning in 1856. Despite his nickname, he made the journey on 10-foot-long skis based on a design from his native country. His legacy is celebrated on both sides of the Sierra, though he was never paid for delivering the U.S. Mail. He is buried in the Genoa Cemetery.

Mark Twain (1835-1910) was the pen name of Samuel Clemens. Called by William Faulkner "the Father of American Literature," Twain began his writing career in earnest as a reporter and editor for the *Territorial Enterprise* newspaper in Virginia City and wrote extensively about Nevada in his book *Roughing It*. Twain is the author of such timeless works as *The Adventures of Tom Sawyer*, *The Adventures of Huckleberry Finn*, and *A Connecticut Yankee in King Arthur's Court*. He held an honorary Doctor of Letters from Yale University. Dragon Crown Books has published two books on his life: *Mark Twain's Nevada* and *The Adventures of Mark Twain in Nevada*, as well as a collection of his short stories, *Dark Twain*.

Sarah Winnemucca (1844-1891) is the author of *Life Among the Piutes: Their Wrongs and Claims*, published in 1883. The first autobiography by a Native American Woman, it contains both her personal history and the history of her people during their first forty years of contact with European Americans. The author was the daughter of Paiute Nation Chief Winnemucca and the granddaughter of Chief Truckee. She worked as an interpreter for the Bureau of Indian Affairs at Fort McDermit beginning in 1871, and was inducted posthumously into the Nevada Writers Hall of Fame in 1993.

Did you enjoy this book?

Recommend it to a friend. And please consider **rating it and/or leaving a brief review** at Amazon, Barnes & Noble, and Goodreads.